THE HORUS HERESY®

THE UNREMEMBERED EMPIRE

GUILLIMAN TURNED TO track the remaining killers. The damned gladius was still stuck through him. He–

At least two shells struck his left shoulder armour behind his ear and detonated. He felt as though his head had snapped off to the right with the shockwave. He felt heat and ferocious pain. He tasted blood and fyceline, his ears ringing, his vision gone.

He fell. He couldn't get up. He was half propped against the desk or an overturned chair.

He couldn't see. He fired blind. It was pointless. He fired again.

He felt a blade against his throat.

'Death to the false Emperor,' said the voice Guilliman had thought belonged to Aeonid Thiel.

'Let me die knowing what you are,' Guilliman whispered.

THE HORUS HERESY®

Book 17 – THE OUTCAST DEAD
Graham McNeill

Book 18 – DELIVERANCE LOST
Gav Thorpe

Book 19 – KNOW NO FEAR
Dan Abnett

Book 20 – THE PRIMARCHS
edited by Christian Dunn

Book 21 – FEAR TO TREAD
James Swallow

Book 22 – SHADOWS OF TREACHERY
edited by Christian Dunn and Nick Kyme

Book 23 – ANGEL EXTERMINATUS
Graham McNeill

Book 24 – BETRAYER
Aaron Dembski-Bowden

Book 25 – MARK OF CALTH
edited by Laurie Goulding

Book 26 – VULKAN LIVES
Nick Kyme

Book 27 – THE UNREMEMBERED EMPIRE
Dan Abnett

Book 28 – SCARS
Chris Wraight
(2014)

Novellas

PROMETHEAN SUN
Nick Kyme

AURELIAN
Aaron Dembski-Bowden

Many of these titles are also available as abridged and unabridged audiobooks.
Order the full range of Horus Heresy novels and audiobooks from
www.blacklibrary.com

Download the full range of Horus Heresy audio dramas from
www.blacklibrary.com

Also available

THE SCRIPTS: VOLUME I
edited by Christian Dunn

VISIONS OF HERESY
Alan Merrett

Dan Abnett

THE UNREMEMBERED EMPIRE

A light in the darkness

BLACK LIBRARY

For Eve and Rich.

A BLACK LIBRARY PUBLICATION

Hardback edition first published in 2013.
This edition published in 2014 by
Black Library,
Games Workshop Ltd.,
Willow Road,
Nottingham, NG7 2WS, UK.

10 9 8 7 6 5 4 3 2 1

Cover illustration by Neil Roberts.
Map by Dan Abnett and Adrian Wood.

A CIP record for this book is available from the British Library.

UK ISBN: 978 1 84970 572 1
US ISBN: 978 1 84970 573 8

See Black Library on the internet at
www.blacklibrary.com

Find out more about Games Workshop
and the world of Warhammer 40,000 at
www.games-workshop.com

Printed and bound by CPI Group (UK) Ltd, Croydon, CR0 4YY

The Horus Heresy®
It is a time of legend.

The galaxy is in flames. The Emperor's glorious vision for humanity is in ruins. His favoured son, Horus, has turned from his father's light and embraced Chaos.

His armies, the mighty and redoubtable Space Marines, are locked in a brutal civil war. Once, these ultimate warriors fought side by side as brothers, protecting the galaxy and bringing mankind back into the Emperor's light.
Now they are divided.

Some remain loyal to the Emperor, whilst others have sided with the Warmaster. Pre-eminent amongst them, the leaders of their thousands-strong Legions are the primarchs. Magnificent, superhuman beings, they are the crowning achievement of the Emperor's genetic science. Thrust into battle against one another, victory is uncertain for either side.

Worlds are burning. At Isstvan V, Horus dealt a vicious blow and three loyal Legions were all but destroyed. War was begun, a conflict that will engulf all mankind in fire. Treachery and betrayal have usurped honour and nobility. Assassins lurk in every shadow. Armies are gathering.
All must choose a side or die.

Horus musters his armada, Terra itself the object of his wrath. Seated upon the Golden Throne, the Emperor waits for his wayward son to return. But his true enemy is Chaos, a primordial force that seeks to enslave mankind to its capricious whims.

The screams of the innocent, the pleas of the righteous resound to the cruel laughter of Dark Gods. Suffering and damnation await all should the Emperor fail and the war be lost.

The age of knowledge and enlightenment has ended.
The Age of Darkness has begun.

~ DRAMATIS PERSONAE ~

On Macragge

ROBOUTE GUILLIMAN	Primarch of the XIII Legion 'Ultramarines', Lord of the Five Hundred Worlds, now known as 'the Avenging Son'
DRAKUS GOROD	Fief commander of the Invictus bodyguard
MAGLIOS	Lieutenant, Invictus bodyguard
VALENTUS DOLOR	Tetrarch of Ultramar (Occluda), Primarch's Champion
CASMIR	Captain, equerry to the tetrarch
TITUS PRAYTO	Master of the Presiding Centuria, XIII Legion Librarius
PHRATUS AUGUSTON	Chapter Master, Ultramarines First Chapter
VERUS CASPEAN	Chapter Master, Second Chapter
NIAX NESSUS	Chapter Master, Third Chapter
TERBIS	Captain
THALES	Captain
MENIUS	Sergeant, Ultramarines 34th Company

ZYROL	Sergeant, posted to Helion orbital plate
LEANEENA	Deck officer, Helion orbital
FORSCHE	Consul of the senate
TARASHA EUTEN	August Chamberlain Principal
VODUN BADORUM	Captain of the Praecental Guard, household division
PERCEL	Praecental Guard
CLENART	Praecental Guard

On Sotha

BARABAS DANTIOCH	Warsmith of the Iron Warriors
ARKUS	Sergeant, Ultramarines 199th Aegida Company
OBERDEII	Scout, Aegida Company

From the storm

EERON KLEVE	(rank deferred in mourning), X Legion 'Iron Hands'
SARDON KARAASHISON	X Legion 'Iron Hands'
TIMUR GANTULGA	V Legion 'White Scars'
VERANO EBB	Captain, Silence Squad, XIX Legion 'Raven Guard'
ZYTOS	XVIII Legion 'Salamanders'

ALEXIS POLUX	Captain, 405th Company, VII Legion 'Imperial Fists'
FAFFNR BLUDBRODER	Watch-pack master, VI Legion 'Space Wolves'
MALMUR LONGREACH	Space Wolves watch-pack
SHOCKEYE FFYN	Space Wolves watch-pack
KURO JJORDROVK	Space Wolves watch-pack
GUDSON ALFREYER	Space Wolves watch-pack
MADS LORESON	Space Wolves watch-pack
SALICK	'The Braided', Space Wolves watch-pack
BITER HEREK	Space Wolves watch-pack
NIDO KNIFESON	Space Wolves watch-pack
BO SOREN	'The Axe', Space Wolves watch-pack
AEONID THIEL	Sergeant, Ultramarines 135th Company
NAREK	Former Vigilator, XVII Legion 'Word Bearers'
BARBOS KHA	Unburdened
ULKAS TUL	Unburdened

LION EL'JONSON	Primarch of the First Legion 'Dark Angels'
HOLGUIN	Voted lieutenant, Deathwing
FARITH REDLOSS	Voted lieutenant, Dreadwing
STENIUS	Captain and master of the *Invincible Reason*
LADY THERALYN FIANA	Navigator, House Ne'iocene
JOHN GRAMMATICUS	Perpetual
DAMON PRYTANIS	Perpetual
USHPÈTKHAR	Neverborn
SANGUINIUS	Primarch of the IX Legion 'Blood Angels'

**Diverse other lords, potentates and commanders,
as the actions unfold**

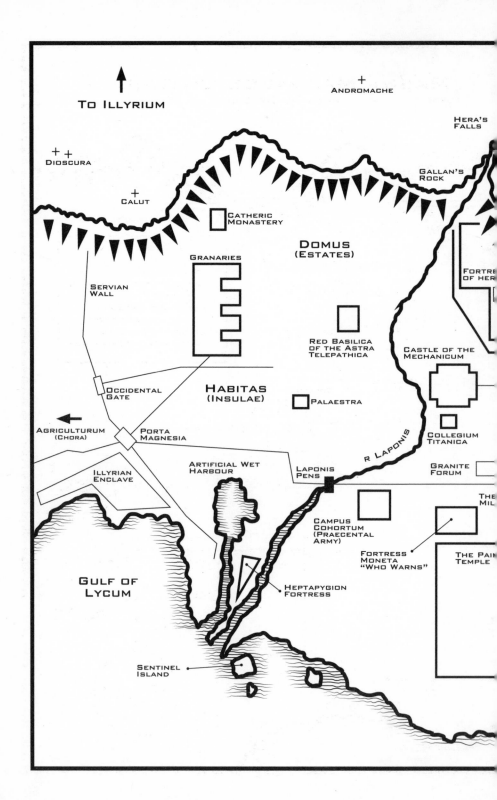

Magna Macragge Civitas
circa 009.M31

HERA'S CROWN MOUNTAINS

CASTRUM

EASTERN KEEP

HIGH SENATE

RESIDENCY

4

3

5

AGILUS BARRACKS

AEGIS WALL

7

PARKLAND

MEMORIAL GUARDENS

TREASURY

NEW SENATE

AVENUE OF HEROES

DIRIBITORIUM

TITAN'S GATE (PROPYLAE TITANICUS)

MARTIAL SQUARE

NYMPHAEUM

VIA DECMANUS MAXIMUS

GRAND COLONNADE

EASTERN CURTAIN

PORTA MEDES

COMMERCIAL DISTRICT

BARBARATHERIUM

STARPORT GATE

HABITAS

LARNIS GATE

FAB PLANTS

ILLYRIAN MONUMENT

LABOURING HABS

LANDING FIELDS

ANOMIE SQUARE

SOUTHERN SUBURBAN HABS

OCTAGON FORTRESS

KEY TO FORTRESS OF HERA

1. PRAETORIUM
2. SACRISTY OF THE LIBRARIUS
3. SWORDHALL
4. LIBRARY OF PTOLEMY
5. TEMPLE OF CORRECTION
6. CHAPEL OF MEMORIAL
7. HERA'S GATE (PORTA HERA)

'No man will ever be forgotten so long as he has children.'

— Konor, consular records

'A capacity for the theoretical is admirable, but a stomach for the practical is priceless.'

— Roboute Guilliman, private writings

'An ambition to save humanity is almost always a disguise for the desire to rule it.'

— attributed to the Panpacific tyrant Narthan Dume, in the era of the Unification of Terra [M30]

1

FIRST, THE APPARITIONS

'Horatio says 'tis but our fantasy,
And will not let belief take hold of him
Touching this dreaded sight, twice seen of us:
Therefore I have entreated him along
With us to watch the minutes of this night;
That if again this apparition come,
He may approve our eyes and speak to it.'

– from *Amulet, Prince Demark* (attributed to the
dramaturge Shakespire), circa M2

THAT PHANTOMS SHOULD haunt Macragge, after all the horrors that had been recently visited upon the planet and the five hundred worlds it held in fealty, came as no surprise to anyone.

The population of Ultramar's Five Hundred World dominion had suffered the atrocity of Calth, the gross treachery of Lorgar, the widespread bloodshed that followed in consequence, and the pan-galactic devastation of the so-named 'Ruinstorm'. Every single one of those billions of souls was in a state of existential shock. The monumental events had left psychological scars, ghost wounds that lingered in the minds of men: combat traumas, griefs and private losses, physical injuries, bitternesses, grudges, stress disorders, warp-fuelled nightmares, and other, less-classifiable after-effects. Calth, the ignition point, barely more than two years past, had haunted the citizens of Ultramar with such phantoms ever since.

No, when the latest apparitions came, the only surprise was that they should be so very *real*.

OVER TEN SUCCESSIVE nights, phantoms stalked the high towers and wall-walks of Macragge City, under the shadow of the Fortress, beneath a night sky that had been a permanent, star-less russet, like blood-soaked black cloth, since the coming of the Ruinstorm two years before.

No stars shone, none that looked healthy or matched any charts, at least. Even the brightest of the capital world's four moons was seldom visible through the inky, cosmological swirl of the enduring warp storm. The corpse of the Word Bearers immense warship the *Furious Abyss* could sometimes be seen in the western skies as the orbital breakers went about their work, but this was merely a sad relic of past bloodshed. During the day, when sunlight fell upon Macragge, it fell only as a tarnished golden haze, as if through battlefield smoke.

It fell upon a haunted city: Macragge City, Magna Macragge Civitas, the greatest city in the Imperial East, a city so mighty that it shared the name of the world it stood on, for the city was the world and the world was the city. Filling the vast lowland plains, from the Hera's Crown peaks in the north to the sea in the south, it was a testament to the power of Imperial mankind, and to one man in particular.

The apparitions appeared only after nightfall. Footsteps were heard in empty corridors where no one walked; voices mumbled from inside block-cut walls or the roots of staircases; sometimes the sound of hasty, running feet rushed down deserted colonnades; once, an odd and mournful laugh was heard echoing through an odeon hall; most often came the aching melody of a bowed string instrument, playing in some cavernous place of eternal echoes.

These manifestations were heard by household guardsmen on night patrol, by cooks and servants, by attachés hurrying to late conferences, by cleaners and servitors, by senators coming to the Residency. They were heard everywhere, from the high Castrum of the Palaeopolis, where the Residency, High Senate and praecental barracks shared the castellated summit with the monolithic immensity of the Fortress of Hera, right down across the demes of the city to the lowliest insulae and worker-habs on the southern coast, from the labouring zones of the eastern wards, and even from the squalid slums beyond the Servian Wall in the west.

It is likely they had been occurring for several nights before they were first reported. Junior staffers and servants had become timid and superstitious in this new age of darkness, and were individually reluctant to speak up and tell their superiors what they thought they had heard in some lonely room or deserted wing.

The Lord of Macragge, the Avenging Son, had issued strict orders that all phenomena were to be reported, however.

'We can't trust the physical integrity of our universe, anymore,' he told Euten. 'Its laws no longer operate the way we think they operate. Everything that might once have been dismissed as a trick of the mind or a figment of the imagination must be taken seriously and investigated. The warp is reaching into us, mam, and we do not yet recognise half of the faces it wears. I will not be taken by surprise again. I will not be infiltrated.'

As I was at Calth. Those were the unspoken words at the end of the sentence. The Avenging Son could seldom bring himself to speak the name of that dear planet. Phantoms of his own haunted him.

Euten impressed the lord's directive upon the staff of the Residency, and the public officers of the Civitas; but ironically it was she who, the very next night, heard a bowed instrument playing in a side chamber of the counting house where there was no player, no instrument, no bow, nor even the space or conditions to produce the echo that had accompanied the tune.

STORIES ACCUMULATED FOR several nights after the chamberlain's report. Spirits were abroad in Magna Macragge Civitas. Their range was wide, but the focus seemed to be the Residency, and the barracks and parklands adjacent to it. Vodun Badorum, captain of the praecental household guard, mobilised sweep parties to watch for occurrences, and record or even challenge them, and he also consulted with agents of the Astra Telepathica and the Mechanicum for advice and counsel.

The Lord of Macragge studied the reports as they came in, and sought the wisdom of his high officers and senior advisors, looking for explanations that could be grounded in science, or at least those parts of human science that lay adjacent to the unknowable laws of the warp.

He also summoned Titus Prayto, a supervising centurion of the XIII Legion's newly reinstated Librarius. After Calth, and the hellish losses inflicted on the XIII by psychic warfare and warpcraft, the Lord of Macragge had effectively repealed the Edict of Nikaea, which had stringently outlawed the use of psykers within the Legiones Astartes. The Edict had been the will of the Emperor, and had been enforced as such. However, the Lord of Macragge felt it had deprived his Legion of its most effective weapon at Calth.

The repeal was his decision to make, and he made it with confidence. There were no brother primarchs to consult, no council to convene, no father to turn to. The Lord of Macragge, like the

City of Macragge, stood alone in the night, besieged by storms that made communication impossible. The Lord of Macragge, Roboute Guilliman, was his own authority more than ever.

He overthrew the Edict, for the duration of the emergency at least, for the good of Ultramar. This exercise of authority was the action of a lord who believed that he wielded the power of the Emperor himself. Until now, only Malcador the Sigillite had been entrusted with such influence, and he had been the Imperial Regent.

And 'regent' was a word used aloud even less often, and with less ease, than was the word 'Calth'.

TITUS PRAYTO, A HOODED giant in cobalt-blue Mark IV armour, came to the Residency directly from the Sacristy of the Librarius, which had been unlocked for use within the Fortress.

His lord awaited in a high chamber overlooking the city. The Avenging Son was working diligently at an antique cogitator. Nearby, his great granite desk was piled with papers and slates. The last rays of smoked gold sunlight shone through the tall, narrow windows. Night was encroaching.

Prayto lowered his psychic hood, unclasped his helm, and stood, respectfully bareheaded, helm tucked under his left arm, the clasps and seal-straps dangling.

'Apparitions walk, Titus,' Guilliman said, without looking up.

'They do, my lord,' Prayto said, and nodded.

'Every night,' Guilliman went on, 'more footsteps. More muttering. And this music. The music is a recurring manifestation. A bowed instrument, or instruments.'

'A psaltery, we think, my lord.'

Guilliman looked up at Prayto with piqued interest.

'A psaltery?'

'From the pitch and tone. A particular high and sharp resonance, though there may be more than one instrument. Some are deeper toned, though the note quality is the same. Perhaps meso or bass psalteries, which have larger sound-boxes.'

'All this from verbal accounts?' asked Guilliman.

'No, my lord. Last evening a high-grade servitor in the pantry of the west dining room made a vox recording.'

Guilliman stood.

'I had not been told. Do you have it?'

Prayto nodded and activated a vox-module clamped to his belt to play back the audio clip.

A few seconds of haunting, plaintive music played: thin, high, long notes that had an ethereal quality.

The clip ended.

'Shall I play it again, my lord?' asked Prayto.

Guilliman shook his head. His mind was such that one hearing was sufficient for him to process all particulars.

'Assuredly a psaltery,' he mused. 'The melody was in the pitch of D, though I do not recognise the tune. So… it can be recorded.'

'Yes, lord.'

'This reassures me somewhat. A psychic intrusion, or some assault of the warp upon our imaginations would not leave a sonic fingerprint.'

'No, my lord,' replied Prayto. 'We seem to be hearing physical sounds, transmitted to us somehow. It would explain why, between us, the Librarius and the Astra Telepathica have detected no trace of psychic activity whatsoever.'

Guilliman nodded. He was wearing the dark, heavy robes of a senator or consul, though cut to a different scale of being.

'Be seated,' he told Prayto, with a sidelong gesture.

Titus Prayto hesitated for a moment while he selected an appropriate place to sit down. The Lord's Chamber was part of a suite of rooms in the upper level of the Residency, which, Prayto knew, had been the private accommodation of Konor, the primarch's adoptive father. Lord Guilliman had changed very little of the decor. The walls were still hung with paintings of people and events that bore significance to the local history of Macragge, but had precious little to do with the greater, galactic narrative of the Imperium.

The main change that Lord Guilliman had made in the decades he had occupied the Residency was to have most of the human-scaled furniture removed and replaced with objects built for a primarch's dimensions: the desk, four chairs, a footstool, and a day bed. There were other items proportioned for the physicality of a Legiones Astartes battle-brother, and Prayto sat upon such a chair. The room, therefore, contained three magnitudes of furniture to provide for the Lord of Macragge and any of the advisors and subjects who might attend him. Positioned correctly, with one of the lord's massive chairs in the foreground, a Legion-scaled item of furniture in the middle ground, and a chair for human build furthest away, it was possible to play amusing and impossible tricks upon the mind, as the apparent recession of the furniture suggested a distance in the room that the walls and ceiling denied. Reverse the positions and the room appeared to have no depth at all.

'The echo,' said Guilliman, returning to the ancient, brass-fitted cogitator on his oversized desk. Like the chamber, the cogitator was an inheritance from his stepfather, Konor. In the old days of Ultramar, before contact with the crusade fleets of Terra brought new technologies, Konor had effectively run the fiefdom from this room with that cold-gestalt instrument from the Golden Age of Technology.

'The echo is part of the sound,' Guilliman said. 'This has been mentioned by several witnesses about several apparitions. The quality of the echo is not an acoustic product of the environment.'

'No, lord,' Prayto agreed. 'The west dining room's pantry would not produce an echo like that. I had it tested by the adepts of the Mechanicum.'

'You did?' asked Guilliman. 'Why?'

'Because I knew you would have ordered such a test if I had not.'

A brief, appreciative smile crossed the Avenging Son's mouth.

'We will solve this puzzle, Titus,' Guilliman said.

'We will, my lord. Assuredly.'

'Bring all new data directly to me, day or night.'

'I will, my lord.'

Prayto rose to his feet, sensing that his audience was ended. Guilliman noticed that the Librarian had been regarding, with some interest, books and data-slates piled on a side table.

'You read, Titus?' the Avenging Son asked.

'Of course, my lord.'

Guilliman demurred with a slight wave of his hand.

'You misunderstand. Of course you *can* read. But I don't mean data, or tactical updates, or informational material. Do you read fiction? Drama? Poetry? History?'

Prayto maintained a solemn face, though he was amused. There were times when Lord Guilliman of Ultramar seemed to know everything about everything, in astonishing detail, yet he could also be childlike in his naivety and not understand very basic things about the people and the culture surrounding him.

'I do, my lord,' said Prayto. 'As I believe someone in this very room said, in the address to mark the recommencement of the Librarius programme, our minds are our primary weapons, so it pays to exercise them well.'

Guilliman laughed and nodded.

'I did say that,' he agreed.

'I read extensively to that end,' said Prayto. 'I find the notions and wisdoms contained in literature and poetry push my mind to places that pure technical reading does not. I enjoy the epic cycles of Tashkara, and the philosophies of Zimbahn and Poul Padraig Grossman.'

Guilliman signalled his approval with a tip of his head.

'All Unification Era, of course,' he said. 'You should explore the classics.'

He crossed to the side table and took up a data-slate. He handed it to Prayto.

'You'll enjoy this,' he said.

'Thank you, my lord.'

Prayto studied the title.

'*Amulet, Prince Demark?*'

'It's drama, Titus. Ancient stuff, from M2 or earlier. One of the few extant works by Shakespire.'

'Why this, my lord?'

Guilliman shrugged.

'My father had me read it as a child. I was reminded of it by current events, so I had it fetched from the Residency biblios. In the ancient kingdom of Demark, ghosts walk upon the palace battlements, and are premonitions of great societal change in the court of that realm.'

Prayto shook the slate approvingly.

'I will enjoy it,' he said.

Guilliman nodded, and turned back to his cold-gestalt machine. The audience was over.

Dit-dit-dit-deeeeet!

The cogitator had an odd, synthesised alert chime. It was an antique device. Every twenty-five seconds, it burbled its little noise, trying to alert the Avenging Son to the new information it had acquired.

Guilliman ignored the chime. He did not need to be told. He

had already noticed the matter that the cogitator was trying to bring to his attention.

A star. A new star. It was the first star that had been visible in Macragge's night sky for over two years.

Guilliman sat, staring through the chamber windows at the star, which glimmered alone in the otherwise bloody, swirling night sky. He had scribbled down its position on a note slate: eastern limits, low on the horizon, rising between the peaks of Calut and Andromache. He had spotted it with his naked eyes fifteen minutes ago, a good three minutes before the cogitator had begun its persistent burbling.

Konor – great Konor, Battle King – had run Macragge, world and city alike, from this room, and with this cogitator. At night, when the mechanisms of bureaucracy had shut down, he had sat here alone, monitoring data-traffic and news-flows. He had sat at his teak desk, looking out of the deep windows, observing his realm. In the daytime, Konor had ruled Macragge from the senate floor. At night, this chamber had been the focus of his authority.

Guilliman remembered that. He remembered his stepfather's intensity, even in repose. As a youth, Guilliman had come to the Residency and watched Konor sitting by the cogitator after hours, reading from the day's reports and slates, reviewing briefings for the next day, looking up every time the data-engine chimed.

Dit-dit-dit-deeeeet!

Until Guilliman came to Macragge, capital world of Ultramar's Five Hundred, Konor had been the epitome of statesman, politician and warlord. No one, not even Guilliman, could have imagined how Konor's adopted son would come to eclipse him.

Roboute Guilliman, a genetically enhanced post-human, one of only eighteen in the galaxy, had fallen to Macragge out of the skies at the whim of fates beyond mortal ken. His blood father, it later transpired, was the nameless Emperor of Terra. Like all of the eighteen sons, all of the primarchs, Guilliman had been stolen from his father's genetic nursery and cast out across space. No one really knew how this action had been accomplished, or by what, or for what reason. When pressed on the subject – and he could seldom be pressed on any subject – Guilliman's blood father had attested that the abduction and scattering of his primarch offspring had been an action of the Ruinous Powers of the warp, an event designed to thwart the schemes of mankind.

Guilliman did not place much faith in this. It smacked of foolishness to suggest that his blood father should be so naive as to be gulled by Chaos so. To have his genetically engineered heirs stolen and scattered in some bizarre diaspora?

Nonsense.

Guilliman believed that a great deal more deliberate purpose had been at the heart of it. He knew his gene-father. The man – and man was far too slight a word – possessed a mind that had conceived a universal plan, a plan that would take thousands or even millions of years to orchestrate and accomplish. The Emperor was the architect of a species. The primarchs were central to that ambition. The Emperor would not have lost them or permitted them to be stolen. Guilliman believed that his father had arranged or allowed the dispersal.

Eighteen perfect genetically engineered heirs were not enough. They had to be tested and tempered. Scattering them across the tides of space and time to see who would survive and who would succeed, that was the project of a true luminary.

Guilliman had fallen on Macragge, and had been raised as a son by the first man of that world to be a ruler, a statesman and a warlord. By his twelfth year, it was apparent from his inhuman stature and abilities that Roboute Guilliman was not simply a man. He was a demigod. He had been tested by circumstances, and he had not been found wanting.

Dit-dit-dit-deeeeet!

Twelve years old, coming into the chamber at night, seeing Konor in his chair, the cogitator chiming, the windows undraped. Twelve years old, already as tall as his stepfather, and already more physically powerful; another year or two and he would have to have furniture, armour and weapons made especially for him.

Dit-dit-dit-deeeeet!

Konor believed in contingency. Any plan, no matter how flawless, needed a back-up. Guilliman believed his blood father thought this too. Contingency was something Konor and Guilliman's blood father agreed on. Their advice would have been the same. Do not believe in perfection, because it can be taken away. Always have a fall-back you can live with. Always know how victory can be achieved in a different way. Always have the practical to compensate for any theoretical.

The Imperium of Man was the most perfect vision of unity imaginable. The Emperor and his heirs had spent more than two centuries making it a possibility. If it failed... If it *failed*, was one to simply despair? Did a man collapse and rail at the universe for compromising his plan?

Or did he regroup and turn to his contingency?

Did he demonstrate to fate that there is always another way?

Horus Lupercal – another of the eighteen primarchs, but, in Guilliman's opinion, far from the best – had been selected as the heir among heirs and, in a miserably short space of time, had been found wanting. He had risen in revolt, twisting some other primarchs against their gene-father too.

The first Guilliman had known of this sacrilege was when Lorgar's bastards had turned upon the Five Hundred Worlds at Calth and, in darkest treachery, had shattered that planet.

Shameless. Atrocious.

Two years had passed, and there was not a second of them when

Guilliman had not thought of Lorgar's treachery and – by exten-
sion – Horus's.

Guilliman would be avenged.

It would be a simple revenge, ultimately, the kind of revenge
Konor had taught him at the cutting edge of a gladius.

Dit-dit-dit-deeeeet!

There was a new star in heaven tonight. One hundred days ago,
Guilliman had set the old cold-gestalt cogitator to alert him to
any stellar changes.

Guilliman had known what to expect if it worked. *If.* Tonight,
he had seen the new star immediately. He had been sitting in his
chair, beside the cogitator, facing the windows, the way his stepfather had passed the long nights.

The star.

A light.

A beacon.

Hope.

Dit-dit-dit-deeeeet!

Guilliman leaned over and pressed the cancel button to kill the
persisting chime.

There was a knock at the chamber door.

'Enter.'

It was Euten.

'My lord–' the old woman began.

'I've already seen it, mam,' said Guilliman.

Euten looked puzzled.

'The… apparition?' she asked.

Guilliman stood.

'Begin again,' he said.

BADORUM, COMMANDER OF the praecental household, had gathered a
squad of men from the night watch in the hallway leading to the

hydroponics gallery. By human standards, they were all large, powerful men, though they seemed like children beside the primarch.

Badorum was a seasoned officer in late middle age. Like his soldiers, he wore steel, silver and grey, with a short cape of cobalt-blue. His strap-hung plasma weapon was chromed and immaculate.

Euten the chamberlain, a tall, fragile stick-figure in a long white gown, led the way, clomping with her staff. Guilliman followed, impatient to arrive, but respectful enough to walk at the old woman's best pace. The approach was dark, as if the lights had been switched off or had failed. The only luminosity came from the lanterns and visor lights of the householders, and the faint green glow of the gallery beyond the door.

Guilliman could already hear it: a psaltery, a bass psaltery, peeling its long, sad, pure notes into the night air. The echo was pronounced. The hydroponics gallery was a large space, but Guilliman was sure it could not have produced quite that kind of echo. The sound seemed to come from the heart of the world, as if it were rising out of some tectonically riven abyss.

'What have you seen?' asked Guilliman, ignoring the rattle of bowed salutes that Badorum and the night watch offered him.

'I was only just summoned, lord,' said Badorum. 'Clenart? You were here.'

The soldier stepped forward and removed his helm respectfully.

'We were patrolling, my lord, and approaching this gallery when we first heard the noise. Music, just as now.'

'Clenart, look at me,' Guilliman said.

The soldier raised his eyes to meet the Avenging Son's gaze. He had to tilt his head back a long way. 'You saw something?'

'Yes, my lord, indeed so,' the man replied. 'A great figure in black. Made of blackness, as it seemed. It stepped out of the shadows and was solid. It was wrapped in iron, my lord.'

'In iron?'

'In metal. It was armoured, even the face. Not a visor, a mask.'

'How big?' asked Euten.

'As big…' the soldier began. He paused. 'As big as him, my lady.'

He gestured down the hallway. Titus Prayto had just come into view, escorted by four Ultramarines battle-brothers.

As large as a Space Marine of the Legiones Astartes. A giant, then.

'Another sighting, my lord?' Prayto asked.

'Can you scan the area?' asked Guilliman.

'I have done so, but I will again,' Prayto replied. 'There is no psychic trace here. The passive monitors would have triggered long before I arrived.'

'But you hear the music, Titus?'

'I do, my lord.'

Guilliman reached out his hand. Prayto, without hesitation, drew his boltgun and slapped it into his primarch's waiting palm. Guilliman checked its readiness quickly and turned towards the gallery door. The weapon was a little too small for his hand. It looked like a pistol.

'My lord,' Badorum began. 'Should we not go in before you and–'

'As you were, commander,' said Prayto. He did not need to read his master's mind to be sure of the determination of his intent.

Guilliman entered the green twilight of the hydroponics gallery. Inside, it was warm and humid. The lights were on some night-cycle pattern. He could hear the gurgle of the water feeding the tanks, and the soft drip of the sluices. There was a pungent scent of grass and leaf mulch.

The phantom music was louder inside, and its echo more profound and inexplicable.

Prayto followed Guilliman. He had drawn his combat sword. Badorum followed him, his plasma gun braced at his shoulder in a sweeping aim.

'I don't–' Badorum began.

The shadows parted in front of them and a figure loomed where no figure had been. It seemed to grow out of the darkness as if it had come on stage through some invisible curtain.

'*In the name of Terra*,' Guilliman breathed.

The figure was no apparition. It was real and solid. More particularly, he recognised it: the iron mask, the unmaintained Mark III plate, the insignia of the IV Legion Astartes. Guilliman knew too well the shuffling, crippled gait that spoke of chronic and unhealing illness. It was worse than when last he had observed it.

'Warsmith Dantioch,' he said.

'My honoured lord,' Barabas Dantioch of the Iron Warriors replied.

'How can you be here, Dantioch? No ships have arrived in weeks! How can you be here without us knowing of your arrival?'

Guilliman paused suddenly. Dantioch's greeting had been accompanied by a distinct echo.

'When last I heard,' said Guilliman, 'you were half a segmentum away, in the Eastern Fringes, on Sotha.'

'Yes, my Lord Guilliman,' replied Dantioch, 'and I still am.'

2
PHAROS

*'And the decree was, "let light be".
And so it was, and it was good.'*

– Proscribed 'Creation Myth', proto-Catheric
teachings [pre-Unification]

DANTIOCH, WARSMITH OF the Iron Warriors, stood in the cold chamber high on the summit of Mount Pharos, and held Guilliman's gaze.

It was extraordinary. There was no lag or delay. The image and sound of Ultramar's lord was an entirely realised presence. It was as though they were sharing the room, except that no echo accompanied Guilliman's voice, and no fume of breath came from his lips, suggesting that the room he actually occupied was smaller and warmer.

'Forgive me, my lord,' said Dantioch. He reached out an iron-clad hand and pressed his fingertips against Guilliman's sternum. There was a slight resistance as Dantioch's fingers slipped into Guilliman's form, causing a slight, spreading ripple of light to shimmer his image for a moment.

Dantioch withdrew his hand.

'I'm sorry,' he said. 'You seemed so real.'

'You are on Sotha?' Guilliman asked. 'We are communicating at this distance?'

Dantioch nodded.

'I am in a chamber known as Primary Location Alpha, near the top of the Pharos structure. We test-started the system three weeks ago, local, and the system has been running for two weeks. Since then I have been attempting to establish communication.'

Guilliman shook his head, marvelling.

'We saw your light for the first time tonight,' he said.

'Roughly when alignment was properly established,' Dantioch noted, 'which in turn allowed this conversation to take place.'

'You are like a star. A new star.'

'I would appreciate any data you can process back to us via this link,' Dantioch said. 'To understand in more detail how we are received will allow us to fine-tune the connection.'

'This is technology of a level we can scarcely dream of, warsmith,' said Guilliman.

'We did not dream of it,' replied Dantioch. 'It was dreamed of by beings who came and went long before us. Yet you suspected its worth, imagined its potential, and trusted me to unlock its secrets. This vision, both literal and metaphorical, is due to you, my lord.'

SOTHA WAS A far-flung world close to the edge of the galaxy's Eastern Fringe. It lay farther out than Graia or Thandros, almost at the limits of both the fiefdom of the Five Hundred Worlds and the span of all Imperial territory.

Not far beyond it, in warpcraft terms, lay the rim of the Ultima Segmentum and the edge of the human galaxy. Past that vast thinning-out of stars and systems lay nothing but the black, heatless void of the intergalactic gulf.

Sotha was a jewel of a world, one of the few Terra-comparable ecosystems discovered so far out in the galactic east. It possessed living oceans and densely forested, mountainous landmasses. There were lower-level animal-forms, avians and insects. Curiously, there were no higher forms, nor any obvious trace of attempted xenos visitation or colonisation. Guilliman and the expedition fleets of Ultramar had always considered the world a particular curiosity: if there was one geo-type almost guaranteed to have been settled during the outward expansion of the Great Age of Technology, it was the rare and precious Terra-comparable planets. For Sotha to have been overlooked or missed by the Great Expansionists seemed unlikely, but there was no evidence that any human presence had reached Sotha, not even a colony that had been established and then died out.

Then the surveyors learned the truth about Mount Pharos, the tallest of all the peaks in the planet's majestic mountain ranges.

Plans for full colonisation were put on hold. A small agri-colony was approved instead, to be based on Sotha in support of a survey mission of archaeologists and xenoculturists assigned to Mount Pharos.

A dedicated company of Ultramarines, the 199th, was assigned to Sotha as permanent protection, and the world was given the classification 'restricted'.

All that had happened one hundred and twenty-seven years earlier.

DANTIOCH HAD BEEN out on the promontory at sunset when the Ultramarines of the protection company came to tell him that signs of contact were finally becoming apparent.

It was about time. The ancient systems of the Pharos, vast quantum-pulse engines of almost inscrutable function, had been running for two weeks. Dantioch had begun to fear that he and the men he worked with had entirely misconceived the purpose and use of the artefacts.

It was late afternoon, the particular moment when the light above the forests and distant sea outside began to skew away, filling the apertures of the summit behind the promontory with a phantom luminescence.

It was the best time to appreciate the sheer magnificence of the structure.

'There is a sign at last?' he asked.

One of the Ultramarines, a sergeant called Arkus, nodded. He was accompanied by two young men of the company's Scout section. The Ultramarines 199th had made the best of their residency on Sotha by taking pride in their specialist duty. They had adopted the name Aegida, or 'shield', Company while operating from the Legion orbital. They had also taken up a symbol as their company icon. Both the Scouts wore it on their pauldrons.

'There are signs, sir,' said Arkus. 'Noises in the… the acoustic chambers.'

'At last,' Dantioch said. He limped across the rocky promontory to follow them inside the mountain, every step an effort for his massive, iron-framed physique. He no longer cared to disguise the attenuated gasps of pain that movement forced out of him. He had been genetically fabricated to withstand superhuman tolerances, and by the damned Emperor, he was withstanding them.

At the threshold of one of the vast apertures which opened like a giant eye socket in the mountainside, Dantioch turned back to look at the evening sky. Beyond the high cloud, he could detect the malicious disturbance of the Ruinstorm. It was easier to see at night, usually, but even in daylight hours the traumatic warp-spasms and ripples shimmering through space were visible.

The trigger point for the Ruinstorm had been the attack on Calth twenty-eight months earlier. Its hideous effects had rapidly spread right across the segmentum, and had engulfed the Five Hundred Worlds of Ultramar.

No one knew how far the storm effects went. Some said they had possessed the entire galaxy. What was certainly true was that they had rendered the Five Hundred Worlds unnavigable except for the most high-risk enterprises. Trade and communication had collapsed. Ultramar, as a single and admirable area of governance, was ruined. Furthermore, all interstellar transit between the Eastern Fringe and the core segmenta, and beloved Terra, was impossible. The galaxy was, in effect, cut in two.

Lord Barabas Dantioch, warsmith of the IV Legion Iron Warriors, was technically a traitor. He was a traitor to the Throne and Terra, because his Legion had crossed the line and sided with the renegade Warmaster, Horus. Simultaneously, he was a traitor to his own Legion, because he had forsworn the Iron Warriors and decided to stand with the loyalists. He stood alone, besieged by the conflicting loyalties of the new, riven Imperium.

Being besieged suited all Iron Warriors, of course, no matter their inclination. No Legion matched them for their artistry in fortification, except perhaps for the VII Legion, the Imperial Fists. The comparative technical excellences of the IV and the VII would be put to the ultimate test, Dantioch was sure, before the Civil War ended. In fact, given that the morality of the Imperium had already been turned upside down by Horus's revolt, it would seem a waste of the opportunity if the ancient rivalry was not tested by war.

For his excellence in siegecraft, and his staunch loyalty to the Emperor, Barabas Dantioch had been recruited by the Lords of Ultramar to help them construct and defend the greatest contingency plan – and perhaps the second greatest heresy – the Imperium had ever known.

Dantioch had accepted the challenge. He had supposed he

would be employed in fortifying the physical defences of Macragge and other key worlds of Ultramar. That was his forte.

Then the Avenging Son had revealed to him the long-sequestered mysteries of Sotha, and Dantioch had realised that the survival of a pocket empire like Ultramar lay less in fortifying its physical defences and far, far more in strengthening its function and operation.

He agreed absolutely with Roboute Guilliman. Sotha offered a way in which they might overcome the Ruinstorm rather than batten down against its wrath.

Dantioch had spent the last nine months working to that end, unlocking Sotha's mysteries and activating the planet's deep-time secrets.

The day's ebbing light shone into the aperture and the great coiled chamber. The interior spaces of the Pharos, each one of them cut from the mountain's living rock by processes that no one had been able to explain, reminded Dantioch of the inner spaces of a great conch shell. They were polished, smooth and curved. There were no straight lines or hard edges. Vast, organically curved chambers led one into another, sometimes connected by smaller, flask-chambers or rounded coils of hallway that felt like tubes or blood vessels. Everything was a polished, gleaming black: a surface treatment of the exposed rock that was durable and resistant to scratching or cutting. It was like a black mirror, yet it gave back very little reflection – just the merest shadow – and held very little light, except for when, at the end of each day, the sunset flooded through the mountain-top apertures, and a curious golden light dripped and drained down through the Pharos chambers, deep into the mountain, like liquid fire running off the polished black walls.

The early surveyors had found the Pharos, men working in the fleets sent out by Guilliman to expand the realm of Macragge, and reconnect with ancient fief-holdings that had been part of the realm before the Age of Strife. This had always been Konor's dream. Konor had ruled Ultramar from Macragge, but his Ultramar was but a shadow, a fraction of the culture that Ultramar had been before the Long Night. Konor had been determined to rebuild the mythical Five Hundred Worlds, and, after his death, Guilliman had set out to achieve his father's ambition. It was while he was rebuilding the Five Hundred Worlds, and making them the greatest empire in the galactic east, that the crusading fleets of Terra had reached Macragge, and Guilliman had finally met his blood father, and learned of his true inheritance.

That the Pharos was an immense structure of xenos origin had been obvious. That was why Sotha had been restricted and placed under guard while it was thoroughly investigated. Guilliman, so forward thinking in other ways, had a natural mistrust of technologies not built by man, especially those that could not be easily reverse-engineered. The Pharos of Sotha was potentially many things, with many possible functions, and Guilliman was cautious of them all. The survey mission was established on the planet, a planet that otherwise would have been rapidly colonised, and a community of settlers founded to support the scientists.

This amused Dantioch. The settlers were simple agricultural workers charged with food production and livestock management. They lived simple, pastoral lives on the lower slopes of the mountain. Forest growth on the slopes was rapid and vital. It had taken several years to clear the entrance apertures just to gain access. Every summer, the farm workers came up from the arable fields in the valley below, bringing their scythes and harvesting hooks, and worked to clear away the year's grass and brush growth where it had begun to choke and invade the gleaming black halls again.

This simple, rural tradition, dating back over a hundred years, had given rise to the protection company's choice of icon.

The people of the farming community did not hold the Pharos in any particular awe. It was simply part of their world. They often used its obsidian apertures as caves to shelter them and their herds from storms. They had also, long ago, discovered the extraordinary acoustic qualities of the linked chambers and halls, and had taken to playing their pipes and horns and psalteries in the deep caves, creating music of unparalleled beauty and mystery.

From the first moment that he arrived to inspect the Pharos, Dantioch had understood that the interlinking chambers had not been intended as occupation spaces, at least not for any creatures of humanoid dimensions. There were often places of near impossible access between chambers: deep, polished drops; smooth sheer curves; untenable slopes. There were no stairs, no measured walkways. In one particular instance, a vast tri-lobed chamber, shaped almost like a stomach, plunged away into a polished tube seven hundred metres deep, which opened in the ceiling of another vast, semi-spherical hall a hundred metres high.

A long, slow process of construction had been undertaken over the years, establishing self-levelling, pre-fabricated walkways of STC design to provide platforms, ladders, stairs and bridges that would allow humans to traverse and explore the almost endless interior of the Pharos.

Dantioch and his Ultramarines escort descended on just such a walkway. The Imperial equipment, solid and steady, locked into place over the rolling, polished curves of the Pharos's chambers, seemed crude by comparison: treated, unpainted metal, cold-pressed from a standard template, stamped with the Imperial aquila, echoing to their footsteps with leaden clatters. When they walked upon the polished black, they made only the softest tapping sounds. The walkways, stairs and platforms were also dwarfed by the gloomy chambers they threaded through, and seemed frail by comparison to the sheened black curves and cliffs.

Arkus and his Scouts patiently led the crippled warsmith to the abyssal plain of Primary Location Alpha. Twice on the journey they passed farmworkers eating supper and playing their instruments. Oberdeii, one of the Scouts, and the youngest of the entire company, shooed them away. The Pharos had been officially out of bounds ever since Dantioch had brought the quantum-pulse engines, deep in the mountain's core, online. They could all hear, or at least feel, the infrasonic throb of the vast and ancient devices.

Dantioch had stood in Primary Location Alpha, and nodded to his escort to withdraw. He had been fairly confident that he understood the function of the Pharos even from the data he had studied before his arrival on Sotha. Guilliman had deduced it too. Primary Location Alpha was, he was sure, the centre of the entire mechanism. Dantioch found himself referring to it in his notes as the 'tuning stage' or the 'sounding board'. It was a vast cave of polished black, with a domed ceiling and an almost flat floor.

Ghosts walked here, images of things light years away, drawn into the Pharos by its quantum processes. They were often fleeting, but always real. It had taken Dantioch two weeks and immense astronomical calculations to tune the Pharos as he wanted it.

As he walked onto the tuning floor, Dantioch saw Guilliman appear before him, as if in the flesh.

He had finally tuned the xenos device to far distant Macragge.

'IT IS AS you speculated, my lord,' Dantioch said. 'The Pharos is part of an ancient interstellar navigation system. It is both a beacon and a route-finder. And, as we just saw, it also permits instantaneous communication across unimaginable distances.'

'You say I speculated, Dantioch,' said Guilliman's image, 'but I never had the slightest clue what manner of technology it was.'

'It is not fully understood by me either, lord,' replied the warsmith. 'It certainly involves a principle of quantum entanglement. But I believe that, unlike our warp technology that uses the immaterium to bypass realspace, this quantum function once allowed for site-to-site teleportation, perhaps through a network of gateways. I also believe its fundamental function lies not with psychic energy, but with empathic power. It is an empathic system, adjusted to the needs of the user, not the will. I will provide fuller findings later.'

'But it is a navigational beacon?' asked Guilliman.

'In many ways.'

'You said it was part of a network?'

Dantioch nodded.

'I believe other stations like the Pharos must exist, or once existed, on other worlds throughout the galaxy.'

Guilliman paused.

'So it is not one, single beacon, like the Astronomican?'

'No, lord. In two ways. I believe the Pharos and other stations like it once used to create a network of navigational pathways between stars, as opposed to a single, range-finding point the way the Astronomican does. Or did.'

'Go on.'

'It is more like a lantern than a beacon, lord. You tune it. You point it, and illuminate a site or location for the benefit of range-finding. Now I have tuned to Macragge, I can, I believe, light up Macragge as a bright spot that will be visible throughout realspace and the warp, despite the Ruinstorm.'

'Just as I see Sotha as a new star in the sky?'

'Yes, my lord.'

Guilliman looked at him.

'I am loath to use xenos technology, but the light of the Astronomican is lost to us because of the Ruinstorm. To hold Ultramar together, to rebuild the Five Hundred Worlds, we must restore communication and travel links. We must navigate and reposition. We must pierce and banish this age of darkness. This is the first step towards our survival. This is how we fight back and overthrow Horus and his daemon allies. Dantioch, I applaud you and thank you for the peerless work you have done, and the labours you are yet to undertake.'

'My lord.'

Dantioch, with difficulty, bowed.

'Warsmith?'

'Yes, my lord?'

'Illuminate Macragge.'

3

FROM THE HEART OF THE STORM

*'Hjold! The sea is set against us, for
it is the sea, and the darkness is set about us,
for it is the darkness, but
we will row on, brothers, backs breaking into each stroke,
we will row on because no other
life or comfort awaits us.
Fja vo! Survive! The sea and the dark are our context!
We will, before eternity, out-row all storms.'*

– from *The Seafarer* (Fenrisian Eddas)

THE HULL HAD been screaming for months. Screaming like a new-born thrown to the night-packs.

Their ship was called the *Waning Crescent*; zeta-class, a courier ship. It was not the proud warship or longwarp they might have hoped for, but they were a small company of Wolves, and Leman Russ had no resources to waste.

Faffnr Bludbroder had felt his heart swell with pride when Russ had given him the duty. It was a duty that had been handed to the VI Legion by the Sigillite. However, Faffnr had felt his heart sag when he realised it was not going to be some great, sharp-edged expedition of battleships and barges, but ten wolf-brothers on a lowly ship to distant Ultramar.

Faffnr had quickened his edge anyway, accepted the fold of parchment upon which his duty was laid out, and bowed to the primarch of the VI Legion.

'*Ojor hjold.* I will do this, lord,' he had said.

They had set out, sworn and dedicated to what was one of the most shocking duties any of the Legiones Astartes might ever undertake.

Three weeks into their voyage, the warp had gone dark, the storm had risen, and the ship had begun to scream. It had been screaming ever since.

Most of the crew, the human crew, had gone mad. The Wolves of Fenris had been forced to kill some, and deprive most of the others of their liberty for their own protection. The *Waning Crescent*, aside from ten warriors of the VI Legion Space Wolves, was carrying gene-stock grain samples and ceramics. Within a day, the violence of the warp storm had smashed all the ceramics in the holds. The screaming... The screaming was...

It was as if the world were ending. The Bloody Sunset of legend, the end of things, the wolf eating its own tail, the end of the great cycle, to be followed only by the cold moonrise of the afterworld. Faffnr had been forced to tie the whimpering shipmaster to his seat. Bo Soren, known as 'The Axe', had stood watch day and night over the Navigator's socket-pit, blade ready to administer mercy. Malmur Longreach, spear in one hand and bolter in the other, had guarded the defibrillating engines. Shockeye Ffyn, Kuro Jjordrovk, Gudson Allfreyer, Mads Loreson and Salick the Braided had patrolled the empty companionways and echoing corridors of the stricken ship in rotation, watching for manifests.

Biter Herek had watched the fore-station.

Nido Knifeson had watched the stern quarters.

None of them had gone unchallenged.

The broiling warp had squeezed out daemonforms, creatures that had pierced the screaming, and slipped in through the hull plates of the ship. The Wolves had been tasked. They had been forced to draw down, stand their ground, and bloody their blades to drive the warp-things back. Malmur had fought two nights in the spastic engine room. Kuro had lost an arm to a tar-blackened maw that had swung in from nowhere. Biter Herek had split a lunging skull in twain with his axe, and had done it every night, to such an extent that it was almost a ritual. As the ship's master clock struck four, the raging skull would appear at the fore-station, and Biter would be ready with his axe to greet it, and split it.

They all had stories, pieces of a saga that none of them would ever live long enough to pass on to a skjald for retelling.

It was a voyage of the damned. They believed that each day, marked out by the increasingly unreliable deck-clocks of the battered ship, would be their last.

Then their voyage and their saga ended in the most unexpected way; not in the jaws of the doomwolf, or a drench of blood spilt by an enemy's blade or teeth.

No, their saga ended in a light, in a beacon.

In hope.

SOMEHOW, DURING THE storm crossing, they had become friends. Eeron Kleve of the X Legion Iron Hands, black in his mourning cloak, and Timur Gantulga of the V Legion White Scars, pale as tundra frost.

Their paths had crossed at Neryx, where Kleve's forces had been caught in flight after the Isstvan massacre that had taken his beloved primarch. A sixty-day fight through the asteroid belt had finally ended when the Sons of Horus, snapping at Kleve's throat, were driven off by Gantulga's strike force.

Word had already begun to spread of the Warmaster's treachery, and Gantulga's force had been hunting for targets. His remit had been to seek confirmation of the atrocity and its perpetrator, but Gantulga had found all the confirmation he needed in the sight of eight warships bearing Horus's mark hounding a battered barge of the X Legion like dogs baiting a wounded bear.

The Sons of Horus had not gone quietly. Knowing their astropathic death screams would swiftly bring more of their kind, the Iron Hands and White Scars had formed up and made a run for Momed, where further Iron Hands were reported to be mustering. Gantulga had transferred to Kleve's barge to share intelligence data just before the assembled flotilla had entered the warp.

Then the storm had struck and they had been lost. Their crossing had begun.

Gantulga did not count the hours or the days. It was fluid to him.

'Time is merely the distance between two objects,' he said.

Kleve had no choice. Settings in his optical implants automatically displayed the track of local time. He would relate the tally to Gantulga, and the White Scar would shrug, as if to note that while the data was practically meaningless, he appreciated the sharing.

When the death of Ferrus Manus had been authenticated, Kleve had decreed that his companies would observe ten years of mourning. But as time was meaningless and fluid within the storm, and merely an arbitrary count in the corner of his vision, Kleve had also declared that the mourning would only begin once they were back in realspace, within the flow of time as it is understood in the physical universe.

It had become his obsession: not deliverance or salvation, not to escape the storm, not even to find the enemy and avenge the fallen of his Legion. He simply wanted to end the crossing and translate again so that he could reset his counter and begin the mourning.

That day, just another period marked for convenience on the shipboard watch, for the bucking, bridling ship travelling through the eternal storm-blackness of the warp, Kleve found Gantulga in an upper wardroom, teaching Chogorian combat slang to some of Kleve's company and a party of remembrancers. Gantulga believed that there might be strategic benefits from having Iron Hands understand the private patois of the White Scars if they were to fight in close cooperation against a remorseless foe who otherwise knew all Imperial codings. The remembrancers were present to learn, and then act as tutors for those in Kleve's company prevented from attending because of watch duties. Kleve had requested his remembrancers set aside their original role, a function that had been established to celebrate the glory of the Great Crusade. Since the treachery, there was nothing pure or worthy to remember. The only thing Kleve felt worth commemorating was the broken past before the fall, so the remembrancers had become willing memorialists.

That day, which was just another meaningless mark in Kleve's stoic timekeeping, and just another non-day to Gantulga, would turn out to be a day to mark after all.

The Iron Hands and the memorialists rose as Kleve entered the wardroom. Gantulga did not. Kleve addressed him directly.

'There is a light,' he said. 'A beacon.'

'This I have heard,' said Gantulga.

'We steer towards it,' said Kleve. 'I have instructed the shipmaster so.'

'Do we know if any of my ships are still with us?' asked Gantulga. Kleve shook his head.

'Is it the light of Terra?' asked Gantulga, getting to his feet. 'Is it the Astronomican, light of the Throne?'

Kleve shook his head again.

'The data is inconclusive. It seems unlikely. Analytically, its pattern is similar, but not the same. However, we are half-blind, and our sensors are hardly reliable.'

'We should steer towards it,' Gantulga agreed. He took out his long, slightly hooked sword, and laid it on the table in front of him. He placed his palms flat on the surface beside it, and made a silent oath of blessing to its trustworthiness and sharpness.

'You draw your sword?' asked Kleve.

'I am a hunter,' replied Gantulga, 'so I know how hunters operate. The light may be Terra. It may be some other hope. But it may also be a lure. So let us go to this light, but let us do so armed until we know what it contains.'

FROM THE HEART of the storm they came, over hours, then days, then weeks: lone ships, wounded vessels, broken flotillas and piecemeal fleets.

They were the lost and the damned, survivors and refugees, men fleeing battles or hunting for them, or simply voyagers seeking shelter from the madness of the Ruinstorm.

And they came to Macragge, the light in the darkness.

Some were ships bringing much needed imports and materials from others of the Five Hundred Worlds. All brought news, or pieces of news. Many were ships of Guilliman's own Legion, storm-lost on their way back from the Underworld War raging on Calth, or the bitter campaign against the traitor sons that snarled across Ultramar as a whole. Some carried more of the wounded Legions – the Iron Hands and Raven Guard, a handful of Salamanders. The stories they brought were the bitterest of all.

'THE AUDIENCE HALL is ready for you, lord,' said Euten gently.

It was a daily practice: the Lord of Ultramar would personally greet representatives of the ships that the light had brought to Macragge. There was some solace and joy in this, sometimes the reunion of old comrades, or the welcoming of a valuable asset. There was also grief and despair, however, and an ever-increasing tally of stories recounting infamy and loss. Guilliman thought his heart had been hardened by Calth to the point at which it had fused like the heavy-metal core of a star, inured to further pain, for a heart can only take a certain measure of pain before it ceases to feel.

He had been wrong.

He was studying a large-scale hololith display of the systems defences: Macragge and its orbital defences, the disposition of the Ultramar fleet elements and the newly arriving masses of ships, the outer weapons platforms and void stations, the starforts and lunar stations, the barrages and decoy hulks, the swathes of mines, the mid-system watch stations and sentry flotillas guarding the Mandeville point, the prowling patrols, the patient battlecruisers, the automated batteries. With dabs of his fingers, he was making adjustments to certain lines, and re-ordering ship positions.

Euten knew this was merely automatic tinkering, the distracted activity of a mind that barely had to concentrate to supervise such strategic complexity.

She knew, from long experience, that Guilliman's mind was elsewhere.

'My lord?'

Guilliman did not look up.

'Three dead,' he said softly. 'Lorgar's boasts were true. Three.'

'My lord.'

Guilliman shook his head, eyes still on the display.

'The stories they bring to me, Euten. That Horus, or any of them, should turn against us, against me, against my father... I cannot begin to process it. My only consolation... My only consolation at all, as I have learned through our bitter fight with Lorgar, is that something has overtaken them, contaminated them. The warp is in their brains. It hardly excuses their actions, but it explains them. They are run mad and are no longer of themselves.'

He looked at the elderly chamberlain. She was upright and slender, supported by her tall staff. Her short hair was as glacial as her gown.

'It is a hard thing to accept, my lord,' she said.

'I thought it would be the hardest,' Guilliman agreed. 'But what are brothers turned traitor compared to the death of three loyal sons? The survivors cannot refute it. Ferrus is dead. Corax, Vulkan, loyal all, and dead. Then, from the mouths of others, this news from Prospero. Magnus defying our father so much that they set the damned Wolves upon him? And now we hear from the Phall System, confirmation that Perturabo has indeed betrayed us...'

He rose to his feet.

'What else? What else, I wonder? Is Terra already burning? Is my father already dead? If half of my brothers have turned to follow Horus's treachery, then who remains? Three of those who might be counted loyal are already dead. Who else? Where is the Khan? Does Dorn burn along with Terra? Sanguinius and his Legion are said to be lost. The Lion has gone into the dark. Have the traitors hunted down the Wolf King and torn him to shreds? Am I alone now?'

'My lord, you–'

Guilliman held up his hand.

'I am just thinking out loud, mam. I will be composed by the time I reach the hall. You know I will.'

She nodded.

'All I can count upon is what I know as solid fact,' said Guilliman. 'Macragge still stands. My Legion still stands. While those two facts remain, there remains an Imperium.'

He pulled a mantle around his broad, armoured shoulders, and fixed the clasp at his throat. He was wearing the ceremonial version of his ferocious, clawed wargear, and carried no weapons. For his daily custom of greeting those coming to his light out of the storm, he carried no personal weapons.

Euten watched her beloved lord fix the mantle. He looked, more than ever, like a monarch. Somehow the very lack of weapons made him seem more powerful.

'We are all we can count on,' Guilliman said. 'The time has long passed coming. We must declare. We cannot afford to lose any more time. We cannot afford to wait to hear if Terra endures or my father yet breathes. For the sake of mankind, as my father would have wished it, the Imperium begins again here. Now.'

He walked towards the chamber door.

'And I will personally kill any bastard who tries to stop me.'

4

IN THE HALL OF THE
LORD OF ULTRAMAR

'Never stand between a predator and its quarry,
Or between a king and his throne.'

– proverb, from Illyrium

'NO ONE KNEELS here,' Guilliman said as he strode into the Audience Hall, but everyone was already bowed. The hall was vast, ornately wrought in silver and gold, the soaring roof supported by a thousand columns with petal capitals. Across the broad floor of black and white mosaic tiles, hundreds of visitors knelt and bowed their heads. Nearly two-thirds of them were Space Marines of the Legions.

'No one bows here,' Guilliman said. 'You are come to Macragge and you are welcome here. Let me greet you.'

Flanked by the imposing Cataphractii Terminators of his Invictus bodyguard, Guilliman approached the nearest group. He raised the leader up, his hands clasping the warrior's shoulders.

'Name yourself,' he said.

'Verano Ebb, captain, Silence Squad, Raven Guard,' the man replied.

'Your loss is my loss, captain,' said Guilliman.

'And your hope is my hope,' Ebb replied. 'I pledge my force to you, lord. I ask nothing but the opportunity to stand with Ultramar and kill murderers.'

'And I'd ask nothing else of you. Your place is here, Verano. Welcome.'

Verano nodded a half-bow and gestured to the squads nearby.

'Sardon Karaashison, Iron Hands, and all of his kinsmen that could be rallied. Beside him, Zytos of the Salamanders and his brothers.'

Guilliman regarded them.

'Do you pledge as Verano pledges?' he asked.

Karaashison was a flesh-spare creature in proud black and white plate. He had left his visor in place, undoubtedly because he had little organic face left beneath it. The visor *was* his face. The lenses of his helm slits glittered red.

'I am, lord,' he replied. 'I will stand with any who stand against Horus.'

Zytos had unclamped the helm of his green armour and stood with it under his left arm. His skin was almost as dark as the black finish of Karaashison's livery. His eyes shone unnaturally brightly, as brightly as the photo-enhanced lenses of the Iron Hands warrior.

'We mourn the loss of our brothers the Iron Hands and the Raven Guard,' he said in a gentle, accented voice, 'and we are bowed and bloodied. But the Eighteenth Legion Salamanders are not in mourning. We have resolved to remain steadfast, and to trust that our primarch, your brother, has survived. Until we see proof, we will not mourn.'

'Is this false hope, Zytos?' Guilliman asked.

'It is pragmatism, lord.'

'It might be argued that the pragmatic approach would be to

accept the worst and move on. Hope can be a burden.'

'Hope can be a weapon too,' said the Salamander. 'Just because we will not mourn, it does not follow that we will not fight. We will pledge to you, and make war at your side, and our fighting shout will be "Vulkan lives!" Your word is our command, my lord, until the day our battle cry is proven true.'

Guilliman moved on to the next group, a huddle of battered Imperial Fists led by a hulking giant. The man had been mauled by war, and had refused all except the most basic medical stabilisation. One arm was truncated, and looked as though it had been gnawed off.

'Alexis Polux,' he began, 'captain of the 405th Company and–'

'I know you, Alexis,' said Guilliman.

'I am flattered, my lord. I was not sure you would remember.'

'I make a point of remembering all the officers my brothers regard as exceptional. I have read your report. The engagement in the Phall System.'

'It was a bloody matter, lord.'

'You displayed brilliant strategic thinking. The Iron Warriors had you outnumbered and outgunned.'

Polux made no reply.

'You escaped in a captured ship? The *Contrador*?'

'It was not an escape. It was an exit, lord,' Polux said. 'Our primarch had signalled our immediate return to Terra. We do not disobey orders.'

'Despite the losses you were forced to suffer by disengaging?'

'I regret the losses,' Polux said. 'More than that, I regret not finishing the job. My retribution fleet had him, lord. We were close to killing the bastard.'

There was silence in the hall. Traitor or not, no one was yet used to hearing one of the Emperor's sons referred to with such disdain.

'Perturabo is my brother,' said Guilliman.

'Apologies, my lord,' said Polux. 'I did not mean–'

'He is also a *thrice-damned* bastard,' said Guilliman. 'Do not guard your words on my account. Alexis, I would have you do two things. First, accept the medical provision we can offer you here, so that you may be restored and renewed. Second, thus restored, stand with me and finish the job you started at Phall.'

Polux hesitated, then nodded.

'I accept both, my lord,' he said, 'but conditionally. I have orders to return to Terra, and I will not disobey them.'

'There is no route to Terra now,' said Guilliman. 'Terra may no longer exist.'

'You think the Throneworld has fallen?' asked Polux.

'I am sure it is the Warmaster's primary target.'

'Then all the more reason why we should rally, re-arm, and move en masse to Terra,' Polux declared.

'How long were you lost in the storm after Phall, Alexis?' Guilliman asked. 'I'm telling you there is no route to Terra. There is only one light in the darkness. We have no choice but to fortify and consolidate here. Besides, I feel I have the authority to countermand your orders.'

'How so?' asked Polux.

'Alexis,' said Guilliman, 'I have seniority. Until someone arrives who outranks me, I have command. I intend to use it. We must save the Imperium. Speculation and indecision are not useful traits at this time.'

Polux glared at the Lord of Ultramar. He was one of the few Space Marines who even remotely matched the primarch's physical scale.

'What have you done here, lord?' he asked. 'What are you *doing* here?'

'I am securing the Five Hundred Worlds, Alexis,' Guilliman

replied. 'I am anchoring what remains of the Imperium on Macragge. We have a beacon, some security of transit, and the possibility of proper recomposition. For all intents and purposes, this *is* the Imperium.'

'Which makes you what?' asked Polux. 'Our Emperor?'

'I do not presume to inherit anything,' said Guilliman, recoiling very slightly. 'Like Zytos, I will wait for proof of life before I take any drastic measures. But if my father is dead and I am the last loyal primarch alive, then yes, I am the Imperium.'

'If those are the circumstances, I will follow you,' said Polux, 'but I caution you that until we know–'

'You are familiar, I'm sure, 'said Guilliman, 'with the Ultramarines' concepts of theoretical and practical?'

'Yes, lord.'

'Everything is theoretical, Alexis. The rest of the Imperium, the security of Terra, the survival of my father. Macragge is the only practical. It's the only thing we know we have, and at such a time of extremity, it's the only foundation I know we can depend on.'

Alexis Polux looked as though he had much more to say on the subject. He held Guilliman's gaze, and nodded.

'Practical solutions are what matter now,' he said. 'Fix me and I will fight at your command. I will fight, at the very least, to learn more of what is practical.'

'Thank you, Alexis,' said Guilliman. 'I welcome whatever expertise you and your brothers can offer in the matter of improved fortification and defence. The Imperial Fists have long been renowned for–'

He stopped. He had become aware of the quiet, steady scrape of a whetstone against a blade.

Nearby, another Iron Hands officer waited with his men and a formation of White Scars for their opportunity to greet the primarch. Guilliman clapped Polux reassuringly on his sound shoulder and moved towards them. They seemed to be the origin of the scraping sound.

'Eeron Kleve of the Iron Hands,' said Kleve, bowing. He and his men were shrouded from head to foot in black cloaks. Now they had returned to realspace, their mourning had begun.

'I am Gantulga,' said the White Scars leader, with more of a snap of the head than a bow. He had a sword, drawn and gleaming, in his left hand.

'Welcome both,' said Guilliman, clasping Kleve's hands. 'Accept my offer of shelter from the storm. I hear you were several ships together, Kleve?'

'A White Scars strike force and my own barge, lord,' answered Kleve. 'Most of us made it through the turmoil in formation. Two vessels were lost.'

'You come to me with blade drawn?' Guilliman asked the White Scar.

'Yes, but with my other hand open,' said Gantulga, offering it to Guilliman. 'We did not know what was in your light, Lord of Ultramar, so I kept one palm empty and a sword in the other.'

'What do you think of the light now?' Guilliman asked.

'I like it well enough,' said Gantulga. 'It is not the trap I feared. But I marked your words to the Imperial Fist. The actions of *Horus*…'

He said the name like a snake-hiss, as if it burned his mouth and he wanted to spit it out.

'The actions of Horus are treachery, Lord of Ultramar–'

'Heresy, I would say,' said Guilliman. 'It was treachery at first. To turn against brothers, to kill for personal advancement and power. But we have seen them, seen how their minds and bodies have been corrupted. Their very belief systems have been warped. This is no longer Horus's treachery. It is his heresy.'

Gantulga nodded. 'Heresy comes in many forms,' he said. 'It can be blatant, like the one which now tears down the stars, but it can be subtle too, accidental. To make example, the building of a new Imperium when the old one is not yet pronounced dead.'

Guilliman's smile was as bright and sharp as the White Scar's blade.

'I am not building my own Imperium, Gantulga. I am preserving what's left of the original.'

With his free hand, the White Scar stroked his long moustaches thoughtfully.

'Then I would make sure of your purpose, Lord of Ultramar,' he said. He sheathed his sword.

'With that blade drawn,' said Guilliman, 'I thought you Scars were preparing impatiently for war.'

They could still hear the scraping of the whetstone. It was coming from behind their group.

'No, lord,' said Kleve. 'That would be the Wolves.'

The men with Kleve and Gantulga stood aside, and the pack of Space Wolves was revealed. They crouched rather than bowed or knelt, hunched and huddled in their armour and pelts upon the black and white paving. One was sharpening his war-axe with long, steady strokes of the honing flat. All of them had removed their helms, but they still wore their tight leatherwork hoods and masks, fright-masks curled in perpetual snarls, worked with figures and spirals. Their eyes shone yellow

'Fenrys Hjolda,' said Guilliman. 'You are far from home.'

Their leader rose out of his squat, unwrapping the fur cloak he had gathered around his forearms, and allowing it to fall loose.

'Not your home, Jarl Guilliman,' he said.

'Let me know you,' said Guilliman.

'Faffnr Bludbroder,' said the Wolf, 'and my pack.'

'Ten of you. A squad.'

'A pack. In fealty to Sesc Company, of the Rout, of the Vlka Fenryka.'

Guilliman glanced at the warrior sharpening the axe. Apart from Faffnr, none of the Wolves had risen or shown any deference.

'That axe looks sharp enough to me, brother,' said Guilliman.

'No axe can ever be too sharp,' the man replied without looking up.

'Bo Soren,' Faffnr growled. 'Ask forgiveness for your tongue.'

The Wolf looked up at Guilliman. He bared his teeth.

'I recognise my failing and will be sure to correct it,' he said.

Faffnr looked at Guilliman. 'Bo Soren can be insolent,' he said, unapologetically.

'Bo Soren is a Space Wolf,' said Guilliman.

'You make a good point, jarl,' said Faffnr.

'Of all today's visitors, you intrigue me most.'

'Are we not welcome to your hall, Jarl Guilliman?' asked another of the men.

'Hush your noise, Herek,' said Faffnr.

Biter Herek let out a low, bubbling growl.

'You are all welcome to my hall, Faffnr Bludbroder. What intrigues me is that everyone else sought a safe haven. From the flight data of your vessel, I see that Macragge was your intended destination.'

'It was.'

'We rode out the storm to get here,' said Biter Herek.

'We have a duty here,' added Bo Soren.

'A duty?' echoed Guilliman.

'Bo Soren has a big mouth,' growled Faffnr.

'Necessarily, for he has a great many teeth to fit into it,' said Guilliman. 'What is your duty, pack-leader?'

'Our duty is what our duty has always been – to do what others will not. To do the unthinkable, if the unthinkable must be thought.'

'Your reputation as the sanction is well known,' said Guilliman, 'and perhaps undeserved. We all serve according to our courage.'

'Wolves serve beyond that. We are the executioner's sons.'

'Who have you come to execute, Faffnr Bludbroder?'

Faffnr hesitated. He reached under his pelt and produced a sheaf of parchment.

'I see no point hiding it,' he said, holding the document out. 'Read for yourself, Jarl Guilliman.'

'No, tell me in your own words.'

Faffnr kept the parchment extended.

'Look at it at least. See the seal of the Wolf King, and beside it the sigil of Malcador. Know where this instruction comes from, and the authority it contains.'

Guilliman took the document, unfolded it and studied the marks.

'Authenticate it if you must,' said Faffnr.

'I don't have to. This is real.'

'You heard the fate that befell Prospero?' asked the pack-leader. 'The Wolves were unleashed to issue sanction to Magnus.'

'Yes. Not so undeserved a reputation after all, eh?'

'Go on.'

Faffnr paused. In the eye slots of his straked and knotted leather hood, his golden eyes blinked once, twice.

'If one can fall, more can fall. More have fallen. *Half* have fallen. It has been decreed that a company of Wolves be sent to the hearth-side of every one of the Emperor's sons, to watch them.'

'For what?' asked Guilliman.

'For signs of treachery, of heresy.'

'And if such signs become visible?'

'Then we are to act.'

'Act?' asked Guilliman. 'You're saying that you are here to watch me? To shadow me? And if you perceive my actions to be in any way untoward, what? You are authorised to enact sanction?'

'By the Sigillite, so authorised.'

Guilliman laughed. 'You would… cut my thread?'

'If needs be. Primarchs are not invincible. Some already sleep upon the red snow.'

Guilliman raised his hand, indicating that his bodyguard should back down. The Cataphractii had cycled up their weapons at Faffnr's last response.

'Faffnr Bludbroder,' said Guilliman, 'do you really think that your pack could take me down?'

Faffnr shrugged. 'Perhaps not. You are Jarl Guilliman and your prowess is the stuff of saga. But we have our duty, and we would try. If you were, say, without your bodyguard and cornered in a room with us–'

'My dear Faffnr, then *you* would be cornered in a room with *me*.'

Faffnr shrugged again.

'We are the executioner's sons, Jarl. Even if you took us all, I doubt you'd leave the room whole.'

Guilliman glanced at a nearby adjutant. 'Find them somewhere to sleep.'

'Your hearth will do,' said Faffnr.

'Then show them to my hearth,' said Guilliman.

THE LIGHT OF the Pharos, the distant xeno-tech of Sotha, illuminated Macragge as a lone, bright beacon in the encompassing dark, and that day it brought one other visitor to the heart of Ultramar: not a storm-lost ship, or a bedraggled convoy; not a broken battle-barge or a cargoboat of refugees.

Not a vessel at all.

It brought a flash, high in the warp-dappled skies above Macragge Civitas, a flash, and then an object falling like a stone, streaking out a tail of fire as it scored through the atmosphere.

✠ ✠ ✠

GUILLIMAN LEFT HIS guests behind, walking back to the door of the Audience Hall with his Invictus guard at his heels and Euten at his side.

Titus Prayto was waiting for him.

'The Wolves aren't lying,' Prayto said.

'I didn't think they were,' said Guilliman.

'Should I–' Prayto began.

'Watch them, Titus? Guard the guard dogs?'

'I urge caution, my lord,' said Prayto. 'The Wolves are mercurial beasts at the best of times, unpredictable and quick to find their temper. It is their asset in battle, but it is not suited to the realm of the court. They are tired and they have endured much. They are living on their nerve-ends. I read this in them.'

'You don't need to have *the sight* to read it,' muttered Euten, casting a disapproving glance over her shoulder in the direction of the Fenrisian huddle. 'And they reek like–'

'Enough, Euten,' said Guilliman. 'Faffnr seems an honest man, straightforward. He made no attempt to hide his duty, or the egregious burden of it.'

'Nonetheless, I urge caution, my lord,' said Prayto, 'precisely because of that. He is like an open book. He is determined to perform his duty even though he knows it is a thankless task. He does not want to make an error. He is aware that the best of us have made many errors so far, not seeing the truth behind the traitors' masks before it is too late, expecting the best because we trust they are our brothers. At Isstvan. At Calth.'

'I understand, Titus.'

'No, my lord, you do not. It means that honest Faffnr is *too* determined not to fail. He will jump at the slightest thing, the merest doubt. He will err on the side of caution, because the alternative failure is too grim to bear. He and his men are a risk to you, because they would rather strike at you in error than allow the slightest possibility of your disloyalty.'

'I have nothing to hide,' Guilliman said.

'Do you not?' asked Prayto boldly. 'What about me? What about the Librarius? We have learned that the Wolves were unleashed on Prospero because your brother defied the Edict of Nikaea. You do the same. Faffnr is looking for the slightest sign. The *slightest* sign. And I am it. I am proof of your heresy, lord. I am evidence of precisely the wretched warpcraft they have been told to hunt for.'

'Your counsel is noted,' said Guilliman. He looked back at the Wolves one last time. 'I think I can handle them. Teach them to come to heel, perhaps. That's why I want them where I can see them.'

'You take liberties with your own safety, lord,' murmured Euten.

'Not now, Euten–'

'You are everything, my lord, and you cannot *be* everything. The only primarch, the only son, the only loyal son we know yet lives.' Euten began to count the roles off on her fingertips. 'You are Lord of Ultramar, king of this world, master of the Five Hundred, commander of the Thirteenth Legion Ultramarines, last champion of the Imperium. You are also the Emperor's proxy, and protector of the Throne. Like the word or not, you will be a regent. You are his surrogate, and possibly his heir. You may indeed, by default, be Emperor already.'

'Mamzel!'

'I will have my say, Lord of Macragge!' the old woman protested. 'You cannot be all of these things. You are too valuable to risk. Let others command the forces. Let the tetrarchs do that! Let others do the dirty work. Delegate! Formally appoint commanders from the forces you are assembling. As a figurehead alone, you are too important. If fate overcomes you, the Imperium is most surely done.'

Guilliman looked at Prayto.

'Tell Mamzel Euten what I am thinking, Prayto,' he said.

'My lord is thinking that he does not wish to call himself regent. If he is building what amounts to a new Imperium, it would be unseemly to place himself on the throne.'

Euten snorted. 'Tell my beloved lord that he may yet have to if there is no other heir!'

'That would make me no more loyal than Horus Lupercal,' said Guilliman. 'I will not countenance it.'

He saw that Prayto was looking at him.

'What, Titus? Something else?'

Prayto hesitated.

'No, my lord.'

Figures approached through the broad hall doorway. Flanked by Ultramarines in artificer plate, Valentus Dolor approached. Dolor was one of the four tetrarchs of Ultramar, the four princes who ruled the master worlds of the fiefdoms that made up the realm, and whose rank was second only to Guilliman's. Dolor's fiefdom was Occluda. He was a giant, and his master-crafted, modified Mark III plate was painted in the Ultramarines livery, reversed – blue for white and white for blue.

'Valentus,' said Guilliman, 'present me with good news and save me from my chamberlain's relentless nagging.'

Dolor looked down at the slender old woman.

'My good and distinguished friend Mamzel Euten is very small, lord,' he said. 'I do not know how she could ever be very bothersome.'

'Flies are small!' Euten snapped. 'Ticks, they are also small!'

'Ticks get plucked out and squashed,' said Guilliman. 'Flies are swatted. Your point, mam?'

'I find myself temporarily without one, lord,' said Euten.

'I do bring good news, lord,' said Dolor. 'I knew you'd want it communicated directly. A ship has put in. The pitiful thing has limped all the way from Calth, carrying the wounded and the weary. A sergeant called Thiel is aboard, and commends himself to your lordship.'

Guilliman smiled.

'Aeonid Thiel. He made a *practical* choice to remain committed to the Underworld War – it will be good to see him. Have him go to the Residency so that we can talk in private. It's been a long time since he was so steadfast by my side at Calth.'

'I will instruct him so,' said Dolor with a courteous head bow. 'Is something wrong, Brother Titus?'

Prayto had suddenly winced, and steadied himself against the wall with one hand. With his other hand he clasped his forehead.

'Something–' he began.

There was a supersonic bang that shook the windows of the hall and made someone present cry out. Looking up through the tall panes, Guilliman saw a streak of fire stride down the sky. For a stricken moment, he thought of Calth, of the *Campanile*, of missiles raining down...

But this looked more like a meteorite, an object plunging through the atmosphere.

Others in the hall had hurried to the windows to see.

'A bad star!' one of the Wolves spat. 'An omen star!'

'A broom star!' snarled another. '*Maleficarum*!'

The fireball was not large. Guilliman could see that. It fell straight down and disappeared behind the towers of the Civitas. There was no explosion, no sunburst of a warhead.

Dolor was already checking a data-slate.

'Reports of an impact, my lord, in the labouring habs of the southern suburbs. Site is just north of the Octagon Fortress, in Anomie Deme.'

'Take charge of this,' Guilliman told him. 'Find out what it was. Find out how in the name of the Throne it passed through our orbital screen and detector grid. And someone check there aren't more of them incoming.'

'At once, lord,' said Dolor.

'Report to me directly when you have anything!' Guilliman snapped.

He turned to look at the room. All eyes were on him, all the visitors: Wolves, Fists, Hands, Scars, Salamanders.

'Find them accommodation in the garrison, see to their needs, and begin to assign them duties,' he said to Prayto. 'Form them into companies, according to their strengths. Let us make an army.'

He turned to leave.

'I'll be in the Residency,' he said. His bodyguard made to follow him.

'Stand down,' he said. 'I go to speak with an old friend.'

5

HE THAT HAS RETURNED

SMOKE ROSE ABOVE the rooflines of the southern city district of Anomie in a grey horsetail.

Alarms were still sounding, and city watch divisions had moved in to isolate the area and hold back residents and labourers from the fabricatories who had gone out onto the streets to look.

Dolor's lifter flew along the broad colonnades and boulevards of Strayko above the moving lines of ground traffic and beneath the sweeping arches and bridge spans. At Larnis Gate, where Strayko Deme became Anomie Deme, the traffic circulation was blocked. A Warhound Titan stood watch on the grassy field by the Illyrian Monument, and another strutted with a muscular, crow-like walk across the upper pavement to take up position behind the fabrication plants along Antimon Square.

Dolor's pilot keyed the authority code, and the sentry Warhound tracked the lifter with its weapons for a second before acknowledging the tetrarch's right to proceed.

In the restricted area around the impact site, the streets were empty, except for rescue and emergency teams. A major fire, sparked by the impact, had half-gutted the old Antimon machine works, the smoke from it staining the sky.

'Not a warhead?' asked Dolor, looking at the scene.

His equerry, an Ultramarines captain called Casmir, was monitoring the information feed on a battle-grade data-slate.

'No, tetrarch, not a warhead. Very little metallic registering in the analysis of its down-track.'

'And it was small, too,' he added.

'It set the machine works ablaze.'

'It probably ruptured something flammable. It went down through the roof at the northern end, and then punched through several storeys. Crews are trying to get to it.'

'How did it get past the damned grid?' asked Dolor. 'In the name of the Throne, this is the most fortified and sky-watched world in the quadrant!'

'I can't answer that, tetrarch,' Casmir replied. 'The data is incomplete. There is no trace of it prior to the point of atmospheric entry. I'll keep working on it, but there is no trace of any in-system plot, not even a cloaked one.'

Dolor frowned.

'So what? Did it just jump out of a ship in orbit?'

Casmir laughed.

'Nothing jumps out of a ship in orbit, tetrarch. Not if it's going to fall like that.'

Dolor looked at the pilot.

'Set us down. Over there.'

The moment the lander had settled, Dolor punched the

ramp-hatch key and exited. His immense, armoured boots crunched across a rockcrete quadrangle covered in glass and ceramic fragments from the machine shop's blown-out windows. Six-legged Mechanicum bulk servitors were firefighting in the steaming ruins of the fabricatory shed's western end, blasting retardant foam from shoulder-mounts. Two of them scuttled past the tetrarch as he approached. They were heading back to the carrier parked in the street to refill their foam reservoirs.

Figures came to meet Dolor. Some were Ultramarines, others were regular humans from the city watch and district medicae. They all snapped to attention.

'Who has authority here?' Dolor asked.

'We have the zone secured, lord tetrarch,' said the leading Ultramarine, his boltgun mag-clamped to his chestplate, 'but Consul Forsche has jurisdiction.'

Forsche stepped forward. He was a solemn, dark-haired man in suit and mantle. He made the sign of the aquila.

'Tetrarch,' he said, and nodded.

'The primarch personally sent me to oversee,' said Dolor. 'Report, please.'

'We've controlled the fires and accounted for all personnel,' said Forsche. 'Some injuries, but no fatalities. All the damage you see is due to kinetic impact and collateral.'

'And the object?'

'We've located it by scan. It's gone down about six floors into the sub-basement, or possibly the sanitation system beneath that.'

'What is it?'

'We haven't cut down to it yet, my lord. A lot of machine shop structure fell into the impact hole after the strike.'

'I want to see,' said Dolor.

Forsche nodded and beckoned for him to follow.

✠ ✠ ✠

GUILLIMAN WALKED ALONE along the private hallways of the Residency, avoiding the public spaces. These quiet corridors, lined in marble and pale wood, had often hosted Konor, pacing for no purpose other than to think. How much of a Battle King's life, Guilliman wondered, was spent in whirring contemplation, compared to the proportion spent in actual battle?

Was that Horus's failing? Named as Warmaster, did Horus take that title too literally, and allow himself to be enflamed past reason by a choleric humour until he was full of violent urges and thus vulnerable to the poisons of the warp? What was it the Wolves had called it? Maleficarum?

Guilliman had always believed that the true purpose of a warlord, or a Battle King, or a warmaster, was not to wage war but to prevent it. War should not be the natural state of life. It should be resorted to only when all other agencies failed. But when war became the only means, a warmaster or a Battle King had to be capable of prosecuting it to crushing compliance.

In Horus, Guilliman had always felt, there was an ugly propensity to love war for war's sake. Was that the human flaw that had led to this calamity?

The eyes of past leaders watched him from gilded frames as he passed portraits of consuls and Battle Kings. How had they managed that balance? What personal struggles of conscience had they endured to keep society safe from its enemies yet unsullied by war?

How would he, Roboute Guilliman, fare when that feat of balance became his to master?

He reached the private entrance into the Residency. The huge pairs of outer and inner doors closed automatically behind him, their hisses sealing him in his private realm.

He paused for a moment in the high chamber, and glanced out of great windows at the single new star shining in the troubled, golden sky, and the wisp of smoke rising from the cityscape in the south. He began unclasping his gauntlets while he scanned the datafeed on the old cold-gestalt cogitator.

There was no new information on the impact. He would wait for the tetrarch's report. Euten had told him to delegate. Dolor was more than competent.

A chime alerted him to the arrival of his visitor. Guilliman put aside the one gauntlet he had unbuckled and keyed the high chamber's public doors to open.

An Ultramarines sergeant with a red helm entered and saluted. His armour was well-maintained, but worn from months of toil and warfare. Guilliman could barely make out the unit insignia. A blade had left a cut down to bare metal across the red visor. On the right pauldron there was a scouring mark, undoubtedly the trace of a flamer's touch. Guilliman noticed all such miniscule details in one glance. Even from the Space Marine's bearing, he could read much. Thiel had always been a confident, almost reckless warrior, but now he seemed subdued and unsure of himself. The unremitting intensity of the Calth war had fused him into a state of constant readiness, a perpetual expectation of threat that even the down-time voyaging back to Macragge had not diminished. Thiel's hand, subconsciously conditioned, never strayed far from the butt of his clamped weapon, as though he believed he might be ambushed at any second.

It was chastening to see a man so changed, so imprisoned by tension.

'You'll keep the armourers busy bringing that plate back to inspection standard,' Guilliman said, as lightly as he could.

'I trust my service has been worth every scuff and scratch, lord,' said the sergeant.

Guilliman smiled. He held out his bared right hand. The warrior hesitated, then took it.

'Good to see you, Aeonid. Good to see you indeed. Come, bring me news of Calth, and forget this formality for a moment. Unclasp that helm. I'll send for wine, or amasec, perhaps.'

'There is no need, my lord.'

'There's every need, Sergeant Thiel. I want to spend some time in conversation with a man who has been devotedly practical since I last saw him. There's too much theoretical here on Macragge.'

'I have seen plenty of evidence to the contrary, my lord. Macragge was always a defended world, a capital world, but such defences we saw as we came into orbital space…'

'Security is pre-eminent, Thiel. Now sit and remove that helm, and talk to me.'

Thiel hesitated.

'With your permission, my lord, I brought battle-brothers I would like you to meet with me.'

'Indeed?'

'They served as my squad in the Underworld War these past eight months. I owe every one of them my life. If it's stories you want, they have plenty to tell, and I would appreciate it very much if you honoured them with a little of your time. They are loyal brothers.'

'They are with you?'

'They wait without, in the anteroom, lord.'

'Bring them in, Thiel.'

At a signal from the sergeant, the other Ultramarines entered: nine battle-brothers, their blue plate as worn and marked as Thiel's. Unit insignia and marks were virtually illegible on all of them. They all exhibited the same quiet intensity as Thiel, so much that it seemed like timidity, as if they were afraid of entering such a bright, luxurious, peaceful environment, or afraid at least of disgracing it with their worn, imperfect armour. Guilliman sighed quietly. What appeared to be timidity was just hard-wired tension that might never unwind. This was the price the accursed Lorgar had made his Ultramarines pay.

He drank in the details again, each untold story plain to see: an armour plate slightly distorted by a melta's brushing touch; a missing finger, sutured and sealed; a gladius with the wrong coloured grip that had been taken up as a battlefield replacement and forced to fit the wearer's scabbard; the pockmarks of a too-close call with Tempest munitions; the slight twitch of a visor from side to side, hunting for hidden killers even here in the Ultramar Residency.

'Each of us was the remainder of a broken squad,' said Thiel. 'Expediency brought us together on Calth.'

'Let me know you all,' said Guilliman. 'Sit. Lose those helms. Tell me your stories, face to face.'

Awkwardly, the Ultramarines began to do as they had been instructed. The situation did not suit them. Two or three seemed unwilling to sit. No one removed his helm. Were they ashamed of their scars? Were they ashamed to show the Mark of Calth?

One had spaced himself back near the main door, a curious placement that was the vestige of squad discipline in chamber-to-chamber fighting. One always covers the exit. Guilliman regretted bringing them in. He should have handled the meeting differently, in one of the squad rooms of the Fortress where they would not have felt so out of place. Guilliman felt a great measure of pity for them: built for war, and then locked into a fierce one, they had become unused to the simple habits of society. They had most probably lived in their armour for the last year, never letting their weapons out of their hands.

They all carried them, bolters and blades, holstered and sheathed. It was odd to see armed men from the warfront in the heart of the Residency. The only weapons openly carried in the private chambers were those of the Cataphractii escort and the palace guard. But Guilliman could hardly ask these weary veterans to check their trusted weapons at a gatehouse. It would be like asking them to surrender something integral, like a hand or an eye. These were the instruments they had depended on for their lives during their tour in Calth's Underworld War, they were part of them, extensions of themselves, and to deprive them–

A thought occurred.

'You lost the sword?' he asked.

'Lord?' Thiel replied.

'The blade that I loaned you at Calth? The one from my collection?'

'Yes. Yes, sadly that was lost.'

Such a small detail. Just one among the hundreds of details Guilliman had absorbed in the last three minutes. It was so tiny, so insignificant, it ought to be ignored, but the past two years had taught him that nothing was too small to ignore. It was in his nature, the way he was engineered, to study every single fact available and notice any discrepancy. To read the potential of anything, the way a card player reads tells.

'Why do you keep your face hidden, Aeonid?' he asked.

'My lord–'

'What kind of sword was it? What type of weapon?'

Thiel did not reply.

His right hand went for the boltgun mag-clamped at his hip.

Guilliman turned cold. Through sheer force of will, he negated dismay, surprise, disappointment, even the desire to curse the fact that he had been tricked, or to vent his hurt at how the treachery had been delivered. There was no practical time for any of those things. They were mere luxuries.

He negated them in an instant, because if he used that instant to indulge in any of them, he would be sacrificing his single, nanosecond opportunity to do one far more important thing.

Which was remain alive.

'BE CAREFUL, MY lord!' Consul Forsche called out.

Dolor paused and glanced back, hoping that Forsche would appreciate the full meaning of his withering look. A human urging a fully armoured transhuman giant to be careful?

Dolor clambered down into the well of wreckage that the object had created with its auguring impact. The fires were damped, and more servitors were cutting away at crumbled cross spars and fallen roof supports. Steam and smoke, mingled in equal measures, rolled up out of the cavity.

Forsche began to follow him, hitching up the skirts of his robe so that he could climb down the side of the debris pit.

'Now *you* be careful,' Dolor growled. 'Stay put. I've been in worse, but you're not dressed for this. Stay put.'

Forsche nodded, and took his place at the lip of the pit. Other members of the recovery crew stood with him, peering down.

Dolor continued to descend. A way below him, he could make out two servitors using las-cutters to slice through a slab of buckled and displaced floor plating.

'We are close to the object,' one of them reported to the tetrarch in a reedy, augmetic tone as he came down to them.

Dolor reached their level and jumped the last few metres onto the slumped decking. He looked up, and saw human faces and legionary visors staring down from several floors above.

'The primarch will reprimand me for allowing you to go down there alone, lord tetrarch,' Captain Casmir remarked over the vox-link.

'There isn't room down here for a lot of us, Casmir,' Dolor replied. 'Besides, he gave me a duty, and I will perform it personally. Anything further from the orbital grid?'

'Nothing yet, my lord. Still processing.'

Dolor looked at the heavy servitors. Braced on their multiple limbs, they were peeling back the section of flooring, using their manipulators to curl the metal plating back like the lid of a food can. As one continued to grip, the other switched back to close cutting work to free twisted bars and connectors. Sparks leapt from shorn and dangling cable work. Fresh smoke swirled up out of the ground as the flooring cap was stripped away.

Dolor moved closer.

'We cannot guarantee your safety,' one the servitors told him.

'Noted,' Dolor replied.

'We have detected something below,' said the other.

'Let me see,' Dolor said. He crouched at the lip of the pit they had exposed and peered down. To either side of him, the servitors activated shoulder-mounted banks of work lights. The dark broiling smoke of the pit became a blinding white haze, defeating even his occulobe enhancements.

'That's useless,' Dolor said. 'Off.'

The servitors obediently shut off the lights. Dolor rose to his feet again.

'Casmir,' he voxed, looking back up the deep throat of the pit. 'My helm, please.'

He'd handed his suit's helm to the equerry before making his descent.

'I'll bring it down directly, lord tetrarch.'

'Just throw it, Casmir.'

There was a slight pause and then the beautifully crafted war-helm appeared, tumbling down through the air into the pit. Dolor caught it neatly and clamped it in place, then crouched again at the lip of the hole, his transhuman eyesight further augmented by the visor's powerful light-sensitive optics.

He saw the shape at once, because it was hotter than the surrounding structures. He saw the heat outline of it.

It made no sense. Why would anyone drop the statue of a man from orbit?

Dolor hesitated. He scanned again, and took another reading. He was not looking at super-heated black granite; he was looking at roasted flesh, burned to charcoal. He was looking at a human-oid figure that had been turned into a seared corpse by the heat of re-entry, then smashed into the ground, pulverising every bone.

'Great Throne...' he whispered.

It was extraordinary enough that it was a corpse. Then full reali-sation sank in. There should be nothing left. Given the fall, the heat, the ablation, the impact, anything organic, including bone, should have been utterly vaporised.

There should be nothing left.

He opened his vox-link.

'I need a full medicae recovery team down here right now!' he called. 'And Casmir? Have this area sealed, vermilion-level security!'

6

TO THE DEATH

'It is easier to forgive an enemy than a brother.'
– proverb of the Five Hundred Worlds

THIEL FIRED HIS boltgun. His men began shooting too.

In that first moment, in that first eye blink, time hung in the air, as weightless as a bar of sunlight. Guilliman's transhuman physiology accelerated from nothing to hyperfast response.

Practical. Read. Move. React. Read everything. No other thoughts. Practical.

He read the storm of bolter-rounds spitting from gun barrels. He read the white-hot muzzle flashes almost frozen mid-belch by the suspension of time as his heightened reactions propelled him to a new state of response. He read the mass-reactive shells in the air, travelling, burning towards him–

Guilliman was already moving, already turning. His right hand was grabbing the edge of a heavy sunderwood chart table, and pulling, overturning it.

Practical. Read everything. So many variables, but so few that will

*make a difference. Extreme close quarters. Outnumbered and out-
gunned. Not even the slightest margin for error.*

Time seeped like resin. The top of the flipping table, heavy as
a drawbridge gate and suddenly rising to meet Thiel like a bull-
dozer blade, took the first four rounds virtually point-blank. The
mass-reactive shells detonated, biting vast wounds out of the
dense, aged hardwood, filling the air with splinters and burning
fibres. One leg of the table came spinning away.

Guilliman was diving sideways behind the exploding tabletop,
full-length in mid-air.

The table completed its overturn and crashed against Thiel and
the Ultramarine beside him, forcing them to backstep. All of
the other visitors were firing. Six bolt-rounds missed the diving
primarch, annihilating a section of the high chamber wall and
several portraits hanging upon it. Others hit the spilled table and
a chair beside it. Another clipped Guilliman's left shoulder guard
and detonated. His plate protected him from the worst of it, but
the heat of the nearest detonation scorched his left cheek and the
nape of his neck, and shrapnel peppered the side of his face.

He hit the carpet, rolling, his tumble distorted by the glancing
impact.

A weapon discharge alarm started screaming. Why so late? The
shooting had begun hours before, days before... No, time was
just trickling like syrup.

*Concentrate! The odds are too bad, in such a confined space. If the
Residency's bodyguard reacts fast enough–*

The Ultramarines who had hung back by the door – of course
one of them would cover the exit for such an ambush! – clamped
a magnetic device onto the doorframe and twisted it. The public
hatches slammed shut. They were locked in together. The primarch and ten would-be killers.

Traitors. Turncoats.

Why?

Guilliman was still rolling. Mass-reactives chewed holes in the carpet, chasing him, filling the air with flock fibres and shreds of matting and underfloor. Mass-reactives punched holes through the furniture he was rolling between, blowing out chair backs and arms. The air was full of cushion stuffing, blizzards of the stuff.

Why? Why Thiel?

Don't think about that. It's just a distraction, robbing focus from all that actually matters.

Practicals. Practicals. Read everything. Move. React.

A throne built for a primarch's stature, punctured twice through the seat back by bolt-rounds, began toppling onto the Lord of Ultramar.

I'm damned if I'll die on my knees–

Guilliman rolled onto his back, put his weight on his shoulders, met the falling throne with bent legs and kicked out.

The throne left the ground, its direction of movement violently reversed. The flying mass of it felled three of the traitors in its path.

I'll die on my feet if I have to die. Even the odds.

Time was still as slow as glue. He could see individual bolt-rounds in mid-air, leaving comet trails of fire behind them. He sprang into the face of the nearest killer. He seized the man's right wrist with his left hand and yanked his aim aside, so that the boltgun barked uselessly at the ceiling. Plaster dust showered like spilled sugar. Guilliman kept his grip tight, twisting the Space Marine around in front of him, turning him into a shield to meet the bolter-rounds crawling through the air towards him. Three rounds hit the man in the lower back, rupturing his plating and blowing out his spine. Guilliman felt the impacts transmitted through the body in his grasp, saw the spinning shards of ceramite armour-plating, fragments of blood and flesh, splashing droplets of blood. He reached down with his oh-so-unarmoured right hand and grabbed the handle of the man's sheathed gladius.

Then he wrenched sideways with his left hand, flinging the dead man aside like a doll. The motion left the gladius drawn in Guilliman's bare right hand. Scaled to the primarch, the short sword seemed little more than a large combat knife. The flying corpse, showering blood, loose-limbed and whirling horizontally, hit two of the other killers in the faceplates and knocked them onto their backs.

Guilliman turned, shearing the blade of the stolen gladius through the extended forearm of the next nearest killer. The veteran's bolter fired once as it fell to the floor, still clamped in the severed fist. Guilliman put his foot in the man's belly and kicked him away, grabbing the hilt of his adversary's sheathed power sword with his left hand as he did so.

A captured blade drawn in each hand, he recoiled sharply, turning his face aside, as a mass-reactive shell burned past his cheek like an angry insect. Then he rotated, burying the edge of the power sword in the side of an Ultramarine head. The helmet parted, so did the skull. Guilliman saw grinning teeth in a skinned gumline, and a dislodged eyeball.

Three down, two of them dead.

But Guilliman was upright, and he was a big target. No matter that time had slowed to a glacial pace, he was not the only being in the room with transhuman reactions. His assailants were of the Legiones Astartes, and that made them the most potent warriors in the Imperium.

Guilliman took his first solid hit: a bolt-round to the shoulder. He felt his armour plate crack and compress, felt the sledgehammer slap of it, felt the searing pain of the fragments that had penetrated his body. A second hit, an instant later, lower back, and then a third, right hip. Dizzying pain. Impact. He was fighting for balance. There was blood in his mouth. He saw his own blood glinting as it ran down the scorched cobalt-blue surface of his leg armour.

Another bolter-round caught him in the left side, exploded, and threw him hard into the room's massive desk, a piece hewn from the granite of the Hera's Crown mountains. He had to drop the gladius to steady himself. Ornaments, trophies and documents scattered off the desk in all directions. Guilliman managed to roll his body against the edge of the desk so that the next round struck its surface rather than him. The polished stone fractured and crazed like glass. Roaring, Guilliman pushed away from the desk, side-stepped another hurtling round, and swung the power sword at the shooter. He felt the collision impact shiver along the blade. The man left the ground, head back, arms rising, as if he had run throat-first into a tripwire. A small dish of blue metal flew off sideways. The power blade had sheared through the cranium of the warrior's helm, carving off a slice of it. Blood drizzled from the perfectly circular hole in the helm's ceramite, the concentric rings of scalp and bone, and then the exposed brain tissue beneath that. He landed hard.

Guilliman wanted to reach for the man's bolter, but another round took him in the chest and blew him back against the desk. They were coming at him. All those he had knocked down but not finished were on their feet again. He groped for the fallen gladius on the desk, missed it, and found a marble bust of Konor's father instead. He hurled that.

It struck one of the killers in the faceplate hard enough to turn his head and smash a visor lens. Guilliman's rummaging hand located the gladius. He hurled that too, like a throwing knife. It impaled the neck of the assassin he had just dazed with the marble bust. The man lurched several drunken steps sideways and collapsed, blood gouting from under his chin.

Guilliman was hit again, left hip. The pain was so fierce he wondered if his pelvis had fractured. Two more shots went past his head to the left, missing him by less than a hand's breadth.

Gasping with pain, the Avenging Son threw himself backwards over the desk in an evasive roll, trying to get its granite bulk between him and the relentless bolters. Stone chips and fragments whizzed out from every fiery impact. The front and top of the desk quickly began to resemble the cratered surface of a moon. One of the attackers leapt on the desk to fire over the side at the sheltering primarch. Guilliman came up to meet him, and put the power sword through both of the assassin's knees with a double-handed stroke that felled the man like a sapling. One leg remained standing on the desk's top, supported by its heavy armour casing.

Guilliman could feel blood leaking inside his buckled, perforated armour. He could feel blood running from the torn tissue of his face and neck. He could hear the palace guard hammering at the high chamber door.

The guard could not open the doors, public or private. If they had no override, then the assassins had brought a system jammer with them. Pre-meditated. Clever. Ingenious, in fact.

Not the actions of bitter, disaffected veterans, nor the behaviour of warp-damaged maniacs.

'Who are you?' Guilliman demanded of anyone and no one. His voice sounded small, enclosed by gun smoke, cinched by pain.

More bolt-rounds came his way in answer, flaring out of the fyceline smoke that clogged the air. Guilliman threw himself flat. Bolts kissed the ruined desk and struck the high windows behind him, creating cobweb patterns of cracks in the strengthened glass. Part of the window drapes collapsed. A picture fell off the wall and its frame shattered. A bookcase toppled over, spilling its contents in an avalanche of paper and leather bindings.

How many had he finished? Five, and one other with a hand severed. Was it five? How many of them would it take to finish him?

He glanced around.

The man he had cut off the desk was sprawled beside him on his back, still twitching. Blood had already stopped jetting from the stumps of his thighs, but the carpet around him was dark and soaking. He was reaching up weakly, aiming his boltgun at Guilliman.

Guilliman rolled and impaled the assassin to the floor with the power sword. The man went into juddering spasms and died.

Guilliman wrenched the boltgun out of his dead grip. Like the one Prayto had lent him the night Dantioch manifested, it was like a pistol to him. It only fitted his un-gauntleted hand. That hand was dripping with blood.

He heard the remaining assassins exchanging guttural, coded words as they fanned around the devastated desk through the smoke to finish him. He didn't understand what they were saying. It wasn't an Ultramarines battle cant.

It didn't matter that he didn't understand.

Practical. Read everything. React.

Their exchange told him plenty. It placed them. Sound and relative angle. He knew, without having to see, that two were coming around the desk to his left, and one to his right.

He went to the left. He came around the desk firing. One kill, solid, a head shot, a red fog. A second, two through the chest.

Something ran into him from behind. His mouth opened wide, a silent howl, as he felt the sharp, cold bite of a gladius blade punching through his back-plate armour and running in under his ribs. It stayed there. It was wedged. Guilliman wheeled and smashed his gauntleted left fist into the face of the swordsman.

The Ultramarine was somersaulted backwards by the force of

the blow. He hit the windows face first, upside down. Despite the cobweb cracks, the glass did not break. The man dropped in a heap on the floor beneath them.

Guilliman turned to track the remaining killers. The damned gladius was still stuck through him. He–

At least two shells struck his left shoulder armour behind his ear and detonated. He felt as though his head had snapped off to the right with the shockwave. He felt heat and ferocious pain. He tasted blood and fyceline, his ears ringing, his vision gone.

He fell. He couldn't get up. He was half propped against the desk or an overturned chair.

He couldn't see. He fired blind. It was pointless. He fired again.

He felt a blade against his throat.

'Death to the false Emperor,' said the voice Guilliman had thought belonged to Aeonid Thiel.

'Let me die knowing what you are,' Guilliman whispered.

A laugh.

'Your killer.'

'What else? What else are you?'

'I am Alpharius,' said Thiel.

Then the hateful rumours from Isstvan, of treacherous masquerade and false colours, were true. The Alpha Legion would employ any means. The deception through which this execution had been accomplished, the impeccable covert approach, it made sense. Guilliman had never had any martial respect for the elusive, cowardly tactics of the youngest Legion, but this had been superlative.

'One thing you should learn from this moment, servant of the Alpha Legion,' Guilliman said. 'When you have to murder a primarch, and you get one at your mercy, do not waste the moment answering his questions when he still has a bolter in his hand.'

Guilliman fired. 'Thiel' was thrown away from him by the force of the point-blank shot. The assassin's blade left a deep scratch across Guilliman's exposed throat. Blood welled.

He rose to his feet, unsteady. His clouded vision began to return. He saw the last assassin, the one whose hand he had chopped off, crawling across the high chamber floor, struggling to find a boltgun.

'Enough,' Guilliman said, and shot him through the back of the head. Then he dropped to his knees and realised how tired he was.

At some point after that, the Invictus guard finally cut through the main doors.

7

GREETED BY DEATH

'There is an art to dying, but it is a dying art.'

– Corvus Corax, Primarch of the XIX Legion

'DOES HE YET live?' asked Valentus Dolor.

There was no response. They had all come in haste, rushing to the Residency, and had entered the medicae hall to find the ashen chamberlain outside a sealed, guarded apothecarion chamber.

'Mamzel, is he alive?' Dolor pressed.

Euten looked up at him. She had been lost in thought. Her frail face was more pale and translucent than ever, drawn more by pain than age. She had been a beautiful woman in her youth, a noted beauty. Now her beauty was her strength, and an intense inner core of belief in, and devotion to, Roboute Guilliman.

The day's events had shaken that.

'Yes,' she replied. 'My Lord Valentus, he lives. He has been most sorely hurt, and it is only chance that spared his life. One lucky shot–'

'I think not chance,' said Phratus Auguston. 'I rather think the martial prowess of our beloved lord saw him through this infamy. His practical–'

'Yes,' said Euten sharply. 'Yes, why not? Let us believe he is an invulnerable god who can do no wrong. Let us believe that death cannot overtake him, or that there are no limits to his energy and capacity. Let us put our trust in him blindly and expect him to deliver us single-handedly from all this–'

'My lady,' said Auguston, 'I meant no disrespect.'

'Did you not?' she asked. 'Really?'

She eyed Phratus Auguston with barely disguised contempt. In the absence of Marius Gage, who had vanished during the battle for Calth in pursuit of the renegade Kor Phaeron, Auguston had been elected to the post of Master of the First Chapter, and thus First Master of the Ultramarines. He was a bullish, aggressive man, and one of the finest field commanders in the XIII. Euten had not favoured his appointment, though she enjoyed no official influence in such Legion matters. She had advised Guilliman to prefer Verus Caspean, current Master of the Second. Auguston was too focused and aggressive, in her opinion, to suit the broader needs of the role. Caspean was wiser, more compassionate, more nuanced. She urged that Auguston should be kept where he would be most effective – in line command, in the field.

Guilliman had not taken her advice.

Euten took a step towards the massive First Master and tapped the chased gold engraving of his breastplate with the tip of her staff.

'Understand respect, First Master,' she said. 'Is this respectful?'

She tapped again. 'No, it is not. No, it does not accord with respect. I do not know my place. I am but a chamberlain of the court, and you are the Lord of Lords in Macragge's Legion. But I am listened to because I am not sparing in my wisdom. Each to his own, Auguston, each to his strength. If you would show our beloved primarch respect, then first do so by accepting his limits. Your vapid praise sounds like false flattery. He is more than human, but he is *only* more than human. The Invictus guard counted eighty-five spent bolter-rounds or impact holes in that chamber. If any one had struck his unarmoured head, *any one*, he would be dead and this conversation would be very different.'

'Lady–' Auguston rumbled.

'Where was the error, today, sir?' she asked, tapping again. 'Was it the bodyguards, for failing to anticipate? Was it the Residency guards, for not scanning the visitors properly? Wait, was it Bado-rum and his men, for failing to police the precinct? It must have been, for they are but human and therefore flawed, unlike the transhumans of the Legion! Or perhaps it was Titus Prayto, or others of his office, perhaps even our Lord Librarius Ptolemy, for failing to foresee the event? Or perhaps it was our avenging Lord Guilliman, for being too tired and burdened with duties, for slipping a moment and allowing someone a quick pass through Residency security because he wanted the relief of a conversa-tion with an old friend? Guilliman ordered the would-be killers through, Master Auguston. He ordered them through, and no one thought to question that authority. Do you know what that means? It means he made a mistake. Let us all help him not to make another.'

Dolor glanced sideways at Titus Prayto, but Prayto had already read the instruction before it had been voiced. He stepped forward.

'No one here disputes your words, mamzel,' he said, taking Euten gently by the arm. 'Let me fetch you water and sit with you. You've had a long and stressful day.'

Euten glared at Auguston a moment longer, then sagged and nodded. She allowed Prayto to lead her from the waiting chamber.

'I have no idea what he sees in her and her counsel,' growled Auguston as the hatch closed. There were thirteen senior Ultramarines in the chamber, the anteroom of the Residency's medicae hall, all of them at least of the rank company commander or Chapter Master. Some laughed. Verus Caspean did not. Neither did the most senior of them, Tetrarch Dolor.

'I am glad you are not of the Librarius, Auguston,' Dolor said.

'How so, my lord?' Auguston replied.

'Because then you would know what I was thinking about that remark,' said Dolor.

Commander Badorum and five of his guards entered the chamber through the southern hatch. They stopped short when they saw the assembly of Legiones Astartes officers.

'My lords,' said Badorum, removing his helm smartly and saluting. 'I came to find out how he fared.'

'He lives, commander,' Dolor said, 'and will live yet.'

Badorum breathed out and nodded.

'No thanks to you,' said Auguston.

'My lord?'

Auguston bore down on the commander of the household company like a Titan lining up on an unshielded kill.

'You screwed up,' he snapped. 'Where were you? Where were your toy soldiers? Your scans? Your surveillance? How long did it take you to respond?'

'My lord,' Badorum stammered. 'Our scanners were jammed. We had no–'

'Excuses,' sniffed Auguston. 'I have a mind to see you relieved of duties.'

'I don't think you can do that,' said Verus Caspean. 'Household is a different chain of command to the Legion and–'

'Close your mouth, Verus,' Auguston spat over his shoulder. 'This is wartime. Wartime rules apply.'

'First Master, the fault was most surely ours,' said Drakus Gorod, commander of the Invictus guard. His voice surged out through the vox unit of his massive war-helm. His armour was stained with blood, Guilliman's blood. He had been one of the men who had carried the primarch to the medicae hub as soon as the high chamber doors had been breached.

'He dismissed you, Gorod,' Auguston laughed. 'He said he could do without you.'

'I make no excuses,' said Gorod. 'We should have insisted. We should have vetted the visitor list, no matter who they seemed to be. Also, the assassins were Alpha Legion. Their jamming tech was exceptional. We could not override it.'

'Let us learn from it, then,' said Auguston.

'Their tech self-destructed before it could be examined and reverse-engineered,' said Gorod.

'Alpha Legion,' murmured Niax Nessus, Master of the Third. 'What have we become, the proud Legions? What has this conflict devolved into?'

'Something we can kill and fight,' Auguston said.

'I think we may need to be smarter than that,' said Caspean.

'I told you to close your mouth,' said Auguston. 'We are one voice here.'

'Then we should decide what that voice says,' Caspean replied.

The hatch of the apothecarion whirred open suddenly. A gust of environmentally stabilised air exhaled at them, like the opening of a void-lock. It stank of blood, of counter-septic gels, of graft cultures and sterilising solutions. The chamber revealed before them was gloomy, illuminated only by the low-light displays of life support systems.

Guilliman had come to the door. He glared out at them like a wounded beast looking out of its cave-lair. He was breathing hard, and his torso, neck and one side of his face were wrapped in juvenat wadding and fixing wraps.

'The walls,' he wheezed, 'are not so thick I cannot hear your bickering. This is not how we behave in crisis.'

'Great lord,' Auguston began. 'You must recuperate and–'

'This is not how we behave in crisis,' Guilliman repeated.

Dolor stepped forward and dropped to one knee, his head bowed. One by one, the others did the same, transhumans and humans alike. Auguston was the last to kneel.

'How may we serve you, lord?' Dolor asked.

'Stand,' Guilliman said.

They stood.

'I will take your private counsel now, tetrarch,' Guilliman said. 'I must do something more than just sit in a bed while I heal. First Master Auguston, you will carry out a full security review of the Residency and the city.'

'Yes, my lord.'

'I'm not looking for blame, Auguston, and I do not expect to hear of any punishment unless a true dereliction of duty can be proved. What I want to know is how they got in so we can prevent it happening again. Give us *practical* information, to improve our practical. Find out how else people come and go, especially the off-world influx. What needs to be monitored more closely? What procedures do we need to improve? Do any of the Alpha Legion – or any of our other enemies – remain among us?'

Auguston nodded.

'My lord,' he said, 'I will have my staff officers detailed to this audit at once and–'

'No, Auguston,' said Guilliman. '*You* do it. Don't hand it off. Oversee it personally. Consult by all means, but consult wisely. Bring in Polux.'

'The Imperial Fist?'

'Correct. The Fists were charged with the defence of Terra. Let us learn from their mouths about the performance of that duty. Am I understood?'

'Yes, lord,' replied Auguston, his jawline tight.

'You think I demean you, somehow, Phratus?' Guilliman asked. 'You think I insult you by giving you a job that is beneath you? You are First Master of the Ultramarines, and that Legion knows no greater responsibility than the security of Macragge. I do not know how this task could possibly be beneath you.'

'Apologies, my lord,' said Auguston. 'It is an honour. I will do this, and I will do it scrupulously.'

'Of course you will,' Guilliman said, nodding. 'The rest of you return to your duties. Assist the First Master in any way he requires, and do your utmost to defuse any alarm or anxiety in the Legion, the Army and the public that has arisen because of this incident.'

'News of the attempt on your life has been restricted to privileged personnel only, my lord,' said Gorod.

Guilliman sighed.

'Nevertheless, it *will* get out, so *expect* it to and be ready to diminish its negative effect,' said Guilliman. 'In fact, I think the news should be made known. If we have enemies on Macragge, they will learn they have failed, and the story will raise the base level of vigilance. Besides, the people of Macragge will be troubled by rumours of an attack on me. I think they would far prefer the fortifying frankness of an account of today's events, especially if it includes the fact that I am very hard to kill.'

HE DISMISSED THEM, and turned back into the apothecarion with Dolor. Suddenly, as soon as the hatch shut, Guilliman reached out to the tetrarch for support. Dolor shouldered Guilliman's weight without a word and guided him back to the bed.

Shrouded medicae personnel, as silent as wraiths, lurking in the shadows, moved forward to reattach nutrient drips and monitors to Guilliman's chest and limbs. Small servitor units were moving around and beneath the bed, scrubbing away the bloodstains and incinerating dirty dressings.

'She was right,' Guilliman murmured as he lay back.

'Lord?'

'Euten,' Guilliman said. 'She advised against Auguston.'

'I confess,' said Dolor, 'I've never liked the man, except when he's been at my side in a fight. Then he has few equals.'

'That is precisely why I chose him to succeed Gage,' said Guilliman. 'I was angry. Treacherous war had wounded us deeply. I wanted a warrior to lead the Legion to vengeance. But our situation grows ever more complicated, and Phratus is no politician.'

'None of us are,' said Dolor.

'Not true. Not if I have done what I set out to do. I didn't raise the Legion solely to build an Imperium and fight a crusade. Crusades are finite. Wars end. I raised the Legion to have a successive function in peacetime too – as leaders, as statesmen, as rulers of the Imperium once it was built.'

Dolor said nothing.

'I always thought of the future, the far future,' Guilliman said quietly, 'where there is only peace. What will our kind do then? What, by comparison, of Russ and his Wolves? What purpose will his kind have when there are no more worlds to conquer?'

'The Warmaster's treachery has given him a few extra years of bloodshed to justify his purpose,' said Dolor.

Guilliman nodded.

'He's probably almost grateful. No, strike that. It's too harsh a judgement, even for Russ, even as a joke. But Russ must wonder, mustn't he, about the peacetime that will someday follow this? What will his purpose be? He believes that his Legion exists to sanction those who become problems to the Imperium. Does he fear that one day that will be him and his kind? That he will face the sanction for being too wild and dangerous for a civilised culture to accept?'

He looked at Dolor.

'Tell me of other things, Valentus. Let us do practical work here rather than theoretical musing. Report to me. What did you find? What fell from the heavens?'

'A body,' said Dolor.

Guilliman's eyes narrowed.

'Human?'

'Transhuman,' said Dolor. 'It is remarkable, lord. We have not identified the corpse or its origin, but I have ordered that it be recovered and brought here to the medicae hall for analysis. The entire impact site is currently being scoured for evidentiary data. I have also taken the liberty of restricting the incident at vermilion-level until we know what we're dealing with. Very few individuals know what has been found, and they are all oathed to secrecy.'

'I trusted the light of the Pharos might bring many things to Macragge,' said Guilliman. 'Lost ships, lost friends, enemies even... I was prepared for the unexpected. But a body, falling from the stars?'

'If I was a superstitious man, lord,' said Dolor, 'I would say it feels uncomfortably like an omen. And if I was a truly superstitious man, I would wonder what else might be coming.'

THE WARP SENT a daemon to kill him.

He felt that he should have been flattered.

The hand-off was made without incident. The assigned stealth-cutter, procured by the Cabal, made no mark whatsoever on the acutely sensitive scanner systems of the Ultramar-humans as it blinked in and blinked out, depositing him by long-range jump onto the Northern Massif under a peak called Andromache.

He woke from the jump, aching and curled in the foetal

position, on the glacier. Blood was streaming out of his nose like water from a tap.

'Thank you so much,' he whispered out loud, spluttering blood, speaking to inhuman gods and demi-deities who could no longer hear him, and who had never cared for his opinions anyway. The stealth-cutter was long gone, a darting spectre, retreating into the outer void. He wondered if any of the souls in Guilliman's would-be empire had even tracked it. He doubted it. A ghost return? A slight imaging artefact? Perhaps. Human technology was highly advanced, but it did not begin to match ancient kinebrach levels.

No wonder the humans were losing. No wonder they were losing to themselves.

No wonder he cared. He was human. At least, he had been *once*, long ago. He worked with the eldar now, though he hated the mother-loving sweet stink of them. He worked with the eldar and the other inhuman breeds of the Cabal that they were in bed with.

In bed out of desperation.

He hated *that* fact even more. He hated the fact that the human race was the reason why the galaxy was dying. G'Latrro had explained that to him in great depth. He had explained it to him when he had first recruited him from the blood-soaked sands of Iwo Jima. The human race, vibrant, innocent and fecund, was the doorway that the warp was going to use to flood the galaxy. Chaos would win because mankind was the weak link that would allow the warp in.

He was a Perpetual. He had been born that way, a natural Perpetual, but the Cabal had enhanced his abilities. He'd been working for them ever since that recruitment on the beach, old-style bullets zipping and fizzing around his head.

He'd been killing people for them ever since: good men. Sometimes, serving the Cabal seemed counter-intuitive. They were very obliging. They explained why a good man had to die, and why it was not a bad thing. The wetwork they had had him perform… *damn*. In Memphis, against the Good Man, and then more than a thousand years later in the City of Angels, against the Brother. Then in M19, against Holiard in the Glass Temple of Manunkind, and in M22 against Maser Hassan in the Spire Terrace before his *Word of the Law* speech.

And then Dume, though no one could persuasively argue against the fact that Dume really *had* to die, by any standards, even human ones.

Things had evolved, of course they had, because of the quality of the opponent. The constant cosmological chess game with the hyper-brilliant, but wayward, Emperor had placed things in flux. The Cabal could no longer quite contain or predict his actions. The mon-keigh was getting above himself.

So, now the ploy was known as the *Horus Gambit*, or the *Alpharius Position*. The purpose was simple: let Chaos win. Let the warp win so hard, so *damnably* hard, it falls in upon itself and burns its fury out. Let humanity be the sword it falls on.

He did what he had to do. He did what they needed him to do. Downside, on an unfriendly planet, bleeding internally and externally from a covert, fast-jack jump, holding himself together and carrying the flesh-tanked sack his weapons were in.

He was high in the mountains, a week's walk from Macragge City. That wasn't the problem. The problem was the daemon that the warp had sent after him.

Three days after his jump, he turned and said to the cold mountain air, 'Show yourself.'

Laughter echoed back, though it was hardly human. It rippled up the deep trenches of the Andromache foothills.

'Come on, sir,' he said. 'Come on, Mister Daemon. I await with interest.'

There was a long, silent, sucking second, then a voice said, *'I know who you are. I have your name. I have possession of you.'*

He sighed, and dropped his pack and his weapons and opened his arms wide to the mountain air.

'You have me then. Take me.'

'Damon,' answered the voice. *'An interesting choice of name, given your trade.'*

'What can I tell you, *daemon?'* he answered.

Silence.

'You have my name,' Damon said. 'What are you waiting for?' His hands were still outstretched. He turned in a slow circle, the snow scrunching under his boots.

'I have your name indeed,' the voice answered. *'And true names are true power. I have your name, and you cannot deflect me.'*

'I know that,' he said.

'So you know I am going to kill you? You know that is what I have been sent to do?'

'Yes,' he said.

'Good.'

He cleared his throat. The atmosphere on the high plateau was thin.

'What is my name to you?' he asked.

'Damon Prytanis,' the daemon replied.

'And knowing my true name gives you power over me?' he asked.

'Yes.'

'You have me, then, child of the warp. You have me soundly. As I die, and as I accept my death, allow me one last boon.'

'Speak it.'

'Tell me, so I know the true name of my obliterator.'

A chuckle rippled through unspace.

'Die forever knowing it,' the voice said. *'I am Ushpetkhar.'*

'I resign. Come and get me,' he said.

The shadow of the void rose and rippled at him. It came at him across the snowfield like a black tsunami.

'By the way,' Damon Prytanis said at the very last minute, 'that is not my true name. Turns out, you have no power over me. But I know you now. I have your true name… *Ushpetkhar!*'

In his pocket, Damon had been frantically getting the vessel ready. He made the appropriate signs and cast the appropriate runes, just as he had been shown. He threw his magic into the onrushing face of the screaming daemon.

The daemon exited realspace in an explosion of fury and indignation. Damon was thrown to the ground.

When he opened his eyes, he realised he was soaked. He was covered in blood, and so was a vast area of the glacier shelf around him. None of the blood was his.

Slowly, badly broken, he got up. Macragge City was still a while away, a long trek down the mountain.

In this manner, the killer calling himself Damon Prytanis came to Macragge.

8

FIRST AMONG EQUALS

'A man chooses his friends; fate chooses his brothers.'
– attributed to Ondrin of Saramanth

THE SHIP CAME out of the darkness, and within its darkness, an endless hunt played out.

It was a human ship, an Imperial ship, a battleship, a flagship, but it was unnaturally propelled through the miasma of the warp by means whose origins and nature would have been deemed heretical to the machinesmiths and forgefathers of mankind.

Behind the battleship, following in its wake, came its fleet. Within those storm-battered hulls, twenty thousand warriors awaited word of a destination, a safe haven.

They were twenty thousand of the greatest warriors in the Imperium. They were the First, and the first among equals.

THE SHIP CAME out of the darkness, and within its darkness, an endless hunt played out.

The huntsman waited in the darkness, listening to the eerie throb of the unhuman device directing the ship's engines. The darkness was oily black, as black as the armour he wore.

The quarry was close, but then, the quarry was always close.

The quarry was supposed to be dead, or at the very least a prisoner, but through his innate guile and wickedness, he had evaded capture and was loose in the ship, haunting its dark spaces and inaccessible extremities. Of course, the quarry was technically a prisoner, because the whole ship was his cell. There was no escape from the ship.

It galled the huntsman that the quarry was at liberty at all. The quarry should have been dead for his crimes long since. The huntsman should have made sure of that, blood or no blood. The quarry was not a sentient being deserving of any respect or mercy. The quarry was an insane animal that needed to be put down, a monster that deserved termination. All the while the wretched quarry was loose on the huntsman's ship, the huntsman's heart burned with rage.

The huntsman had sent warriors to locate the quarry and kill him, to section the ship, deck by deck, to smoke the monster out of hiding, and end his curse. But the quarry – the creature of darkness, the haunter of the eternal night that glowered in the unlit hold spaces and hull structures that were a feature of any warp-capable ship – had killed the men, and killed the men sent after them, and the men sent after them. The quarry had trapped them, and murdered them, stalked them and tricked them, left their bodies swinging from hold spars as warnings, left their heads in void-locks as messages, left their butchered remains impaled on inter-deck stanchions and pipework as bloody promises.

The huntsman was a noble soul, though to those who met him in battle, he often appeared to be a monster too. Few, if any, knew the true workings of his mind. He kept his own counsel, and walked his own path. He was hard to know.

He was a noble soul, nevertheless.

He refused to send any more men into the darkness to their deaths. He refused to order any more men to do what he was not prepared to do. He had had all but the primary decks evacuated and sealed; then he had put on his armour, the black armour etched with Martian gold, and had become the hunter. Every day for sixteen weeks, he had entered the unregulated spaces of his ship and hunted through the darkness for his quarry.

Every day for sixteen weeks.

The ship came out of the darkness, and within its darkness, an endless hunt played out.

The huntsman could smell the quarry. They had come close many times in the past sixteen weeks. There had been two brief scuffles, from which the quarry had fled when he had realised that the huntsman was hard to ambush. There had been times when the quarry's brittle whisper of a voice had gusted out of the darkness to taunt the huntsman. There had been messages left in blood. There had been traps and counter-traps, hours of stalking, slow progress through the dark and juddering spaces of the ship, testing every shadow for the one shadow that wasn't a shadow at all.

The huntsman halted, crouched, balancing his dense but agile form on a cross-spar that ran like a rock bridge over the ravine of an exhaust shaft. A dark green blackness glowed far below. Thermal vents opened and a stream of hot air blew up the shaft like a desert wind. It stirred the huntsman's long, golden hair. He paused, unclasped it, re-gathered it and tied it again to keep it out of his eyes.

There was a scent on the dry wind. One part in a billion, but the huntsman could smell it.

Old blood. Pain. Adrenaline. Hatred.

The quarry was close. He was hiding below, on one of the sub-level walkways that lined the throat of the exhaust shaft. In sixteen weeks, the huntsman had never got such a precise fix.

The hot air was venting from below, and the huntsman was downwind of the quarry. Doubtless, the quarry couldn't hear him because of the machine noise echoing up the shaft space.

Silently, the huntsman rose and leapt. He landed twenty metres away on another cross-spar, and ran along it like a tight-rope walker before clambering into the girder-work reinforcing the shaft wall. He descended. Every few metres, he stopped and scanned, hunting with his eyes, his ears, his sense of smell.

Close, so close…

There. The huntsman froze. He could see the quarry. He could see him for the first time. The quarry was hunched on a gantry about thirty metres below the huntsman's position. He looked like a ragged hawk, roosting on a ledge. The quarry was look-ing down. For some reason, he was expecting the huntsman to approach from below. For once, his uncanny powers of augury and foresight had failed him. The quarry was waiting, hunched, silent, ready to strike.

The quarry had no idea the huntsman was above him.

The huntsman drew his sword, oil-damp and silent, from his scabbard. He lined up to make the leap – less a leap, in fact, more a pounce. It would be an impact kill. The huntsman's weight and momentum would crush the quarry into the unyielding gantry, and the sword's edge would finish it.

It would be quick, which was more than the quarry deserved, but long overdue.

The huntsman flexed his arms, loosened his neck, and made ready for the leap. There was no room for error. The quarry was not a creature to underestimate. The huntsman leaned forward, holding onto a girder with his left hand for support, tensing his legs, ready to–

'*My lord,*' his vox system woke up and crackled.

Below, the quarry looked up, his head snapping upright at the sound. The huntsman saw the quarry's pale face: surprise, and delight.

'Close!' the quarry squealed up at the huntsman. 'So close, but confounded!'

The quarry started to laugh. He darted off the gantry and dropped away into the shaft, arms spread, tattered cloak fluttering like ragged wings. He dropped into the darkness of the exhaust pit, leaving his scornful laughter in the hot wind behind him.

The huntsman rocked back. He bit down his rage. He activated his vox-link.

'Speak,' he said, his voice low and seismic, 'and for your sake, make the content worthwhile.'

'*My lord,*' said the vox. '*There is a light.*'

'A light?' the huntsman growled.

'*A beacon, my lord. We have detected a strong but unknown navigational beacon.*'

The huntsman hesitated.

'Have an assault squad waiting at the agreed exit hatch to meet me,' he said. 'I'm coming out. Let's see this beacon.'

FIRST MASTER AUGUSTON was waiting for him on a battlement of the Moneta Fortress overlooking the landing fields of the starport. The First Master was accompanied by several of his key subordinates and a number of officers of the city. They had finished delivering their latest reports and were silent. Auguston was gazing up at the light of the Pharos, the new and only star in the turbulent sky.

Auguston's suit system registered the approach of another, and he turned to regard Alexis Polux as he came along the battlement to join them. Auguston was used to being one of the largest beings in any given place, excepting the Avenging Son. There was something dismaying to him about the Imperial Fists captain's size.

'Lord Auguston,' Polux said, with a respectful bow of his head. 'My apologies that I was prevented from joining you sooner.'

Auguston acknowledged him.

'It was suggested to me that you might assist with your expertise, captain. You have three days' worth of security inspections and protocol reviews to catch up on.'

'Again, I apologise,' said Polux. His wargear had been cleaned and mended, and his damaged arm was strapped across his chest in a juvenat sling. 'The Master of Ultramar ordered me to heal and make ready for the coming war. I have been two days in the grafting suites.'

Auguston glanced at the repairs to Polux's arm. Instead of a simple augmetic replacement, the Apothecaries had elected to fix a flesh graft grown from seeded organics, vat-cultured. Inside the semi-transparent sleeve of the sling, beneath the layers of nutrient wrap and growth hormone gel, Polux wore a new hand and arm of living flesh which had been bio-typed to his own. It was still growing, still forming, the new bones still knitting. Flooded with oxygenated blood, the hand was almost crimson.

'Will it take?' asked Auguston.

'The prognosis is good,' said Polux. 'Another two days and rejection can be ruled out. It should be serviceable within a week.'

Auguston nodded. He gestured for one of his aides.

'As I said, we've been conducting the review for three days. I have had a summary prepared.'

The aide handed Polux a data-slate.

'How fares the primarch?' Polux asked.

'He–' Auguston began. 'He fares well, I understand. Given that it has been merely three days, he shows remarkable signs of recovery.'

Polux didn't do more than quickly scan the data-slate. He turned and looked out over the port fields, then eyed the shadows of ships at high anchor far above and the cloud-bank shapes of the orbitals.

'I don't believe it's a simple matter of protocol reviews,' he said.

'You haven't even begun to look at the slate–' Auguston started to say.

'I can study the close detail later. Believe me, First Master, I have been considering Macragge's security all the while the Apothecaries worked on my limb. This is a magnificent port facility, but it is not secure.'

'What?'

Polux looked at Auguston.

'I said, it is not secure.'

'Are you trying to anger me, Captain Polux?' asked Auguston, stepping forward. Polux noticed that most of the aides and juniors escorting him took a step backwards. They did not want to get caught in the First Master's wrath.

'No, lord,' replied Polux calmly. 'I am trying to help. I took very seriously your great primarch's request.'

'Then look before you speak!' Auguston spat. 'Since the crime that was Calth we have fortified the system, the planetary approaches, set guards and defences, launched new platforms, and fortified the city, especially the starport areas and–'

'You have done all of these things,' Polux agreed. 'But you have done them all while preserving the original nature of this world and this port. Macragge is a capital world, sir, and this port is its great harbour. Macragge rules an empire of five hundred worlds, sir – the realm of Ultramar. It may even come to rule over the Imperium. It has a port that reflects that role, a port built for trade and commerce, a port built to serve the mercantile needs of peace. Yes, you have fortified it. But it is still not secure. It may withstand an assault, but can it filter out the illegal entry of our enemies? I believe it is reasonable to expect that those killers who meant to take the life of your primarch are not the only intruders currently here on Macragge.'

'Is this how your kind would protect Terra?' asked Auguston scornfully. 'To cast away all of its original purposes and make it nothing more than a razor-wired rampart?'

Polux nodded.

'I fully expect that my primarch will have encased Terra in armour. I fully expect that the Imperial Palace is no longer a palace but the greatest fortress in the galaxy. This is a war like none we have ever contested, sir. It will make casualties of us all if we do not respect it, or if we are too precious about our possessions.'

'So what? We stop trying to fortify and preserve what we have, and instead simply rebuild it?'

'Yes. In times like this, it is not enough to bar or board up a window, my lord. You must brick it shut so that the window no longer exists. The reconstruction work needed on the city, and especially the port, will be costly and time-consuming. You must begin work on the construction of a fortified military port. There are remedial actions that can be made while construction is planned and executed.'

'Such as?' asked Auguston.

Polux gestured at the ships at anchor overhead.

'Let nothing, and I mean nothing, come within firing distance of Macragge until it has been inspected. I suggest using some of the outer starforts in mid-system as way stations. Let no ship land, or send landers to the surface, until the identity of both the ship and its occupants have been verified by eye and gene-code.'

'That will slow all trade and imports to a crawl!' said one of the city officials.

'It will,' Polux agreed, 'but it will also slow down the ticking of the doomsday clock.'

'What of our veterans, returning from Calth and the other war-zones?' asked an Ultramarines captain beside Auguston. 'Must their passage be delayed in this ignominious way too?'

'I think after what happened in the Residency,' grumbled Auguston, 'we know the answer to that. What else, Polux?'

'That,' he said, pointing at the orbiting wreck of the *Furious Abyss*, now clearly visible as it crested the horizon.

'It's dead,' said Auguston, 'and what's left of it is being disman-tled by reclamation teams. What of it?'

'It's a hazard to navigation,' Polux replied, 'and furthermore, it is a military threat. Effective sabotage could knock it from orbit, and drop every megatonne of its metal bulk on this city. The enemy is not beyond such tricks, First Master. That corpse-ship must be towed beyond the orbit of the outer moons and disman-tled there.'

'Anything else?'

'Orbit-to-surface teleporting must be restricted, and all entry to the planet by craft or teleport forbidden, unless it comes through the designated area of this port. I suggest the installation of upgraded void shields to cover the lower orbital tracks and the port area, enough to close it down if necessary. I also suggest a proportion of the orbital sensor systems and auspex modules be re-tasked to cover the surface of the planet.'

'Why?'

'I'm talking about a new philosophy of defence, First Master. You have fortified the system, the planet and the city in case of another Calth. You have more than enough ships and battery sys-tems to fend off any openly hostile approach to Macragge. But the incident in the Residency proves that an open assault is not the only way our enemies may come for us. Treachery comes in different scales, sir. A small percentage of your auspex modules could be retrained to cover the entire surface of this world without significant impairment of the early warning or system scanning watch processes. If anyone lands a ship or uses a drop pod or a teleport system outside this restricted port area, you'll know about it. Do not assume you can keep them out, sir. A planet is a vast area. Assume they will get in, and make sure you see their footprints when they do.'

Auguston pursed his lips. He was annoyed at the way the Imperial Fist had schooled him in basic defence analysis, and made the conclusions look so obvious, but he also knew that including most of Polux's suggestions in his report would make it look as though he'd done a particularly thorough job.

'You're worth listening to, Polux,' he said grudgingly.

'I take that as high praise from you, sir.'

Polux looked up at the light of the Pharos.

'You have hung up a lamp to draw travellers here out of the storm, my lord, and that is right and just, and the only way that a fair and noble civilisation can survive. However, you must scrutinise who and what the light brings to you, and how disguised their real motives are. I would certainly like to know more about your "new Astronomican". Understanding its function and process may assist me in making good recommendations for Macragge's protection. I do not even know where it is situated, or what manner of technology allows it to function.'

'That is classified,' said one of the aides, 'but I am sure the primarch will permit you to discuss basics with the warsmith.'

'Did you say warsmith?' asked Polux.

The aide nodded.

'Warsmith Dantioch has led the operation to activate the Pharos,' said Auguston.

'An Iron Warrior?' Polux asked, his voice low.

'Is that a problem, captain?'

GUILLIMAN WALKED WITH a slight limp, though it would mend. His throat and one side of his face looked as though he had been dragged along rockcrete by a Scimitar jetbike.

He had dressed in a loose tunic and robes to cover the extensive bandaging around his torso, and had refused the armoured bodyglove for reasons of mobility and comfort. He told his advisors that he would not be making a similar error again. However, until he was healed enough to wear full war-plate, he accepted the heavy belt slung with a refractor field generator, which he wore under his robes. To it, he had holstered a Maetherian ray-pistol, a formidable piece of archeotech from his personal collection.

Titus Prayto and Drakus Gorod of the Invictus accompanied him wherever he went, the Librarian and the heavy-armoured beast, ready to sense danger and dispense violence.

So escorted, he returned to the Residency for the first time since the attack. He had ordered that nothing be touched or repaired until he had the chance to review the scene. Titus Prayto read very cleanly the psychological intent of this. Guilliman wanted to face his daemons. He wanted to look directly at the circumstances in which he had nearly died. Prayto could sense the underlying tension in the primarch like a tremble in the air. It disquieted him. When the greatest beings in the universe registered stress or tension, it was time for all things living to find cover.

They came up the hallway. The carpet was dappled with dark stains, a trail of blood where Gorod and his men had carried Guilliman out. Ahead of them was the door that the Invictus guard had cut open.

Men waited for them at the doorway: a pack of men.

They looked up, yellow eyes alert, heads cocked, the moment

Guilliman and his escort came into view. They had been huddled around the doorway, resting or sharpening their blades. None of them had dared cross the threshold into the primarch's inner chambers.

Guilliman approached. Faffnr Bludbroder's wolf pack rose to meet him, not as a challenge, but as an honour guard.

'This isn't my hearth,' Guilliman said, looking at the pack-leader.

'No, jarl, it's your door,' Faffnr agreed. 'Your door will do, for now.'

Guilliman nodded.

'We were told not to go in. Told it was your orders,' Faffnr added.

'They were my orders,' Guilliman agreed.

'Dogs must always wait at the doorpost,' Gorod rumbled out of the depths of his Terminator plate, 'until the master lets them in. Good dogs, that is. Good dogs stay at the edge of the firelight, waiting for scraps, until they are allowed near the hearth.'

Faffnr turned his head slowly and stared into the Cataphractii's gargoyle visor. His eyes were unblinking. One of his men leaned forward and whispered something into the pack-leader's ear. A half-smile crinkled Faffnr's lips, exposing one fang.

'No, Bo Soren,' he said. 'I can't let you do that. Though it would be funny to watch.'

Faffnr glanced up at Guilliman.

'You'd let your warrior speak to me like that, jarl?' he asked.

'It's exactly what you were thinking,' said Titus Prayto.

Faffnr looked at Prayto. He sniffed, and then chuckled and nodded.

'It was, *maleficarum*, it was. True enough. We have a low opinion of ourselves, I suppose, but a high opinion of our loyalty and obedience.'

'What about *your* obedience, Jarl Guilliman?' Faffnr asked side-long of the Avenging Son, his stare fixed rigidly on the Librarian's face.

'Is it questioned, Wolf?' asked Guilliman. 'Because I use the Librarius in defiance of the Edict? The Edict was made before this war was begun. It is obsolete. We need the Librarius if we're going to survive. Does that make me disobedient?'

Faffnr let out a deep, wet growl, like a jungle beast. His eyes stayed on Prayto's face.

'He thinks it might make you courageous and decisive in your obedience,' Prayto told Guilliman, holding Faffnr's stare, 'to pursue your loyalty through decisive, unilateral and perhaps unpopular choices. He thinks that's why you are a great leader.'

Guilliman nodded.

'Tell him the rest while you're in there, *maleficarum*,' said Faffnr.

'He thinks he will, nevertheless, keep a very close watch on you, lord,' said Prayto.

'A day without a clumsy threat from you is not complete, is it, Faffnr?' asked Guilliman. 'Really? Again with this? Me, alone in a room against a squad of ten? In case you've missed recent events, I've already done that.'

Faffnr Bludbroder shrugged.

'They were Alpha Legion. Not Wolves.'

'I did it unarmed.'

Faffnr broke his gaze from Prayto and looked at Guilliman. 'I never said it wasn't well done,' he replied.

Prayto smiled.

'Will you let my pack guard your hall, jarl?' asked Faffnr. 'We've come a long way to protect the Emperor's peace.'

'I think that responsibility is fully covered,' rumbled Gorod, his words grinding out of the helm-vox, one by one, like heavy calibre rounds from a chain-fed weapon.

'Not well enough, looks like,' replied Faffnr.

'Not even nearly well enough,' added Bo Soren.

'You may cross my threshold, Wolves,' Guilliman said. 'You may approach the fireside. I'll permit it. But do not obstruct Gorod or his men. Can you be obedient in that respect?'

Faffnr nodded. His men broke and stood aside.

Guilliman entered the room where he had nearly met his end.

The furniture was shattered. The great desk was scarred and gouged like a meteor. There were holes in the walls, the floor, the ceiling. Pictures had fallen from their suspensions and broken. One portrait of Konor still hung, but the entire area of the face and shoulders was shot away. Hanging canvas shreds and fibres stilled in the gentle air-circulation.

All the corpses had been removed, but the carpets were still dyed with the lifeblood of the Legiones Astartes, and the walls were speckled with yet more blood that had dried and looked like black paint or spatters of tar. Parts of the wall and chunks of heavy furniture were peppered with pieces of exploded plate armour, shards of ceramite flung out from exploding wounds to embed like shrapnel. The main windows were crazed with spider-web patterns. One series of cracks looked like a coiled snake: a multi-headed coiled snake.

Guilliman drew a breath. He knew he was in a slightly heightened state. He was reading symbols and portents into things that had no significance.

He closed his eyes. For a millisecond, the noise and fury of the moment came back, filling his head, every last moment relived in flaring, vivid–

He opened his eyes again.

'My lord?' asked Prayto.

'I'm all right,' Guilliman said. He looked around, and moved forward, each step crunching scattered glass chips into the carpet. Konor's cold-gestalt cogitator, and the stand that had housed it, was a smashed wreck on the floor. A falling body had crushed it.

Guilliman stared at the debris for a moment. The living history of Macragge, the rise of Ultramar, the fortunes of the Five Hundred Worlds, had all been witnessed and monitored by that ancient device. It was strange. The loss seemed to carry more emotional weight than had been provoked by the sight of his stepfather's disfigured portrait. Guilliman felt unexpected levels of sentiment rising within him.

'I will need–' he began. His voice cracked slightly.

'A replacement device,' Prayto finished quickly. 'I will speak to the adepts of the Mechanicum at once about furnishing you with a new cogitator system, a cognis-signum application device that will enhance data processing.'

Guilliman nodded.

'I feel...' he began to say to Prayto. He stopped. Gorod was waiting behind them at the door, the Wolves in the doorway behind him. Guilliman walked to the windows on the far side of the room and stood with his back to the doorway, staring out. Prayto went with him.

'You feel pain and sadness,' said Prayto, 'and you do not want the others to overhear this.'

Guilliman nodded again.

'It is a delayed reaction, lord,' said Prayto.

'To an attack? I've lived through wars, Prayto – I've fought daemons, and my own brothers. I've taken worse wounds than this.'

'That was not my meaning, lord.'

'Then what? To the loss of an old cogitator?'

'I think that was just the trigger, my lord. It was an heirloom. It had personal meaning to you.'

'Then what, I say? A delayed reaction to what?'

'To Horus,' said Prayto.

Guilliman sighed deeply.

'Make sure they come no closer,' he said to Prayto.

Prayto nodded, letting the unspoken thought finish in his mind.

Because I do not want those Wolves to see me with a tear in my damned eyes.

EUTEN FOUND HIM alone in the room. Prayto had gone to meet with the Mechanicum, and Guilliman had sent Gorod and the Wolves out so he could have time for reflection. He heard her greet Gorod and grumble at the feral wolf pack as she came through the outer door.

He had raised one of the larger seats onto its feet. The back was shot out of it, so the shredded leather padding looked like ruptured blubber. He had placed it in front of the cobwebbed windows, and was sitting, leaning forward, elbows on his knees.

'Do you bring me the day's agenda, mam?' he asked, without looking at her.

'I do not,' she replied. 'I have dealt with most matters. You need time to think.'

'I never stop thinking, mam.'

'Then you need time to focus, my lord. The hour has come to commit.'

He glanced at her, though he still sat forward.

'I have already committed. You know this. Macragge, and the Five Hundred Worlds... They *are* the Imperium. *Imperium Secundus.* The contingency that we never even dreamed might be necessary is now a practical.'

She nodded.

'You continue to evade my meaning,' she said. 'What I mean is, I think it's time you admitted it to more than just me and your closest confidences. It has been your private theoretical – now you must declare Imperium Secundus *formally* and *publically.* You have to have strength in your conviction, and not shrink from the more unedifying aspects of it. If you do not have faith in it, then neither will a single soul in the Five Hundred Worlds.'

He opened his mouth to answer, but said nothing.

'What is it? What makes you hesitate?' Euten asked. 'Is it a fear that you are usurping every bit as much as Horus? Or is it–'

'Grief,' he said quietly. 'Grief that my father, and Terra, and the grand dream of the Imperium are lost, and the only way for our civilisation to survive is to consolidate here. It is a burden I never looked for, mam, and it is made heavier by sorrow.'

He looked out through the crazed glass and surveyed the towers and stacks of Macragge Civitas, golden in the sickly warp-light.

'You think I should make a formal declaration because I look weak, don't you?' he asked.

'Yes,' she said, nodding. She adjusted her grip on her staff to ease her stance and rest her back. 'The morale of Ultramar has never been lower. Calth, the Ruinstorm, the war against the sons of Lorgar and Angron – these things have battered us, but the assault on you… My lord, it has shown us that even the most precious thing we have left is not safe.'

Euten glanced around at the cold devastation of the chamber. Her eyes lingered on the smashed cogitator and a broken bust of Konor.

'Just an hour before… before *this* happened,' she said, gesturing at the room with her slender left hand, 'I lectured you about how vulnerable you are. I am sorry if my tone was hectoring. I am not sorry that my words were true. This is all we have left of the Imperium, and you are the last precious prince. You cannot be all the things you once were. You are too valuable to be risked. You are too important to be diluted with a surfeit of roles.'

'This isn't a conversation about declaring Secundus, is it?' he asked.

'There is no point declaring Secundus if Secundus has an empty throne. You must declare *yourself*.'

'What?' he asked, a mocking laugh behind the words. 'Emperor Guilliman?'

'Regent at least, my lord. Don't look at me like that. I know how you hate the word.'

He stood up.

'Euten, I cannot. I cannot command and rule. I cannot administer this empire *and* be its figurehead.'

'I told you, you must delegate,' she said. 'No one else can possibly be head of state. No one else can possibly be regent. You are the last primarch, my lord. The last loyal son. The *only* loyal son. Become what you must become. Invest yourself as the rallying point of Imperium Secundus. Be Imperial, and reveal your renewed strength, your resolve, your mettle and the glory, like a phoenix rising from these ashes. Leave the everyday mechanics of Imperial business to others.'

'That is my point,' he replied. 'I trust no one else to oversee those mechanics. I have done it for so long. I… trust no one else… Not even you, dear lady.'

'Because I am not capable?' She sniffed, though she was mocking.

His reply was typically honest.

'Because you are old, Lady Euten. You are human and old. I do not know how much longer life will let you stand at my side. I cannot rely on you being here, and I do not trust anyone else.'

'A good answer,' she said. 'But, you know… I have known you since you were a child, Roboute. I know when you are being careful with the truth. This is such a time. For all your logic, none of the things you have said are the real reason you will not declare yourself Imperial Regent.'

'Is that so?' he asked.

'You know it is.'

He sighed.

'Then let me say it once. I cannot build an empire and put myself on the throne, even if I *am* the only candidate. It smacks of hubris, of arrogance, of overweening pride and foul ambition.'

'It smacks of Horus Lupercal,' she said.

'Oh, indeed. It will diminish me in the eyes of those who yet respect me, and it will simply confirm the doubts of all those who do not. "Look at Guilliman," they will say, "taking advantage of this crisis and naming himself king. Look at his unseemly eagerness. Look how fast he jumped in to take unwholesome advantage of the situation!"'

'I am glad to hear you admit your misgivings at last,' she said. 'But it is the only *practical* action to take. You always taught me that practical trumps theoretical.'

'But in this matter, the theoretical stinks,' he said. 'I have been holding out hope that one other brother might still come to me. Rogal, stars, but I would hand the throne *selflessly* to him! Sanguinius, in an *instant*! These are worthy heirs! These are *noble* brothers!'

'And if they were willing, it would validate Secundus,' she nodded. 'Their sanction would reinforce your choices.'

'Any loyal son,' murmured Guilliman. 'Right now, I would take any loyal son.'

'Even Russ?' she asked.

Guilliman laughed.

'He's a barbarian,' he said, 'but he is still a king. And he is loyal in ways that shame us all. Yes, even Russ. Perhaps we need a truly fierce monarch to see us through this new strife.'

'And you, as his conscience, would keep his crown clean,' she said.

'Of course,' he said. He sighed deeply again, and looked around. 'Have the Residency staff clear this room. Strip it. Make it new. I'm hungry. I think I'll feast with the Wolves tonight.'

He looked at her.

'Rest easy, mam,' he said, 'by morning I will have made my

decision. If I am going to declare as regent, you will know it soon, and we can prepare for the announcement.'

'There is no one else fit, my lord,' said Euten.

'There is no one else at *all*,' he replied. 'So I suppose it will have to be me.'

THE SCORCHED CORPSE that had fallen on the southern deme of Magna Macragge Civitas had been taken to a private, secure suite in the lower levels of the Residency's medicae hall. The exits to the area were guarded and locked, and only authorised personnel were allowed in and out, or even to know the nature of what the lab suite contained.

Valentus Dolor, Tetrarch of Occluda, arrived unescorted, and strode down the long, echoing hallway to a series of iris valve hatches. Ultramarines guards bowed to him and let him pass. The hatches scraped as they dilated, one by one.

Captain Casmir was waiting for him in a stark laboratory chamber of zinc and galvanised steel. The place was lit by greenish lights, and smelled industrial. A massive iron casket lay on a raised plinth in the main area of the room. There were heavy armourglass viewing ports built into the sides and top of the casket, so that the body, suspended in embalming solutions, could be examined. Instrument locks in the sides of the casket also allowed for surgical tools to be inserted so that tissue samples could be taken. All that could be seen through the ports was a thin, scummy murk. Several medicae technicians were working around the casket.

'Do we have an identity?' Dolor asked his equerry.

'No, lord,' replied Casmir. 'But we have answered one question.'

He offered Dolor the data-slate he had been holding. Dolor took it and read.

'Careful analysis of orbital watch records has finally revealed how our dead stranger arrived,' said Casmir. 'You see the brief spike there? A teleport flare in the upper atmosphere. Non-standard teleportation pattern.'

'So he materialised in the upper atmosphere, out of nowhere?'

'And then fell,' Captain Casmir said, 'all the way to the surface, burning like a meteor as he cut through the atmosphere.'

'Do we know anything about the origin point of the teleportation?'

'The flare pattern is being examined, but I doubt it, my lord.'

Dolor handed the slate back and took a few steps towards the casket.

'The more we learn, the more of a mystery he becomes. I–'

He stopped short. Some monitor alarms had started to buzz. A few amber telltales lit up along the console beside the plinth. The medicae technicians reacted in surprise and backed away for a second.

'What is it?' asked Dolor. 'What's happening?'

'I don't know, lord tetrarch,' said one of the technicians.

'It makes no sense,' said another.

'It must be a system malfunction,' said a third.

A new alarm started to sound.

Dolor stepped closer to the casket, his hand on the hilt of his sword. He peered in at one of the murky portals.

'Someone explain to me what's going on,' he snarled.

There was a sudden, very violent bang. Even Dolor jerked back.

The sound had been made by an impact from inside the casket. Something had struck one of the glass portals very hard.

Dolor looked. He blinked. Pressed against the inside of the armourglass – bloody, raw and peeling with blackened, burned meat – were the palm and fingertips of a large human hand.

'Open the damned casket!' Dolor ordered, drawing his sword. 'In the name of the Five Hundred Worlds, whatever's in there isn't dead at all!'

✠ ✠ ✠

THE SHIP CAME out of the darkness, and within its darkness an end-less hunt paused for a moment, for the first moment in sixteen weeks.

Deep in the almost lightless void of the ship reactor's vast heat sink, the quarry paused, a nocturnal ghost, condemned to be absolutely alone for the rest of his life.

He crouched on a rusting stanchion above the smoking furnaces of the ship's engines, and wrapped his arms around his body. His cloak was tattered and black. What little light was coming off the smouldering embers of the drive chambers beneath him caught along the razored lines of his claws.

He felt the bump, the ripple, the heave of transition. He heard the arrhythmic flutter of the engines as they dimensionally cor-rected. He felt his guts twist and his sinuses pinch. It made him whimper.

The ship had made a translation into realspace.

The quarry tilted his head back and began to laugh. He peeled back cracked lips to expose teeth that, had there been any light, would have showed as blackened and rotting. His laughter, as sharp and shattered as a calving glacier, fell away and echoed down the sink.

The rules had just been rewritten. In realspace, the ship was no longer a finite prison. He was no longer the quarry.

The rules had just changed, and people were going to die. A lot of them. *All* of them.

At long last.

THE SHIP CAME out of the darkness.

'Translation complete,' Captain Stenius called from the high, railed platform of the bridge. 'Realspace positioning achieved.'

Below him, on the main fore-station deck, the bridge crew, plugged into their various consoles, chattered back and forth, sharing and updating the surge of realspace data as fast as their automatics would allow.

Stenius turned to look at the ship's lord. The low light of the flagship's bridge hazed off Stenius's smoked-silver augmetic eyes. The captain's face, immobilised by nerve damage, hadn't registered an expression for decades.

The ship's lord, the huntsman, knew, however, that there was a smile of relief locked away in that unmoving flesh. He sat on his titanic, engraved throne, a shadow at the back of the flagship's vast bridge space, a monarch with no realm.

He raised his head, acknowledging Stenius, and looked at the main display. The light was astonishing: a beacon of some sort, a world thoroughly illuminated. His ship, miraculously, with all of its fleet in sequence behind it, was ploughing into a stellar system lit up by the greatest intergalactic lighthouse that he had ever seen.

The system was armed and defended. Already, challenges were coming in on all channels. He could read starforts heating up weapon banks on the strategium display, interplanetary bands of defence, mine-belts, gun-stations powering batteries, and interceptor fleets turning hard in response to the pulse of their abrupt arrival.

Of course they would. Of course they would react so urgently. What the huntsman was bringing with him was one of the greatest war-fleets in the Imperium; perhaps *the* greatest.

'This isn't the Terran Solar System,' he said.

'Not even slightly, my lord,' replied Stenius. 'It's not even the Solar Segmentum.'

'Answer me, now. Where is this?' asked the huntsman. His voice was barely audible.

Lady Theralyn Fiana of House Ne'iocene, the flagship's Navigator, stepped off the elevator platform from the navigation pit and approached the huntsman's throne. The nephilla had much damaged her. Her withered form was supported on either side by her brothers Ardel Aneis and Kiafan.

'You are correct, lord,' she said, in the whisper that was all she could manage. 'This is not Terra, and that is not the light of the Astronomican. I cannot yet account for the presence or nature of the beacon, but it has drawn us out of the storm. It has done it in ways that–'

'What do you say to me, lady?' asked the huntsman.

Fiana shook her head.

'I cannot explain, my lord,' she whispered. 'There is something at work here, some technology I cannot explain. Not psychic. Empathic. It is as though the light showed itself to us because it knew what we wanted. It knew where we wanted to be.'

'Expand on this,' the huntsman said.

'Despite the storm, my lord,' the Navigator whispered, 'despite the turmoil of the warp, we have arrived precisely where it wanted us to be. This is Macragge. This is the heart system of Ultramar.'

The huntsman rose. He stared at the planet ahead of them.

'*By my father's dead gods…*' he breathed.

'Orders, my lord?' asked Captain Stenius. 'We are bombarded with challenges – vox, pict-feed, psychic and sub-vox. We have been target-locked by sixteen of the starforts and platform systems, and two of the three nearest intercept fleets are moving in to acquire firing solutions. They will start shooting very soon.'

He shrugged.

'Of course, my lord,' Stenius added in a more hushed tone, 'our shields are raised. We can cut right through them. We can burn and splinter Macragge if you so wish. An order is all I require.'

The huntsman held out his left hand. 'Vox,' he said.

Servitors, gilded and cherubic, flew a master-vox horn into his grasp and braced it for him.

'To my brother, Lord Guilliman,' the huntsman said, 'on all channels. I bid you welcome from afar. I wish to alight at Macragge and parlay with you. It is I, Roboute. It is the Lion. Respond.'

9

TRAITOR TO MANKIND

'Those who affect masks, and steal their way through shadows, and take the names of others as their own, are more deadly than any blooded warriors.'

– Gallan, *On Espiel*

'THE LION?' ASKED Warsmith Dantioch softly. 'The Lion himself? Is it true?'

A degree of trial and error had allowed them to permanently stabilise the vision of Primary Location Alpha in the Chapel of Memorial, adjacent to the newly founded Library of Ptolemy in the Fortress. The chapel, now an oddly lustrous place thanks to the permanence of the Pharos link, was the site for all audiences with far-away Sotha.

'The Lion himself, sir,' Titus Prayto replied. 'His fleet translated in-system just a few hours ago.'

'So the Lion emerges,' murmured Dantioch. 'He comes to support Lord Guilliman, I trust?'

'It would appear so, though he brings with him a fleet force of Dark Angels that might have split the planet in two,' Prayto said.

It was a curious experience to be at once standing in a candle-lit chapel and looking into a gleaming, abyssal cave of the tuning floor.

'So, he is our salvation,' Dantioch said.

'He is our hope,' Prayto corrected. 'It appears he has twenty thousand Dark Angels with him. That number could turn any tide.'

Prayto paused.

'I sense unease in you, Titus. You greet me with today's momentous news of the Lion's arrival, but there is another reason for this conversation.'

'You "sense"?' Prayto replied with a quizzical smile.

'Now, now, sir, I am no psyker,' replied the warsmith. A heavy, high-backed seat had been set on the tuning floor so that Dantioch did not have to stand throughout the audiences. Some of his tactical conversations with Guilliman lasted for hours. The warsmith eased his position a little and succumbed to a rasping cough. 'The quantum tuning of the Pharos device is empathic, and the more I use it, the more I am aware I can read demeanor. What do you hesitate from saying?'

'Alexis Polux of the Imperial Fists has requested an audience with you, sir.'

Dantioch stiffened slightly as the hulking Imperial Fist stepped into the communication field beside Prayto and became visible. Polux had removed his helm. He gazed directly at Dantioch's masked face.

'Captain,' said Dantioch.

'Warsmith,' Polux replied.

'I have been advised of your actions in the Phall System, sir,' said Dantioch. 'I am used to the sons of loyal Legions regarding me with suspicion, but I imagine you have more cause to distrust me than most.'

'I reserve judgement,' replied Polux.

'This means of communication,' Dantioch said, 'as I was reminding the Librarian, enhances empathic vibrations. You hate me. I can feel it.'

'I have not quite done killing Iron Warriors, sir,' Polux replied.

'I am quite sure the Iron Warriors have not done killing Imperial Fists, either,' Dantioch said, 'but I stand apart from their actions. Do not judge me by–'

'Sir,' said Polux, 'Primarch Guilliman has asked me to assist in the provision of security and fortification for Macragge and its system. I have made it my business to personally inspect all potential flaws and weaknesses.'

'You feel that I am a weakness?' asked Dantioch.

'Your Legion has turned,' said Polux, 'yet you are here, charged no less with the control of a device at once vital to Ultramar's survival and yet technologically still a mystery. That is a dangerous combination. The navigational viability of the Five Hundred Worlds is entrusted to a man who might be an enemy. How better to undermine the fortress of Ultramar than to get inside, and gain a position of trust and vast responsibility? I would know if this is your siegecraft, purposed to bring Lord Guilliman's domain down.'

'You are direct at least,' said Dantioch, 'but if you learn to read the tuning field's vibrations, you will see my true intent well enough. Besides, if I had been seeking to undermine Ultramar, captain, it would have fallen already.'

'You seek to distance yourself from your traitor-kin,' said Polux. He pointed at Dantioch with his crimson, grafted hand. 'That mask is not helping.'

Dantioch's iron mask was fashioned to resemble the emblem of the IV Legion.

'The mask hides nothing, Polux,' said Dantioch, 'and it does not come off. Rather than reminding you of my association and origin, it should remind you how far some will go to remain loyal. This tells you something about mettle, sir. This mask shows you that some men will wear a badge of shame forever, so that no one forgets the bonds they have broken in order to remain true.'

Dantioch slowly rose to his feet.

'The Imperial Fists and the Iron Warriors, Polux,' he said, sadly. 'Let us not debate, let us simply agree that of all the Legiones Astartes, they are the greatest in warcraft, the finest exponents of fortification, either of building defences or of overwhelming them. Together, sir, with our talents and vast experience pooled, we can make Macragge impregnable.'

He coughed again, looked to his side and took up a data-slate from the heavy arm of his seat. His gauntleted hand shook slightly at the effort.

'Now that the Pharos is operational,' he said, 'I have been giving time to the consideration of defence in the Macragge system. Speculation, really. Some suggestions. A number of integrated schemes that might work well.' He looked at Polux. 'This might be the way to prove my loyalty to you, captain.'

'How?'

'We talk,' said Dantioch. 'Every day, if necessary. I share every plan and idea I have with you. Every secret of my warcraft, including concepts the Iron Warriors have regarded as private lore since their foundation. I will betray my traitor-kin, captain. I will tell you all of my secrets, until you see through this mask and believe that only a truly loyal warrior could give up so much.'

GUILLIMAN FINISHED READING the report, and then looked at Euten.

'Why didn't you wake me?' he asked.

'You needed rest. Besides your injuries, you spent too long drinking that foul brew with the heathens last night.'

'Mjod is… an interesting concoction,' Guilliman agreed. 'As for the Wolves, I like their honesty. I like much less battle-brothers who hide their intentions and make guile a weapon.'

'Battle-brothers in general?' Euten asked. 'Or one in particular?'

'I am thinking of one brother especially,' said Guilliman.

He rose from his day bed.

'Is it really the Lion?' he asked.

'In such strength,' she replied, 'that he could have been a serious threat, had he not come peacefully.'

'Of all of them… Why did it have to be *him* who found a way through the storm?' Guilliman whispered.

Euten pretended she had not heard. She waited patiently.

'I admire him,' Guilliman said, more audibly, looking at his stoic chamberlain. 'Throne, who wouldn't? It's impossible *not* to admire him. But there is always a shadow on him. He dwells in secrets, he plays his cards too close, and he walks by himself when he pleases. There is… too much of the wild forest in him. He should be as noble as any of my beloved brothers, but we have never been close, and there is too much about him that is sly. This will be an interesting reunion. I wonder what agenda brings him all the way to Ultramar.'

'It could be nothing more sinister than shelter from the warp,' replied Euten. 'You'll find out. The Lion is coming. I suggest you put on full plate and welcome him in a manner that befits his eminence. Any loyal son, you said. Well, one has come to you out of the storm.'

IN THE OPINION of most rational observers, the Primarch of the First Legion Dark Angels was the most potent and potentially dangerous individual to visit Macragge since its illumination.

There was another strong candidate for that title, however, though his arrival was rather more clandestine.

Sometimes, he used the name John.

The immigration halls of the Helion orbital plate were vast, but now they were overcrowded and had begun to smell. Helion was the outermost grav-adjusted hard anchorage circling Macragge, and the largest and oldest of all the capital world's orbital plates. Battleships, bulk carriers, barges and gross tenders clung to the edges of it like piglets to a sow's teats.

Macragge, a gleaming grey marble whorled with white cloud, rolled slowly beneath the floating island.

John had been trying to find a way off the Helion plate since he'd arrived there six days before.

'This is cruel! Cruel, I tell you!' sobbed Maderen, holding her hungry baby against her neck. She was twenty-one, Terran standard. Her baby – John forgot the name of the poor thing, but knew he could fetch it out of her mind in a moment if he had to – had been born aboard the filthy refugee ship from Calth. The newborn's father, an Army regular in one of the Numinus regiments, had died back on Calth, and had never seen his son. He had never even known he was going to *have* a son.

Maderen was marked, a sunburn blush on the right side of her pretty face. The child was marked too, John noticed. An extra toenail on the underside of the second toe, left foot. The Mark of Calth, legacies of a biome corrupted by toxins, munition dust, heavy metals and solar radiation.

'Cruel,' she whispered, subsiding.

'I know it is,' John said, soothing her. He could smell the stale odours of his own body, and the reek of the hall around them. There was crying and wailing everywhere, echoed by the orbital's unforgiving acoustics.

'What is Guilliman thinking?' asked old Habbard. He coughed, shaking his head. 'I thought he was a kind king, a noble man. But he keeps us penned like animals.'

'I thought he was a warrior,' grumbled the sulking youth, Tulik. 'Some warrior. He let Calth get scoured to ashes.'

'Come on, hush, all of you,' John said. 'We've all been through hard times. Our beloved primarch... and let's be respectful, shall we, old man?'

John looked at Habbard, who shrugged and nodded in apologetic agreement.

'Our noble primarch,' John went on, putting his hand on old Habbard's shoulder to reassure him, 'he's been through a hard time too. He's hounded here. Enemies at his door. I'm sure he's doing his best to look after us all.'

'*This* is his best?' Maderen asked.

'I was talking to the guards, last shift,' John said.

'*Guards*, now? *Guards*, is it? Why would they have to guard *us*, poor damned victims in all this?' Habbard asked.

'Shhhh, now, old fella,' said John.

He dropped his voice to a conspiratorial whisper, and edged up the persuasion in his psyk.

'Enemies at the door,' he told them, the wide-eyed circle of desperate refugees crowded into the corner of the gloomy hall. 'The guards are as much for our benefit as anything. These are bad times, we all know that. Bad, dark times. God knows, an age of darkness. Security's tight. It's got to be. They want to let us down to the welcome camps in the city, but they have to hold us here while they check us out. Check identities. Confirm our status as metics.'

'Metics?' Tulik asked.

'Resident aliens,' John said. 'It'll be a temporary classification until we are assigned full citizenship. Anyway, they're using the orbitals as way stations, to process us as we come in. That's what the guards told me last shift, okay?'

Some of them smiled because they were reassured. Some of

them smiled at the comfort of his odd vocabulary, the 'okay' thing. Some of them smiled because he had managed a subtle adjustment of their amygdalae.

'Please,' said Maderen, 'can't you talk to them again, Oll?'

'Okay,' he said.

HE TRUDGED UP the grilled staircase to the main landing deck. He heard moans and complaints from below as the ghostly blue light of the ultraviolet sterilising lamps came on. Every few hours, the lamps bathed the holding halls in a radiance that made everyone feel nauseous. The ultraviolet wash was meant to keep them clean of lice and bacteria.

He fought to hold back the misery of the thirty thousand refugees in the deck pens below. The weight of it could easily unbalance a mind as sensitive as his.

Yet coming up was harder still. On the main deck, he was obliged to contend with the constant pain of the Thallax guards. The towering Mechanicum meat-borgs watched over the entire yard area, brutal and spare, glowering like butcher-birds, striding around on piston-limbs.

John wasn't sure which was harder to handle, the empathy or the knowledge. He hated the psykana backwash of the Thallaxii. He could smell their pain. He could feel and see that behind every polished, blank faceplate was a human skull, with its spinal column still attached, screaming in agony, neurally threaded to the unforgiving steel frame that it wore.

He also knew why the orbital was being guarded by a Thallax-heavy retinue, however, and that fact was difficult to deal with. He could read the order sequence plainly in their howling, fizzling brains.

The plate had been staffed by Mechanicum automata with a skeleton staff of Ultramarines supervisors in case it had to be sacrificed at short notice. Helion could be auto-destructed with a minimum loss of Legiones Astartes.

'*Return below!*' the nearest of the Thallaxii commanded, pistoning towards him, pneumatics puffing, weapons cycling.

'I want to talk to the officer in charge,' John said.

'*Identify yourself,*' the automaton said.

'You know me, Khee-Eight Verto. We talked just a while ago,' he said.

'*Accessing records,*' the machine replied, hesitating.

'What's the problem here?' asked the bay supervisor, approaching them. The supervisor was an Ultramarines sergeant. John hot-read him in a flash. *Ambitious.*

'Sir, I was just asking about waiting times and conditions,' John said.

The Ultramarine looked down at him. Helm off, the warrior was oddly out of proportion, a too-small head on a too-big body.

'What's your name?' asked the Ultramarine.

'Oll Persson,' said John. He'd been wearing his old friend's identity ever since he'd joined the refugee ship during a stop-over at Occluda. Oll was an easy role to play. He'd been a farmer on Calth after all, and his name would be on the population lists. It was easier to play an old friend. There were fewer cover details to remember.

'You've come from Calth?' asked the Ultramarines sergeant. *Zyrol*, John read. His name was Zyrol.

'Yes, sir,' John lied.

'What were you back there?'

'A farmer, sir.'

The Ultramarine nodded, compassionate. 'These are tough times, Oll,' he said.

'They are,' John agreed.

He felt a sudden, unexpected twinge of guilt. He thought of the real Oll Persson, his very real friend. He thought of the task he'd set for Oll, the danger he'd put him in. He thought about all the things at stake. Right now, Oll was cutting his way across–

No.

John regained control, regained clarity. He couldn't afford to think that way. Worry and fear made him vulnerable.

'There are a lot of women and children below,' John said, gesturing towards the holding decks. 'God knows, they could use proper help and not confinement here.'

'"God?"' asked the sergeant.

'Apologies, sir – a slip of the tongue. Old habits die hard.'

'You're what? Catheric?'

'Yes, sir.' Play the role. *Play the role.* 'Renounced, of course.'

'So, what are you, a spokesman?' asked the Ultramarine.

'I guess. We've been here a while, sir. Days. Before that, ten months on a carrier from the ruins of Calth. We thought–'

'I know it's bad, Oll,' said the sergeant. John read the legionary's ambition more closely, and saw it for what it really was – a kind of nobility. Sergeant Zyrol wanted honour. He wanted promotion. He wanted the transverse broom-crest of a centurion. To earn that, he knew he had to be just like his primarch: open and honest, compassionate, caring, serious, truthful, firm, effective. This was not an act. This was his belief model. It was in his gene-code.

'Women and kids down there,' John said. 'Waiting… It's getting hard for them, do you see? To be at the doorstep of sanctuary and yet denied.'

'New protocols, Oll,' replied the sergeant, with a shake of his head. 'First Master Auguston brought them in. We are obliged to hold, question and search them. Trust me, we hate to do it. You people deserve all the support Macragge can give you.'

Auguston. The name flamed up in the sergeant's mind. These

new security measures weren't Ultramarines protocols, in John's estimation. XIII Legion security was all about guns on walls. This was Iron Warriors style countermeasures… Long-term planning, arm's-length caution. No, given the way the cards had fallen, not IV Legion. No, more like…*VII tactics*. Imperial Fists. John probed harder, caught a quick memory flash of Zyrol watching his superior Auguston taking the credit for a security scheme orchestrated by someone called Polux.

Auguston. *Arsehole*. Note to memory. Adjust, a new strategy. Zyrol was not going to bend, nor was he going to bad-mouth his arsehole superior, but he was noble. He wanted to be like Guilliman. He wanted to stand for honour and duty.

'What's that, sir, over there?' John asked, pointing across the vast hangar space of the orbital deck.

Zyrol sighed. 'The dead,' he replied.

About half a kilometre away, across the rockcrete and adamantium cargo floor of the orbital's western dock, sarcophagus capsules were being unloaded via suspensor webs into the open maw of a cargo lander.

'The dead?' John echoed. He was pushing a gentle mental finger into the sergeant's frontal lobe dopamine system.

'We're repatriating the fallen of the Thirteenth to the Memorial Gardens for interment.'

'You…' John paused for effect. He amped his emotions so that tears would well. 'You prioritise the dead over the living?' he asked.

'It's not like that, Oll,' the sergeant protested, suddenly guilt-stricken.

John shook his head and walked away. It was all right. He'd already secured from Zyrol's surface thoughts the name of the officer in charge of landing schedules.

✠ ✠ ✠

John shed the Oll Persson guise as easily as one might take off a coat. He adjusted, and became Teo Lusulk, a fleet Intelligence officer assigned to the orbital. He gained access to a prep room, and acquired a clean flightsuit and a carrybag to stash his possessions in. He was particularly careful with one item. It was heavy, but not much bigger than a short sword. John had wrapped it in silk cloth, and he further bundled it inside his dirty clothes.

As he changed garments and cleaned himself up, John allowed the Mark of Calth that he had psyko-somatically applied to his left cheek and forehead to begin fading.

He walked into the busy control ring levels of the orbital's western watch tower. The great arched windows were open to permit a view across the grey cityscape of the titanic plate, the shoals of ships beyond, glinting in hard light and sharp shadows, and then the bright and vast sweep of Macragge, painfully lit against the throbbing darkness of the void. Operational code magenta, he decided. If the day's status was higher than scarlet, the window ports would have been automatically blast shuttered.

Passing as someone you were not was all about confidence: the confidence of body language and mind-state. John simply walked through the bustle of fleet staffers and servitors, passing Thallaxii sentries and Ultramarines security without even glancing at them. He was stopped, once, at the hatchway into a strategium.

'Papers and ident,' the Ultramarine said, his voice a glottal drawl emanating from his vox-grille.

'Of course, sorry,' John replied. He made a show of searching his flightsuit pockets. At the same time, he planted a thought-seed in the Ultramarine's head.

'Apologies, Lusulk,' the Space Marine said, waving him through. 'Didn't recognise you, friend.'

The strategium was humming with dataflow. Tactical officers, intelligencers and Mechanicum adepts worked around the glowing hololithic display tables. John picked up a data-slate and pretended to consult it as he moved closer.

He read dispositions. Near orbit and high anchorage were both packed tight as a drum. So many ships. Close to a third of the Ultramar warfleet by the looks of it, and another big fleet had recently taken up station in Macragge's polar range.

Were those Dark Angels ships? *First Legion*? Holy hell. Holy shitting *hell*.

John looked closer, reading the fine detail. There was a stand-off. It was subtle, but none of the Dark Angels vessels were out of gunsweep from either the Ultramarines warfleet or the principal weapon orbitals. Shit, what did Guilliman think his brother-Legion was going to do?

Of course. Of *course*. The answer was 'almost anything'. The galaxy had been turned upside down. No one trusted anybody.

What else? What the hell was that navigation beacon? Since when did Macragge have an Astronomican?

Except it wasn't an Astronomican. John could feel it. He could feel the light of it pulsing in his brain and heart and spine and balls. It was xeno-tech. Guilliman was using some kind of xeno-tech to pierce the warp storm and make the Five Hundred Worlds navigable. Holy, holy hell. The galaxy *had* turned upside down. Even sane men were resorting to desperate measures.

The xeno-tech was ugly. It was an ugly light – an old light, like a lamp lit aeons earlier. John didn't like it. It reminded him of something, something that had lurked deep in the Acuity he had shared with his alien puppet masters in the Cabal; a species memory, a memory of old time, of pre-humanity. It was tech that had taken others across the gulf of stars long before man, long before the eldar, even.

The feeling made him shiver. It made him fear for his own kind, for mankind, even though he had been a traitor to his kind for longer than he cared to remember.

He was an agent of the Cabal. He wondered for how much longer. John Grammaticus had a conscience, despite all evidence to the contrary. How much longer before he would finally be forced to acknowledge what his conscience was telling him and pay it some heed? How much longer before he let it guide his actions?

The galaxy had turned upside down. What else had to happen before he finally told his alien masters to go screw themselves?

His alien masters would kill him, of course. *Permanently*, this time.

John crossed to the next hololithic display table, a downsweep view of Macragge.

He bumped into a good-looking female officer, who was turning away from the table.

'Sorry,' he said, picking up the data-slate she'd dropped. She smiled.

As he handed it back to her, he got a decent hot read as his mind brushed hers. Her name was Leaneena, which was nice but not important. More significantly, he took her console access codes out of her head, like plucking individual whisker bones out of the cooked flesh of a good piece of fish.

John got to the table, and keyed the code into the fascia panel. He had data access. He started to work, carefully and methodically, trying not to make it look like he was gorging on information. He pulled up meteorological views, disposition spreads and data-slides. He dragged as much of it as he could over to his borrowed data-slate, his hand moving through the motion-conductive light-cloud. Some of the data was rebuffed and wouldn't copy to his device, because his clearance wasn't high enough. He copied what he could and memorised what he couldn't.

It was extremely demanding, keeping up a psyk disguise in such a crowded and vigilant environment. John reckoned he could do it for thirty minutes, tops, before his control started to fray. This was his one shot at learning how the ground lay.

He looked at Macragge. According to the Cabal, his target was down there somewhere, some*how*.

John had been many things for them: procurer, suborner, spy, panderer, recruiter, persuader, provocateur, iconoclast, thief.

He'd never been an assassin before.

He rotated the table view and rolled the three-dimensional globe of Macragge around on its axis, flicking aside the meteorological overlays and air traffic schemes. He wanted security data.

He got it. He'd been hoping for a teleport entry, but that was clearly out of the question. Some supremely clever bastard had retrained a modest proportion of the orbital auspex systems to watch the surface. Clever. Oh, *very* clever. Any teleport burst would be seen and logged. The same applied to unauthorised drop pods or landers. That was definitely Imperial Fists thinking. You can't keep everyone out. What you can do is know if they have got in.

What else? Well, authorised planetfall was restricted to the primary starport, and the primary damn starport looked wide open, but it wasn't because starship-quality void fields had been set up to close down the lower orbital tracks and the entire port area at a second's notice. So, zero chance of stealing a lander and then pleading code ignorance on the final approach. They'd just slam him out of the air.

John Grammaticus sighed. Sweat was starting to bead on his forehead.

It looked as if he was going to have to go with a crazy improvisation that had crossed his mind earlier.

TEO LUSULK BECAME an Army officer called Edaris Cluet, who was attached to the repatriation process. As Helion plate was overtaken by the terminator and night fell, Cluet boarded a bulk transport and stood, solemn and dignified in his mourning uniform, alongside other officers of his stripe, beside a row of sarcophagi. A fanfare sounded.

Lifting on hot blue burners, the transport rose and moved out of the orbital bay.

10

A PRIDE COMES
TO ULTRAMAR

'Enter every city as though you are its first-born master.'
– Fulgrim, Primarch of the III Legion

THE SIX GREAT war horns of the ancient Battle Kings sounded across
the storm-lit Civitas, screeching out long, rasping blasts in unison.
The horns, hollowed from the tusks of an extinct beast, had once
been wheeled into battle on giant cart-engines in the vanguards of
the armies that Konor and his forebears had taken to war. Now,
they were placed in the minarets of fortified towers around Martial
Square and the great wall of the Fortress.

As their hoarse bellows died away, like the fading roars of a
monstrous bull or glacial pachyderm receding into myth, the
sharper fanfare of the XIII began – silver trumpets and carnyx,
eight hundred of each, swelling with bright, triumphal joy.

In full, magisterial wargear, like a golden and azure demigod, Guilliman stood on the platform of the colossal Propylae
Titanicus, the 'Titan's Gate', that formed the northern entrance

of Martial Square. It was a pylon gate, large enough for even the largest engines of the Collegia Titanica to pass beneath without stooping, a fact that had been demonstrated twice that morning. Titan's Gate had been draped with the colours of the XIII Legion for the occasion, flanked on either side by the drop banners of the Titan Legions and various Army regiments, along with the standards of the V, VI, VII, X, XVIII and XIX Legiones Astartes.

Guilliman breathed in, ignoring the dull wound-ache in his back and the cramp of his healing lungs. From his vantage over-looking the nine hundred-hectare square, paved in polished azurite and marble from the quarries of Calut, he could see the Avenue of Heroes, the central axis of the Civitas. Its pavements only one-thousandth part engraved with the names of the fallen, led due north to the massive glacis of the Aegis Wall that sur-rounded the Castrum. Above that majestic, cliff-like rampart rose the implacable towers and halls of the Fortress of Hera, dwarf-ing the Residency, the Agiselus Barracks and the High Senate, each one a vast building in its own right, but which clustered like small children in the skirts of the Legion Fortress. The Fortress and its surrounding structures on the high Castrum were collec-tively known as the Palaeopolis, or 'Old City'. Behind that vista, stabbing into the sky, climbed the distant mountains, the points of Hera's Crown, usually ghost blue at that time of year, but now a submarine green thanks to the storm-light.

To the east of the square lay the imposing domes of the new Senate House and the Diribitorium, the municipal buildings that dominated Circe Deme, a district of habitas and industry, which ran east across the valley to the Porta Medes, and the fine farming country beyond where many consuls kept their estates. Circe and its neighbouring demes were collectively known as the Neapolis, the New City.

To the west lay the river Laponis, shining like smoked glass in the daylight, which wound between the vast black ziggurat castle of the Mechanicum and the vertiginous Red Basilica of the Astra Telepathica. No birds ever flew in that part of the sky. This was a fact that Guilliman had noted from the moment the basilica was first raised and inhabited.

To the south-west of Martial Square lay the geographic centre of Magna Macragge Civitas, the point at which the north-south running cardo of the Via Laponis crossed the east-west running Via Decumanus Maximus. The spot was marked, at a circular intersection guarded by herms and blackwork statues, by the Milion, a milestone marker from which all measurements in the Civitas and, technically, the entire realm of Ultramar, were measured. It was from the top of that milestone, his hands red with traitor blood, that Guilliman had made his first rallying speech during Gallan's revolt, the uprising that had left his beloved stepfather dead.

Due south of where he stood, the Grand Colonnade led straight and true from the south end of the square all the way down to the starport fields and the coast. The airspace had been cleared. Guilliman could smell the sea, and even glimpse the distant glitter of its racing waves.

It was nearly time.

The intensity of the trumpet fanfare shivered the air, but he knew it would soon be drowned out by the roar of braking jets and landing thrusters.

Guilliman felt a kind of gladness. The arrival of his warlord brother threw up many questions and troubles, but it at least marked a state change in the affairs of Ultramar. Whatever else it might be, this was a turning point.

It was also an excuse to take pride in the glory of Macragge and the XIII. It had been a long time since his Legion had assembled in full and formal regalia for the sheer magnificence of it. Nothing since Calth, not even the hard-fought victories and bloody feats of retribution, had caused them to celebrate.

The arrival of the Lion called for nothing less. The galaxy contained only eighteen primarchs. The conjunction of even two of them was a singular moment when the balance of the cosmos was temporarily and specifically weighted, especially when those two were, perhaps, the most feted and respected war leaders of all.

This was a day to be marked, so that all of Macragge – *all of Ultramar!* – knew it. This was a moment. The lord of the Dark Angels deserved such respect, and by the high towers of Terra, Guilliman knew his warriors deserved to feel pride too.

Guilliman was accompanied on the platform by Gorod and the Invictus guard, by Auguston and fifteen officers of the XIII's senior ranks, by ninety-four senior Army and fleet commanders, by high officers of the senate and the Mechanicum, and by twenty centurion-ranked warriors of the Legiones Astartes, representing an officer cadre for the other Legions that had come to Macragge. Of high officers of the XIII present on Macragge that day, only Valentus Dolor was noticeable by his absence.

The first fanfare of the trumpets had ended. As the second volleying blast began, the clean, silver notes of the horns lofting like a flock of bright eagles into the summer sky, the war horns of the Collegia Titanica began to boom in harmony. Forty war-engines, representing all eight of the Titan Legions pacted with Guilliman, the engine-forces of the forge worlds Tigrus and Accatran, stood on station around Martial Square, or flanked the Grand Colonnade to the starport gates. The assembly included nine Warlords and two Imperator engines, the *Ijax Ijastus* and the *Death Casts Its Own Long Shadow*, which had taken up positions on either side of the platform, and stood like vertical cities, bristling with guns.

The air did more than shiver. It threatened to split.

Guilliman allowed himself a smile. He glanced to his side, and saw Euten grimacing and covering her ears.

He beheld the scene again. This was his empire. It was magnificent. He would never use the phrase 'his empire' out loud, of course, but it was. He had founded it and fought for it, and he knew that, one day, he would die for it too. Below him, the polished marble paving slabs of Martial Square gleamed in the storm-light and the eerie luminosity of the Pharos, the single star in the sky. Around the vast square lay the Magna Macragge Civitas, one of the greatest cities of the Imperium. It wasn't the city that mattered – it was what the city bred. It was what the city could produce.

Guilliman had assembled an honour guard of nine thousand Ultramarines around the edges of the square. They stood in perfectly mediated blocks behind their respective company standards, their polished wargear glittering in the daylight. Between each company formation was assembled either a mechanised armour formation or an Army battalion, the soldiers kneeling in obeisance beneath their fluttering vexils held aloft by their bannermen. Guilliman was offering his brother an honour guard of almost forty-seven thousand fighting souls, not to mention the million or more civilians crowded into the adjacent streets and thoroughfares for a glimpse of the Lion-lord and his famous warriors. Euten had told Guilliman that street hawkers and vendors were doing a brisk trade in cheap icons and tin badges displaying the iconography of the First Legion.

'So my people think he will save them when I cannot?' Guilliman had asked as he strapped on his ceremonial plate in the Residency's fitting chamber.

Euten had blown a raspberry.

'They celebrate the moment, you foolish boy,' she replied. 'They welcome his arrival. He is noble and he is loyal.'

Guilliman had nodded.

'Are you jealous of him?' Euten had asked.

'No!'

'You are. You *are*. Because he is the Lord of the First, the first born. I never thought I would see such jealousy in you, my dear lord. It does not become you, but it is also rather sweet.'

Guilliman had growled something indecipherable, and then demanded that his armourers adjust the servo fit of his pauldrons.

'Of course,' Euten had added, thoughtfully. 'He is Lord of the First, and thus the first of your equals, but he was not the first found.'

'*What*, woman?'

'Horus was the first lost son to be found. Look how well *that* ended, my lord.'

Guilliman had looked at her and laughed. He couldn't stop himself. It had felt good.

'First is not always best,' Euten had said, also laughing, 'my *eighth*-found Lord of the *Thirteenth* Legion. Look who has an empire.'

Still smiling, Guilliman had looked at her.

'Be careful what you say,' he had told her. 'Whatever I have, my *beloved brother* Horus almost has an empire.'

'The point is,' she had replied, 'the people of Macragge know that *two* primarchs are, logically, better than one.'

The trumpets screamed, lifting him from the memory. An aide stepped to Guilliman's side, and presented him with a gene-reader data-slate.

'Your authority to open airspace, my lord?' the aide bowed.

'Given,' Guilliman said. He took the slate and kissed the screen. Such ultimate authorities required a direct gene-sample, and it was often too cumbersome for a fully plated warrior to remove a power fist or gauntlet to affect a dermal read. A kiss had become the expedient and understood custom. Guilliman knew that some, like First Master Phratus Auguston, preferred to spit on slates rather than kiss them. It had the same effect, but it lacked humility.

The deep systems of the Civitas accepted and interpreted his genetic order. Overhead, the starport airspace opened and the void shields slid aside. Ships descended from the shadow of a fleet lying out in the atmospheric murk.

First, Stormbirds, painted void-black, the leading edges of their wings flecked in dark, dark green, the colour of ancient forests. Behind them, in formation, landing ships, Thunderhawks and Thunderhawk bulkers, and troop landers.

They were not just in formation. They descended in perfect, *perfect*, aerial synchronicity. The ships came down like formation dancers, in a precisely integrated and orchestrated ballet.

He's showing off, Guilliman thought. He smiled. *I would too, if the situation were reversed.*

The ships began to land, four by four, in perfect sequence, along the top of the colonnade where it met Martial Square. The timing of their touchdowns was almost embarrassingly precise. Four, then four, then four, each group together. Their downdraft obliterated the trumpet fanfare and even the constant howl of the Titan war-engines.

Drop hatches and ramps opened and released with similarly pin-sharp timing. Formations of Dark Angels strode down the ramps onto the colonnade and entered the square. They stepped as one, each beat perfect, each warrior gleaming and uniform. As the marching companies entered the square, they began to spread into wide, double-ranks from their ten-by-ten blocks. The spread was seamless. Squads widened and melted into and through each other, forming a perfect double-wall, all still marching in step, never missing a beat. The drill discipline was the most impressive Guilliman had ever seen.

He's showing off, he thought again.

Not missing a beat, the Dark Angels formation rotated its edges to form a horseshoe with the open end facing the platform of Titan's Gate. Two thousand warriors deployed in sublimely orchestrated marching order. Then they began their weapons drill, all marching on the spot as they tossed, spun and rotated their bolters, or threw swords and standards aloft and back again in precise returns. Beat, beat, beat, beat, *beat.*

Guilliman noticed details of particular weapons carried by the Dark Angels – beam and projectile weapons of various kinds that even he did not immediately recognise. The First Legion had arsenals containing devices unknown to all the other Legions. The Dark Angels had been the first created, and their history predated all other institutions of the Legiones Astartes. They were, in many regards, the prototype. It was said that during the latter years of the Unification War and the first years of the Great Crusade, before the other Legions had been constructed, the Dark Angels had known and done things that no other Legion was privy to. They had built their strengths and identity in that era, in isolation.

That identity had needed to be complete. When there was only one Legion, that Legion had been obliged to contain all special-isms. Guilliman knew that the six hosts or 'wings' of the Dark Angels represented specialisms of every school, at subtle variance to the standard order of the *Principia Bellicosa.*

Guilliman had also heard tell of secret orders and mysterious hierarchies within the ranks of the Dark Angels; hierarchies of knowledge, trust and authority invisible to outsiders. It explained some of their curious insignia, which sometimes bore no relation to rank or company structure.

Like their lord, the warriors of the First Legion were coded, shrouded and ciphered. They kept secrets well, perhaps too well. This was a legacy, Guilliman believed, of the formative days when they were alone and had no other Legion to rely on.

Without any sign of a signal, the Dark Angels suddenly stopped their drill and froze, as one singular form. Perfect. *Perfect.*

He's really *showing off*, Guilliman thought.

His helm-vox beeped. Guilliman looked at the mantle display. The ident-tag read *Dolor*.

'I'm busy,' he said.

'*Of course you are, lord,*' Dolor replied over the link. '*I would not trouble you if it wasn't important. I need to show you something.*'

'Again, dear friend, this is not the time.'

'*Agreed. Come to me as soon as you can. But do not pact anything with your noble brother that you can't undo… until you have seen what I have to show you.*'

'You unsettle me, Valentus.'

'*Greet your brother. Commit to nothing. I have a practical here that you need to appreciate.*'

The link cut.

'Everything all right?' Euten asked him.

Guilliman nodded.

'They're very, very good at that marching drill thing, aren't they?' Euten said, gesturing at the square below. The Dark Angels ranks had begun moving again. They had peeled meticulously into tempered, marching cohorts that crossed diagonally through other cohorts to create perfect new shapes: diamonds, squares, triangles, curved lines, a six-pointed star. Point leaders were turning and marching back into their packs, inverting the march order. It was annoyingly impressive.

'I imagine they must get plenty of time to practise,' Guilliman replied.

Euten looked at him and covered her mouth with her hand.

'That's the most acid thing I've ever heard you say, Roboute,' she declared.

He grinned at her.

'Brace yourself, mam. My big brother's come to stay. The acid is only just starting to flow.'

Down below, on the polished marble stage of the Martial Square, the Dark Angels finally finished their display. Polished bolters clamped to their chests, they formed a V-shaped fan of squads leading back to the ramp of the lead Stormbird.

The Lion emerged.

Despite himself, Guilliman felt his heart skip and his lungs pump. The Lion. The *Lion*. There were brothers that he could look down on, and was happy to, and there were brothers that he could admire. Rogal, Magnus and Sanguinius, and, damn him, even Russ. He could admire them for what they were. But there were only two brothers that he had ever actually looked *up* to, only two brothers that he had ever actually admired.

There were only two brothers that he felt shadowed by when they were present.

Lion El'Jonson and Horus Lupercal.

The Lion emerged from his lander stony-faced, bareheaded, his long golden hair trailing in the wind. So beautiful, so deadly, so empty, so unreadable. He carried his war-helm under his left arm, and marched with the same perfect discipline that his men displayed. To each side of him came his voted lieutenants, in identical step. Beloved Corswain was commanding the First Legion elements on the other side of the Ruinstorm, so the Lion was braced by Holguin and Farith Redloss. Holguin carried an executioner's long sword upright before him in his two hands, the tip of the six-foot blade rounded over like a butter knife. His pauldron was marked with the crossed swords of the Deathwing. Redloss carried a massive war-axe, haftwise across his chest. His pauldron bore the skull-in-hourglass of the Dreadwing. All three wore black artificer armour worked with red Martian gold.

They approached along the echelon, entering the square.

Guilliman sighed.

'Bastard. Always showing off,' he murmured.

He looked at his aides, nodded, and began to walk down the steps to meet his brother. The Wolves followed him. Guilliman stopped and looked back up the steps.

'Really? Right *now*, of *all* times?' Guilliman asked Faffnr.

'My watch-pack walks where you walk, jarl,' said Faffnr.

'Even my own Cataphractii aren't following me at this moment, Wolf.'

'We could, lord,' Gorod growled from the platform. 'Indeed, we could also hose the unwanted off the steps in an unbelievable storm of shot, if you so desired.'

'Enough,' Guilliman said. He looked at Faffnr and the Wolves. 'You see how I spare your lives?'

'No one spares our lives, jarl,' Faffnr replied. 'They're not for sparing. Never have been.'

'With… *respect*,' Biter Herek whispered to his pack-leader.

Faffnr nodded. 'Obviously, obviously. Like Biter here says. Goes without saying. With respect.'

Guilliman hesitated, painfully aware that he was halfway down a staircase, in front of a million and a half people, pausing to converse with a band of barbarians while his noble brother waited below.

'I appeal to your honesty, Faffnr Bludbroder,' he said. 'This moment isn't about me, is it? It's about you, and the Angels, and the feud.'

Faffnr paused.

'It is,' he replied, nodding. His men, hunched and ugly, nodded too.

Guilliman sighed. 'Let's do it then. But do not embarrass me or I'll gut you all myself.'

He turned and resumed his walk down the steps from the plat-form. He was aware of the Wolves closing in behind him as a ragged and unseemly bodyguard.

'By the void,' Guilliman hissed at them. 'You know you're mak-ing me look like an idiot! Like a heathen king of Illyrium!'

'Sorry and all that, jarl. Honour demands it,' Faffnr replied, a hot-breath whisper at Guilliman's shoulder.

'You're a pain in the arse, you know that?' Guilliman said.

'Indisputably,' Faffnr returned.

Guilliman walked down to meet the Lion. The Lion walked up to meet him.

It was a long wait. The distance between the landing site and the gate was over a kilometre. The two primarchs made slow progress towards one another.

When they were at last face to face, there was a moment of silence. All the grand fanfares had died away. Even the crowd noise had ebbed.

The Lion looked at Guilliman. The Avenging Son looked at the Lion. The Lion's black armour was richly engraved and inlaid with red gold. The chestplate and pauldrons displayed all the intercon-nected icons and symbols of his Legion, the complex heraldry of the Dark Angels hierarchies, visible and invisible. All the secret hosts, thrones and powers of the First Legion's secret structure were represented there, united by the central insignia, the six-pointed hexagrammaton. He wore the pelt of a forest beast across his right shoulder, and the golden badge of a shrouded urn at his throat.

'Brother,' said the Lion.

'Brother,' Guilliman replied.

'Well met.'

'Not before time,' said Guilliman.

'You do me a great honour with this show of force,' the Lion said, gently indicating the square around them.

'And you do me an honour with this display of drill,' Guilliman said.

The Lion smiled, nodding, appreciative.

He handed his war-helm back to Holguin.

'Has it really been so long, Roboute?' he asked and abruptly embraced Guilliman in a clash of armour.

'No, no,' Guilliman replied, swallowing hard. His war-helm had been knocked out of his grip with the abruptness of the Lion's embrace, and was rolling on the marble paving behind him. 'It's good to see you,' he said, forcing control of his voice.

The Lion broke the embrace and nodded. He bowed, picked up Guilliman's fallen helm and rose again, handing it back to him.

'Good to see you too, brother,' he said. 'And good to see your extraordinary light. You must tell me all about that.'

'I will. But, there is another, more immediate matter,' Guilliman said, hoping his composure had remained intact. 'Of... protocol,' he added.

'The Wolves?' replied the Lion.

'Just so,' said Guilliman.

The Lion nodded and turned away from Guilliman. He looked down at Faffnr Bludbroder.

'Name yourself, Wolf. Let's get this done.'

'I am Faffnr, dear lord.'

'Are you of Sesc? I recognise the markings.'

'I am, lord.'

'Let's take the smack, Faffnr. Will it come from you?'

Faffnr Bludbroder straightened to his full height. The feud between the Angels and the Wolves had existed since Dulan. It was a ritual for them to field champions every time they met.

'Yes, lord,' Faffnr said. 'I crave you advance your champion.'

Both Holguin and Redloss stepped forward.

'I'll be my *own* champion,' the Lion whispered. There was a hint of a smile on his lips.

'No,' said Faffnr.

'So, the Wolves of the Rout are cowards, I take it?'

'*No*,' snarled Faffnr.

'Then take your strike, Wolf,' said the Lion, 'and make it count.'

Faffnr sighed and swung his axe at the Lion. Guilliman flinched as the blade cut the air beside him. It was a sensationally good strike. Faffnr had betrayed no cues, no hint of muscle tension, no focus of powered plate. The blow had just come. Guilliman wondered if it would have taken him by surprise. He was forced to admit that it might have.

The Lion caught Faffnr's swing with one hand, blocking the haft with the blade edge millimetres from his face. Faffnr grunted involuntarily as his strength was met and fundamentally matched by superior power.

Then the Lion delivered his return blow. It came with his left hand, not enough to maim or kill, almost pulled, but fast, faster than Faffnr's superb swing.

It knocked the pack-leader onto his knees and left the Lion holding Faffnr's axe.

Faffnr Bludbroder rose to his feet again.

'Satisfied?' asked the Lion, tossing the axe back to him.

'Honour is satisfied, lord,' Faffnr assented, catching it. He nodded and backed off, waving to his pack to do the same. Holguin and Redloss both grinned with unbearable insouciance.

'Then tell Bo Soren to guard his manners, Faffnr,' Guilliman said over his shoulder without looking back.

'I will, Jarl,' Faffnr returned. Guilliman heard a hard slap and a muffled curse.

He looked at the Lion. He'd never realised before that the Lion was very slightly taller than him.

'Shall we, brother?' he asked.

'The famous Fortress of Hera?' asked the Lion. 'I would be disappointed not to see it.'

IT WAS LATE afternoon.

At the Occident Gate in the mighty Servian Wall, at the very western edge of Magna Macragge Civitas, the gate-guards were processing incomers. There was a steady tide, tricksters and blackmarts flowing in to the evening markets of Laponis Deme from the slums of the Illyrian Enclave behind the high wall, or agrics flocking to the city granaries with sweating payloads of grain from the chora on bulk-servitor wagons.

'Name?' asked the gate officer, a senior ranked man in the praecental division. The man looked important and he bloody knew it too.

'Damon,' replied Damon Prytanis, huddled on the back gate of a servitor freight car in his smelly black fur coat. 'What's going on?'

'What do you mean what's going on?'

'In the city? All that airshow? The damned horns?'

'The First Legion has come to us,' the officer replied proudly.

'The First Legion, eh? The Lion's mob? Big news.'

'It is,' the officer agreed.

'Big news,' Damon repeated, nodding. His heart sank. Too many serious players for comfort.

'Ident,' the officer reminded him.

Damon shrugged and nodded and held out his open, empty hand. It generally worked. The gesture was so automatic, guards usually saw what they wanted to see.

'Good, all right,' the officer said, waving him on.

Damon passed through the deep, cold shade of the Occident Gate on the back of the jolting servitor car and entered the western edge of the city. This was his target city, his bloody destiny, probably. It was not promising. Down at this skunk-end of the low-qual deme it was still gross, cheap-built *habitas*, tinkermarts and slum runs, and would be for many kilometres before a traveller could reach the handsome domi and wide estates of Xanthi Deme in the low, rolling country west of the river.

Damon dropped off the back of the trundling bulk-car and started walking down the busy highway, skirting Illyrian caravans and grain cargoes.

He suddenly had a bad feeling. He liked to call it his first sense because, according to his blessed mother, he had not been born with any.

'Hey!' a voice called out from behind him. 'Hey, *you*! Fur coat man!'

Damon cursed. The gate officer had only been temporarily convinced. Damon took a look back, and saw a squad of praecentals moving from the gatehouse in his direction. They were picking up pace and shoving slower-moving pedestrians out of their path. Most of the locals shrank back. The praecentals looked like overgroomed show-guards, but they were tough, well-trained, and they carried serious authority.

They were also well-armed. Damon saw plasma weapons and intimidating blades.

'Halt!' one of them shouted. When Damon didn't, the officer started barking at the pedestrian traffic.

'Out of the way! Give us a clear shot!'

A *clear shot*? Encouraging. Welcoming. Reassuring. Times were worse, and tensions far hotter, than he had anticipated, and he had anticipated a fair bit.

It was a moment to switch out, to revert to the skills he'd honed hunting and being hunted over an unimaginably long period. The hindbrain temptation was huge. There were only a handful of humans in the galaxy possessed of equal to or greater experiential skill than Damon Prytanis. He'd met two of them, and one of those was his current target. The other was a surly, uncooperative rogue.

Yet another of his kind was the Emperor of Man. Damon had never met the fellow, and didn't much want to. He sounded like a total *dunkhole*.

Smiling, he reverted.

Damon ducked to his left very sharply, racing down an alley into the warren of stenopoi, the maze of narrow streets in this most densely packed quarter of Laponis Deme. He collided with no one and knocked over nothing. People just got out of his way or, if they froze, he went around them. He made two more turns, another left and then a hard right, following a dank, high-walled lane under the arches of a major aqueduct. Washing had been strung out to dry on lines below the arch and between the walls, and he could smell cook-pots and pipe smoke.

The guards were fit, and close behind him, moving fast and with determination, despite the encumbrance of their armour and wargear.

He saw the hazy grey shapes of the giant granaries ahead of him, and thought for a moment that he might reach them and hide. But the praecentals were efficient. A second squad had appeared, crossing a chain-dropped canal bridge ahead of him to work back through the stenopoi and pin him between them and his pursuers.

He realised he was going to have to get wet. It disappointed him to have to contemplate blood-business so early on, but it also partly pleased him. He'd been in the mountains for too long, and he was cold and hungry and fit to hurt someone. He'd been sent to Macragge to perform a mission he didn't want to perform, and challenge a man he didn't think needed to be challenged.

Damon Prytanis was in an ugly mood, and by cornering him, the praecentals had offered him a chance to vent that frustration.

He carried four weapons. They had come with him in a sack of living flesh in order to survive, as metallic items, the extremity of the fast-jack teleport. The sack had been bred for purpose in a Khu'Nib replicator vat. Once he had cut it open and killed it to get at his weapons and kit, after his painful arrival, its meat had fed him for six days.

Four weapons: a matched brace of Zhul'kund *murehk* – elegant, long-snouted, knob-gripped sling pistols, the best kind. Eldar shuriken weapons were Damon's favoured firearms, for what they lacked in range and accuracy they more than made up for in rate of fire and penetrative effect. This pair had come from Slau Dha's personal battle-casket, an uncharacteristic gesture of generosity that had been made, Damon was sure, to emphasise the importance of the mission. One was called (in High Idharaen) *Guh'hru*, which meant 'Bleed-to-death', and the other was called (in the demotic and corrupted slang of the Crone Worlds) *Meh'menitay*, which meant 'Death Looks in Your Eyes and Finds You Entirely Wanting'. He kept them holstered under his fur jacket, in a make-shift double-shoulder rig he'd made from the indigestible skin of the flesh-sack.

The third weapon was a short-pattern chainsword, not much longer than a gladius, which dated from the interminable wars of the pre-Unification Era of Terra, and which had been designed as a secondary, close-protection weapon for the retinues of a Panpacific nobleman called Kendra Huul. The sword came from Damon's private collection, and he knew its provenance well, because he'd been the retinue member it had been carried by, and he had given it its name: *Huul's Doom*. He wore it across his spine, once again under his heavy fur jacket.

The fourth weapon was a small red-glass bottle that lay in the

right-hand pocket of his fur coat, jumbled in among the other
odds and ends of his trade.

Damon side-stepped into a range of shadows, darted under the
eaves of an old stable block, and pulled himself back against a
stone partition wall to wait.

Six men coming from behind, six more from up ahead, Praecentals all. All of them were packing plasma weapons, and wielding
quality blades if it got nasty-close, blades they knew how to
handle. They were armoured in the head, torso, shoulders, groin
and legs. Guilliman did not stint on the materiel budget for his
householders, so that armour was plasteel at the very least, probably with a ceramite underveil.

Nothing a murehk couldn't puncture, but he'd need to let them
get very close to ensure hard, wet kills.

He reached under his coat and drew his pistols, *Guh'hru* in his
right hand and *Meh'menitay* in his left. He held them up, muz-
zles aimed at the storm-streaked sky. With his thumbs, he stroked
the studs that activated the almost silent gravitic accelerators and
brought them cycling up to power. The wraithbone grips began
to feel warm.

The sound of racing footfalls had ceased. Damon listened and
heard, over the gurgle of the nearby canal and the distant street
sounds, a terse, hushed back and forth: vox chirps, a search pattern inter-signalling as it spread out.

Come for me then, he willed them.

The first two appeared to his left very suddenly, turning around
the end of the stable block with their plasma weapons aimed.

Snap. He was already moving. They had the drop, but he beat
them to it. His guns came down, side-by-side, as he moved and
fired.

He squeezed each trigger with the lightest of touches, a pulse
technique that the eldar called the *Ilyad'than*, or 'feather-finger'.

Shuriken technology was amazing. The gravitic accelerators shoved shots out of the weapons at abnormal velocities, and ammunition was a solid core block of plasti-crystal that the gun sliced off and hurled one monomolecular disc at a time. It was so efficient a system that a single over-generous squeeze of the trigger could unleash hundreds of razor-rounds in a second or two.

The Ilyad'than technique allowed the shooter to fire off crisp bursts of five or six discs at a time, preserving the solid ammunition core and avoiding messy overkill.

Damon was well-practised. *Guh'hru* spat four monomolecular discs through the armoured chest of one guard, and *Meh'menitay* did the same to the other. Dark slits, suddenly welling blood in extravagant quantity, appeared in their chest plating as they fell backwards. One dropped onto the path, the other toppled over a rail into the dirty canal.

Damon swung around as a third praecental appeared around the opposite end of the stable block behind him. Turning, he fired *Guh'hru* straight-armed, and put two discs into the man's face, which ruptured messily inside the frame of his helmet. The man dropped to his knees, then flopped onto his front, kicking a squish of blood up out of his head on impact.

No pausing now. Voices were raised. The men had heard the distinctive shriek of sling guns, a sound no being who had faced the eldar ever forgot. Damon ran towards his first kills. The corpse in the water was face down and slowly sinking into the green, algae-thickened murk, supported by the air caught in his cape. The man on the path was on his back, his eyes as wide as full moons, blood leaking out of him in astonishing quantities, turning the earth pathway into terracotta putty.

Damon knelt and made an adjustment to the man's weapon. Then he started to run back the way he had come.

'Here he is! Help me!' he yelled over his shoulder as he ran.

Damon threw himself sideways into the far end of the stable block, putting a heavy wall between him and the canal.

He heard other praecentals approaching, heard their outraged curses as they saw the kills.

Then one of them said, 'Wait, wait! What's that sound?'

A plasma weapon's powercell on overload, you numbwit, Damon thought.

It went off like a bomb, blowing out the far end of the stable block where it overhung the canal. Damon emerged into the smoke, finished off the one man that the blast hadn't killed with a swift headshot, and counted the other bodies. It was a jigsaw. He had to make sense of the bloody, half-cooked chunks. Four. Two more still close, then. And more squads would be on their way.

How many more would he risk? How many more would it take to slake his frustration?

He looked down at the canal. The water was very still, suddenly.

'Oh, come *on…*' he began.

Gahet looked up at him, an impossible reflection. The telepathic consult was like a hot wire through his brain.

+You waste time and expose your presence unnecessarily, Damon.+

'I'm blowing off steam,' Damon growled back, hurting.

+Fulfill the duty you must perform for us.+

'All right, just stop–'

+Find him and secure the prize. Make him perform his assigned task, or, if he will not do it, perform it *for* him.+

'All *right*, damn you!' Damon winced.

He turned away from the canal. The two praecentals were rushing him along the towpath. One fired, scorching the air beside Damon with plasma heat, a very near miss.

Damon pulled up his guns, firing both.

+What are you doing?+

'Finishing things,' Damon replied.

He could hear the other squads moving in. Wet. It was going to get bloody wet.

'I'll do your job, Gahet,' he said, with no respect at all, 'once I'm done here.'

11
COMMUNION

'Let us start with the truth, and move on to more interesting matters.'
– attributed to Malcador the Sigillite

TWO LEGIONS SLOWLY marched, side by side, along the Avenue of Heroes, towards the Castrum and the Fortress, like a half-black, half-blue river. On the right-hand side of the column marched the Ultramarines; on the left, the Dark Angels. Behind the main column came the remnants of the other Legions, and then the Army units and the Titan engines. Crowds cheered and waved from both sides of the vast route.

'The last time this many banners were carried aloft must have been on Ullanor,' the Lion said.

'I think so,' Guilliman agreed.

They were walking side by side at the head of the procession, half-shaded by the Legion standards being carried at their heels. Holguin and Redloss escorted the Lion, and Gorod and his lieutenant, Maglios, flanked the Avenging Son.

'It is a glorious feeling,' the Lion said, 'and one we deserve. Your warriors, after the ordeal of Nuceria and the many battles of Lorgar's "shadow crusade" – mine after Thramas and the fury of the warp.'

'You will tell me, I hope, about the Thramas Crusade in detail,' Guilliman said.

'I will.'

'You fought against Konrad? Against the Eighth Legion?'

'Traitors all, sad be the day. I have prisoners aboard the flagship, including his First Captain, Sevatar.'

Guilliman glanced sideways at his expressionless brother.

'Have you interrogated him? Have you rooted out the cause of this treason?'

'Have you?' asked the Lion. 'In your wars against Angron and Lorgar, have you identified their argument?'

'It is the warp,' replied Guilliman. 'It is an infection, a pollution of the soul. On Nuceria, the horrors I saw heaped upon Angron by one he considered a comrade... Our brothers, even the Lupercal, have not turned against us. They have *been* turned.'

'I think so too,' the Lion replied. 'It is a hard thought to hold. I cannot imagine having cause to turn against our father and Terra, but I can at least conceive of the possibility of a cogent argument for dissent. This treason... it spreads like a plague. It is contagious.'

'It is. Which is why, I imagine, you came to me.'

The Lion glanced sideways at Guilliman.

'Roboute. Such a question.'

'Your ships were not lost, brother. They were heading for Macragge when the storm struck. I have read the flight-logs. Did you fear I'd turned with Horus and become a threat to our father? Have you come to sanction me, like Russ's wolf pack?'

The Lion laughed.

'My dear Roboute, I did not think for a moment that you had turned. I thought you'd done much, much worse.' He looked at

Guilliman. 'I think we both know you *have*.'

He glanced at the Castrum ahead, the towering bulk of the Fortress of Hera.

'That is quite a place,' he said. 'I am impressed. I expect a proper tour and inspection.'

The Memorial Gardens lay to the east of the Avenue of Heroes. John Grammaticus watched the glittering column move by, banners aloft, heading up the titanic street to the Porta Hera, a cyclopean gateway in the Castrum wall that he could see from six kilometres away.

It was a display of force, John had to admit. The Legions were good at that. They were good at killing too, and the vanguard, the Army and the Titan engines... a god-slaying force. John was especially impressed by the retinues of the so called 'Shattered Legions'. They suggested a human resolve that John knew the Cabal doubted. They stood together, despite their losses. They fought on.

We always have, he thought. *Watch us for just a moment, though a moment to you might be ten thousand years to us, and you'll see. We are not children. We have morals and souls.*

The Memorial Gardens were far too civilised. Walls of inscribed stone flanked oblong pools of pale water lilies and beds of rushes and vein flowers. The Ultramarines dignified their dead. They engraved their names upon the flagstones of the Avenue of Heroes, and again here in the gardens, and also on the black marble walls of the Chapel of Memorial in the Great Fortress.

It was the gardens where the dead were actually interred, in pre-built catacombs that lay beneath the beds and pools.

John had a vision of the day when, after endless centuries of war, there would be no room left on the flagstones of the avenue to fit more names, and the catacombs would be full, and the walls of the chapel would be covered. Where would they commemorate all their dead then?

He blinked back the thought.

The funerary shuttles had been cleared to land on the raised stone decks of the garden compound. Eight of them, wings hinged up like butterflies, sat side by side on the landing terrace. Their cargoes of sarcophagi would be unloaded later. Because of the parade, there weren't enough Legion personnel available to conduct the rites and deliver the dead in respectful silence to their resting places.

John was content enough, however. As Edaris Cluet, an officer of repatriation, the funerary flights had got him to the surface of Macragge and deep inside the great Civitas. The Ultramarines solemn respect for their fallen had allowed him to circumvent almost all of Macragge's complex layers of planetary security.

Most of the other crews from the repatriation flights had gone to the edge of the landing terrace to watch the procession pass along the Avenue. A few were running systems checks on the landers, which were parked on the deck with their canopies up and their loading ramps down.

Time to slip away. Time to step out of Edaris Cluet and find a new person to hide in.

John picked up his pack, slung it across his shoulder and walked quietly away through the lawns and bowers. The jet-black mourning uniform was sober and smart, and, because it was austere and lacked any rank pins except the golden ultima-and-omega of the Funeral Watch, it suggested he was of a higher rank than he actually was. In a city of uniforms, he could pass for almost anyone and not be called on it, except by those with the most expert and detailed knowledge of Legion liveries.

All eyes were on other, grander things. Unchallenged and unobserved, he walked up the northern pathway of the gardens, passing under box-hedge arches cut for transhuman statures, and along flagged walks shaded by stately yew and sorona trees.

The planners had built the gardens to be appropriately noble and quietly sorrowful. The grey-leaved canopy turned even the day's bold light into a kind of dusk. The flagstones, the commemoration walls, and the entrances to the crypts were all of Saramanthian bluestone. The water lying in the long, oblong, black-reeded pools was as dark as veils. The silver shivers of ghost carp moved under the silent mirrors of the water. The lilies drifting on the surface of the pools were grey, like tear-stained handkerchiefs.

Mirrors…

A breeze hissed through the trees around him. John tensed. Ripples radiated across the surfaces of the pools. He was aware of the distant bombast of trumpets, war horns and cheering in the distance, but it felt as though the volume had suddenly been turned down.

John's eyeballs prickled. His mouth dried. A pulse began to tap in his temple.

'Please don't do this now,' he said, quietly but firmly. The Cabal was trying to summon him. They were trying to establish a psychic communion, most likely using one of the pools nearby as a flecting surface.

They were trying to keep track of him. They would want to be sure he was staying true to the task they had given him.

He swallowed hard. The breeze hissed again, rustling grey leaves. The heavy object in his carrybag trembled slightly, as if sensitive to the immaterial stirrings around him.

+Please.+

This time he spoke with his mind, not his mouth.

+Please, I'm tired. I've only just got here and I'm at my wits' end. Let me get safe and rest. Come to me later when I can take the burden of a communion. *Please.*+

The breeze stirred. Who would it be? Gahet, he of the Old Kind, most probably, but John suspected the unsympathetic persistence of Slau Dha, the eldar autarch.

+Please.+

He turned and resumed walking, but his skin was still prickling. The faraway sounds of the parade had become so muffled that John felt as though he was underwater.

He glanced at the pool next to him, involuntarily. The surface had frozen, like dark glass, *scrying* glass. Below the surface, silvered fish had stilled, suspended, tail-fins mid-stroke.

A shadow fell across the flecting surface, and it wasn't his. He flinched as he saw the dark, rising crest of an eldar war-helm, the impossibly tall, attenuated figure, a scarecrow-god, the dimensions of its slim, long-boned form running the whole length of the pool.

'I said *not now*!' John spat.

He turned, tearing his eyes away from the shadow and striding down the flagstoned path away from the pool. There was a buzzing in his hindbrain. The leaves hissed.

'Leave me alone!' he growled over his shoulder. 'Leave me alone!'

HE LEFT THE gardens and entered the oddly quiet streets. Everyone in the deme was lining the Avenue of Heroes. His head stung from the attempted communion, and his hands were shaking.

They had to be careful. The Cabal had to be more careful than that. From his reviews, in the guise of Teo Lusulk, of Civitas security, John knew that the XIII had reinstated their Librarius on a world-wide protocol. There was also a formidable contingent of the Astra Telepathica on the planet. Psykana techniques would be interlacing the defences. A raw conduit like the one Slau Dha had attempted to forge in the gardens might well be detected.

Detection by the Librarius would make his work very much more problematic, and would probably end his life. This life, anyway. He was tired of dying.

Shaking, he saw a fairly grand tavern on the corner of the next emptied street. Lights burned inside. It was an up-scale place for senatorial officers and the political echelons of the Civitas. The whole neighbourhood adjoining the Memorial Gardens was elegant and well-to-do.

He went inside. The place was a grand salon of gilded ormulu and chandeliers, with rows of tables under the high, frescoed ceiling and in booths along each wall. It was empty, aside from a few waiting staff and servitor units, and they saw to him quickly.

John took a table in one of the booths, the nearest he could find, and sank back into its comparative privacy. The seats were high backed and upholstered in leather, and the booth was formed from panels of coloured glass that rose from the tops of the seat backs to form partitions. At the back of the booth, the wall above the seats was a large crystal mirror in which John could watch the foot traffic coming in and out of the tavern without drawing attention to himself.

His hands were still shaking. One of the aproned serving staff brought him a jug of water and a beaker, and the large amasec he'd ordered as he'd walked in.

'Will you dine, sir?' the servant asked.

Food was an excellent idea. John had been poorly nourished the last few weeks as it was, and a decent hit of carbs and protein would help smooth out the after-sting of Slau Dha's approach.

'Bread,' he said. 'Salt butter. Something gamey or some chops.'

'We have a haunch of coilhorn deer.'

'That will do. Some root vegetables.'

The servant nodded.

'Are you not watching the parade, sir?' the servant asked.

'Are you not?' John snapped.

The man shrugged.

'I'm working, sir,' he said.

John nodded, and tried to warm up a smile.

'Me too,' he said. 'Besides, when you've seen one Space Marine march past you, you've seen them all, haven't you?'

The servant laughed as if this was a reasonably funny observation, and went off to take the order to the kitchen. John poured a beaker of water. His damned hands were still trembling, but food would help take the edge off.

So would the spirits. He raised the amasec. He needed to use two hands just to keep it steady.

A sip. Warmth. Better. *Better*.

He put the heavy glass down, felt the tension slip out of his wrists.

There was a mark on the white tablecloth between his hands. A dot. A second dot appeared beside it.

Spots of blood.

His nose, his damned nose was bleeding!

He shook out his napkin and wiped his face. He hoped no one had seen. He could move the water jug to cover the bloodspots. That damned Slau Dha had done a real number on him.

John took another sip of amasec, relishing the way that its burn counteracted his nerves, and checked the mirror at the back of the booth again, half-expecting to see centurions of the Librarius bursting across the tavern threshold.

Mirror. Oh, *stupid*! Oh *so* stupid! His anxiety had made him clumsy! Mirrors and glass and reflective giltwork *all* around him!

Hotwire pain jabbed in his head through the base of his skull.

'No! *No!*' he gasped.

A little dribble of blood came out of his right nostril, ran down his mouth and chin, and dappled the white linen. No hiding that.

'*Please!*'

The mirror above the booth-back frosted as though the room temperature had dropped forty degrees. John refused to look at it even though a force, a physical pull, was trying to tilt his face up by the chin to stare.

'No! Not now! Leave me alone!'

He forced himself to look down. He stared at his drink instead, the oily surface of the amasec, which was rippling because the hand clasping the heavy glass was trembling so hard. He looked at the constellation of dark blood-spots on the table cloth, marks that all the careful arrangement of beakers and jug could not hide.

In the freshest of them, where the glossy blood had yet to soak into the linen, he saw reflections forming: a crested helm. John moaned. The amasec in his glass stopped rippling and froze. The glass frosted cold under his fingers. The crested helm reflection appeared in the amasec too.

John groaned aloud, and closed his eyes.

'Slau Dha, you f–' he gasped.

'Not Slau Dha.'

There was silence. No sound at all except John's stumbling breath. The voice had not been that of the cruel autarch, steel sharp and cold-edged.

It had been as dark and dense as ebony.

John opened his eyes.

The entire tavern had suspended. The candle flames, frozen, radiated a cool blue light, and that light sparkled off the chandeliers, the sconces, the ormulu, the mirrors, the stacked shelves of clean glasses for wine and amasec. Daylight falling into the grand salon through the tavern's handsome windows was stained blue too, as if by very diluted ink. John could see serving staff across the room, poses locked mid-gesture, mouths open in mid-exchange.

Silver shoals of ghost carp hung, stilled, in the blue air above the tables.

The eldar stood at his table. His lean frame in its form-fitting armour, combined with his crested helm and flowing robes, made him seem extravagantly tall and thin, like a gaunt spectre of death, or a skeletal giant.

'Not Slau Dha,' John murmured, surprised by the sound of his own voice. 'You, again.'

'Again,' the eldar replied from behind the beautifully terrifying visage of his helm.

John's latest mission for the Cabal had begun on a world called Traoris. He was sent there to acquire a weapon, and then to use it to–

To betray his species more than he had ever betrayed it before.

John had struggled with his conscience for a long time, but this had brought him to the brink. The acquisition of the weapon that lay wrapped up in his carrybag had been miserable, and the prospect of what he was supposed to do with it more miserable still.

The one ray of hope had been an intercession that had taken place during the Traoris mission: a psykana communion visit from the very same eldar who manifested before him.

John had not been told the being's name, though he had suspicions, but he had been offered consolation, an alternative to following the Cabal's plans.

Not all eldar were of the same mind, it appeared. The Cabal wanted to sacrifice mankind to snuff the power of Chaos out. This nameless eldar lord opposed that thinking. He saw mankind not as a firebreak but as a true ally against the rise of the Archenemy. It seemed, and this notion troubled John more gravely than he cared to admit, that the eldar were at war with themselves over what to do about the human civil war.

'You promised me hope,' John said.

'I did.'

'On Traoris, you promised me hope. An alternative.'

'I did,' the towering figure replied.

'But there was nothing,' John complained. 'You offered to place information in my mind, information that would make me understand things in new ways. You offered me a conduit for the transfer of new thoughts.'

'I did.'

John sneered. 'There was only one thing true about it. You said the conduit would hurt, and it did. I learned nothing else, no new perspectives, no alternative thinking. I don't know what you did to me, or why, but I was just being used again, wasn't I?'

'You learned a great deal, John Grammaticus, you just don't know you did yet.'

John laughed. He laughed a dirty, mocking laugh and shook his head. He looked up at the impossible silver fish frozen mid-stroke in the blue air, and the servants locked in an eternal conversation.

'You know what, nameless lord?' he said. 'I am sick to death of you xenos-breeds and your enigmatic little un-meanings. Say what you say, plainly. Say something true. Or get the hell out of my head.'

He snatched up the amasec to take another sip, but the solid reflection of the eldar still lay across the liquid, so he set it aside, untouched.

'Think, John Grammaticus,' said the eldar quietly. 'Think, and you will recognise that you know much more than you knew you knew. Through the conduit, I placed data and ideas in your head, but they were too dangerous to be left in your surface thoughts. All the while you were on Traoris, or making your way here, there were any number of chances you might be read... by the notions of the warp, by your enemies, by the Dark Apostles, by your slave-masters the Cabal. They would each have killed you for thinking such thoughts, so I ensured they would not surface until the time was right.'

'When will that be?'

'When you are come to Macragge, in the realm of Ultramar.'

'I'm here. I don't know anything different.'

'Don't you? Think.'

'Come *on*...'

The eldar reached up and unclasped his war-helm. He set its sculptural form on the linen cloth beside the spots of John's blood. His pale face, tinged blue in the psyk-light, was similarly sculptural, taut and high-boned. His long dark hair was bound up tight to fit beneath his helm, and there was a rune inscribed upon his forehead. There was nothing human about the intelligence in his dark eyes.

Slowly, and with a dignity that seemed almost comical, he sat on the bench of the booth across from John. He was too tall and slender to fit the human space well. The long bones of his arms and legs just *too* long. Folding himself into the seat made him seem gangly, like an adolescent.

Once seated, he spread his hands on the cloth, palms down. The fingers were as alarmingly long and slender as his limbs. Even sitting, he was taller than John.

'Think what you know,' the eldar said in his ebony voice. 'Do you have the spear?'

'Yes,' John answered, realising he had shot an incriminating glance at the carrybag on the seat beside him. Not that the eldar would have been under any illusion that the weapon was anywhere else.

'And you know what to do with it?'

'I know who I'm supposed to see killed with it, if that's what you mean.'

'What else might you do?' asked the eldar.

'I don't know,' said John. 'Sit here forever and talk riddles?'

'Who am I?' asked the eldar.

'I don't know. You never said,' John replied. 'I have no way…
you–'

He hesitated, swallowed hard, wished the damn reflection
wasn't in his drink so he could gulp it down.

'Eldrad Ulthran, Farseer of Ulthwé Craftworld,' he said in a very
small voice.

'Indeed. See, then, what you know?'

'How did I know that?'

'The conduit put it in your head on Traoris so that you would
know it now. It is one of many ideas the conduit put in your head.'

'Is this the truth?' John asked.

'What else might it be?' Eldrad replied. His spider-leg fingers
gestured to the rune-marks on his armour, his crested helm and
his brow. 'Are you a scholar of the path-signs and world-symbols
of the eldar lexicon? Do you recognise the marks of Ulthwé?'

'No,' said John.

'But you know them well enough now.'

'What else do I know?' asked John. He thought for a second and
then held up his hand to mute any response. 'Wait, if we're dealing with truths, farseer, tell me this. Why have you come to me?
Why have you made such ridiculous efforts to commune with
me? If you passed ideas into my mind months ago on Traoris
that would be secure until the very act of coming to Ultramar
unpacked them, so I could know *then*… what the hell? What else
have you got to tell me? This communion has placed us both in
huge danger of being detected.'

'It is a risk worth taking, when set against other risks, though I
agree this conversation makes your position here more precari-
ous by the second. The Ultramarines Librarius is already aware
of a psykana event. Fortunately, in eight minutes' time, this

communion will be eclipsed by another, more powerful psykana event in the city, followed by a considerable crisis. Both will divert attention from you.'

'If we haven't got much time, speak fast. What do I need to know?'

'Almost everything you know already. Now you are here on Macragge, the ideas will unlock. The "unpacking" process, as you referred to it, may take a day or more, and ideas may come in strange orders, but do not be frustrated. It will give you all that you need.'

Eldrad leaned forward.

'I am here to warn you. That was my imperative. Since our communion on Traoris, I have foreseen new things, new dangers. It has been worth the effort forging this link just to make you aware of them.'

'What dangers?' asked John.

'Two things,' replied the Farseer. 'The Cabal may be beginning to suspect that your resolve is not all that it might be. They may make an effort to reinforce your commitment.'

'I've been expecting that. But thanks for the tip. What else?'

'It may be connected to the first thing. Someone is hunting you, John Grammaticus.'

'I see. Are they here, or–'

'They are here, or will be soon.'

'Good to know.'

Eldrad nodded.

'My departure is overdue,' he said. 'Yours too, John Grammaticus. Use the fade of this communion to slip away. Do not stay. Find a safe place and unpack your mind. Choose your path. We are bound together, human, in the target of your mission, and in the matter of Earth.'

'You said that before. You don't just mean "earth" as in soil, do you? You mean it literally but not *just* literally. You're using the *old* meaning too, aren't you? The old name for Terra?'

There was no answer. Eldrad Ulthran was no longer there. John looked around. Time was still frozen. The silver fish still swam in the air. The servants' conversation was still paused.

The light was still blue.

But it would not remain so for long. John felt a prickle in his ears and a warmth in his spine. He could hear sounds returning, as though from far away. Ten, fifteen seconds and the aura would be gone.

He looked at the table, at his blood spots on the cloth. The reflections had vanished at least.

He picked up the amasec, sank it in one gulp, then snatched up his carrybag and left the tavern just before the blue light fled and noisy reality resumed.

A LITTLE UNDER eight minutes later, and just nine streets away from the tavern in Ceres Deme, physical reality failed briefly, and a mouth into the warp yawned open.

Members of the Librarius of the XIII Legion, in concert with adepts of the Astra Telepathica, were monitoring the psychic landscape of the Civitas, and had already detected the farseer's communion with John in the tavern, though they had not identified it. A rapid response squad of Librarius officers and Cataphractii Terminators had been sent to the tavern location in armoured Land Speeders and heavy skimmers.

The warp-tear occurred in a scriptorium in the Via Edirne, south of the Memorial Gardens and east of the Avenue of Heroes. The moment it took place, psychic wards in the Red Basilica and the Sacristy of the Librarius pealed out their warnings. Two attuned adepts in the Basilica suffered debilitating strokes.

The fast-response force was immediately and urgently diverted to the Via Edirne.

The scriptorium had been closed and locked for the afternoon so that the scribes and rubricators who worked there repairing and transcribing old books could attend the parade.

In the gloomy, unlit chambers, lined with shelves of manuscripts, filled with lecterns, and stinking of cochineal and mixing oils, papers began to rustle. Books and bound manuscripts on the shelves and desks began to shiver and rattle, or fell onto the floor, or spilled open as if a strong breeze were rifling their pages, or an invisible scholar was speed-reading them. Locked cases of more valuable books began to quiver, the chains and padlocks rattling, as though the rebellious tomes wanted to break out and fly free, flapping their pages like wings.

More than anything, it appeared as though the density of words held in that one place was what had drawn the warp's wild attention and anchored it there.

Reality split.

It sheared open like a fruit torn in two by hungry hands, shreds of pulp and pith stringing across the breach.

It cut like a silk curtain.

It opened like a mouth, like a wound.

Light welled, like unstaunched blood.

The skin of reality sliced open along a jagged diagonal scar, torn by the tip of a ritual athame wielded on the far side.

The blade-cut peeled back corporeal reality on either side like excised flesh. A foul breeze exhaled into the scriptorium, billowing loose leaves further into the air, until the chamber was a blizzard of fluttering pages.

A figure stepped through the slice. He was huge, and armoured in full plate. In his fist, glowing and dripping with immaterial aetherplasm, was the ritual athame.

A second figure stepped through after the first, sword raised. Like the first, he was clad in the dark red and ritually inscribed armour of the XVII Legion Word Bearers. Like the first, he wore no helm, for no helm could ever contain the twisted horns and scalp spikes that adorned their skulls. Their eyes were slits the colour of hot night.

They were once-proud warriors of the Legiones Astartes who had willingly allowed daemon-things to spawn and grow inside them parasitically. They were Unburdened.

Their names had become Ulkas Tul and Barbos Kha, dull inhuman echoes of the names they had been baptised with. They were members of the Dark Apostle Erebus's retinue, and had learned their evil craft directly from him.

They were vile things, their plate covered with scraps of parchment, all of which bore the insane scriptures of a now-mad creature who had once been the most insanely loyal of the Emperor's sons: Lorgar.

A third figure stepped through behind them. He was a Word Bearer too, but he was helmed, and his armour was grey, scraped back to the metal, and bore no inscription other than the Legion's crest. The warrior's plate resembled the colour of the scheme worn before the war, before the Fall.

The third warrior lacked the Neverborn traits that invested his companions. A massive Legion-issue sniper rifle was slung in a case over his back. He carried his bolt pistol, drawn and ready in his hand.

He was not ready, however. He shuddered as he stepped through the reality-slice, and then dropped to his knees with a crash, shaking the wooden floor of the scriptorium. Pages swirled around him, covered with words. Some had started to singe and burn.

With his free hand, Barthusa Narek tore off his helm. Beneath it, his eyes were masked by a tied blindfold. He had insisted on that. He had seen nothing of the crossing, but he had felt it well enough.

It was not a sensation that he ever wished to repeat. He had no idea how his brothers had ever embraced it, except for the fact that they were insane.

He began to pull off his blindfold, but the trauma he had experienced finally swept him away. He pitched forward onto his hands, and threw up. Stinking black bile squirted out of his mouth and plastered the floorboards between his hands. Burning scads of paper fell around him like snow as he heaved, prostrate and humiliated.

With a shudder, the slice in the world behind him sealed again, and the sickly light faded. The swirling, burning papers began to cease their turmoil and scatter back on the floor as the wind died.

'This is the place, Narek,' said Barbos Kha, the Neverborn-blessed with the athame. Kha wiped the blade clean on his tongue, and kissed it. 'As close as we can get.'

'M-Macragge?' asked Narek, still on his hands and knees, spitting out toxic bile to clear his throat. He shuddered and gagged again. More bile jetted out of his anguished, gaping mouth.

'Macragge,' agreed the horned thing with the knife. 'Sanctuary City of our sworn foe. As the divinations said, this is the place.'

'I th-thank you for your trouble, brothers,' said Narek, trying to steady himself and rise. 'I could not have reached this place otherwise.'

'Then do what you must, Narek,' hissed Ulkas Tul, the other horned thing. 'Whatever your great mission is, whatever your hunt – it will be your last.'

'I know,' said Narek. Slowly, trembling, he got to his feet. His gut felt hollow. There was a disgusting taste on his palate. He held his bolt pistol in trembling hands that were splashed with flecks of tar-black vomit.

'You are pathetic,' announced Barbos Kha, turning away. Kha's bat-tongue flicked the air, tasting it, like an insect. There was a

particularly unpleasant growth of hair and tumour on the back
of his powerful, corded neck where it rose above the gorget seal
of his armour.

'We could kill here,' he purred to Ulkas Tul.

Ulkas Tul smiled back. It was not a smile anything human ever
wanted to look at.

'No,' Narek said, spitting to clean out his mouth. 'No, you
should go. You got me here, and I am thankful for it. But coming
here is suicide. To enter the fortress city of our enemies–'

'We are aware of the dangers,' Barbos Kha said. He began to play
with the athame.

'But we can cut our way out anytime we like, unlike you, Narek.
Now we're here, we can have sport.'

'May Lorgar watch over you,' Ulkas Tul told Narek. 'Barbos Kha
is right. There is sport to be had here. We are in the belly of the
beast. Kha and I will do as we please. We will take many lives
before we leave. Maybe Guilliman's.'

'My brothers,' Narek said, 'if you go on a spree, you will ruin my
mission. I need to disappear. I need to work and hunt. You will
spoil this for me if you go killing.'

Barbos Kha kept toying with the athame that had cut open the
warp for them.

'Look at you, Narek,' he said, 'so impoverished. Our transit
alone left you gasping and sick.'

'You have mocked us, burdened one,' Ulkas Tul said. 'You have
scorned our conjunction with the warp, refusing to take it into
yourself. Yet you were quite happy to make use of our magic to
get you here.'

'You are right, brother,' said Narek nodding. 'I have dishonoured
you and the glory you serve. Forgive me.'

'Not good enough,' said Kha. There was something horribly
insectile about the way his mouthparts moved independently.

'You used us to get here. You used my knife.'

'You used my divination to find your target,' Ulkas added.

'We only brought you because of where you wanted to go,' Kha gurgled, saliva welling out of his maw and dripping onto the floor. 'Magna Macragge Civitas, home of our enemies. We will kill now, and then depart. That is the price we claim for your transfer.'

'Yes, I dishonoured you,' Narek said. 'I am not worthy of the magic you wield. But you must go now. *Now.*'

'Is he threatening us?' Ulkas asked Kha.

'No, no, not at all!' Narek told the daemonic twins. The smell of them was quite awful. Flies were humming around them, flies born out of nothing.

Narek turned his head aside, spat out another fat gob of black phlegm, and looked back at his travelling companions. He tried to smile a reassuring smile at what remained of two men who had once been his sworn comrades. It had taken every ounce of his guile to persuade the pair to assist him at Traoris starport, and every scrap of his stamina to tolerate their presence ever since. His weakness was not false, for the warp-transit had harrowed him, but he was overplaying it to keep them pliant.

'Then you presume to give us orders?' asked Ulkas.

'I presume only the Word,' said Narek.

He paused and wiped his mouth with the palm of his left hand.

'I believe in the Word of our primarch,' Narek continued simply, 'and I believe that Word makes us loyal to the Emperor. We are of the Word, and thus we are of the Emperor. It was *ever* thus. I despise the steps my Legion-kin have taken to embrace the Outer Dark. Too many steps, too far. You, Kha, and you, Ulkas. You have polluted yourselves and our Legion. Yet I thank you. I thank you for bringing me here. You have done a great service to the loyal Seventeenth.'

They both glared at him, confused.

'What are you saying, Narek?' Kha asked.

'I'm saying receive my thanks,' Narek replied, and put four bolts from his pistol through Barbos Kha's skull.

Fragments of horn, bloody meat and brain tissue spattered out in an explosive burst that was driven from within by an eerie flicker of fracturing warp-light.

Barbos Kha toppled backwards. Narek was fast, but not as fast as he had been in his glory days, thanks to the augmenting bionics that had repaired his leg.

Ulkas Tul came at him howling, swinging his blade. The light of dead stars blazed in his lidless eyes, and his lips had peeled back to reveal a screaming maw filled with serrated, blackened tusks.

Narek tried to shoot, but the blade ripped the pistol out of his hand. Too slow. The cross-strike came back and the sword scratched a deep gouge in his ceramite chestplate, almost splitting him entirely, as surely as Kha's athame had split time and space.

Narek smashed the blade aside with his forearm, and backed away. Ulkas would not be denied. The Unburdened swung again, another potential kill-strike. Narek threw himself backwards, ducked further slashing cuts that would have severed his armoured torso cleanly, and then bypassed Ulkas's guard and landed a ferocious punch in the beast's snout.

Teeth broke. Bits of them went flying. The Unburdened monster lurched backwards, crashing into two script lecterns and shattering them. Still toppling, he caught himself against a heavy shelf to stop his fall, but Narek was not going to let up. Ulkas's guard was down, his sword flailing. Narek came in and delivered two more punches into the side of Ulkas's skull with his gauntleted fist, crushing his ear, cracking his brain pan.

Raging, Ulkas smashed back at Narek, catching him a glancing blow that removed the two smallest fingers of Narek's left hand with the edge of his sword. Narek rolled away from the pain and the jetting blood, and delivered a huge, angry, power-amplified punch with his right fist, which sent Ulkas flying the length of the scriptorium chamber.

He hit the far wall, demolishing shelves, crushing books. Another blizzard of pages filled the air.

Ulkas fell on his hands and knees, found his blood-stained sword, and got up again. He saw Narek across the chamber and came at him, charging, his sword drawn back for a two-handed strike.

Narek had already dropped the case from his rifle and pulled it to his cheek, aiming. He felt the kill-notches against his skin.

He had time for one shot. He had pre-loaded a specialist bolt-round for penetration and range, a custom-built core and propellant shell manufactured by his company armourer. Over-kill, at this distance.

Narek didn't care. He enjoyed the explosive red murk Ulkas's head produced as it burst off his neck.

Ulkas kept coming.

Narek remained calm. Time had almost frozen for him. A sniper's greatest strength was steadiness and patience, even when the world around him was moving at high velocity.

The sniper rifles of the Legions were all massive weapons, and Narek's gun, the infamous Brontos-pattern, was a particularly huge and unwieldy brute. It was long and heavy and cumbersome, and gauged for bolt-rounds, an almost impossible trade-off between muzzle velocity and round impact. The bolt shells had to be tailor-made to compensate for range with an added propellant stage.

The *Brontos* had an automatic bolt return, a fixed sequenced powered cycle that chambered each round from the short-packed magazine.

It also had a manual racking handle for faster returns.

Narek calmly racked the bolt handle and fired again as the headless thing bore down on him. The first shot had been overkill, but the second...

Ulkas's torso disintegrated in a crimson blitz of meat, sheared electro-fibre bundles and armour shards. His ruined body collapsed at Narek's feet.

Narek rose out of his firing crouch and lowered the smoking bolt rifle from his shoulder. His transhuman biology had already stopped the blood flow leaking from the stumps of his missing fingers.

Something twitched nearby. Kha's corpse was still quivering. Narek slotted back the bolt of his rifle and put a final shot through Kha's chest into the floor. Kha's corpse jolted like someone slammed by cardiac paddles as the round went clean through him.

Silence.

Paper crackled as it burned and settled.

The chamber reeked of toxic blood.

Narek shook himself. 'Wake up,' he muttered. 'This is done but there is so much still to do.'

The enemy would be closing in, without a doubt. He had to move, and lose himself. The Ultramarines wouldn't take him. He wouldn't allow it, not this early. Not like this.

He had work to do, the holiest work that any legionary had ever undertaken.

He had to deliver his Legion from evil.

Narek bagged his rifle and exited the scriptorium. Outside, in a dank insulae, he cowered, hearing landspeeders approaching and gun-teams deploying.

He took out the piece of parchment that Ulkas had given him before their departure, and looked at the words written upon it.

Grammaticus: the divined location of Grammaticus.

Narek closed his eyes and let his mind dwell on his target.

John Grammaticus, human, Perpetual, and pawn of the xenos-breeds. He and John had played regicide against one another on Traoris.

This new playing board, this *Magna Macragge Civitas*, would see the endgame.

Narek of the Word fled into the darkening streets.

12
BROTHERS

'The Salamander is a sufficiently convincing example that
everything which burns is not consumed,
as the souls in hell are not.'

– 'Saint' Augustine

TETRARCH DOLOR CAME to attention as Guilliman strode into the Residency's medicae hall. The primarch was still wearing his ceremonial war-plate, and seemed too big and regal for the sub-level confines.

'My lord,' said Dolor. 'Your brother has arrived, I gather?'

'He awaits upstairs,' Guilliman replied. 'There is conversation to be had.'

'How does he seem?'

Guilliman's solemn face permitted a slight smile at the subtlety of the question.

'Like himself, Valentus. Like the Lion. He is suspicious, and I fear he has already, in his mind, decided to oppose the future we are trying to secure. I have yet to explain myself and my decisions to him. He has yet to show me that he accepts or even understands what I am about.'

Dolor nodded.

'He is waiting,' Guilliman added, dryly, 'and I have excused myself and come to you, because you asked me to do so, and I know you would not waste my time or divert me unless it was critical.'

Dolor nodded his head again, more a bow of appreciation.

'It is, my lord,' he replied. 'You need to see this. I believe you may be shocked. In truth, I cannot count whether it is reason to rejoice or mourn. Also, I would have spared you this concern when you are occupied with your noble brother, but... you need to know this. You need to be in possession of this information before you take any further steps.'

Guilliman studied his friend's face, but transhuman features were notoriously hard to read for microexpressions.

'Then just show me,' Guilliman said.

Dolor ushered his lord through the doorway into the guarded areas of the secure suite. Status bars on the wall plates displayed the fact that the area was held at vermilion level security. The long line of guarded iris valves opened and closed behind them as they walked.

'This concerns the object that fell from the sky, doesn't it?' Guilliman asked as they walked.

'Yes, lord.'

'The transhuman corpse?'

Dolor did not reply directly.

'You've established an origin?'

'Yes, lord.'

'An identity?'

'Yes, lord.'

Guilliman glanced at him sharply.

'Something else?' he asked.

'Something else indeed, my lord,' said Dolor.

They reached the gloomy inner chamber where the iron casket lay. Captain Casmir and Titus Prayto were waiting for them. They bowed to the primarch and fell into step as Dolor led his lord through the laboratory chambers and into the isolation block beyond. The area was reserved for hazardous material and viral quarantine work. It was a long row of brightly lit cells, stark and white, each with a hermetically sealed armourglass wall facing into a common corridor. The corridor was lined with Ultramarines guards, and high-ranking medicae personnel worked at cogitation and cellular-sampling arrays that had been set up in the walkway facing one of the cells. Power cables snaked from the consoles across the grilled deck in fat rubber loops.

'Surely the mortal laboratory would have been a better venue for dissection,' Guilliman began.

'I authorised the transfer of the patient,' Dolor replied simply.

Guilliman stopped in his tracks so abruptly that Captain Casmir almost bumped into him.

'You said *patient*,' Guilliman said quietly.

'My lord, I did,' said Dolor. 'By the stars of Ultramar, my lord, he is alive.'

'How?' asked Guilliman. He asked it first of Dolor, a mix of anger and incomprehension crossing his face.

'How? *How?*' he repeated, turning to look at Casmir, Prayto and the suddenly tense medicae personnel.

'He... healed, my lord,' said Prayto.

'Healed?' Guilliman snapped. 'He fell out of the damn sky! From orbit! He burned to a crisp and dove deep into the Civitas like a meteor! You don't *heal* from that!'

'And yet–' Dolor began.

'May the old gods come and strike you all down as either liars or incompetents!' Guilliman yelled. 'Whatever else, you said, Dolor, you told me he was dead! Organic residue. A corpse. A cremated corpse!'

'I did not lie,' Dolor said calmly. 'He was utterly dead… Utterly. All life sign was extinct, all brain function. There was no viable organic tissue on his charred bones whatsoever. Your best physicians and analysts confirmed this, and so did all the instrumentation of the medicae hall.'

He paused.

'He was dead, lord. And then… he *was not*. Life returned where life was not and could not be. He *healed*.'

'You do not heal from death!' Guilliman roared.

'It appears you do, my lord,' said Prayto quietly, 'if you are one of the sons of mankind's Emperor.'

Silence. Guilliman turned to look at Prayto.

Titus Prayto held his master's stare and nodded confirmation.

Guilliman turned away and strode towards the occupied cell. Guards and personnel darted out of his path. He reached the thick armourglass wall, stopped a few centimetres from it, and stared inside.

The cell was a bare white space. A single male figure occupied the left-hand corner away from the glass. He was sitting on the floor, his back against the walls, his forearms resting on his raised knees. He was naked. He stared ahead, towards some distant spot that was not in the room.

He was a massive form, heavily muscled. The fire of his long fall had shrivelled his corpse but his stature, so much greater than human, was obvious now that he was restored to life. He possessed a primarch's build, a being scaled to fit only the largest chairs in Guilliman's Residency.

There were no marks on his body, no hair. By whatever means he was healing, it was still happening. Every part of his skin was

raw and bloody as some miraculous process brought living tissue
out of burned residue.

'I don't...' Guilliman began, his breath making a fog on the
surface of the glass wall. 'Who is he?'

'It is Vulkan,' said Dolor.

Guilliman gasped in pain and recognition. 'You are sure?'

'I'm certain,' said Titus Prayto.

Guilliman raised both hands, and placed the palms against the
armourglass on either side of his face, peering in. He paid no
heed to the fact that both were jacketed in full ceremonial plate
and massive, ornate lightning claws.

'Let me in there,' Guilliman said, staring at his brother.

'No, my lord,' Dolor replied.

'*Let me in there, damn you!* My dear brother is returned to me!
Twice! Once from the death that I thought had befallen him on
the traitor's field, and once from the death that delivered him
here! Let me in!'

Guilliman slammed his clawed and armoured fists against the
unbreakable wall in frustration. The sound shook the cell.

Vulkan looked up, brought out of his reverie. Eyes as blood-red
as the healing flesh of his body fixed upon Guilliman. They fixed
upon the massive, clawed figure standing at the glass.

'He sees me,' Guilliman said. 'Let me in there!'

'My lord–' Dolor began.

Vulkan lunged. With an anguished scream of rage and horror,
he leapt up and threw himself across the cell at Guilliman. The
attack was so sudden and so violent that Guilliman started back
from the protective armourglass in surprise.

Howling words that meant nothing and sounds that meant
every pain in the galaxy, Vulkan hammered his fists against the
glass, until it was slippery with blood and tissue-fluid from
his healing, still-forming flesh. His teeth were brilliant white

enamel chips in his screaming mouth.

His eyes were glaring circles of blood.

'Don't! Brother, stop!' Guilliman cried out in alarm. 'Brother, it is me! It is Roboute. Calm yourself!'

'He does not hear you, my lord,' said Dolor miserably. 'He does not hear any of us.'

'The Salamanders who have come to your hall were right, my lord,' said Titus Prayto. 'Vulkan lives. But whatever he has endured, it has driven him mad. Your brother, my lord, is quite insane.'

THAT THREE OF the Emperor's sons were present on the same world at the same precise moment was a truly auspicious conjunction, whatever the circumstances.

For different reasons, none of them knew that the true number of primarchs who had converged that day on Macragge was, in fact, *four*.

Deep in the pitch-black, unregulated spaces of the First Legion's flagship, the *Invincible Reason*, the quarry exhaled slowly.

It was time. *Time.*

Visions flickered through his head like a broken, mis-cued pict-feed. Visions had always flickered through his head, since his earliest childhood – visions of the future, of the possible, of the probable. Of the next, and the next after that.

It was the visions that had driven him mad.

Just now, though, the visions were coming to him more cleanly. They were bearable, tolerable. They were not the prescient night-mares of a galaxy in flames and a doomed future. They were not the hellish sights of a corpse-universe that came to him too often and caused him to devolve past the point where life – his or any other – retained any value.

The quarry breathed carefully. The visions firing behind his blood-rimmed eyes were calm and trustworthy. The ship had translated into realspace after weeks of travail through the storms of the warp, and suddenly he had clarity.

He knew who he was: a lord of the dark. A master of the lightless. A night haunter.

No, *the* Night Haunter: Konrad Curze. *Konrad Curze.*

'Konrad Curze,' he whispered to himself, speaking his name like a benediction. A benediction, or a death sentence.

He knew who he was and he knew his purpose. At that moment, in the bleak and bloody years of Horus's revolt, Konrad Curze understood his purpose the most cleanly and most perfectly of all the Emperor's eighteen sons.

The pitiless void had shown it to him. The endless night, his friend and tormentor, had shown it to him. His dreams had shown it to him.

Terror, pain, iconoclasm. All would pay. All of them, every soul, every one. They would all scream with him.

The mighty *Invincible Reason* creaked and groaned around him as its titanic superstructure, a billion tonnes of alloy, settled and unstressed from the tensions of warp-transit. Curze knew where they were. He had envisioned it, so he knew that it was almost assuredly true. They occupied high orbit above the grey-sheened glory of Macragge.

Macragge. Ultramar. The thought of the self-righteous Guilliman made Curze want to piss acid. His blood-brother the Lion was his blood-*enemy*, as the Thramas fight had proven, but Guilliman...

Toad. Reptile. Fool. As bad as Dorn, as bad as Vulkan. So blindly indoctrinated into the belief that the future would be a noble, golden age. So insufferably honourable. So eager to please their father. So eager to cry, 'Look at me! I have built an empire just for you! Just like yours!'

Jump up and down all you like, little child. Boast all you want. They were all going to pay. They were all going to understand the truth, the truth that only Curze saw. He would bring them down once more in fire and fear, until they were as broken as him. Perhaps, if he provoked them far enough, one of them might even kill him. Curze was waiting for his end. He welcomed it. If he could force one of his oh-so-noble brothers to deliver it, and thus reduce themselves to his level, it would serve a sweet, delinquent purpose.

Guilliman. Proximity and fortune had raised him up the list of priorities. Guilliman was an icon to topple and break. Guilliman, and his world along with him.

Curze closed his eyes. Visions played. He saw the streets of Macragge Civitas carpeted with bodies. He saw the towers and spires ablaze. He saw blood. He saw–

The red visions struck him with the force of arterial spray. He composed himself. It was too soon to devolve. He had work to do. He had to retain some focus. Anger was only useful when it was forged as a weapon. The same was true for terror. He knew both intimately.

It was time, time to leave the ship. Now they were back in realspace, the *Invincible Reason* was open and unbarred.

First he had to break *out* of the ship. Then he had to break *into* Macragge. Guilliman was a toadying cur, but he was no amateur. His defences would be sound.

The Night Haunter was not put off for a moment.

Visions flowed through his head like a river, the surface shot with reflections.

Curze mostly trusted them, for they were almost always true. Only occasionally, when fate shivered its spine, did a vision prove to be a false promise. He usually knew when they were lies. He certainly knew when they were questionable. He was always aware that he was playing a chance. With each vision, he had to decide if it would prove true or false, trustworthy or untrustworthy. He decided whether to act on a vision or not, and he calmly accepted when those decisions were wrong.

The current stream of visions seemed particularly dependable. Curze decided to follow their hints.

One in particular kept coming to him: a vision of rust, of a hard-void seal, of a sign. *Cargo Load Hatch 99/2.*

He smiled.

Sixteen minutes later, Curze exited the flagship's hull by shearing through the second cargo hatch of the ninety-ninth deck. The ninety-ninth was one of the unmediated spaces in which he had been sealed and hunted by his brother.

The shredded hatch blew out into the nearspace glow, cascading bright fragments of debris after it. Curze saw the world below, lit by the rising star. He saw the hard edges all shadows possessed in the contrast of the void. This was a stern, geometric night to haunt.

He saw the orbital plates circling below the standing fleet like artificial continents.

He had long since lost his helm. He simply held his breath as he flew out of the ship, and bounded, weightless, along the skin of the hull. The sheer cold of the hard vacuum was bracing.

Curze squatted beside Hatch 22/3, waiting for it to open. Prescience had shown this to him too. Hatch 22/3 was where the repair crews would emerge if a cargo hatch blew on the ninety-ninth.

It took them eighteen seconds. The hatch opened and light shafted out. The Night Haunter tilted back, so as not to be seen immediately.

It was not a repair crew, however. It was an assault squad of Dark Angels, warriors wearing the marks of the Stormwing, braced with boarding shields.

Curze shrugged. Sometimes the reflections were unreliable. The Lion, it seemed, had anticipated that Curze would try to break out. He had set his men on alert. Full marks, brother. Full marks.

He would kill them anyway.

Curze paused for a second to see if Hatch 22/3 reconciled in any way with the recurring visions he had had of his death. Was this it? Was his last moment rushing up at him?

No. His mind simmered, confident. His death lay somewhere and some*when* else.

The first Dark Angel pulled himself clear into the weightless space, one hand on his shield straps, the other on the hatchway rail.

Curze lunged at him hard and fast, the way a shark slams into a swimmer. A crunch, a single wound trauma that nothing could survive.

The Night Haunter's claws took away both the gorget and the throat of the Dark Angel as he came clear of the hatch. Vast beads of blood bobbled away into the vacuum.

The man fell away, limp, trailing balloons of blood, his head held on by a twist of metal and a shred of gristle.

As the first victim went by, Curze took his shield from him and slammed it into the face of the warrior emerging from the hatch behind him.

The impact was hard. Things broke – a skull, primarily – beneath all of it. The blood oozed out of the crushed faceplate in oily, weightless bubbles.

The blow knocked the man back. Curze reached in and scooped him out through the hatch so he could get at his next kill. The dying Dark Angel was propelled away from the hull so hard that his twitching form quickly overtook the drifting, rotating corpse of the first victim, and dropped towards the bright, grey planet below. It began to glow blue and then burn like a shooting star.

Curze went in through the open hatch. He re-entered the ship feet first. He was moving so fast, shadows barely stuck to him. His heels met the shield of the Dark Angel advancing behind the first two, and kicked the warrior back down the gullet of the hatch's void-lock. The man dropped heavily.

Landing on a foot and one knee in the gate beside the Dark Angel, Curze slew him before he could rise again by slamming down the edge of the captured boarding shield and crushing his throat.

Now there was confusion. *Now* there was reaction. Possibilities flew fast. Curze obeyed the visions. He responded, reacting to things that had not yet occurred.

Two Dark Angels came at him, firing. Bolter-rounds burned silently across the narrow space of the gate. Curze could hear, through vox-chatter or his visions, the outrage and profanity they were screaming, because of his attack and the murder of their brothers.

They wanted him dead.

Their wish would be entirely denied.

Curze tilted, and stopped the shoal of bolter-rounds with the captured shield. One, two, three and four, five and six, he swatted them aside. He felt the impact of their detonations transmitted up his arm. Flickering reflections had told him where each blazing shell would be before it had even been fired.

Curze went for the poor bastards. He removed a head with the long claws of his right hand. He eviscerated a torso with the long claws of his left.

Conflicting arterial geysers hosed the ceiling and wall.

Another Angel, a veteran of the Deathwing, rushed at Curze. Curze impaled him upon the claws of his left hand. Blood squirted in a torrent as the poor fool bled out around the adamantium hooks rammed through his torso.

The killing was only just starting.

The visions told him that a great many more Dark Angels were closing in on his location.

That meant that a great many more lives were about to end.

'I SELDOM COME to this chamber,' Guilliman said, 'but when I do, it reassures me.'

The Lion followed him into the room. Guilliman's Cataphractii bodyguard held the broad doors open for him.

'You give me a tour of the most magnificent fortress stronghold beyond Terra itself,' The Lion said, 'and believe me, I am impressed, Roboute. But you decide that this tour should include a chamber you seldom visit?'

He stopped, and looked around.

'I see,' he said, nodding. His lieutenants stood in the doorway behind him. He nodded to them, dismissing them.

'Leave us,' Guilliman said to Gorod. The warriors of the bodyguard turned, and closed the doors.

The two primarchs were alone for the first time.

'The Fortress of Hera is a true achievement, brother,' the Lion said quietly. 'It is more than I could have believed. It exceeds my imaginings.'

He smiled and glanced at Guilliman.

'That was not a slight, Roboute. I have never doubted your abilities. But I stand in awe of your achievements. The Fortress. Macragge. The Five Hundred Worlds of Ultramar. All of it.'

Guilliman pursed his lips. 'I do what I was bred to do, brother,' he said. 'What *we* were bred to do.'

'Ah, *that*,' the Lion murmured, as if contemplating things that Guilliman could not possibly know.

'The Fortress is robust,' Guilliman went on, a little stiffly. 'It serves me and it serves my Legion. It is fit for purpose.'

'It is entirely and magnificently practical,' the Lion replied.

'Truly, a wonder. I have no doubt it will endure for a thousand years or more. But you were always practical, Roboute. You, Rogal too. Men of the head. Led by your brains, by your processed data, not your emotions. That's why the two of you have the best and most efficient Legions in human space.'

The Lion tapped his brow with one long index finger.

'You think, and you apply that thought, and you don't let emotions cloud you. Not like Vulkan, or dear Ferrus, or Jaghatai.'

'Or Russ,' Guilliman added.

'Heavens, no!' the Lion laughed.

'Terra help me, *Russ.*'

'So, this,' the Lion said, gesturing to the long table. 'This surprises me. A work of emotion, not logic.'

The light of the late afternoon, discoloured by the storm, flooded the chamber through high windows. A long table, carved from stone, dominated the length of the room. Around it were twenty-one chairs, all built for the scale of a primarch. Each one was cut from the same mountain granite as the table.

The chair backs were draped with banners. The great seat, at the head of the long table was draped with the pennant of Terra. Two of the other pennants were plain and made of bleached, un-dyed cloth. The other eighteen were the banners of the Legiones Astartes.

'You did this?' The Lion asked.

'Are you mocking it?' asked Guilliman.

The Lion shook his head.

'It moves me. You still believe in a day when all of us, *all of us*, can sit at a table with our father, as equals, and talk of the matters of empire.'

'All of us,' Guilliman nodded.

'You made this room in anticipation of that?'

'Yes, many years ago. Does that make me sentimental?' asked Guilliman.

'No, brother,' said the Lion. 'It shows you possess a soul.'

He set his hands on the back of one of the chairs bearing an un-dyed banner and leaned.

'Two will never come,' he said.

'Yet their absence must be marked,' replied Guilliman. 'Places must be left for them. That is simply honour.'

The Lion straightened up, and slowly pointed, in turn, at the banners of Horus, Magnus, Perturabo, Mortarion, Curze, Angron, Alpharius, Lorgar and Fulgrim.

'Others will never take their seats, unless as conquerors,' he said.

'I know,' said Guilliman. 'Yet their places must be kept. I believe in the Imperium… In the continuity of the Imperium.'

'That it will endure?'

'That it must endure. That we must make it endure.'

'Without a doubt,' replied the Lion, 'but this is a universe of uncertainty. We know the names of many of our traitor enemies, but not all.'

'No?'

'I am certain there is more treachery to be revealed.' The Lion looked at the draped banner of the Fifth Legion.

'The White Scars?' asked Guilliman. 'You suspect them too?'

'The Khan is a mercurial figure. Who of us can say we know him or trust him? His nature is rebellious, and he keeps himself much apart from us. Only one brother stands close to him, and that is Lupercal. The Khan always had great affinity with Horus Lupercal.'

'And on this basis…'

'Tell me your theoretical simulations have not suggested this?'

Guilliman was silent.

'And don't pretend you haven't run multiple theatrical simulations on all of us, Roboute,' the Lion sneered.

'I won't,' replied Guilliman. 'You are quite correct. The projections concerning the Khan were troubling. But neither of us have heard a single whisper that he has turned too.'

'We have not,' The Lion agreed. 'But until I arrived here out of the warp storm, I had not seen confirmation of Magnus's treachery either. That was data you could impart to me, data that you had only just come upon. We knew they had ignored the Edict, and that Russ's hounds had been unslipped to chastise Magnus, but neither of us knew the grim outcome – the fate of Prospero, the full disgrace of the Fifteenth. This is a universe of uncertainties. What *else* do we not know?'

Guilliman paused. Then he turned to look the Lion in the eye.

'You have made it plain that I am one of your uncertainties,' he said.

'Brother–'

'You mistrust me, and my motives,' said Guilliman. 'You have told me so, clearly. You suspect me of a treason at least as great as Horus's, if not deeper.'

The Lion sat in the seat marked with his Legion's banner, and placed his armoured hands flat upon the table in front of him.

'Imperium Secundus,' The Lion said, staring down at his mailed hands. 'You do not deny it. You are establishing a second Imperium on the corpse of the first.'

'No,' replied Guilliman.

'No?'

'No. I am trying to keep the flame alive. This is not about empire-building, or thrusting for the main prize. I have an empire already! Ultramar! Five Hundred Worlds! Brother, I do this only so that *we* may persist. Terra may have fallen, and our father may already be dead. Whatever the facts, the Ruinstorm prevents us from knowing the truth. I am not taking this moment to move to my advantage, and I am not using the crisis as an opportunity to usurp. I am not Lupercal.'

The Lion looked up and held Guilliman's stare.

'I am simply keeping the flame alive,' said Guilliman. 'If we need another capital world, another figurehead, then let us have one, if it keeps our father's vision of the Imperium alive. If Terra burns, then Macragge lives. The Imperium endures. Do you know the real difference between me and Horus Lupercal, brother?'

'Tell me.'

'I don't want to be Emperor,' Guilliman said.

The Lion didn't reply.

'Help me do this, brother,' said Guilliman. 'Help me keep what is left together. Help me preserve the human intent. Don't make argument with me and misinterpret my motives.'

'I want to trust you, Roboute,' the Lion replied, 'but I have always been wary of your ambition.'

Guilliman sighed and shook his head.

'I cannot be more open with you. It is ironic. With respect, my dear brother, you come here full of doubts about me, yet you have always been one of the most opaque amongst us. You are a man of secrets, Lion, or at least of silent privacy. No one knows your mind or fully appreciates your intent, not even our father. Yet *you* doubt me?'

A tiny tremor of irritation crossed the Lion's noble face.

'Hard words,' he said.

'But true,' Guilliman replied, 'and perhaps I should have spoken them before now, long before. I do not doubt your loyalty or your prowess, but you and your Dark Angels are secretive beings, my brother, and Caliban is a world of mystery. I am wounded that you come to me with distrust when no one knows you well enough to know *your* heart.'

'You have never spoken this way before,' said the Lion.

'There has never been a time before,' replied Guilliman. 'The universe has never closed in so tightly around us to squeeze the words out. I will be plain. I have never had the courage before. I have always been too in awe of the noble Lord of the First.'

'The Master of the Five Hundred Worlds in awe of me?' laughed the Lion.

'You know it. You know we all were. When Horus was named Warmaster, he did not much care that he had succeeded above me, or Rogal, or Ferrus. What he truly savoured was being chosen over *you*.'

Guilliman felt a curious wash of relief at having spoken so candidly. He saw, though he wondered if it was his imagination, that the Lion seemed uncomfortable when confronted by such openness.

'Your Imperium, then,' said the Lion, 'this Imperium Secundus, this great scheme of survival... How do you intend to proceed? Do you intend to declare yourself regent?'

'I do not,' Guilliman replied. 'I will not found an empire and then crown myself. Such arrogance would confirm every doubt and suspicion lurking in the minds of men like you. I need a figurehead for the public to rally around while I fight to keep the mechanisms of Imperium turning over and protected.'

'But...' the Lion began. He looked pointedly at the great central seat, draped with its Terran standard. 'Who then? Surely it must be blood?'

'Agreed,' said Guilliman. 'It must be a primarch.'

'My dear Roboute,' said the Lion. 'There are only two of us here. What exactly are you proposing?'

13

FALLING ANGELS

'The strength of your enemy is also his weakness.'
– *Martial Stratagems*, 123rd Maxim

'I AM, I confess, uneasy with the suggestion,' said Titus Prayto.

'I understand,' Guilliman nodded. 'Then you refuse?'

'I do not refuse orders, my lord,' Prayto responded quickly.

'It is not that kind of order. It is a request that you could choose to deny.'

Prayto looked at his commander. They were alone in the Residency, out of earshot of even Gorod and the Terminator bodyguard, and out of mindshot of any psyker.

'I would neither deny a request, my lord,' said Prayto.

'But I put you in a difficult position?'

Prayto nodded.

'I am not sure I want to spy on the mind of a primarch.'

'I'm sure you're in my mind all the time, Titus,' smiled Guilliman.

'No, lord. Surface thoughts only, and only then when they are too bright for me to screen them out. I never pry unless invited.'

'Then perhaps I should not presume, and explain my thinking to you in words,' said Guilliman.

He sat down, and stared out of the repaired window ports at the distant glimmer of the new star.

'We stand at the brink. Imperium Secundus needs a figurehead to unite it. I had postponed that choice, for it had to be a primarch, and I was the only primarch present. It was unseemly–'

'No one would have refuted you, lord,' said Prayto.

'It would have been unseemly,' Guilliman insisted. 'I prayed for a loyal brother to be delivered through the storm. When all hope seemed extinguished, I resigned myself to taking the regency with all the humility I could gather. Then the Lion appeared.'

'You would declare him your regent?'

'Of course... but...'

'You don't trust him?'

'Yes, I do. No matter how closely he plays his secrets. The problem is, I don't believe he trusts me. If I am going to let him in, Titus, if I am going to declare him into a position of power that I cannot undo, I have to be sure of his agenda. Once he has been ratified as regent, we cannot unseat him if we are disappointed by the character he reveals.'

'Not without insurrection,' said Prayto.

'Which we will avoid, for reasons of toxic irony if nothing else. I need to know his mind, Titus.'

'I see, my lord. We are essentially vetting the new Master of Mankind.'

Prayto rubbed the bridge of his nose thoughtfully.

'It is difficult,' he said. 'It is as with the Wolves, only on a greater scale. Like the Wolves, the noble Lion undoubtedly understands the authority of the Edict of Nikaea. The Librarius of the Ultramarines is already evidence that you are prepared to overrule the word of the Emperor. If I am caught probing his mind...'

'Will you be caught?'

'I will endeavour not to be. At the Feast of Hosts tonight, I will use the background rush of many minds in company to get close. Understand, I do not know his capabilities, and he is famously closed. Also–'

'Yes?'

'There has been odd activity this afternoon. At least two incidents were detected by the Astra Telepathica during the parade. We are still processing their findings, but it is possible that one or more powerful minds are at liberty in the precinct of the city.'

Guilliman nodded.

'Keep me appraised. Titus, if you can tell me that the Lion trusts me sufficiently, I will declare him. He is the only choice... unless you can tell me that poor Vulkan is no longer insane?'

'I cannot, lord.'

'I do not care which, Titus,' said Guilliman. 'Search the mind of one primarch or heal the mind of the other. Whichever is easiest. Whichever serves us best.'

THE SURFACE. THAT was the next goal.

Curze dropped feet first, a flutter of crow-shadows, and landed at the bottom of a deep extraction vent overlooking one of the *Invincible Reason*'s eight massive dispersal decks.

Below him, like seeds ready to be sown, hundreds of drop pods were loaded in their cradles over the chutes to the void hatches.

He could commandeer one and drop–

No. A vision came, and it was firm. An undeniable reflection. Guilliman's city was protected from aerial and orbital assault by field screens and vast automated batteries. In his mind's eye, Curze saw a single drop pod falling. Its descent was rapid, but not rapid enough. Detection systems awoke. Auspex trembled.

Fire control systems calculated intercept. A spear of green energy from the surface struck the diving pod and converted it into an expanding cloud of fire and fluttering debris.

Another vision, slipping in and overlapping the first, showed him that a similar fate awaited any ship or lander that attempted planetfall without the correct code signal. But the codes wouldn't resolve in his mind. He imagined that they were being randomly generated on a minute by minute basis.

A third vision showed him the pointlessness of trying for the teleport assemblies. The Lion had ensured that they were all deactivated to prevent exactly that kind of escape route.

The Lord of Night bared his teeth and whined. How could one man get to the surface? How could one man–

Another vision. Curze smiled. *One* man could not.

They were still hunting for him on the upper decks of the flagship. Curze had wearied of the killing, and had slipped away, leaving false trails and brutal traps to delay and occupy his would-be captors. No one suspected that he could have reached the dispersal decks in the ship's belly so quickly.

Curze slid out of the vent base, and slunk along the side of the vast deck, using the shadows of the great stanchions and kinetic brace-beams. He was moving parallel to the lines of drop pods in their cradle framework. He studied them carefully, checking their status, though this only confirmed what the visions had shown to him.

He was far from alone on the dispersal deck.

Launch control was a large operations room overlooking the bay. Alongside the servitor station personnel, there were twelve drop officers on duty. From the moment Curze let himself into the room, none of them lived for more than thirty seconds. They took the launch permission codes with them as they died, but that didn't matter.

Codes were for minions and menials. The Lord of the First could launch his drop pod blizzards with a simple gene-sample override.

Curze picked up a data-slate that had fallen onto the deck beside the headless body of the launch station's commander. He wiped the blood off it with the tattered hem of his cloak. *'Full assault drop'* was already pre-selected and waiting.

Curze stuck out his dark tongue and slowly, almost lasciviously, licked the cold screen of the data-slate.

From a shared genetic root-source, one brother's gene-sample was as good as another's.

The slate pinged.

Genecode accepted.

Launch authorised.

Assault swarm launch in thirty seconds.

Twenty-nine.

Twenty-eight.

THE LION RAISED his goblet. 'To the Lord of Macragge, for your welcome,' he said.

'To the Lord of the First, for your faith,' Guilliman replied, 'and to the Imperium, for its endurance.'

They drank, and around them, along the dressed tables of the great dining hall, their men echoed the toasts and drank.

There were a thousand guests present at the long tables – the highest ranking Ultramarines had gathered and were seated with the Dark Angels counterparts of their specialisms, along with senior consuls, delegates from the Army, the Astra Telepathica, the various fleets, the Mechanicum and the Collegia Titanica, and representatives of all the other Legions that had come to Macragge.

As soon as the toasts were given, music began, and tides of

servitors flooded out of the kitchen doorways to serve the first of many courses.

Guilliman and the Lion took their places across from each other at the principal table. Glow-globes drifted in the vaults of the hall's high roof, and the tables were lined with fluttering candelabras, which combined to fill the hall with a golden light – a luminosity that reminded many present of the numinous aura of the Emperor.

Three seats away from Guilliman, Titus Prayto watched the Lion and waited for his opportunity.

He closed his eyes for a second, screening out the background noise. He was uncomfortable. There was a terrible tension that–

Prayto started and stood up, his eyes wide.

'*Great Terra!*' he cried. Despite the scale of the hall and the size of the company present, all talking ceased, and all eyes turned to him.

'Titus?' Guilliman asked, confused.

Prayto stared at the Lion.

'I felt it,' he said. 'I felt it there. The surge of minds. Hundreds of minds suddenly alert with anticipation. What did you do, my lord? What did you just do?'

'I have no idea what you're talk–' The Lion began, but his words were cut off by the sudden chiming of multiple alert monitors, swiftly followed by the blare of the palace klaxons.

Guilliman threw back his chair and stood up.

'Report!' he demanded.

'Mass orbital launch,' Auguston reported, reading off his data-slate as he rose to his feet. He looked at Guilliman in disbelief. 'The Dark Angels flagship has just... It has just launched a full drop pod assault on Macragge Civitas.'

'What?' Guilliman cried.

'Four hundred drop pods,' Auguston said. 'Primary assault

spread formation. This city is targeted. Planetfall in four minutes.'

'Assault swarm confirmed by all stations,' Gorod reported.

Guilliman's dress sword was in his fist and aimed, tip-first, across the table at the Lion.

'Is this your treachery?' he snarled.

'No!' the Lion replied, not flinching from the blade hovering at his throat. Some of his officers had drawn swords at the threat to their master, and he waved them back urgently. There were far too many weapons drawn in the hall already.

'I have done nothing,' the Lion hissed. 'I have not authorised anything!'

'The grid does not lie!' Auguston barked. 'Drop pod swarm! From your ship! *Inbound*!'

'You *attack* me?' asked Guilliman.

'I swear not!' The Lion said. He glanced at the Dark Angels nearest him. 'Stand down. Someone explain this!'

Holguin held out his data-slate.

'Signal is confirmed. The *Invincible Reason* has launched a drop pod assault. Impact in three minutes and counting.'

'Condemned from their own lips!' Auguston cried.

'This is a mistake!' Farith Redloss shouted at the Ultramarines First Master. 'A malfunction! A mis-launch!'

'How exactly do you *accidentally* launch a drop pod assault, brother?' asked Guilliman.

'This is a malfunction,' the Lion insisted to Guilliman. 'I swear so.'

'Accident or not, the pods will not reach the city,' said Guilliman. 'Our shields are raised. Our batteries have full lock. We will burn them out of the sky.'

The Lion swallowed hard and stared directly at Guilliman.

'This is a mistake, brother. A terrible mistake. I swear it. And I implore you, spare my warriors.'

'Your warriors?'

'Four hundred drop pods. A great number of battle-brothers. Please, Roboute, this is a mistake. An error.'

'All this time, while we talked of the future, your drop pods were loaded and ready with assault troops?' Guilliman shook his head. 'What do you suggest I do, brother? Lower the city shields?'

'Yes,' replied the Lion. 'Drop your shields and allow the pods to make controlled landings.'

'Two minutes!' Gorod cried.

'You cannot open the city to them, lord!' Auguston yelled. 'It is too great a risk! You must fire and eliminate them!'

'Please,' said the Lion, his gaze not leaving Guilliman. 'I did not authorise this.'

'But it is an attack force you had prepared and held in waiting?'

'A precaution. You would have done the same.'

'We must fire now!' Gorod roared. 'While they are still in optimum range. You must give the order!'

'Please,' said the Lion one last time.

Guilliman glanced sidelong at Prayto. 'Tell me,' he said.

'Your brother is closed to me, but I can see enough to know that he is telling the truth. Perhaps not the whole truth, but enough of it. He did not authorise this attack. He is horrified by it.'

Guilliman looked back at the Lion. There was a long pause.

'Your orders, lord?' Auguston insisted.

'Hold fire,' said Guilliman. 'Power down. Lower the shields and let them land.'

'My lord?' Auguston gasped.

'Do it!' Guilliman ordered. He returned his gaze to the Lion as Auguston spoke a rapid series of orders into his vox.

'Do not make me regret this, brother,' Guilliman said.

IN THE NORTH-WEST deme of the great Civitas, Damon Prytanis paused halfway through the supper he had just purchased.

He was in Xanthi market, just north of the shadows of the granaries, where the day's trade of clothing and livestock had shifted
to farm produce and hot food in the late afternoon. He had
bought a pastry stuffed with fish and vegetables from a trader
with a clay oven, and then taken himself over to the market's skirt
wall nearby, so he could sit with his back resting against the foot
of the wall and eat his fill.

He heard a murmur of voices, a change in the tenor of the crowd
around him. Something was happening.

He lowered the half-eaten pastry, and got to his feet, wiping the
grease off his lips as he munched.

Somewhere in the central part of the vast Civitas, alarms were
sounding. People around him were pointing at the sky.

He looked up, and saw immediately the multiple heat trails
slicing the darkening sky high overhead.

A massive drop pod assault. Unmistakable.

'Holy living Emperor,' he said out loud.

THE LEAVES OF the trees above him suddenly shivered in an evening
breeze that had come out of nowhere.

John Grammaticus, his carrybag slung across his shoulder, was
already walking quickly through the glade to find a patch of open
ground where he might better see the evening sky.

He had taken shelter in the ornamental parkland at the foot of
the Castrum's mighty Aegis Wall and tried to sleep for a while,
curled up on a grassy bank behind some lofty bluewoods, hoping
that rest might help his mind unpack.

The commotion had roused him. He'd heard it, but he'd felt it
too, felt it between his eyes like a sharp pain, the sudden agitation of hundreds of minds. It had come to him almost before the
sirens had started to wail.

He saw the drop pods filling the eastern sky like a meteor

shower. Their flame trails stretched out behind them in bright orange tongues.

John wondered exactly what he was seeing. A new enemy – that seemed certain, a new threat bearing down upon them all. He remembered the farseer's enigmatic remark: *In eight minutes' time, this communion will be eclipsed by another, more powerful psy-kana event in the city, followed by a considerable crisis. Both will divert attention from you.*

This had to be that 'considerable crisis'. Which faction was this? Which wayward brother? Which friend-turned-foe?

John reached out with his mind. He wanted to dredge for something he could use, something that would give him an edge in the hours to come. If he knew what was about to transpire, he could decide the best place to shelter from it, or the best allies to seek out.

What he got first was *surprise*. John blinked. At this range, he would not have expected to be able to reach specific thoughts or individual minds, but the unity of this hot-read shocked him. The warriors in those distant drop pods were *surprised*. The decision to launch an assault had come suddenly, without warning.

John reached harder, searching for more defined information.

He hit something else. It made him gasp and recoil. He'd touched a single mind, a dark thing, a midnight thing, quite unlike any mind he had ever touched before. It was ferocious: a black, hot, repellant presence, radiating energy rather than light; like a neutron star, hyper-dense and menacing.

John didn't know what it was. John didn't *want* to know what it was. He just knew that it was a greater threat than the four hundred drop pods and the armoured squads they contained.

'Don't let it in,' he said to the evening air. 'Don't let it in.'

Why weren't the city batteries firing? Why weren't the orbital weapon systems lighting up? Why was this being allowed to happen?

'Don't,' said John. 'Don't let it come here. Don't let it land.'

There was a pop, a slight but noticeable change in air pressure. A breeze hushed through the bluewoods again. John felt it. He smelled ozone.

The void shields protecting Magna Macragge Civitas had been lowered.

'No!' he cried. He turned and looked up in fury at the palace high above him, towering over the trees and the grey cliff of the Aegis Wall.

'You idiots!' he shouted, as if they could hear him. 'Raise the shields. Raise the damned shields!'

He could hear the howling of the incoming drop pods. Two screamed low overhead, trailing streams of blue-hot ablative burn, their braking jets beginning to fire. To either side of him, more pods flashed across the gleaming towers and high blocks of the Civitas, riding the flame-plumes of their retros. The noise was deafening.

John started to run. He began to sprint up the slope into the trees, heading west along the hem of the parklands towards the main Castrum gate. He had to get into the palace. He had to find someone he could trust and communicate a proper warning.

Hell was coming to Macragge.

Something crashed into him and knocked him down. John rolled, dazed. He tasted blood in his mouth. He couldn't clear his head. What... what?

There was a weight on him, a terrible crushing weight. A huge, mailed hand closed around his throat. Over the roar of the braking jets and the thunder of the pods landing in open areas all across the city, John heard a voice.

'Well met,' said Narek of the Word.

'MUTE THE DAMNED alarms!' Captain Casmir ordered.

One of the medicae staff turned to a console and tapped out a code. The alarm sounds and flashing lights in the quarantine corridor of the Residency's medicae hall shut off. Through the heavy bulkheads and sealed hatches, the alarms sounding through the rest of the great palace precinct came soft and muffled.

The cessation of the lights and sirens did not placate the confined primarch.

Vulkan continued to hammer his bleeding fists against the armourglass wall as he had done since the alarms first sounded. He was howling, his mouth wide, in despair, like a trapped animal. The mess of plasma, blood and half-formed tissue his fists and forearms were leaving on the glass was miserable.

'What's wrong with him?' asked the chief attending medicae.

'You're the damned surgeon!' Casmir returned. 'I thought it was a response to the alarms. Our Lord of Nocturne has clearly suffered through extremity. I thought the alarms had triggered some traumatic response.'

'It wasn't the alarms,' remarked a junior medicae nearby.

'What?' Casmir barked, turning on her. She bowed her head.

'Sir, I simply said that it wasn't the alarms,' she replied in a low voice.

'How do you know?' Casmir asked.

The young woman looked nervously at her superior, the chief attending.

'I spoke out of turn,' she said. 'I'm sorry.'

'Junior Physic Patrishana is one of our most promising novices,' the chief attending told Casmir. 'Patrishana, please... Explain your comment.'

The young woman nodded. She turned to her console and punched up a data review on the main lithoscopic display.

'I was monitoring the vitals of our... honoured guest,' she said. 'Please, if you will, observe the time-count indicator on this replay, captain. I have slowed it to one-tenth speed. Although it was close, so close as to suggest cause and effect, as you'll see...'

'Great Hera!' Casmir whispered. 'He began his agitation three full seconds before the alarms started. As if...'

The young woman looked up at Casmir.

'Exactly,' she said. 'As if his response, like the alarms, was to something else.'

Casmir looked at the glass wall and the screaming figure beyond it.

'What does he know?' he asked. 'What does he know that we don't?'

TREADS CLATTERING OFF the basalt pavers, the Land Raider growled into Barium Square, just off the Via Laponis – the *cardo*, or north-south 'heart street' of the Civitas. Barium Square was a broad and pleasant area, the popular haunt of scholars and academics who used the many libraries and rubricatories there. Through to the west, the cross-streets afforded an excellent view of the majestic Titanicus collegium and the even more massive castle of the Mechanicum. In the centre of the square was a broad grass sward like a little green island, boasting a grove of handsome grey seamwood trees and some ornamental shrubs. Scholars would sit on the benches there on summer days and talk as they ate lunch.

Smoke fumed from the shrubs, and the grass was scorched. The drop pod had felled two of the seamwoods when it landed, and destroyed an ornamental bench. Its landing pads had cracked and dug up the pathway too.

Sergeant Menius of the Ultramarines 34th Company led his squad out of the Land Raider. He fanned them out with a gesture, weapons ready. The orders had come down from the First Master. Active and duty sentry squads were to attend and secure every landing site. Reports were already flooding back from across the Civitas of sites secured. The Dark Angels squads emerging from the landing pods had immediately submitted to the XIII Legion details, handed off weapons, and allowed themselves to be escorted to the holding centre at the Campus Cohortum. Some, it was reported, had apologised and begged for forgiveness from their battle-brothers.

There were also reports of minor property damage. No matter how carefully you tried to park a drop pod, it was not a subtle device.

Menius checked the area, and compared his visor data with the flow from the Land Raider's more comprehensive auspex array. The square was quiet. Residual vapour rose off the drop pod, which sat at an awkward angle amongst the trees. Heat residuals were much hotter on the infrared display. It was bleeding out the fury of its atmospheric entry.

No contact. No *life trace*.

'Power up,' Menius voxed to the Land Raider's driver. He heard the gunpods heat up behind him, and he rejoiced in the tight, metallic clatter the turret mounts made as they traversed, tracking for a target. Menius had killing power in his fists, in the hands of the battle-brothers around him, and almost excessive killing power in the vehicle behind them.

They wouldn't need it.

Throne, this was already quite clearly a terrible mistake, and their brothers, the Dark Angels, were freely entering submission.

What was wrong with this one, then? Menius wondered. *No life traces? What, a bad landing? It didn't look that bad.*

'Summon an Apothecary on standby,' Menius voxed to his sub-altern. 'There's something off here.'

Bolters ready, the squad closed in on the smoking pod.

'Hello?' Menius hailed via his helm's augmitters.

The evening light had gone an odd, blue colour, as before a storm. Shadows had turned grey. Menius was aware that every move they made was accompanied by an over-loud sound. Every footstep, every grind of armour, every hum of power-support.

The city shields had not yet been re-fired. Menius could hear the distant chop and hum of the Thunderhawks and Storm Eagles despatched to cover each and every landing site. He could see some of them in the distance above the rooftops, circling as they probed neighbouring districts with their stablights. According to vox-data, his air cover was inbound and would be with him in two minutes.

'Hold steady,' Menius told his squad. 'Stand and cover me.'

He approached the drop pod. The hatches were wide open.

'Hello?' he called again.

Nothing.

He approached the nearest hatch and peered inside.

The pod was empty.

Must have been a misfire. An empty pod, mis-launched. The word was, the whole swarm had been due to a malfunction.

'Clear the area!' Menius ordered. 'Secure!'

He turned away from the pod and scanned the square. For a moment, he thought he might have glimpsed something moving along the portico of the Tigris Library. He dismissed it as his imagination. Nothing could move so much like a shadow, so jittery, so much like a flock of crows.

'Sergeant?'

'What?' Menius asked, turning.

His subaltern was facing him.

'We scanned the interior,' the subaltern said.

'And?'

'The entire interior is coated with blood, sergeant.'

'What did you just say?' asked Menius.

'Blood, sergeant, about eighteen litres of it.'

FROM THE PORTICO above Barium Square, Curze watched the Ultramarines trolling around the drop pod. *So* stupid!

Curze had targets elsewhere, and he intended to find them, but the stupid Ultramarines were so terribly inviting.

He'd never killed one of Guilliman's. It was enticing, even though they did have a big, bad Land Raider with them.

The Night Haunter stood up, proud and tall, and opened his wings and his dreadful claws.

'*Death*,' he murmured, as a sentence.

Eighty-eight seconds later, Sergeant Menius and his entire squad were dead and the Land Raider was on its side and burning.

Konrad Curze had come to Macragge.

14

DEATH IN THE FORTRESS OF HERA

'I am a brother to dragons and
a companion to owls. My skin is black upon me
and my bones are burned with heat.'

– from the Old Earth religious text known as 'Job's Book'

'OUR GUESTS, MY lord,' said Verus Caspean, Master of the Second, 'are being escorted to the Campus Cohortum.'

'Any resistance?' asked Guilliman.

Caspean shook his head. He had a sleek skull with very tightly cropped grey hair, and high cheekbones framing a blade of a nose. The shake of his head made Guilliman think of the warning sway of a mountain hawk.

'Our guests have made no resistance,' he replied, again stressing the word 'guests'. 'They have allowed themselves to be escorted to confinement.'

'Have they surrendered weapons?'

'Some of them have, lord,' said Caspean, 'but we have not made that demand of them. As per your instructions, we are treating them as respected battle-brothers, and regarding this as the unfortunate accident their lord claims it to be.'

'How many?'

'A strength in excess of five companies… as our Legion would consider it. I have little patience with their "wings" and cohort divisions.'

'So… enough to kill this city?'

Caspean paused.

'Easily,' he replied. 'Whatever else I think of them today, I am in no doubt of the capability and ferocity of the First. If we had dropped the city shields and their intent had been malicious, the Civitas would be burning, and the death toll unthinkable.'

'Tell me when they are all confined,' Guilliman said. 'Have their drop pods recovered and transported for holding at Fortress Moneta. I will not have the reminders of an invasion, no matter how peaceable and unintentional it may have been, littering my city and scaring my population. Has Auguston made the announcements?'

'Yes, lord,' said Caspean. 'He has made two statements over the Civitas address system, and they are being looped on the civilian datafeeds. I was impressed. He was quite reassuring. He insisted that there was no cause for general concern, and that it was merely a practical training exercise conducted in conjunction with the Thirteenth.'

'Whose idea was that?' asked Guilliman.

'Auguston's. It also helped that Holguin of the Dark Angels stood with him during the address and added his voice to the statement.'

'For that we can be thankful,' said Guilliman. He glanced along the length of the room. Through open doors, in an adjacent part of the Residency, he could see the Lion sitting alone, deep in thought.

'Have the confined officers interviewed,' Guilliman told
Caspean. 'Make it a polite but firm debriefing. Make sure their
story matches my brother's. This may well be an accident, but I
want to know how it happened.'

Caspean saluted, his mailed fist clunking off his breastplate. He
turned and left the chamber.

Guilliman turned and looked at Valentus Dolor. The tetrarch
was waiting attentively by the windows.

'An accident?' Guilliman asked.

'A strange one,' Dolor replied, 'but why would you not trust his
word?'

'Because he is the Lion.'

'He seemed mortified.'

Guilliman snorted. 'He had a drop force loaded and waiting. A
readied invasion. As he received my toast and sat at my table, he
had an assault force of five companies set to fall upon this city.'

'Consider, my lord,' said Dolor, 'if the situation were reversed,
and we stood, at fleet-strength, off the proverbial green shores
of Caliban, would you not have done the same? Would you not
have had your finest prepped to move without any delay if the
need arose?'

Guilliman did not reply.

'I think you would,' said Dolor with a sad smile. 'In fact, I know
you would. The core values of theoretical and practical would
not have allowed you to do anything else. These are dark days,
the darkest we have known. The events of this night are his fault.'

Guilliman shot another glance down the length of the chamber
to look at the brooding Lion.

'My brother?' he asked.

'Yes, but not the one you stare at,' said Dolor. 'I mean the Warmaster. This blight of conviction, this loss of faith, this caution
and suspicion that means that the proud sons of the greatest

family in the cosmos cannot trust one another… It is down to him and what he has done.'

Guilliman realised he had clenched both of his fists. He forced himself to uncurl them.

'I believe I would have shown more trust in him than that,' he said.

'Would you?' asked Dolor. 'Do you? The long shadow of the Lupercal means we play our cards closer to our chests than ever. We keep our secrets tight. Have you, for example, told your brother of the one who resides, howling like a bedlam fool, in the medicae hall?'

'I have not,' Guilliman hissed, quickly raising his left hand to excuse his spark of anger.

'Then think of your secrets and the reasons you keep them, while you examine his.'

'Good counsel as ever, Valentus,' said Guilliman. 'Wait upon me here. I think it is time my brother and I talked more frankly.'

Dolor made his salute and a respectful bow of his head. Guilliman walked through the doors into the chamber where the Lion sat. The Lord of the First occupied one of the large-scale chairs. A fire had been lit in the chamber's grate, and the Lion was intently watching the flames as they softly consumed the wood.

What was he thinking? Of forests, dark forests beloved by him, similarly consumed? It was a burden. Guilliman reminded himself that at least he knew the fate and status of his home world. What fears filled the Lion's heart when he thought of his forested fortress, now presumably inaccessible beyond the Ruinstorm's wrath?

'Not the evening of feasting and good comradeship I was expecting,' said Guilliman.

'Nor I,' the Lion agreed, looking up.

'How much would you have needed, brother?' Guilliman asked.

He walked to a side table and poured wine from a jug into two goblets of frosted white glass.

'How much what?' asked the Lion.

'Provocation,' said Guilliman. 'How many lines would I have had to cross? How many failings would you have needed to detect in me and my Legion?'

'What, to attack you?'

'Yes. It may indeed have been prudent, brother, but you came to my world fully prepared to strike at me if I was found wanting. Your men were loaded and ready, your pods primed, the vectors set. You have admitted to my face that you came here with no qualms about sanctioning me if I was found fit to sanction. So what would it have taken?'

The Lion took the goblet that Guilliman proffered.

'Your ambition, Roboute. It was always your greatest strength and your greatest flaw. No two brothers more ambitious than you and Horus. It has seen you build an empire. If I had come and found you stealing another, then I would have struck.'

He rose to his feet and sipped the wine.

'Honesty is your other great strength, brother,' the Lion said. 'Again, it is another strong trait you share with Horus.'

'That name can only be spoken so many times within the Residency before I reach for my sword,' said Guilliman.

The Lion laughed. 'Quite so. But my point is a valid one. Before… before he fell, Horus was an honest creature. Noble and honest. I always thought of the two of you as very alike. Admire him or despise him, one was never in any doubt as to his ambitions. He was honest. He made no secret that he wanted to be the best of all, the first amongst equals, the first son by merit and not numerical fact. He wanted to be Warmaster. He wanted to be heir. His honesty was naked.'

'But that honesty has gone.'

'Indeed it has,' said the Lion. 'When he fell, however he fell, his honesty peeled away from him. He became a lord of lies, a great betrayer, a being capable of the worst deceit and falsity that we can imagine or even bear to think of. But you are honest still.'

The Lion looked at Guilliman.

'When I came to you, you opened your heart to me. You told me of your fears, of the wounds you carry, of the principle and nature of your fight, and of your intentions for Imperium Secundus. That stayed my hand, to see the honesty in you still.'

He took another sip of wine. The goblet was made of white Servian glass, and it glowed like a chalice. It contrasted sharply with the dark gauntlet that held it, with the armour hued a shade of black known in the ancient language as *calibaun*. The goblet had more warmth in it than shone from the Lion's pale skin. The wine looked like blood.

'Part of your honesty, Roboute,' he said, 'was to remind me that I am not an open book. I have always found it hard to trust and be trusted.'

'But you are admired and beloved—'

'That is not the same thing at all. I have my secrets. Men may keep secrets for good reasons.'

'Then if we are to put this behind us, and step forward from this day side by side as allies, I must open my heart further,' said Guilliman. 'There is something—'

The knock of a fist against the chamber door interrupted him. Guilliman paused, annoyed, wishing to unburden himself fully now that he had begun. Yet he knew full well that no one would knock without a pressing reason.

'Enter,' he said.

It was Niax Nessus, Master of the Third.

'I apologise for the intrusion, my lord,' he said, 'but it is

imperative that you see this. Also, your noble brother's voted
lieutenant wishes to speak with him urgently.'

Farith Redloss stood in the doorway behind Nessus, flanked by
several of Gorod's hulking warriors.

'We will continue this conversation in a moment,' Guilliman
said to the Lion, drawing Nessus to one side and taking a data-
slate from him. The Lion went to the door and stepped out to
meet Farith Redloss. Redloss moved his lord down the hallway a
little away from the bodyguards. He passed the Lion a data-slate
marked with the First Legion's icon.

The Lion read it.

'Tell me this is not so,' he said.

'It is confirmed.'

'This? *This* is the cause?' the Lion growled.

'It took a gene-print to launch the assault. We have swabbed the
device. It is confirmed.'

'Then he's on the surface?'

'Ingeniously so,' said Redloss. 'He used the lives of our battle-
brothers to make Guilliman throw open the door for him.'

The Lion's lips trembled in rage. 'Find him,' he whispered.

'Lord, I–'

'*Find him.*'

'The Ultramarines will not permit free movement in the Civitas
precinct, My lord, so–'

'Then be ingenious. Find him.'

Redloss nodded.

'Will you tell him, lord?' he asked. 'Will you tell Guilliman?'

'WE CANNOT EXPLAIN it,' said Nessus to his lord in a low voice. Guilliman thumbed his way through the slate's datalog for the third time.

'A squad dead?'

'Menius's troop, in Barium Square, not less than thirty minutes ago. They were not just killed, they were silenced. They were torn apart.

'This isn't the work of the Dark Angels...'

'It does not look like their handiwork at all, nor would that answer make much sense. Why this one incident if all the others stood down peacefully?'

'Something else was in that pod,' said Guilliman.

'Indeed. Theoretical, it slew the original occupants and took their place. We're analysing the blood found in the pod now.'

'What has he brought here? What has he brought to my world?'

'Your noble brother?' asked Nessus. 'My lord, this may be something he has no knowledge of. He–'

'It was on his ship. It was in his pod. It killed his men. He must know what he has brought here.'

Guilliman looked at Nessus.

'Inform Auguston. We raise our security status to Ready One, city-wide and in the Fortress. Mobilise in strength. Household and Legion. Scour Barium Square and the routes out of it. Genetraces, footprints, blood trails, anything. Access security picters in the deme. Something or someone must have caught a glimpse. I want to know what this is and where it's going. I want it found, and I want it stopped before it kills again.'

Nessus snapped off his salute and turned to leave the room. The Lion was re-entering.

'What have you brought here?' Guilliman asked.

'I'm sorry? What?' the Lion replied, pausing in the doorway.

'If my face is anything like yours, brother,' said Guilliman, walking up to him, 'and I believe it is a great deal more open, then we have both been recipients of disturbing news. So, I ask again... What have you brought here?'

'Farith Redloss was simply confirming the facts of the incident,' said the Lion. 'A mechanical failure, probably the result of storm damage. I wanted an answer quickly, and it has been provided. The pod drop was–'

'No,' said Guilliman. He took another step towards the Lion. 'We just spoke, brother to brother, of the need for honesty. We spoke more freely than we have ever spoken. You told me that my honesty is why you stayed your censure, and admitted to me that you could be far too closed at times. We agreed that only true honesty would allow the Emperor's loyal sons to stand against the darkness and drive it back. So we start. Now.'

Guilliman held up the data-slate that Nessus had given him so that the Lion could read the report on its screen-surface.

'What is this?' Guilliman snarled. 'Tell me what you have brought to Macragge, or by the name of Ultramar, I swear I will put you through that wall.'

'You will *try*...' the Lion replied, stiffening.

'Damn you, brother! Trust me and speak the truth now or we are done and finished! What have you brought to Macragge?'

The Lion sighed.

'Konrad,' he said.

THE WALL WAS high, high and mighty, but it was just a wall. Walls could be climbed, and gates opened. Veins could be opened too.

Less than a shadow, Curze rippled up the Aegis Wall like a black autumn leaf fluttered upwards by the night breeze. Above him, like a geometric mountain, towered the bulwarks of the Fortress.

The sons of Ultramar marched from this great bastion, so eager to boast of their prowess and their fortitude, so eager to celebrate their courage.

Curze reached the rim of the wall and vaulted onto the parapet. He looked back over the city below, a sea of lights. The night sky, with its one foul glowing star, shimmered behind the re-lit void shields.

Sentries on circuit were approaching. He could see them in his mind before he smelled the dry heat of their power armour. He opened a shadow, slid into its embrace and extended his claws.

He was inside the Fortress of Hera, inside the cradle of the haughty Ultramarines.

Tonight, at last – and long, long past time – they would know fear.

JOHN WOKE. HE was in a basement or cellar, tied to a wooden chair. There was a tang of blood in his mouth.

The Word Bearer sat facing him on a metal crate. His weapon lay across his lap in its case. John's carrybag stood on the floor at his feet.

'What do you want?' John asked.

'To renegotiate and then conclude the business we began on Traoris,' said the Word Bearer.

'Narek–'

'Call me lord. Show me respect.'

'I do not feel I am in a position to negotiate much,' said John. His head hurt, but he reached out with his mind anyway. Perhaps…

No. It was futile. John's initial suspicions had been correct. The torc around the Word Bearer's throat was a powerful psychic hood. Narek had come prepared.

'You want it,' said John. 'Take it.'

Narek did not reply for a while. He kept his gaze fixed on John Grammaticus. Then he put aside his cased rifle and reached down to the carrybag. He took a bundle out of it, unwrapped it, and held the fulgurite spear up in the half-light. It didn't look like much: a forked spearhead of dull grey mineral, unfinished, no longer than a gladius.

But it was a piece of the Emperor's psychic lightning, fused into a fulgurite in the sands of Traoris. It was a weapon of extraordinary power. With it, one could kill a god.

Or, most certainly, one could kill the son of a god. Even the one son-of-a-god who was impossible to slay otherwise.

'It is potent,' said Narek. 'I can feel the life in it, the power. It is… *godlike.*'

'It is a fragment of divinity,' said John. 'Or something as close to divinity as we will ever know.'

'I could take it, and leave you dead,' said Narek.

'This is entirely what I expect,' said John.

Narek turned the spearhead over in his hands.

'One thing has become clear to me,' he said, 'through my pursuit of you here and on Traoris. This is a powerful weapon, but you… you are a notable being too. You would not have been charged with the recovery and use of this if you were not something… special.'

'I'm just an agent for–'

'You are a Perpetual.'

John faltered. 'I–'

'So old, so rare, so forgotten. You are the legend of a legend, the myth of a myth. But the Word Bearers are the keepers of the word and the lore, and in our histories are even the ghosts of myths remembered… the old ones. The long-lived ones. The eternal kind. The first and last. The Perpetuals.'

'It's more complicated than that,' said John, 'a lot more complicated than that in my case. I–'

'The details don't matter,' said Narek. 'I know what a Perpetual is capable of. I understand. After all, we are all proof of what the oldest and most powerful Perpetuals can do.'

'What is that?'

'Build an Imperium.'

John let his head drop and he exhaled slowly.

'Just kill me, Narek,' he said.

'Has your life been so endless that you long for death?'

'I know when I'm beaten,' John replied.

There had been a flash of truth in the Word Bearer's remark. John was tired. But death was not a permanent state in his case. The Cabal saw to that. If he could goad Narek enough, death might become an escape route and–

'The spear is powerful, John Grammaticus,' said Narek, 'but I fancy it is even more powerful when one of your kind wields it. So you become, you see, part of the weapon.'

'There is some truth in that,' said John. There seemed little point lying.

'Then I will take you both, you and the spear. As one, you will be my weapon, for the purpose I have ordained.'

'And what would that purpose be, Narek?'

'Respect!' hissed the Word Bearer.

'What would that purpose be, my lord?' asked John. 'I know why I want the spear. I know what deed is expected of me. What do you intend to do with it?

'I intend,' said Narek, 'to perform holy work. I intend to cleanse the soul of my Legion of the daemonic pollution that contaminates it.'

He held up the speartip. Despite its dull finish, they could both see the tiny flashes of power that coursed through it.

'I intend to save the Legion of the Word Bearers,' said Narek, 'and you are going to help me accomplish that.'

'How?' asked John Grammaticus. 'What exactly do you intend to do?'

'I will cleanse the soul of my Legion,' said Narek, 'by seeking out and slaying Lorgar Aurelian.'

'MY LORD. MY lord, no!' Gorod cried.

'Curze?' Guilliman roared. With one hand he had smashed the

Lion back into the wall. He held him there by the throat. 'You brought that monster to my world?'

'Unhand me,' said the Lion.

'Answer!'

'I have not resisted you, Roboute, but you molest me. Unhand me or we will swiftly discover which of us is the superior combatant.'

'My lord!' Gorod repeated. The bodyguard had closed around them, hoping that they would not be obliged to drag the primarchs apart. They did not want to lay a hand upon their master, the Avenging Son.

Guilliman did not loosen his grip.

'Tell me how this happened. Tell me about Curze!'

The Lion's hands remained at his sides. He did not resist the fury and the formidable pressure pressing him into the wall, but it was plainly a feat of determination not to.

'Since Thramas, I have held several officers of his Legion prisoner,' the Lion said, 'including that bastard known as Sevatar. Curze was on my ship too, loose in the unregulated decks. I hunted him. He could not escape, but I could not capture him. It appears he has now... made his exit.'

'Upon your arrival, this wasn't the first thing you chose to tell me?' asked Guilliman. 'That one of the worst of our traitor brothers hides within your flagship?'

'In hindsight, I could have been more... open,' said the Lion. 'In truth, as we are speaking plainly, I was ashamed that I could not confine him. I would gladly have brought him before you in chains, on his knees and pleading, so we might have sequestered him in your darkest dungeons. While he was free, however, he was my problem, my *curse* to contend with.'

'But you didn't,' said Guilliman, 'and men are dead because of it, and more will die, and we are at each other's throats.'

'Quite literally,' said the Lion, looking down at Guilliman's crushing hand.

Guilliman released his grip and stepped back. The Lion stood up properly.

'That will not happen again,' said the Lion.

'It might,' replied Guilliman.

'Not that way around.'

'Don't test me, brother!' Guilliman snapped. 'Can you not see the anger in me?'

'I can, but I am better at hiding things, and you clearly cannot see the anger in me. That will not happen again.'

'Then make sure of it. Your men will help my men find this monster,' Guilliman said.

'Agreed.'

'No more lies, Lion. No more secrets.'

'Agreed. Let me contact Holguin and–'

Alarms started to ring throughout the Residency.

'Perimeter breach. The Fortress,' said Gorod, reading the data-flow off his visor.

'Which means?' asked the Lion.

'Well, unless you have any other surprises you haven't told me about,' said Guilliman, 'he's here. He's on the Castrum. He's in the Fortress. Curze is here.'

His eyes widened. His mouth opened and looked as though it was screaming, though no sound came out.

'I don't like this,' said Captain Casmir. 'What's he doing?'

The medicae staff shook their heads. Behind the armourglass, the insane primarch flexed his hands and howled without sound. His dark skin was still healing and still bleeding. He resembled some grotesque revenant, some grisly spectre that had fled death and returned from the grave.

'Get someone!' said Casmir.

'Who?' asked the chief attending.

'I don't know! Tetrarch Dolor! Guilliman himself!'

Several aides began to back away to do as he ordered, but no one wanted to take their eyes off Vulkan.

There was a sense of power in him, terrible power and terrible purpose. Madness still invested his eyes, but it was focused now, as though all his wrath and pain had been concentrated into one thing.

He was mouthing something, over and over again.

'What is that? What's he saying?' asked Casmir.

'He's just raving,' the chief attending replied.

'No, that word…' Casmir stepped forward. 'Read his lips. He's saying…'

Casmir turned and looked at the medicae staff and the guards.

'He's saying… *Curze*.'

Vulkan screamed the name of his tormentor. He locked his bloody fingers together and began to smash his fists against the glass like a pounding hammer in a forge, like the working, toiling beat of a smithy, making and unmaking, shaping and unshaping. The armourglass wall, smeared with the blood of his previous blows, shivered. It vibrated.

It cracked.

'Seal this level! Now!' yelled Casmir. 'Seal it!'

Vulkan's fists kept pounding. The glass cracked more broadly.

Then the whole wall exploded in a blizzard of fragments.

Vast, dark, murderous, Vulkan stepped out of his cage. Casmir and other Ultramarines rushed forward in desperation to restrain him, but he threw their armoured forms aside as though they were dolls.

Vulkan was free.

In his madness, he would not be stopped.

Not again. Not by anything.

15

KILL ALL THE SHADOWS

*'I know you are my eldest brother; and, in the
gentle condition of blood, you should know me…
You are the first-born; but the same tradition takes not
away my blood, were there twenty brothers betwixt us:
I have as much of my father in me as you.'*

– from *As You Alike* (attributed to the dramaturge Shakespire), circa M2

'MAKE YOUR REPORT!' Guilliman demanded into his armour's vox-link. He strode along the grand colonnade that linked the Residency to the Fortress proper, with the Lion and an assembly of bodyguards from both Legions at his heels.

'Captain Terbis, my lord,' the vox scratched back. Overlapping ambient noise suggested a great activity at the other end. *'We've… we've found three men dead in the Portis Yard, strung from the Aegis Wall with wire.'*

'Our own men?'

'Three Ultramarines from 27th Company. Roster confirms they were on sentry duty. Wait! Stars of Ultramar! One's still alive! Hurry! Hurry, cut him down! Cut him down–'

'Wait!' the Lion cried, grabbing Guilliman's arm. 'Tell them no! Tell them–'

Despite the distance, they felt the blast. The vox-link scratched out, dead. A haze of red light glowed over the fortress wall, casting an infernal wash across the stately buildings of the Palaeopolis.

'Terbis!' Guilliman yelled into the vox. 'Terbis!'

'He mines the bodies,' said the Lion. 'I've known him use the method several times. He takes munitions and grenades from those he slays or maims, and sets them with time or motion triggers on the fallen. Such is his insidious poison. He spreads terror. We cannot trust our own dead.'

Guilliman looked at Gorod.

'Issue a warning to that effect. All channels.'

'Aye, my lord,' rumbled Gorod.

Before the Invictus commander could begin the task, another ripple of blasts shivered the night air. This time, the detonations came from the direction of the Sword Hall. Beyond the Fortress wall, Guilliman could see flames scudding from the lip of a roofline. He looked at the men with him and drew his gladius.

'He will commit no more injury,' he said, 'no more insult, no more outrage. Let it be known, we hunt him with maximum prejudice. No matter he is our brother, all warriors are hereby notified to stop Curze with lethal force.'

ON THE PIERED western walkway that skirted the Praetorium, Titus Prayto held up his hand sharply.

'Stop. Stop dead!'

At his side, Captain Thales and his assault squad came to a sudden halt.

'What do you sense?' asked Thales.

'Something… He's here. Or, he was here,' said Prayto. To the east of them, the blast of a grenade rang through the inner yards. Alarms and bells sounded from all quarters.

'He's… everywhere, it seems,' Thales murmured. 'Are we sure he is alone? It feels like a strike force has infiltrated the Fortress.'

'We know nothing for sure, but I feel he is alone,' said Prayto. 'This is his art. He moves fast, and unpredictably. He leaves death and traps where he walks. Thus he is everywhere and nowhere, and so terror mounts.'

Prayto looked back along the walkway. Something had made him halt their urgent advance. He unclipped his lamp pack.

'We are Ultramarines, captain,' Prayto added. 'He can sow all the terror he likes. We shall know no fear.'

Prayto had set his lamp to ultraviolet so that it might further enhance his transhuman ocular implants. He shone it along the walkway. The night's shadowed darkness was mottled with the glow of distant flames.

'There,' Prayto said. The hard light of his lamp caught wires stretched taut between the piers of the walkway at shin height. It showed them as sharp white lines.

'Trip wires,' he said. 'He's wired the walkway. Thales, close off this area. Tell everyone not to enter by the western gate. You three, start clearing these wires. Make them safe.'

The Ultramarines moved forward, clamping their boltguns to free their hands. Another blast, from the direction of the Library, lit the night above the walkway's roof.

'My lord!' one of the men called out.

'What have you found?' asked Prayto.

'These wires, my lord… They are just wires. They are tied between the piers, but there's nothing attached to them.'

Even his traps are traps, Prayto thought. *He binds us and blocks us, merely with the idea of death…*

'More confusion,' Prayto said to Thales and the men. 'Every

action is designed to wrong-foot us, occupy us, delay us. He is the opposite of all he does.'

Prayto turned to look back down the walkway, the way they had come.

The shadow standing silently behind them smiled at him.

Prayto was fast, but a rush of inimical malice flooded his brain with stunning force. It was as though Curze had kept his corrosive mind hidden, and now suddenly allowed Prayto's sensitivity to read it.

Claws scythed the air. Prayto felt pain deep in his side. The impact hurled him sideways into one of the corridor's stone piers, which he bounced off with a clatter of plate. Before he even hit the ground, he was covered in blood.

It belonged to Captain Thales. The officer was still standing, but his head had been removed. A considerable volume of blood was jetting from the stump of his neck, plastering the walkway like torrential rain.

One of the squad members got off two shots: bright flashes and deafening noise in the covered space. Almost instantly, the man sailed backwards through the air, his boltgun spinning out of his slack grip, his chest plating ripped open like torn foil.

Despite the terrible wound in his side, Prayto got to his knees. Bringing his bolter to bear, he fought to discern which of the night's shadows was Curze.

There? *There?*

'Kill all the shadows!' he roared, and opened fire. The remaining men fired too, wildly, in all directions. The searing light of gunfire dispelled the darkness, and the furious bolt-rounds ripped into the stone work of the piers and the walkway, filling the night air with dust, micro-metal fibres and fyceline fumes. They kept firing until their magazines were empty. The pulsing, juddering flash of the shots showed them nothing but the emptiness of the shadows.

Curze had already moved on.

But Curze had let Prayto taste his mind.

Prayto had him.

Half-unconscious with pain, the Librarian opened his vox-link.

FIRST MASTER AUGUSTON heard the roar of bolter fire and turned.

'That sounds like a whole damned squad unloading!' he roared. 'Where is that?'

The sergeant beside him checked his auspex.

'Locator places the weapon discharge in the western walkway, my lord,' he reported. 'Beside the Praetorium.'

Auguston's squad turned, weapons raised, as warriors approached along the hallway. It was the Lion's man Holguin, and a band of his Dark Angels.

They faced each other uneasily for a moment.

'Anything?' asked Auguston.

'He left grenades seeded in the beds of the ornamental garden,' replied Holguin, 'and two more of yours dead outside the Sacristy.'

'I will have his head on a spike,' said Auguston.

The vox crackled.

'*This is Prayto! Respond!*'

'Auguston,' the First Master replied.

'*He was here, Phratus! At the Praetorium. Where are you?*'

'In the hall of the Eastern Communication.'

'*Then he's coming your way, Phratus. I can sense him. He's coming your way and he's coming fast.*'

'Titus? Titus?'

The link was dead. Auguston looked at Holguin, his combi-bolter raised.

'You hear that, Dark Angel? It appears we may be the ones to end this.'

Holguin was holding his executioner's blade.

'It is an honour I am happy to share,' he replied.

Auguston gestured, and the Ultramarines spread down the long, high-ceilinged hallway. The Dark Angels moved to the left, covering the closest of the doorways.

'This is Auguston,' the First Master said into his vox. 'I have it on good authority that our tormentor is moving into the Eastern Communication, heading towards the Chapel of Memorial. Available squads close in. Block access to the Sword Hall and the Temple of Correction.'

He waited.

'Respond!' he hissed.

There was a shiver on the vox, distant static, like the dry skeleton of a voice.

'*Roboute…*' it said.

'Who speaks?' Auguston demanded.

'*Roboute…*' the dry crackle repeated. It was almost crooning the name.

'Flames of Terra,' Auguston said, looking at Holguin. 'He's even inside the damned vox.'

A bang made them all turn. The light bank at the far end of the Communication went out. Quickly, in sequence, the other light banks along the hallway went out, each one with its own bang. Darkness marched towards them along the hall.

The lights went out overhead, and then behind them. Then the lights were extinguished all the way to the far end of the Communication.

Silence. No emergency power cut in. No secondary lighting. It was as though the darkness had obeyed Konrad Curze, and all light had fled from him in panic.

Every helm visor lit up, Ultramarines and Dark Angels alike. High resolution enhancement searched the darkened Communication for movement. Auguston and his men saw the area as a green twilight.

'*Roboute…*' the vox whispered.

Suddenly, Holguin was moving. The massive, round-tipped executioner's sword caught the infralight on its edge as it swung. There was a shadow, just a shadow… No, even less than that. Just the hint or memory of a shadow. The blade caught something, a tatter of night.

Then there was an impact, bloody and crunching. Holguin lurched backwards and crashed against the wall. The Dark Angels beside him seemed to pivot oddly. His side came open, armour and torso parting to release blood and slippery organs.

Auguston began firing. They all began firing.

In the rapid, hellish flash of the multiplying gunfire, Auguston turned full circle, hunting for his foe.

He suddenly found a face immediately in front of his, just centimetres away, staring straight into his soul. The face had eyes like black suns, and skin as white as a bone desert, made sickly by the green infralight. Long, ragged, black hair half-stuck across the cheek and nose, glued by the blood of dead men. The mouth leered, revealing blackened teeth and blue gums. The leer stretched the mouth open impossibly, inhumanly wide.

Auguston heard laughter.

He lunged at Curze, firing his combi-bolter. The face and the shadow, even the insane laughter, all vanished in a moment. In dismay, Auguston saw that his shots had felled a Dark Angels on the far side of the hall.

Other men were still firing. It was madness, confusion. All discipline was lost. It had scarcely been seconds since the first instant of the fight. Auguston realised he was bellowing, expressing his fury as desperate non-words.

Was this fear? Was this *actually* fear?

He saw a legionary, an Ultramarine, struck into the air. The warrior had been touched by nothing more than a piece of shadow, the tatter of a butcher-bird's black, ragged wing, but the impact was as though he had been fired from a cannon. Flailing, he struck one of the hall's great windows, shoulders first, and went through it in a blistering cascade of broken glass.

The helm of an Ultramarines sergeant rolled along the stone floor at Auguston's feet.

There was still a head in it.

'Face me!' Auguston roared. 'Face me like a man! You coward! You night-thing!'

Curze's answer was a clawed hand that punched through ceramite, armoured under-mail and fibre-sheaves into the living gut.

Auguston fell forward, blood spewing out of the eviscerating wound. So much blood had come out of the dead Ultramarines and Dark Angels that there was almost a pressurised tidal flow along the Communication's floor. The darkness stank of blood – the blood of good Space Marines.

Curze paused for a second, a towering, skeletal shadow in the twilight, one clawed hand raised, clutching steaming ropes of Auguston's viscera as some ragged trophy.

'I'm not dead yet, you bastard,' Auguston spluttered, bubbles of blood-froth bursting at his lips. Soaked almost head to foot in his own gore, he came at Curze with the executioner's sword clenched in his right fist.

From inside the candle-lit Chapel of Memorial, the sounds of the Night Haunter's campaign of terror could be distinctly heard: the alarms, the frantic vox, the sounds of running feet, gunfire, the random detonation of grenades and other devices from the east, the west, from every quarter.

'It sounds as though a war rages through the Fortress,' said the vision of Warsmith Dantioch.

'Be thankful you are not here,' replied Alexis Polux. 'I have heard many tales of Curze's malevolent and vicious talents, but this night he seems to be excelling himself.'

Polux glanced around as power failed in the hallway outside the chapel. He could smell burning. He drew his bolt pistol, favouring his right hand, not his healing new one.

'I believe our audience for the day is over,' said Polux. 'I must take my leave and assist my brothers in halting this madness.'

'Then I bid you farewell in your efforts, Polux,' said the warsmith.

Polux glanced back at Dantioch icily, as if the earnest wishes of an Iron Warrior were more of a damnation than a blessing.

Three Ultramarines suddenly entered the chapel, weapons drawn, hunting for targets. When they sighted Polux, they lowered their aim.

'Has he come this way?' demanded the officer.

'Curze? No,' replied Polux.

'This area must be secured,' the officer told the two legionaries with him.

'You think he's close?' Polux asked, walking towards him.

'He's everywhere,' the officer replied grimly. 'The order came "Kill all the shadows". I thought… I thought that was nonsense at first. But he is like a daemon.'

'He is a son of the Emperor,' Dantioch said from the lustrous vision of Sotha's tuning floor behind them. 'He is a demigod. It is not possible to overestimate his potential.'

Dantioch had risen uneasily from his high-backed chair and come to the very edge of the communication field.

'Beware,' he said suddenly, looking around as he responded to the empathic vibrations of the quantum field. 'My dear brothers, beware–'

All the candles in the chapel blew out. The sudden gloom was wreathed with tendrils of grey smoke roiling from the wicks. Now the greater proportion of light came from the polished cavern on

Sotha, falling into the night-struck chapel through the communication field, and illuminated the room in an uncanny fashion.

The chapel had four sets of double doors, one at each compass point. The doors at the north end splintered open, demolished by brute force. Two figures came through, locked together, reeling across the chapel's broad, paved floor. One was First Master Auguston, a raw-headed spectre drenched from head to foot in blood, Holguin's long blade in his hand. The other was darkness manifest – a bigger, crueller, more elongated shape, an insubstantial horror, the fleeting ragged shadow left on the ground when a rook flies fast across a winter sky.

Polux and the Ultramarines rushed forward. The combatants were so interlocked that it was impossible to take a shot without risking Auguston. Polux hesitated, watching in horror. The Night Haunter seemed as a wraith, a mosaic, a suggestion of claws, of a ragged cloak, of long hair straggled and streaming, of a face white as a bared skull, of a black leering mouth.

'He's here!' the Ultramarines officer yelled into his vox. 'The chapel! The chapel!'

Auguston fell, broken, spent. He landed on his knees and, for an instant, Polux could see the appalling damage that had been wrought upon him. The First Master had been ripped open and gutted, half his face torn off. That Auguston was still moving spoke to his courage and transhuman thresholds.

The executioner's sword was no longer in the First Master's hand. Hurled, it crossed the chapel like a spear, and impaled the Ultramarines officer through the neck before he could repeat his call. He fell, drowning noisily in his own blood, air whistling out of the holes in his throat.

Polux and the two Ultramarines opened fire, but there seemed to be nothing to hit.

'For Terra's sake, Polux!' Dantioch yelled from the edge of

the communication field. 'Flee! You can't fight him. Flee now! Regroup!'

Claws came out of the smoking darkness and sheared through one of the Ultramarines. The other ran forward, firing repeated shots that hit nothing except his slain comrade. Darkness twisted around him, and his head turned through one hundred and eighty degrees with a brittle crack. The Ultramarine fell across his comrade's corpse.

'Polux! Run, brother! Run!' Dantioch yelled in exasperation.

Polux had frozen. He turned slowly, bolt pistol raised, darkness melting and flowing around him. Silence hissed and breathed like a living thing. He could feel the monster close at hand. He could feel stinking evil circling him in the darkness. Nearby, Auguston let out a terrible gurgling sound. Spasms shook his kneeling form as death finally overwhelmed him. He toppled onto his side.

'You've killed many tonight, monster,' Polux told the darkness, still turning, still hunting. 'None I doubt as great a warrior as that man now expired. None I doubt that put up so furious a fight against your evil. I hope I last half as long.'

The silence breathed.

'Moreover,' said Polux, 'I hope I bathe in your blood before the night is done.'

'To your left!' Dantioch yelled.

Polux swung and fired. He heard something. Had he actually made contact? Drawn blood?

'To your right!' Dantioch shouted.

Polux turned again and fired two more rounds. The warsmith was using the field's empathic vibrations to read the darkness and detect the Night Haunter's movements.

'Where now?' Polux yelled back. 'Where is he?'

'At your back!' Dantioch roared.

Polux wheeled, but he was not fast enough. He took a glancing blow that knocked him to the floor, hard. The bolt pistol skittered away from him across the flagstones.

'*Move!*' Dantioch cried.

Polux rolled sideways desperately. Claws came out of nothingness, sweeping in a downstroke that split the flagstones where he had been lying.

He struggled forward on hands and knees, groping for his fallen weapon.

'No! Keep moving!' Dantioch yelled.

Polux hurled himself aside again as the claws came again and again. He was almost on top of the fallen Ultramarine. Heedless, frantic, Polux wrenched the executioner's sword out of the man's neck.

'Left! Left!' Dantioch cried.

Polux struck left with the long blade, once, twice.

'Ahead!'

Polux swung another blow. With this one, he felt a contact through the hilt. Speckles of black blood dotted the flagstones. He had left a mark. He would make a good account of his death, as Auguston had.

'Right! And behind!' Dantioch shouted.

Polux put his weight into the sword as he turned, and felt the heavy blade rebound off claws. There was a shower of sparks as the Caliban-forged steel deflected Curze's talons. Polux followed the block with another swing, and then another wild strike, hoping to keep the monster at bay.

The Dark Angel's sword was so large that Polux realised he was instinctively using both hands; old hand and new, clamped expertly around the grip.

He feinted left and then chopped into the darkness to the right, and then ahead.

'Guide me, warsmith! Where is he?'

'There. To your left!' Dantioch exclaimed, pointing uselessly at the dark within the darkness.

Polux struck hard to his left. He could smell the stink of something in the gloom, feel the heat of its rage. It was an unwashed smell, the smell of a diseased animal. It was like fighting all the beasts of Inwit's nightside at once.

'Left. Now!'

Polux roared at the effort as he struck with the blade. He connected again. He felt it.

'Did I cut you?' he asked the darkness. 'Do you bleed?'

The answer was a blow to the face that smashed Polux to the floor. Dazed, he tried to recover. His mouth was full of blood.

He could hear Dantioch yelling his name, telling him to move. He couldn't clear his head.

Another blow, a kick most likely, caught him in the belly, and sent him rolling across the chapel floor. The sword was no longer in his grasp. There was no air in his lungs. He spat blood.

He had ended up right at the edge of the communication field, bathed in the eerie light of Sotha. Dantioch was standing over him, yelling in helpless rage and frustration, apparently centimetres away yet actually light years distant. The warsmith's anguish was terrible: he could do nothing but watch, and cry at Polux to get up, and scream obscenities at the thing in the dark.

Polux tried to rise.

Everything went very still. He could hear Curze breathing, panting like a dog. He was aware of the Night Haunter beside him, standing over him, the tips of the long, long talons slowly, almost delicately, scraping across Polux's armour, about to flex and strike.

'Yes, I bleed,' rasped a death-rattle voice, 'but not as much as you are about to, Imperial Fist.'

Polux flinched, braced for the kill-stroke.

A gauntlet seized his left hand and pulled. It pulled with

immense power. It pulled him sidelong and out of the way, so that Curze's scything deathblow missed entirely.

Polux looked up to see who could have entered the fight and intervened. But only three were present: Polux, the shadow of Curze and the warsmith.

Dantioch had a tight grasp on Polux's new left hand. The air was cool, and smelled entirely different. The acoustics around him had changed. Polux was no longer in the chapel.

He was on the tuning floor on Sotha.

'Dantioch…?'

'I don't have an answer…' the warsmith replied.

They looked back. Curze, a towering, leering shade, cheated of his prey, gazed back from the darkness of the chapel. He reached out a handful of talons and tried to touch them, but they were as solid as smoke. Where Polux had passed across, Curze could not.

'You will tell me,' Curze hissed, spittle flecking between his blackened teeth, 'how this is done. How this is achieved?'

'The faith and will of good men,' replied Dantioch. 'When they stand together against infamy, the galaxy fights for them.'

'I would hardly put my trust in the galaxy,' Curze hissed. He was so thin, so tall, a cadaverous herald of death. 'I have seen what it dreams of, and it is quite run mad.'

His leering smile faded away.

'Now come back where I can kill you,' he said.

'I believe neither of us will accept your offer, Night Lord,' said Dantioch. 'Furthermore, I believe you are about to have more pressing matters to concern you. Auguston and Polux have between them kept you here longer than you meant to stay.'

Behind Curze, light flooded into the chapel as two sets of doors opened, the south and the west entrances. Framed in the south, blade drawn and flanked by Ultramarines, stood the Avenging Son.

'Back off,' Guilliman told his men. Rage smouldered from him like a heat haze. 'This wretch is mine.'

'No,' said the Lion, leaving his Dark Angels at the threshold of the west doorway and striding forward. 'He's *ours*.'

'Well now,' murmured Konrad Curze, hooking down the left-hand corner of his lower lip thoughtfully with the tip of one extravagant, bloodied claw. 'Interesting.'

16

BLOOD BROTHERS

'I may call you kin, but you are un-kind. You are entirely not of me.'
– Ferrus Manus to Konrad Curze, reported

CURZE STEPPED AWAY from the communication field and faced his brothers. Guilliman and the Lion approached him, Guilliman to his left, the Lion to his right.

Guilliman clutched his gladius – not his most magnificent weapon, but a favoured piece. He had made more kills than he had truly cared about with that utilitarian blade than any fine sword in his arsenal. He had a gleaming combat shield strapped to his left arm. He was bare-headed.

The Lion's hair was loose, his jaw set. He held a charged longsword that Farith Redloss had passed to him. It was known far and wide as the Lion Sword, said to have been forged on Terra by the Emperor's own armourers. It shone with a pale inner light.

'Not a man intervenes,' Guilliman said to the Ultramarines and Dark Angels crowded at the chapel doors.

'This is between us,' the Lion agreed. 'Farith, you may strike down any other who tries to engage.'

'You heard that, Gorod,' said Guilliman. 'The same applies.'

Both Gorod of the Invictus and Farith Redloss made murmurs of acceptance.

'You do not come to my world and do this,' said Guilliman, stalking Curze. 'You do not enter my house and do this.'

'I do what I please, brother,' Curze replied. They could smell the stink of his breath from across the chamber.

The Lion glanced sidelong at Auguston's pitiful remains.

'You have piled up too many corpses this night, Konrad. My legionaries, and too many of Roboute's. This warrior, the Master of the First, is an especially grievous loss.'

'He was pugnacious,' Curze hissed. 'Even when I'd taken out his gizzard and lights, he kept walking.'

'Bastard!' Guilliman snapped.

'Master Auguston fought like the champions of legend, my lord,' said Polux from the gleaming field. 'He defied death to fight on. I have never seen its like.'

'And you have defied corporeal physics to escape me, Imperial Fist,' Curze whispered, his words issuing as though they had been ground out between millstones. 'Come. Does no one else wonder at that?'

Guilliman was close to Curze. He began to loop and spin his gladius.

'Brother has killed brother,' he said. 'As we were raised, that is unthinkable, but brother has killed brother. Every time, it has been a heretic son who has slain a devoted brother: Ferrus, Corax, Vulkan.'

'Ahh now,' murmured Curze. 'Tut tut tut, Roboute. Vulkan lives.'

'Then I rejoice,' said Guilliman, 'but I believe it is past time that the heretics paid a price. A blood price. I think it is past time that a devoted son put a heretic in the damned ground.'

'Agreed, sevenfold,' said the Lion in a low, hunting voice.

Curze faced them. He stood tall, taller than either of them – a stark figure of lean, long bones and hollowed frame. He looked like a starved giant, towering yet emaciated. His tattered black cloak flowed from his shoulders to the ground like the furled wings of a wounded bird. His slender arms hung at his sides, the huge, slack power claws making his hands disproportionately long. He tilted his head back, his hair lank. He closed his eyes.

'Brother,' he said. 'And you, brother. Come and get me.'

Guilliman surged forward. The Lion was faster. Guilliman was robust and dazzling, but the Lion was elegant. The Lion Sword described a buzzing arc in the air as it circled, leaving a bright after-image briefly stamped on the vision of all the legionaries watching.

The blade scythed at Curze's head. He did not move.

Then he was smoke.

The power claws of Curze's right hand snapped out and drove aside the stinging bite of the Lion Sword. The claws of his left met Guilliman's gladius and deflected it.

Guilliman struck again, driven by fury, and cut through something.

It was only shadow. Only the tatter of a cloak.

Talons snapped back at him. He raised his shield. Razored claws ripped sparks off its surface and shredded its edges.

Guilliman hacked again. Nothing. Shadow. *Shadow*!

The Lion rotated like a dancer, and swung the famous Lion Sword sidelong at Curze with a two-handed grip. Curze ducked, evaded, and rotated in turn, punching away Guilliman's next strike as he did so. The Lion tilted and swung his sizzling blade in a strike designed to unseam Curze from the groin to the throat.

But Curze was no longer there.

He had flickered left and blocked the upswing. Then he smashed his hand into the Lion's face.

Blood burst from the strike. A talon had punched clean through the side of the Lion's neck. The Lion reeled backwards, his hand clamped to the wound to staunch it.

Some of his men mobbed forward in alarm.

'*No!*' the Lion yelled.

Guilliman slammed his ragged shield into Curze and drove him backwards. He stabbed twice with the gladius, rapidly, like a striking snake, and drew blood on the second jab.

'Bastard!' Curze hissed.

His talons struck Guilliman and knocked him aside, leaving four long gouges in his chestplate.

Guilliman recovered, sweeping in low with his blade, and then high on the return. Struck, Curze spun away and fell. When he rose, his right cheek was open to the bone.

'Now we start in earnest,' he hissed.

'Now we *finish* in earnest,' the Lion spat, coming at Curze with his sword ready.

Curze moved again, sliding into darkness. The blade ripped through smoke and shadow. The Lion turned and engaged again, striking once, twice, three times, each blow blocked by swift and savage claws.

'Oh sweet Terra,' Polux said. He looked at the warsmith. 'Do you feel that?'

'I do,' agreed Dantioch. 'I do most assuredly.'

The quantum field's empathic effect was resonating through both of them.

They could both feel it. A truth, Curze's truth. The efforts of Auguston and Polux had *not* delayed Curze too long. They had *not* kept him in place so that he might be trapped.

He had built this as a trap all along, a trap to kill one or more of his brothers.

'Get out, my lords!' Polux yelled. 'Get out now! He has wired the Chapel! Get out, for the love of mercy!'

Driven back by Curze's claws, Guilliman looked at the figures of Polux and the warsmith in the glow of the communication field.

'He has *what*?'

'*Get out, my lord!*' Polux screamed.

Curze knocked the Lion's blade aside.

He paused, and his black-toothed grin reappeared. It was a grin of triumph.

'I have, since birth, been a staunch friend of death,' he said. 'I have learned that death is lonely, and so enjoys making new and lasting friends. Roboute? Great Lion? Let me make your introduction.'

Curze clapped his clawed hands.

The seventy-five grenades wired around the eaves of the Chapel triggered.

In a sheet of white flame and fury, the Chapel of Memorial ceased to be.

17

HEARTH AND HOME

'Death does not discriminate. It is so even-handed,
so scrupulously fair, that it seems not fair at all.'
– Eeron Kleve, X Legion Iron Hands

'TELL ME, I implore you, what was that?' Euten asked the captain of
the praecental guard.

Vodun Badorum shook his head.

'Mamzel, it is hard to say. Reports from the Fortress are… con-
tradictory. Some say it is the Night Haunter, unleashed upon the
Castrum, others claim it is an entire *host* of night haunters. There
are reports of attacks and incidents on every level of the Fortress
and–'

'But you cannot tell me what the blast was that shook these very
walls?' she snapped.

Badorum shook his head again. At his side, four of his praecentals were urgently conducting conversations by vox, trying to
gather accurate intelligence from the Fortress.

'Then I will trust my own eyes,' Euten announced, and stood up abruptly. Badorum had, previously, ordered her to be escorted into the private wing of the Residency for safety, but now she marched straight across the outer hall to the head of the main staircase. He hurried after her, calling her name. The August Chamberlain Principal moved with surprising speed when she wanted to.

Down below, at the foot of the staircase, warriors milled and waited. They looked up at her as she strode past. They were all Legiones Astartes, all castaway visitors to Macragge from the Shattered Legions. The lower halls of the Residency had become their barracks.

Like her, they awaited news.

'Mamzel. My lady!' one called.

Euten did not stop for him. She crossed the landing, opened the glazed doors to the west balcony and stepped into the night. Badorum followed her.

The night was especially dark. The Pharos glowed frostily like a white lamp in fog. A swathe of black air hung across the great Civitas below the wall.

From the unlit balcony, in the cold night, they had a direct view to the Porta Hera and the cyclopean eastern ramparts of the Fortress proper. Smoke and, in places, flames rose from the Fortress at several locations. They were all dwarfed by the huge coil of underlit smoke belching from the inner part of the Fortress into the night. It reminded Euten of the great, grumbling volcanoes in the far north of Macragge.

'Great Darknesses!' she whispered, that old Illyrian curse. 'What has been done?'

'Mamzel, you must come inside,' said Badorum.

'The Chapel of Memorial is burning, Vodun,' she said, staring at the appalling view.

'I think perhaps so,' said Badorum. 'Or perhaps the Praetorium.'

'It is the Chapel,' she insisted. She turned to look at him.

'We must know something of what is transpiring in the Fortress. Guilliman is in there.'

'And the Lion too, both gone to hunt their fell brother, who makes war on us tonight.'

'War. Mischief. Dissent. Terror,' Euten said, uttering each word as though she were spitting out pebbles. 'The Night Haunter searches for one victim above all others: Ultramar. Macragge Civitas is the last stable, loyal place in the galaxy, Vodun, for our lord has made it that way, steadfast when all else withers and fails. This is what Curze has come to murder – our peace, our faith, our fortitude.'

'They will stop him,' said Badorum.

'Will they? Or by dawn, will there be panic and rioting in the streets of the city? Will terror reign and blight the hearts of the citizenry? Will Macragge catch afire and blaze, the last true stronghold lost?'

'No, my lady,' he said. 'Come, please, I fear it is not safe. Come, please, within.'

Euten allowed herself to be walked back into the Residency.

'My lord has taken almost all the Ultramarines on the Castrum into the Fortress with him, and he has in addition his noble brother and good strengths of Dark Angels legionaries. Furthermore, the gates and base of the wall are guarded to prevent access to the Civitas.'

'The monster Curze got in, Vodun. He can get out again, I expect.'

'With every passing second, he has less and less surprise on his side, mamzel,' Badorum replied.

She stopped at the head of the staircase and looked down at the patiently waiting Space Marines: Salamanders, Iron Hands, Raven Guard, a White Scar or two.

'What have we here, Vodun?' she asked.

'My praecentals hold the Residency, mam,' the commander replied. 'Lord Guilliman's direct order. He made me pull my men back from the Fortress.'

'Because the praecentals would be outclassed?'

'This hunt is a task for the Legiones Astartes at the very least. It is no small thing to corner and kill a primarch.'

'We have not used our full resource,' she said. She took a few steps down the staircase and addressed the waiting warriors.

'My dear battle-brothers, worthy souls – this night is a grim one, a darkness through which we must abide and come out whole, together.'

'We have come through much already, my lady,' said one of the Iron Hands. 'We have learned to endure. It is the steel in us.'

Many of those around him nodded.

'Well spoken, Sardon Karaashison,' Euten said.

'We are yet in ignorance, lady,' said a Raven Guard captain near to Karaashison. 'We are merely obliged to wait, robbed of action and purpose.'

Euten nodded. This was a problem that had yet to be overcome. Since the light of the Pharos had been turned on Macragge, nigh on a thousand souls had come to the city from the Shattered Legions of Isstvan. They were sequestered in the Residency, and in several other barracks across the city. They were a resource of great potential, and their resolve and determination, having been witnesses to treason and atrocity, was beyond doubt.

A way had not yet been found, however, to resolve them into one force. Guilliman had begun to find duties for some, as suited their specialisms, and it was, of course, straightforward to place Iron Hands with Iron Hands and Raven Guard with Raven Guard. But to alloy them more permanently threw up problems of differences in Legion practices and methods, of motivations and loyalties, of intentions and desires. Would the flesh-spare leaders of the Iron Hands form a command backbone to a force of survivors? Would the Raven Guard or the Salamanders be content to follow that? Could command be shared? Could orthodoxies be matched? Could the survivors be inducted as additional squads to the Ultramarines or the Dark Angels?

As things stood, the Shattered Legions were hard to wield as one force. In an emergency, such as the one that presently hung like a shroud across Macragge, they could not be deployed with unified effect as could the Ultramarines or the Dark Angels.

The question of it had vexed Guilliman. Euten had seen him struggling to resolve the issue many times in the previous few days.

'The individual character and characteristics of the Legions is what invests them with their strengths, and makes them wonders,' he had said to her. 'The idiosyncrasies of composition and method are pre- cisely why there are eighteen Legions, rather than one Legion eighteen times the size. But it is a weakness too, a mortal flaw, when it comes to forging them together as one. It makes one long for a formal, martial codification that would burnish away the rough edges, clean out the differences, and provide for a perfect, easy fit.'

'I sympathise with your ignorance, Verano Ebb,' said Euten. 'We all dwell in darkness this evening. I will tell you what I know, which is too little. Through guile and skill, and by exploiting the good faith of good men, Konrad Curze has made a visitation to our city this day.'

There was a general murmur of disquiet and anger.

Badorum, at Euten's side, held up a hand for quiet.

'To my best knowledge,' the chamberlain continued, 'he is loose in the Fortress, seeking to undermine the authority of Ultramar by breaking morale and the rule of law, and by magnifying hatred and fear.'

'These were always his weapons,' said an Iron Hands officer in mourning robes.

'They always were, Eeron Kleve,' said Euten with a solemn nod. 'And they always shall be, until he is stopped or finished. My lord Guilliman and the noble lord of the Dark Angels are even now in the Fortress hunting for him. I pity any man, any demigod even, who has the like of those two at his heels.'

Another general murmur filled the entryway, but this time it was more emphatic and eager.

'I dare say,' said Euten, 'that against a foe like the Night Haunter there is no such thing as too much help. If you can, go from here to the Fortress and add your power to the hunt. But hear me well… Do not do this thing if you are not prepared to respect and follow the commands of Ultramarines or Dark Angels officers. The field is theirs tonight. Order and discipline must be maintained, especially against a foe whose singular purpose is to breed disorder and chaos. There is no room for pride or individual action, battle-brothers. If you can obey and serve, then my lord will be glad of you.'

'We will not abuse this trust, my lady,' said Eeron Kleve.

'Horus, cursed be his name, has done one good deed in this great treachery,' said Verano Ebb. 'He has made the greatest and truest sworn comrades of those he has wounded.'

'It gladdens my heart to hear it on this cold night, sirs,' said Euten. 'As Chamberlain Principal, I own the full authority of the Lord of Ultramar in his absence. So with that power and pitch of command, I charge you all to go from here to the gates of the Fortress, and make perfect war upon the Night Haunter. Serve Guilliman, serve the Lion, and serve Macragge. Let no disobedience weaken this endeavour. May your blades, before dawn comes, run wet with traitor blood.'

The gathered legionaries, all looking up at her, made immediate salute, crashing mailed fists against their breastplates.

'We march for Macragge!' declared Timur Gantulga.

It was odd to hear the cry uttered in a strong Chogorian accent, but in an instant the declaration was echoed with vigour by his fellow White Scars, and then by every battle-brother in the hall. The war cry of Ultramar was coloured and invested by the accents of cold-hearted Medusa, of lofty Deliverance, of feral Fenris, of fire-forged Nocturne, of glacial Inwit and distant, holy Terra.

'My lord Badorum,' said Euten, turning to him. 'Make it known by my seal and authority, via all channels, that this force of warriors is coming to the Fortress to render aid. Have the gates opened for them, and have them admitted and assigned without delay. Let us not waste this intent.'

'At once,' he assured her.

'And, Badorum,' Euten added, 'make sure my lord Guilliman personally knows that I am sending this strength. Tell him they are of one resolve and ready for his command.'

'I will,' he said.

He had neither the heart nor the words to tell her that, since the blast that had ripped through the Chapel of Memorial ten minutes past, no contact had been made with Guilliman or the Lion at all.

'GOROD!'

The fief commander of the bodyguard turned his massive armoured form and saw Titus Prayto approaching him. Prayto was limping and clutched a deep and bloody injury to his side.

'Tell me,' said Prayto.

'I tell you squarely, Prayto,' rumbled the Cataphractii, 'I am a man of no honour. I have failed in my duty. My oath was to protect him, and I have not done so.'

He looked at the Master of the Librarius.

'Guilliman is dead,' Gorod said. 'So too the worthy Lion.'

Behind them, across the courtyard, the great Chapel of Memorial was blazing in the night. Its roof and upper walls had collapsed. The heat was so intense that even armoured legionaries had been driven back while rescue crews were summoned.

'No,' said Prayto.

'I may wish on every minute of every day for the rest of my life that it was not a truth to be spoken,' said Gorod, 'but it is plain. Curze has struck the foulest blow of all. He rigged the chapel, and made it so that our lord and the Lion found him there. Curze was bait in his own trap. He has murdered our master, and with him the noble king of Caliban. I only hope that this crime has cost him his life.'

'No,' Prayto repeated.

'Why do you refute me?' asked Gorod. 'With my own eyes—'

'Drakus,' said Prayto, 'I have, perhaps at penalty to my own soundness of thought, touched the mind of Konrad Curze. He showed it to me, so that I might know the nightmares that live there and be driven mad. Drakus, listen. I feel it still… still, in my head!'

Wincing and drawing sharp breath as he moved, Prayto looked around.

'Curze lives. And if he escaped this conflagration, then so could better men.'

'He knew what was coming. He planned his exit.'

'If Lord Guilliman had died, Drakus, I swear I would have felt that too. He trusts me and lets me wait at his shoulder. I would have felt the instant of his annihilation.'

'Then I do not know how or where he lives,' said Gorod. 'Forgive me, brother, but you have taken a great wound. I wonder if your perceptions are as sharp as they might be?'

'In this, they are.'

Farith Redloss approached them. The Dreadwing commander showed no expression in his face.

'A signal has come, of reinforcement sent from the Residency. You are to open the western gates. There is no trace of Curze, nor of...'

His voice fell away, wordless.

'Master Prayto declares them all living,' said Gorod, 'despite the evidence of this inferno.'

'Then Master Prayto gladdens my heart. You have hard proof, brother?'

'I have my mind,' said Prayto. 'We must find them. Indeed, we must find Curze in particular. If he is still at liberty, then he will use this great confusion to sow greater woes. Let us open the gates, bring in the reinforcements, and lock the Fortress down entirely. I will attempt to focus. Perhaps with the aid of other Librarians I can locate the villain in the darkness.'

'You need attention,' said Gorod. 'That wound must be dressed and bound. You should go to the medicae hall at once–'

'The medicae hall has suffered attack too,' said Farith Redloss. 'I heard that it was sealed while the trouble was contained.'

'Wait,' said Prayto. 'Curze struck all over the Fortress, but the Residency too? So far I had not heard of his acts extending beyond the precinct of the Fortress.'

'I say only what I have heard,' said Farith Redloss.

'Are we haunted by more than one foe tonight?' asked Gorod.

'Let us concentrate on the one we know about,' said Titus Prayto.

THE EASTERN GATES of the Fortress rumbled open, letting the stench of fire and smoke out into the cold night air. Attending without, on the pavements and colonnades that linked the Residency to the

Fortress, the battle-brothers of the Shattered Legions roused and moved inside.

Niax Nessus awaited them, with senior officers of his Legion and the Dark Angels.

'We are glad of your arms,' Nessus said directly. 'Confusion is our enemy. We have good reason to believe that the Night Haunter is still active within the bounds of the Fortress. He must be found. You will divide into search squads, and pair each squad with a team of Ultramarines or Dark Angels. You will move in concert, watch each other's backs, and confirm each other's sweeps.'

'I have assigned areas,' said Holguin. The Dark Angels had, it was clear, taken an almost crippling blow in combat. His determination to proceed was inspiring. 'Brothers, Curze is evil and cunning manifest. At any sighting, sound the warning, stay in formation and maintain discipline. He has devoured too many good lives tonight by declaring misrule and disarray.'

'He is a killer, right enough,' Nessus agreed. 'Take no chances with your lives, or the lives of the brothers around you.'

Ultramarines officers moved forward and began marshalling the reinforcement force.

'I have studied his art,' Gantulga said to Kleve as they awaited assignment.

'His art?'

'Little is written of the Night Lord's methods, but what is recorded is stimulating.' The White Scar paused. 'He fancies himself a hunter, a stalker of prey. That is how he styles himself, at least. But it...'

'What, friend?' asked Kleve.

'It is not convincing. I say that as a hunter myself, and as one who knows hunters. What I have seen so far of his work in the Fortress – it is expertise of a sort, but it is not hunting.'

'His design is to spread terror and disruption,' said Kleve.

'And to wound, and to punish,' Gantulga said. 'He risks himself. He places himself at great jeopardy to strike these blows, as though he cares not for his own fate.' He paused and looked back along the gatehouse to where the sentries were preparing to close and bar the eastern gates. The night outside, framed by the massive gate arch, was as cold, black and unfathomable as darkened glass.

'Unless,' he murmured. 'Unless, Eeron Kleve, he *is* a hunter at heart.'

'What do you mean, Gantulga?'

'A hunter takes risks,' said the White Scar, 'but never excessive ones. He always protects himself, so that he may hunt again. A wolf stalks a herd, and perhaps causes panic, so the herdsmen drive the animals into a tight fold and pen them. Does the wolf persist? No. It is too open, too exposed. The herdsmen are alert, and they have gathered in numbers. To try to take from the fold would draw down their slingshots and arrows. That is an unacceptable and unnecessary risk for a hunter. So, while the herdsmen are occupied, guarding the herd, the wolf turns to where they are not – the larder, the granary, the stables, the bird cages.'

Gantulga turned, abruptly, and hurried towards the closing gates.

'What are you doing?' Kleve called after him, starting to follow. 'The chamberlain was quite specific! This is no time for individual action or improvisation! We are here only if we conform to discipline and command! Gantulga! We have a duty!'

The White Scar turned and looked back at the Iron Hands legionary for a second.

'We do,' he said, 'but he's not here. We are here, all of us, circling the herd. He has done what he can, but it is too dangerous for him to be here. There are too many of us. So he has gone where we are not.'

'The Residency,' said Kleve, understanding.

'The Residency,' Gantulga agreed.

HE FOUND A HALL. It was unlit. It was a private place. His eyes saw all the details, despite the darkness. This was a room for trophies and keepsakes, a room where a proud man kept the relics and reminders of his career: books, charts, coats of armour, weapons.

This was not merely a man, though. Even in its raving delirium, his mind recognised that. This was more than a man. This was a master of worlds, a demigod.

Here hung blades of great scale – falchions and broadswords, powered glaives and hooked axes. Here were suits of plate and wargear master-crafted for state occasions. Here were the scrapes and notches of their service. Here were mantles and cloaks, robes and banners, the raiments and decorations of kingship.

He reached out with bloody hands.

The enemy was close.

He needed to be ready.

'HELLO?'

There was no one there.

Euten paused, and then shook her head. Her nerves were taut. She was jumping at shadows.

She had retired to Guilliman's withdrawing chamber, so recently refurbished and repaired that it seemed half-empty. So many items needed to be replaced, and so very many never could be. The walls were bare of paintings. The newly installed cognis-signum cogitator device purred softly, and seemed cold and clinical compared to the ancient machine it had replaced.

She poured herself a drink, a small amasec.

The night was bleak outside the windows, cut only by the baleful glow of the Pharos. She tried to ignore the way the low clouds were side-lit and ruddy from the fires in the Fortress.

She sat, but could not settle. Setting down her glass, she went to the chamber doors. An officer of the praecental guard stood guard outside.

'My lady?'

'I am bothered, Percel,' she said. 'Is there really still no word from our Lord Guilliman? Please, good sir. It has been overlong.'

'I will check again, my lady,' the officer replied.

Euten went back into the room and resumed her seat. Her drink remained untouched. She tapped her fingers on her knee.

Her back ached. Her joints were sore. How miserable it was to be human and old, no matter the sciences that prolonged the mortal span. Euten resented the way that her life and capabilities were slowing down. Oh, to be transhuman in measure – to be so strong, to possess such vitality.

The day is not far off, she thought, when I will be of no more use to him, when I will need to be cared for like a child, and my part in his life will finally be over. Soon thereafter, I will be gone from this vale altogether. Have I done enough for him? I have stayed the course, stayed it well, from the days of Konor to this dark night. Surely I can serve him yet–

A noise. Was that a knock at the chamber door?

'Come?' she called out.

No one came. A cloud passed across the solitary star, briefly.

Why was there still no word from the Fortress?

Euten rose and crossed to the door.

'Percel?'

There was no one in the hall. Glow-globes sizzled softly in their sconces.

He has gone as I ordered, she decided. He has gone to seek word.

The chamberlain went back into the room. She felt that she might fidget herself to death with nervous energy. She felt great agitation. It was ridiculous to be so, in a well-lit chamber, in a fortress-palace, guarded by the best soldiers in Ultramar. It–

She froze.

The name was written plainly on the wall. It had not been there when she had gone to the door. It was there now.

Roboute.

It was written – and Euten knew this even though she knew not how she knew it – in the still-warm blood of Officer Percel.

Horror clenched her. It drove the air from her lungs and the power from her voice. Her heart had never beaten so fast.

On the desk, there was a switch for the alarm. It seemed to be leagues away from her.

She turned slowly, turned in a full circle, waiting to set eyes upon the grinning thing that she knew must be waiting behind her.

There was nothing there. Nothing. *Nothing.*

Yet the letters of her master's name still trickled red down the wall.

'Who is here?' she hissed.

No answer.

'Who? Who is here?'

Nothing.

She looked around, hunting for detail. That name, daubed across the wall.

'I am not afraid of you,' she said. 'I am August Chamberlain Principal of the Five Hundred Worlds, and damaged fiends like you do not frighten me. Show yourself. Be a man and confront me. I dare you.'

What other details had changed while she had gone to the door?

Her glass. *Her glass.* It still sat where she had set it upon the side table, but it was no longer full of amasec. The spirit had gone. The glass was filled with blood.

Terror touched her heart. She could not fight it. Its fingers were like ice. Like a child, she fell to the floor and scrambled behind the nearest piece of furniture, staying low, crawling into shadows. Maybe she could hide. Maybe she could–

Officer Percel was waiting for her beneath the sofa. His severed head at least. His eyes were glazed. His mouth was half-open, as if in the middle of some great and dismaying surprise. He stared back at her from between the sofa's elegant bluewood feet.

Euten recoiled.

There was someone standing over her, right behind her. His shadow fell across her. He was huge, silent and powerful, and he stank of blood and war.

She wanted to ask him, *beg him*, to make it quick, but her voice would not come out at all.

He put a massive hand on her shoulder. She flinched.

'He's here,' the shadow said. 'Stay down.'

She turned and looked up. Axe raised, alert, Faffnr Bludbroder stood over her.

'You stayed,' she whispered.

'We don't leave the hearth,' he replied. He looked down at her. 'Stay down. Run when I tell you. I will protect you with every drop of my blood.'

Still cowering, Euten looked around. As silent as falling snow, the other savage members of Faffnr's pack were creeping into the chamber, weapons ready, ears pricked for any sound or motion. Their silence was extraordinary. They padded like…

…*like wolves on snow.*

Faffnr sighed. 'Now we have it,' he said.

Konrad Curze came out of somewhere. It was not exactly clear where. It might have been a shadow, or a fold of drapery, or even merely a tiny crack in the wall. He manifested. He was monstrously vast, a black shadow, power claws unfurled like the flight feathers of a raven. His hair was a halo of filth. His mouth was impossibly large, a yawning, blackened maw that stretched the thin white flesh of his angular skull as though it would split it. His right cheek was slashed to the bone and clotted with dark blood.

The Wolves went for him without hesitation. Their blades were thirsty.

Only Faffnr stayed his place, loyal Faffnr, covering her, defending her with his blade and body.

'Run now,' he told her.

'I can't run,' she said, barely able to get up.

'*Hjold!* You'll damn well run if I tell you to run, female!'

A blur. Bo Soren swung his axe, but it was stopped dead by curved talons. Shockeye Ffyn lunged with his longsword, but cut only smoke.

Gudson Allfreyer came at the beast, but was smashed aside, spitting blood and broken teeth. Mads Loreson tried to swing, but was blocked by the reeling Allfreyer.

A primarch. A squad of the Legiones Astartes. One locked room. The *same* locked room. How would history repeat itself? How would it be *revised*?

The Wolves were the Emperor's executioners.

But Curze…

Malmur Longreach, spear thrusting, and Salick the Braided, axe low, attacked together. One struck home, for blood spattered the floor and the furniture around Euten, but both were knocked aside. Kuro came in, Biter Herek, then Nido Knifeson.

Blades hammered off armour and drew flinty sparks from whirling claws. Curze grabbed Salick by the throat and threw him across the chamber into the wall. Biter Herek buried his axe in the depths of Curze's darkness. Blood sprayed. Mads Loreson went down on one knee, clutching at his torn throat, trying to stem the blood gushing from it. Kuro Jjordrovk sailed across the chamber and demolished a chair and table as he landed.

Curze was laughing. His pale, harlequin face was split by a maniacal grin of delight in bloodshed. He threw Shockeye Ffyn through the chamber windows, which detonated as one sheet like a glass bomb. He kicked Biter Herek to the ground and cracked his skull with a vicious, armoured, driving elbow. He took Gudson's sword away, broke it across the Wolf's back, then drove the broken blade into Bo Soren's cheek. Malmur grappled with him, and Nido Knifeson joined him.

Both were cast aside, bones snapping and armour cracking.

'I told you to run,' Faffnr said.

'I'm sorry,' Euten replied.

'Last chance,' he said, raising his axe and rushing the Night Haunter.

Euten found her feet. She got up and tried to run. A Wolf, bleeding and writhing, lay in her path, another to her left, and a third against the wall, who appeared dead.

The doors were close.

Something flew over her, a huge thing. It hit the doors ahead of her and smashed them down entirely.

It was Faffnr Bludbroder.

The pack-leader lay in the wreckage of the doors, and did not rise.

Euten stopped. She turned.

Konrad Curze bowed to her. He was a smile made of shadows and smoke and sickness. He was wickedness itself.

'Tarasha,' he sighed. A smile should not be that wide.

'He will kill you for this,' she said.

'He's dead, Tarasha,' Curze replied.

All her strength left her. Grief felled her. She dropped to her knees.

'No...'

'I killed him,' Curze cooed. 'Roboute and the Lion both. I have studied his story, of course. As the little emperor he pretends to be, he does so chronicle himself. I have heard of you. Tarasha Euten, Chamberlain Principal, and to all intents a mother to him. A *mother.'*

Curze sighed.

'Thanks to the genius of my father, my kind does not enjoy the luxury of mothers. You are rare. You are a *rare and obscene thing,* you ragged witch. I wish Roboute had been alive to suffer the damage of your death.'

Euten rose to her full height and looked the monster in the eye.

'Go to hell, you bastard,' she said.

Curze drew back his claws.

Something entered the room. It entered with great speed and force. Euten felt the rush of it, the shockwave. She recoiled, reeling, stunned.

Suddenly, her killer was no longer in front of her.

Curze was being driven towards the exploded window by an elemental force.

It was clad in mismatched armour plate and mail, all purloined from Guilliman's trophy hall, armour built to fit a primarch's scale. It wielded a battle mace, a fine piece that Roboute had used early in the Great Crusade.

The elemental force, raging and screaming, its skin sheened with blood, smashed Curze backwards and drove the mace into his slender chest.

The elemental force had a name, though it did not know it or remember it.

That name was Vulkan.

Locked together, he and Curze tumbled out of the chamber windows and into the precipitous gloom beyond.

18
DEATH DENIED

*'There may, perforce, be one end of time, one end
of the long thread, that playeth out to such dimension that it
out-spans all things, and all things loseth their measure beside it:
the edges of our cosmos, the puissance of our gods,
the endeavours and limits of life, all would be found less
than the extremity of time. Indeed, so far may time extendeth
that it outstretches even death itself, so death itself must perish.'*

– from *The Night Sound of Insects*, by the Sage of Sanaa [antiquity]

THE PRIMARCHS, WRESTLING and falling like rebel angels, dropped into the night.

The lower roofs of the Residency slammed up to meet them. Their mutual impact shattered tiles and broke finials from the caps of the roofline. Near to the site of their impact, the sprawled body of Shockeye Ffyn lay at an angle over a gutter pipe where he had landed before their plunge.

They were still a long way up. The Residency was of considerable height. Behind them lay the Aegis Wall and the even more significant drop off the Castrum of the Palaeopolis into the out-spread

Civitas. To the west of them, the night wind blew in thick smoke from the burning Fortress.

The jarring force of impact barely interrupted their fight. Vulkan rolled across the broken tiles and rose at once, swinging the mace; it wasn't a warhammer, but it was close enough to register in his damaged mind. Curze squealed in pain and indignation, and writhed at his attacker, lashing out with his talons.

'You live! You live!' shrieked the Night Haunter. 'Still your damned life plagues me! Still you won't let me take it! Why do you still deny me? Why won't you let me take it? Eventually even *you* must die!'

Vulkan's answering howl was incoherent. He slammed his mace home, and drove it against warding claws. Sparks billowed out in the night wind.

'I have killed two brothers tonight!' Curze yelled. 'A third would make this hour most perfect in outrage! And your life, yours of all lives, so inextinguishable, would be the greatest trophy of all!'

Vulkan did not understand the words that were being yelled at him. He understood very little. His mind had been destroyed by unbearable pain, by suffering, by the meticulous and ingenious torment that Curze had forced him to endure over a period of months. Curze had annihilated Vulkan's spirit and sanity, but he had been unable to terminate his actual life.

He had discovered that Vulkan possessed one inhuman trait that the other primarchs did not. This vexed Curze immeasurably. It offered a challenge that a being raised on murder, blood and terror could not resist.

All Vulkan saw was his tormentor, his abuser, the man who had killed him over and over again in search of a way of killing him permanently; the brother who had, through the uttermost cruelty, revealed Vulkan's immortal gift. The rage to exact vengeance consumed him.

The claws of Curze's left hand ripped across Vulkan, stripping away part of his borrowed plate in silvered metal shavings. Vulkan drove the head of his mace into Curze's left shoulder-plate with a swift, short-arced blow, and then swung the weapon sideways into Curze's head.

The haft, not the head, caught Curze across the cheek, and sent him reeling. He tried to rally, and turn to check his opponent, but shattered tiles slithered under his feet. He fought for a second to control his position.

Vulkan exploited that second, and drove a ferocious two-handed swing into Curze's wavering body.

Plasteel cracked. Curze screamed, knocked clean off the slope of the roof. He pitched and fell, dropping ten metres onto the next shelf of the Residency roofscape. Grey slates, mined and shaped in the high peaks of Hera's Crown, burst under him like sheet ice, throwing chips and slivers into the air.

Arms wide, Vulkan leapt off the roof and dropped feetfirst. Curze was not going to escape him.

On the slates below, Curze stirred. He looked up, saw Vulkan plunging towards him, and rolled desperately to avoid being crushed beneath his brother's armoured bulk. Vulkan's landing shattered more of the slates, and sent some large pieces whipping into the wind as shrapnel.

Instantly braced, Vulkan swung from the waist and drove his mace's head at the sprawled Curze. The Night Haunter half-leapt, half-folded himself aside. The mace punched a significant hole through the roof, but the head wedged there for a second.

Curze retaliated, laughing with insane glee. He embraced Vulkan with his left arm, pulling their faces almost tenderly cheek to cheek. He drove his right arm in, a sharp understroke, palm up.

All four primary finger points stabbed into Vulkan's side, coring through armour, underplate, flex sub-suit and directly into his torso. Blood gouted. Vulkan's head snapped back and he clenched in pain, his blazing eyes closed. Curze held onto him, pulled the claws out, and repeated the stab.

Vulkan wrenched himself away. His side, left leg, and the tiles beneath him ran with blood. He staggered, and then fell onto the roof with a clatter of armour and cracking slates. He twitched violently and fell still.

Curze spat out clots of blood and phlegm. The wind whipped at his filthy hair.

'See?' he demanded. 'This is death. Learn to accept it, brother!'

Vulkan's eyes snapped open.

'Oh,' said Konrad Curze in disappointment. 'That was quick.'

GANTULGA RACED UP the central staircase of the Residency, sword in hand, with Eeron Kleve close behind him. Vodun Badorum and details of praecental guardsmen were already rushing to the private quarters across the landing and along the main corridor.

'He's here!' Gantulga roared at them. 'Have a care. He's in this house!'

'Curze?' asked the guard commander.

'Of course, Curze!' Kleve growled.

Badorum barked orders to his men, orchestrating their advance. Weapons snapped up, aimed and ready. Powerfeeds whined to charge.

'We have heard a terrible commotion from the private quarters,' Badorum told the White Scar and the Iron Hands officer.

'Get behind us,' Kleve told him, 'and ready those plasma weapons to fire.'

Gantulga led the way, slowing his advance to a prowl, his sword raised and ready. Kleve had his rotor cannon braced and armed. He swung the heavy thing from side to side, hunting for a target.

The main doors to the inner rooms had been smashed down.

Euten knelt in the wreckage of the doorway, wiping blood from the brow of the crumpled, half-dead Faffnr Bludbroder.

'Mamzel!' Kleve cried, and ran to her. Gantulga flew past them into the chamber, and took a quick inventory of the scene. The place was wrecked, the floor littered with hurt and dying Space Wolves. The night's cold air was gusting in through destroyed windows.

'Great stars of Ultramar,' Vodun Badorum murmured.

'He was here, then?' Kleve asked the chamberlain. 'Curze?'

Euten seemed too shaken to move, speak, or even look up. She was wiping blood from Faffnr's head with a strip of cloth torn from her gown.

'He was here,' she said at last. 'The Wolves… They held him at bay. I think several have paid with their lives.'

Voices came from the hallway outside, ordering the praecentals to move aside. The tetrarch Valentus Dolor entered, escorted by Niax Nessus, Holguin of the Dark Angels, and a squad of Ultramarines. Eeron Kleve had voxed their alarm on all channels as he and Gantulga had rushed back to the Residency.

'Your concern was correct, Kleve,' Dolor said grimly.

'Gantulga made the call,' said Kleve.

'Your instincts are sharp, White Scar,' said Holguin.

'Not sharp enough to save lives,' said the White Scar, 'nor to put a net upon him.'

'Where did he go?' Dolor asked. 'My Lady Euten? Where did he go?'

'The Wolves held him at bay,' she repeated quietly. 'For as long as they could, they held him at bay. Then… then he was going to kill me. But Vulkan stopped him.'

'Vulkan?' asked Niax Nessus.

'It was Vulkan,' said Euten.

'That is not possible,' said Holguin.

'I know him,' said Euten. 'I have seen his likeness often enough. It could have been no other. He came upon us like a tempest, a storm-force. Curze was his sole intent. They clashed. They fought. The combat drove them back through the casement, out into the night.'

'The lady is in shock,' said Holguin. 'She does not know what she is saying.'

'I fear she does,' said Dolor.

'It is madness!' Holguin replied.

'Yes,' said the tetrach, 'but not of the kind you think.'

Nessus had reached the smashed windows and stood at Gantulga's side.

'I think there's movement down there,' said the White Scar. 'Movement on the lower roofs. You see?'

Nessus nodded. He opened his vox.

'This is the Third Master. We have located the Night Haunter. Move assault squads to the south side of the Residency. I want two Storm Eagles in the air, covering the lower roofs. Make it fast! Illuminate the roof tops and secure the yards so that no one can cross them. Invictus guard inside the Residency. When Curze sees his exit routes blocked, he will undoubtedly attempt to break back inside. I repeat the instructions you were given earlier – lethal force is not only permitted, it is expected.'

'Let's move,' said Dolor. 'With a purpose! I want to be there for the kill. Badorum, get medicae teams for the Wolves, and for the Lady Euten. Secure this level.'

'Wait!' Holguin hissed. 'Tell me… tell me what you meant about Vulkan.'

Dolor paused.

'Vulkan lives, Dark Angel,' he said. 'He is not in his right mind, but he lives, and if the Lady Euten was speaking the truth, it is likely that Vulkan is holding Curze in combat on the rooftops as we speak.'

'Vulkan lives?' Holguin echoed.

'Who cares if Vulkan lives!' Euten exclaimed, rising to look at them, her hands and sleeves bloodied. 'What of the Lion and our dear Lord Guilliman? What of them? Curze told me they were dead! Curze told me to my face that he had murdered them!'

They looked at her.

'Is it true?' she asked. 'Well? Someone speak! Someone say something!'

FLAMES SURROUNDED THEM. White-hot, incandescent flames, so bright they hurt their eyes, so hot they would turn even the hardest plate to quicksilver dew.

Yet they felt no heat. A cool freshness surrounded them. A space... a silence.

'You are alive, my lords, I am pleased to say,' said Warsmith Dantioch.

He stooped, with some effort, to help Guilliman to his feet as Alexis Polux went to the aid of the Lion. Ultramarines from the 199th Aegida Company rushed onto the tuning floor of Primary Location Alpha to assist, and then hesitated at the strange wonder of the encounter.

Guilliman took in the polished black cavity of the vast cavern around him, then looked back at the vision of the fire-wracked chapel shown to him by the communication field.

'Sotha?' he asked, his voice dry.

'Yes, my lord,' said Dantioch.

'We are on Sotha?' Guilliman repeated.

'I... Yes, my lord,' said Dantioch, 'and I am glad of it, for if you had not been here, you would have been there.' He gestured to the sun-hot blaze of the chapel.

'You brought us here?' asked Guilliman.

'No, lord,' said Dantioch. 'The Pharos did. Perhaps as a

by-product of its process, perhaps deliberately.'

'Deliberately?'

'I am beginning to suspect this mechanism possesses some... sentience,' said the warsmith.

'I am beginning to suspect, brother,' said the Lion, 'that you are dabbling in technologies that no one, not even our father, would play with.'

Polux had stood the Lion up against Dantioch's heavy seat and was examining the wound in his throat. Both Guilliman and his brother had taken several injuries during their contest with Curze, but the neck wound was the worst. It had stopped bleeding at least.

Guilliman leaned over, turned the Lion's head with his hand, and regarded the wound.

'That needs packing before it opens again,' he said.

'What, no comment, Roboute?' asked the Lion. 'Of all the things that trouble me about you and your dealings, brother, we had not even begun to discuss your extraordinary beacon. It was the first thing I saw as I approached Macragge, and thus the first hint I had that–'

'But you saw it,' Guilliman snapped. 'That's the point, brother. You *saw* it. It worked. It is as vital to the function and survival of the Imperium as a regent to watch over it!'

'Yet you seem to know nothing of its function or potential,' said the Lion. He pushed Polux away and stood up. 'Am I to believe that we have been transported across space some... *unimaginable* distance from Macragge?'

'You are,' said Guilliman. He sighed. 'Brother, it was with the greatest reluctance that I explored and then authorised the use of the Pharos beacon. I am fully aware of the great unknowns that attach to it. It was a calculated risk.'

'I feel your calculations may be too optimistic,' said the Lion.

'Do you?' asked Guilliman. 'Yet you are alive. Had we remained in Curze's trap, that would not be the case.'

The Lion sniffed.

'Furthermore,' said Guilliman, 'I know I am not the only one who makes use of prohibited technology. The warp signature of your flagship, brother... Did you think the technicians of my fleet and the adepts of the Mechanicum would not analyse it? When were you going to tell me about that? Or was that a secret you hoped to keep, like the fact that Curze was at large aboard your vessel? You keep too many secrets, brother.'

The Lion looked away. 'We will debate this further,' he said. 'Now, we must return. We came here. We must go back at once.'

'That will require some consideration,' said Dantioch.

The Lion glared at him.

'My lord,' Dantioch added, with a slight bow of his head.

'We will go back, just as we came,' the Lion insisted.

'At the very least, my lord,' said Dantioch, 'I must spend some time re-tuning and focusing the device. I cannot send you back into that.' He indicated the seething fire beyond the field.

'Why am I even talking to you?' the Lion asked.

'Because the warsmith, appointed by me, made this Pharos device work,' said Guilliman. 'He knows more about it than any person alive. If anyone can return us, it is Dantioch. I suggest you address him in a more civil tone.'

The Lion looked at Dantioch.

'It is hard to trust the face of an enemy,' he said.

'He is no enemy,' said Alexis Polux firmly.

'Then, warsmith,' said the Lion, 'explain how this device works, and how we may be transported back. My Navigator saw it as empathic rather than psychic. She said it showed us where we wanted to go.'

'Your Navigator is perceptive, my lord,' said Dantioch. 'This is a site of ancient technology of pre-human origin. My study has shown that it is indeed empathic in its resonance. A principle of quantum entanglement, I speculate. Unlike our warp technology, it does not use the immaterium to bypass realspace. I think it was part of a much larger navigational network that once existed. By tuning it upon Macragge, we have achieved a navigation guide to conquer the Ruinstorm, as well as instantaneous communication.'

'How did we get here?' asked the Lion.

'I am still pondering that, my lord,' said Dantioch. 'I had wondered if, in its original form, the network might have allowed for site-to-site teleportation on a scale we could scarcely imagine. I had presumed that function was lost, as it would require other gateways or beacon sites. I was wrong.'

He looked at Polux.

'The successful transfer of Alexis to this place teaches us the most, I think,' said Dantioch. 'The communication field was already providing me with enough empathic resonance for me to be able, with some success, to detect Konrad Curze in the darkness and forewarn my friend. Then, when his life was in true jeopardy...'

Dantioch paused.

'I wanted to save him. I wanted to reach out and take his hand, and save him from that monster. I think the empathic field responded to my great need and opened to allow it. Just as, when the two of us saw you, my lords, in peril of your lives, our will to save you opened the field again.'

'So it cannot be controlled or set?' asked Guilliman. 'It cannot be switched on and directed? It simply responds to an innate, inarticulable need?'

'I'm afraid so, my lord,' said Dantioch, 'which supposes that, if we cannot access or generate the appropriate emotive, empathic urge, we may not be able to return you to Macragge.'

There was a longer pause.

'Of course, there is also the fact,' Dantioch added awkwardly, 'that we do not know with any certainty that the process works in both directions.'

There was an even longer pause. The polished, mirror-black dome of the cavern surrounded them with cool silence.

'Then you had better find me a ship,' said the Lion. 'A fast one.'

19
MORTALITY

'Common needs make for the strangest strangers comrades.'

– Zerksus, *Proverbs*

'LOOK, I'VE TOLD you – I cannot help you,' John Grammaticus said to the Word Bearer.

'And that is still not an acceptable answer,' Narek replied. 'My efforts to secure you involved a great deal of planning, preparation, effort and sacrifice. I would–'

'Listen to me,' said John. 'I am the agent of a xenos power. The Cabal runs me. It owns me. I am here on their bidding, sent to perform a task that has been pre-ordained.'

'And?'

John strained against the ropes that lashed him to the chair.

'And? They are watching me. If I step away from my course, if I… defy them and refuse to complete my mission, they will come for me. And you too, if you are with me.'

'They can try,' Narek mused.

'They will do more than try,' said John. 'They are quite resourceful. And determined.'

John relaxed and dropped his chin.

'God knows, warrior, I should dearly love to see Lorgar brought down and finished. The galaxy would be a better place for it.'

'"God"?' Narek asked. 'There are few true gods any more. Only the daemons of the warp that pollute the hearts of men.'

'And the demigods that men have fashioned and manufactured,' John countered. 'Creatures such as Lorgar, polluted by the warp, are only as dangerous as they are because they were already primarchs. Mankind has made gods in their own image, and those gods have proven false.'

He looked at the Word Bearer. Narek sat, his face half in shadow, listening.

'Believe me,' John said, 'I would help you if I could. I despise the Ruinous Powers more than all things. I would fight against any part of their influence.'

Narek stood up.

'Then tell me,' he whispered, 'what is your task? What is it that you must perform for your alien masters? What duty must you complete so you can be finished with your service and free to help me?'

'They want no less than you, Narek,' said John. 'They want a primarch dead.'

Narek grunted. 'Whose life do they seek?'

'That of Vulkan,' said John Grammaticus.

'Why?'

'Their motives are too complex to explain easily,' said John.

'But Vulkan is here? He is here on Macragge?'

'So I am informed. His arrival has been foreseen. He vanished by teleport into the aether more than a solar year ago, and was presumed lost – but I understand that the strange properties of the Pharos have brought him here, across the void.'

'I care for none of that, human,' said Narek. 'Nothing except my Legion. Let us find Vulkan. Slay him as you are bidden. Then you can help me.'

'Oh,' John sighed, 'if only it were as simple as that.'

'Explain.'

'I've been tracking his mind since I arrived on Macragge,' John said. 'Tracking him so I could find him. And I've learned that... well, Vulkan is mad. Utterly insane.'

'How?' asked Narek.

'The best I can read it, he was tortured, extensively and extravagantly over a long period of time. It has quite broken his mind. In his state, he is ridiculously dangerous.'

'So we will be cunning,' said Narek.

'That's not all,' said John. 'It is possible to kill a primarch. They are demigods, but they are still mortal, to an extent. Enough firepower, venom, or explosive force...'

John looked straight at the Word Bearer.

'There is a reason the Cabal armed me with this specific weapon to take down Vulkan. They know that he has a very particular, unique trait. He doesn't die.'

'What?'

'Like me, he is *functionally* immortal. He resurrects, even from the most catastrophic demise. To kill an entity like that, you need something really special. And that spear, Narek of the Word, is a ritual weapon if ever there was one.'

Narek glanced down at the fulgurite spear. It was lying on the top of the carrybag at his feet.

'Oh,' said John, 'and according to my instructions, I can't do the deed myself. I have to deliver the spear to another primarch who is willing to strike the blow.'

He paused.

'So, Word Bearer… I have to kill an unkillable, immortal demi-god who has the power of fifty men and also happens to be violently insane. Do you still want a part of that?'

Vulkan screamed his anguish. He swung the mace. The sweep of it made the air howl.

Curze dodged the almost certainly lethal blow. He turned, bolted along the length of the roof slope, and leapt over a broad gap onto the green-tiled crest of the Southern Portico.

Vulkan gave chase. The blood on his armour had already dried. The punctures that Curze's claws had made in his torso had closed. The internal organs that had been shredded and torn were re-forming. Vulkan cleared the gap as easily as Curze had done, and landed on the end of the portico's long roof.

He arched his back and turned the mace in a huge, one-handed rotation, launching it headfirst at the fleeing Curze.

Released, the mace flew like a missile. It struck Curze high on the left shoulder, and knocked him onto his face. He slithered down the slight incline of the roof. The mace crashed off the tiles beside him and slid to rest.

Vulkan came bounding along the roof to reach his enemy. There were lights in the yard below, dancing stab lights that chased hard, bright beams up at the roofline. There was the chop and whicker of gunship engines.

He closed on Curze. Curze struggled to rise. At the last second, as Vulkan's powerful hands grabbed at him, Curze rolled over to face his brother. He had hold of the battle mace.

He drove the weapon into the side of Vulkan's head. His jaw broke. Teeth shattered audibly. Blood squirted from his ear and nostril.

Vulkan staggered backwards, but did not fall. Curze came at him, pressing his advantage. He struck Vulkan twice more in the body with the stolen mace.

Powerful lamps flooded them with white light. They became two silhouettes trading blows in a colourless glare. Two Ultramarines Storm Eagles, engines howling, circled the portico roof, while dozens of others filled the skies over the Fortress.

One of them came in, almost at the level of the roofline, and sprayed two warning salvos of fire from its twin-linked heavy bolters. The grouped blasts blew out great sections of the portico roof, directly behind Curze. Flames, dust and fragmented tiles erupted in all directions.

Curze, furious at the intervention, turned and shrieked directly into the lights of the Storm Eagle. The gunship had a confirmed lock on him, and its weapons blazed.

In a huge bound that spread his cloak behind him like wings, Curze leapt clean off the portico and landed on the hull of the Storm Eagle. Its engines immediately started to wail as it recoiled from the roofline. Its nose dipped as it turned out.

Curze clung on. He punched his right fist through the cockpit canopy, and seized the human pilot-serf by the throat, the blades of his claw encircling the man's collar.

'Away from here,' he hissed over the screaming engines and streaming wind.

The pilot looked at him, eyes wide, choking.

'Now!' Curze added.

Unsteady, yawing badly to starboard, the Storm Eagle turned and began to move across the gate yard away from the Residency. It was running at less than rooftop height.

'Climb,' Curze insisted over the headwind. 'Climb!'

The gunship began to gain altitude.

Behind it, Vulkan braced himself and leapt too. He slammed onto the gunship's starboard tail wing on his belly, and held on. The impact made the gunship sway laterally as it continued on its slow, advancing hover.

Vox channels went wild. The squads of Ultramarines in the Portis Yard and Residency quadrangle started to fire in a free-for-all at the wavering gunship, realising that it had to be sacrificed if Curze was to be stopped.

Bolt-rounds and las-bolts clipped and boomed off the Storm Eagle's armoured hull. Sparks leapt and shrapnel flew. Fireballs bloomed and left scorched patches on its armoured skin.

Curze looked down the hull of the Storm Eagle and saw Vulkan. The gunship's nose was coming up. It was approaching the line of the Aegis Wall. Curze kept his hand clamped around the pilot, threatening to shear his head from his shoulders.

'Over!' he said.

Vulkan clawed his way up the wing, over the starboard engine cowling. Curze judged the weight of the mace in his free hand. He waited until Vulkan clambered clear of the cowling. Then he hurled the weapon with a vicious snap-sling of his arm.

The mace's head struck Vulkan in the face. He lost his grip, and flew sideways, into the Storm Eagle's tail assembly, which he tried to grab hold of.

He failed, and fell off the gunship's stern.

Vulkan plummeted about thirty metres. He neither landed on the yard inside the Aegis Wall, nor fell the greater depth of the wall and Castrum on the outside.

Instead, he struck the top of the wall, smashing into the castellations with a force that broke his spine. Then he dropped, limp, and folded onto his side on the wall-top walkway, a bright mirror of blood leaking out of his shattered body, his life seemingly extinguished once more.

The gunship, with Curze clinging to its cockpit assembly, continued over the wall. Ferocious hails of gunfire chased it from the yards and wall-top. It slugged on. The Castrum dropped away. Curze was high over the city and the parkland.

'*Down!*' he hissed.

The pilot gurgled. He had been bleeding profusely since Curze had first smashed the canopy in his face, and seized his throat. The gunship began to bank towards the towers and spires of the city.

Gunfire continued to track it from the walls and battlements. The second Storm Eagle, searchlamps blazing, thundered over the Aegis Wall in pursuit, taking a far more direct and aggressive path than its stricken twin. The other gunships aloft circled back to allow the Storm Eagle to take its kill.

Curze glanced back, the night wind lashing his hair, and saw it gaining.

'Down!' he ordered.

The Storm Eagle began to drop fast. The spires, city halls and residential citadel spires north of Martial Square rose to meet it, their windows lit. Raid sirens were blaring down in the streets. Curze could see the criss-cross light streams of traffic in the streets below. Titan's Gate, immense and unlit, was a black henge, a silhouette against the distant bright radiance of the landing fields far to the south.

'Down!' Curze ordered again.

They were lumbering low over the high tops of towers and domed vaults, or even between the bulk of the tallest spires. Their course was arching east of Martial Square, swinging towards the high, block shapes of the Treasury and the new Senate House.

The Storm Eagle chasing them began to fire. Bright heavy bolter fire spat orange darts through the night, shots that reflected off the high windows of the towers on either side of them. They found their mark. Parts of the tail assembly burst away in a shower of spalled metal and a gout of burning gases.

The gunship that Curze was riding lurched, its engines straining. They were losing height very fast, nearly smashing into the north face of the Consular Record Building. The starboard wing-tip raked a flurry of squealing sparks off the building's stonework.

Curze had been watching his visions all the while, letting them play through his head like that damaged pict-feed, sorting the true from the false, the trustworthy from the untrustworthy. His entire operation since planetfall had been guided and directed by his visions.

Vulkan. Vulkan was the only part of it that his visions had not shown, nor even hinted at.

He saw glass now. *Water, fire.* A specific dome.

More shots hit the diving Storm Eagle from behind. A greater chunk of it exploded and broke away. It fell rather than flew, no longer controllable, a chunk of mangled debris arcing like a meteor to impact, trailing fire and wreckage. Twenty metres above the roof-tops. Curze saw the dome, the particular dome. He let go of the pilot's throat and jumped, falling away from the plunging gunship.

Feet first, he hit the dome of the building, a great and ornate crystal canopy, which shattered under him. Pinwheeling in a torrent of glittering fragments, he fell hard and hit water in a plume of spray.

The Storm Eagle, leaving huge, jumping yellow flames in its wake, continued on for another five seconds, and struck the east facade of the Treasury building fifteen metres above the street. It made a dazzling orange fireball that punched through the wall and incinerated the chambers within, and simultaneously spat back into the night sky, lofting and expanding and raining burning fuel and micro-debris. A nanosecond after impact, as the fireball was forming, the Storm Eagle's munitions payload went off, and a second, larger, brighter fireball engulfed the first, blooming like a small sun over the Treasury Yard. The orange glare was reflected in a million windows, except in the nearby streets where the blast blew all of the casements out.

Curze surfaced in a spray of water and shook his head. He was in the principal Nymphaeum of Magna Macragge Civitas. A large, circular building with columns supporting the famous crystal dome, it housed the oldest of the natural springs that had been worshipped in the days of the Battle Kings as sacred to the water spirits.

Curze thrashed to the edge of the stone pool and rose out of the water, letting it stream off him onto the flagstones. He glanced back at the spring-fed pool, polluted with fragments of smashed crystal. The clear water was stained. There was a fair measure of blood in it.

Not all of it belonged to Curze, not by any means.

He smiled, a black crescent in the sloshing blue twilight of the Nymphaeum. He walked towards the exit, towards a night-bound city lit by the fury of burning wreckage.

Curze understood cities at night. The secret was, you either made them darker, or you made them burn.

He waited for the visions to show him where to go next, and which of those things to do.

TETRARCH DOLOR STRODE along the walkway, on top of the high Aegis Wall, staring at the fireball blooming over the eastern Neapolis. The night sky was full of circling, beating gunships.

Verus Caspean waited for him.

'Is that a kill?' Dolor asked.

'His escape vehicle was brought down east of the Martial Square,' said Caspean.

'Can we confirm his death?' Dolor asked.

'Not yet, lord tetrarch,' replied Caspean. 'Forces are on the ground. We're waiting for word.'

'I want a body,' said Dolor, 'preferably one I can spit on. Burned bones at least.'

'Yes, lord tetrarch.'

'Less with the "lord tetrarch", my noble and good friend, Verus,' said Dolor. He looked Caspean in the eye. 'Phratus has fallen. Until the Avenging Son can be found, I have authority in the Fortress, and I directly name you First Master to succeed Auguston.'

'My lord.'

'We must surely maintain and reinforce the chain of command in this black hour, Verus,' said Dolor. 'You will perform the duty in superlative fashion.'

'Thank you, tetrarch,' said Caspean, saluting and bowing.

'We will know no fear, First Master Caspean,' replied Dolor, saluting back. 'Make your respect known!'

The Ultramarines around them clattered out brisk salutes.

'Will we know no fear, Valentus?' Caspean asked. 'This night may have seen the violent death, in the space of one full hour, of *four* of the Emperor's sons.'

'These bold and dread facts are yet to be confirmed,' replied Dolor.

'One might be,' Caspean replied. He led the tetrarch along the defensive platform to a section of the battlement that was wet with blood. Ultramarines stood all around, their heads bowed.

Vulkan lay in a broken heap, on the walkway, surrounded by a wide slick of his lifeblood.

'In the spirit of our brothers, the Salamanders,' said Caspean, 'Vulkan lived. But he does so no longer.'

Dolor was about to reply when the vital sensors of every man in the vicinity, including his own, went off. They had all been set to maximum yield earlier that evening, in the hope of detecting the Night Haunter as he hunted through the dark.

A brand-new life trace had been detected within five metres of them.

'Great Terra!' Caspean exclaimed.

Vulkan sat up in the pool of blood. He gazed at them, his eyes like the hearts of red suns.

'My lord,' said Dolor, taking a step forward. 'My honoured Lord Vulkan, we–'

Vulkan ignored him and got up. He took several deep breaths as if scenting the air, and gazed over the lip of the Aegis Wall towards the hot fire burning in the Treasury quarter.

'My lord,' Dolor urged, 'will you speak to us? Will you tell us where you have been, what has befallen you, and how you come to us? My lord, I–'

Vulkan didn't look back. He jumped onto the rampart of the Aegis Wall, spread his arms wide, and stepped off.

He fell, magnificent, like a cliff-diver, head first into the dark green space of the parkland below the Castrum.

20
ALIGNMENT

'Cut in darkness, and you are called a monster;
cut in starlight, and you are proclaimed a god.'
– *The Nocturniad*, Eleventh Cycle.

THEY HURRIED THROUGH the subsystem of Strayko Deme, moving through the ancient but well-maintained network of sewers, out-falls and storm drains that lay beneath the paved streets and refined avenues. Occasionally, light fell upon them through drain gratings or grilles, and where it did, it was tinged with flame.

'Why are we moving?' John asked. Narek had unbound him, but hustled him along on a leash of dirty rope tied around the Perpetual's neck.

'You heard the blast.'

'It could have been anything.'

'Tell me it wasn't.'

'I can't tell you anything, Narek–'

'Respect!'

'I can't tell you anything, *my lord*,' John Grammaticus repeated in a low voice. 'This close to that torc you're wearing, I'm limited to virtually nothing. And I'm in pain.'

'That is a shame.'

'Tell me what you know then.'

Narek came to a halt. They had just entered the cistern of a wide storm drain, circular in cross-section. Dark, pungent water rippled around their feet as they came to a stop.

'Some form of aircraft crashed, not far from where I had you secured. The authorities of the city will be closing in. I can fight Ultramarines well enough, but perhaps not *all* the Ultramarines. So, we're moving.'

'To where?'

'Wherever I can find. Come on.'

John paused.

'Come on!' Narek hissed, snapping on the rope. John lurched, his neck jerked painfully.

'Look, Narek. *My lord.* I could help more than this.'

Narek of the Word looked at him carefully.

'You are full of mind-tricks and deceit, John Grammaticus… or Caeron Sebaton… or whoever else you ever are. Our business on Traoris taught me that.'

John nodded.

'Yeah, I bloody am.' He ran an index finger around the inside of the noose to loosen it. 'If I could escape from you, Narek, I would. There, I'm honest, at least. You are dangerous. You're never more than a few moments away from killing me, and you don't trust me. But this, Narek of the Word, this is not a good position for either of us to be in.'

John stepped towards the frowning Word Bearer. Oozing water rolled around his ankles.

'There are worse allies to have than a Space Marine,' he offered, 'just as there are worse allies to have than a Perpetual. Of course, that's true only if they get to work to their strengths. Take off the torc.'

'No.'

'Take it off.'

'No,' said Narek. 'I am no fool. You are high-function. You would… blow out my brain with an aneurism with one thought-blink, and leave me dead. Or something.'

John shrugged.

'I suppose,' he said. 'Though that would be worst case, and at least it would be quick.'

'You could do that?' asked Narek.

'Of course I couldn't!' John snapped. 'I'm a telepath, not a telekine. I can do all sorts of things, Narek. I can read your mind, or let you read mine, speak any language, be anyone I like, surveil the area for psykana sensitivity, or even look into the ghostly filaments of the near-past and near-future… None of which sound like bad ideas, right now. It would be good to have more immediate combat intel than "something crashed so we had to run".'

Narek grunted.

'I could read disposition,' said John. 'I could tell you where the Ultramarines are. I could guide us. I could alert us to proximate activity. I could find what we're looking for.'

'You're dangerous,' Narek whispered.

'So are you. And right now, *my lord*, I think leaving me hooded is making this situation even more dangerous than it has to be for both of us.'

'I don't trust you,' said Narek, clenching his steel-gloved fist around the rope to yank it again.

'I know,' John replied, 'but you want to use me as a weapon to assassinate your dear, beloved primarch, so I think you'll probably have to start trusting me at some point, or that's never ever going to become a practical possibility. Weapons need love, respect, careful handling and a chance to excel in their particular way. Ask your sword. Ask that ridiculously large damned rifle of yours.'

John took a step closer. The rope between them slackened.

'Narek, trust is the issue here. Let me open my mind. Let me allow us to see each other's thoughts. There's a lot of common ground, I think, more than you'd imagine. We're never going to be alike, you and I, but I think we're *aligned*.'

'Aligned?' the Word Bearer asked, his voice very small and hollow.

'Yes. We're in alignment. We're not like the hands of a clock at midnight. We're never going to point in the same direction. But think of the hands at six o'clock.'

He paused.

'You know what a clock is, right?'

'I've seen them,' Narek nodded. He was more used to digital chronometer displays.

'At six o'clock, the hands point in opposite directions, but they make a straight line,' said John. 'They are in alignment.'

'I see.'

'Do you?'

Narek nodded. 'It is a metaphor for cooperation between two individuals who have conflicting aims, but many common values.'

'Right. Shit, that's right.'

Narek hesitated.

'I am alone,' he admitted eventually. 'I have turned against my Legion. I have killed a certain number of my brothers. But my Legion has turned, so I am an outsider to all others. No loyalist would ever trust me, no Imperial Fist or Iron Hand, and – since Calth – no noble Ultramarine. I am cursed at every turn. All I can do is make amends. All I can do is cleanse and restore my Legion, for it was once so great! It was beautiful, John Grammaticus. It was the truest expression of the Emperor's word.'

'I'm sorry for your loss,' John said, 'and I'm not mocking you when I say that. You scare me half to death, Narek of the Word, but I admire you. The way Horus's war has played out, the brothers of the Word Bearers are on the wrong side. You've thrown yourselves in with darkness. So, understand me. I'm astonished by you, by your resilience and loyalty to the original high principles of your Legion. The cosmos believes all Word Bearers to be traitors, heretics and rebels, but you, alone, have rebelled against their rebellion. I admire that. That's why I'm even considering helping you in your cause.'

He shrugged.

'But I wish you'd let me read you, so I could be sure the tale you're spinning me is true. The Word Bearers manipulate truth. Your story could simply be a way of obtaining me and the spear *for* Lorgar.'

'It is not.'

'Prove it.'

Narek thought for a long time.

'A comrade would be welcome on my lonely mission,' he muttered. 'A battle-brother, an ally. Even... a person in alignment.'

'Take off the torc,' John said. 'Let's find out where we are. Let's get in alignment.'

Narek paused.

'I do not trust you, John Grammaticus,' he said.

'I know,' John replied, 'but there's no one else here, and you need to trust someone.'

Narek hesitated, and then reached out and removed the noose from around John's neck. He slung his cased rifle over his shoulder, took a breath, and drew his bolt pistol from its holster.

He aimed the weapon at John, and, with his other hand, reached for the control stud on the side of the psychic torc.

Narek pressed the stud. At a deep, psychic level, there was a local suspension of vibration. The aching dullness that had been hobbling John's hind brain for hours began to dispel.

It was an unpleasant, nauseating experience. John staggered, and rested his hand against the wall of the storm drain. His mind was rapidly becoming aware of its environs, an overload of restored psychic feedback.

Narek watched him warily. He unclasped the torc and handed it to John.

John took it.

'Do not make me regret this,' Narek said.

'Oh, he won't,' said a voice from behind them.

Narek turned with transhuman speed to locate the source of the voice. His pistol wavered, aiming, seeking a solid target.

Damon Prytanis stepped out from behind the curve of the brick-built drain, an oddly slovenly figure in his dirty fur coat. He had a shuriken pistol aimed in each hand.

'Sorry I'm late,' he said brightly, and opened fire. 'The Blessed Lady sends her regards.'

Narek fired once, but projectiles had already punched into his hand, arm and shoulder and ruined his aim. The discharged bolt shell shot wild and struck the ceiling of the drain tunnel.

Damon's fusillade ripped across Narek, a blanket of whizzing monomolecular discs. Damon Prytanis employed none of the feather-finger restraint he had used against the praecentals to conserve ammunition. This was a fully armoured Space Marine. The blitz of razor-rounds shredded into Narek of the Word, and explosively peppered the tunnel wall behind him. John had to dive into the ooze for cover.

'Johnny-boy!' Damon yelled, still shooting. 'Come to papa! It's time to depart!'

Narek went down into the sluice water, hurt and gagging, his plasteel fingertips scraping on the limed brick walls.

John got up and staggered past him towards Damon Prytanis.

'You bloody idiot!' John yelled. 'I had him. I had him right where I wanted him!'

Damon nodded. 'Right. Eating out of your hand. You'd virtually broken that torc's restraint, right? You were right in his head.'

'No! I was negotiating. I had him. I was persuading him!'

'Screw that,' said Damon. 'Life's way too short. That's your trouble, John. You like to solve problems the hard way. You don't like to get wet. You're too genteel. Let's exit.'

They started to run along the drain, side by side, towards the next outfall.

'What are you doing here?' John asked him. He slowed his pace for a second and winced.

'What?' Damon asked. 'What's up?'

'My head. It's been blanked for too long. Everything's coming back. Perceptions. It's not pleasant. I asked you a question, Prytanis. What are you doing here?'

Damon grinned.

'The usual. Gahet asked me to check you were performing according to schedule.'

'You're my insurance?'

'Positively, yes.'

'And if it looks like I'm falling down on the job?'

Damon Prytanis shrugged, *Guh'hru* in one hand and *Meh'menitay* in the other.

'Guess I'd just have to mess you up to teach you a lesson,' he said. Then he laughed.

'I'll tell you what you've messed up,' said John. 'This whole *entire* assignment. The Cabal should never have sent in the cavalry.'

'Cavalry, am I? You know something, I actually was, once. Seventh Cavalry. Tell you what, those Lakota–'

'You know what I mean,' said John.

'So do you. You know they had to,' said Damon. 'You were wavering.'

'I was not.'

'You so were. This job needs to get done, and done fast. Vulkan has to die. That's the way it has to go. That's the order of it all. You've got this spear thing?'

John gestured with the carrybag in his hand.

'Good,' said Damon. 'Good for you. That's all that matters. Let's get this done. I'll be there as your support. Your... *guarantee*. So tell me, Johnny, how is this supposed to work? Gahet was not specific.'

'I place the spear in the hands of a primarch, and in his hands, that spear becomes capable of slaying another of the eighteen.'

'Vulkan.'

'Yeah.'

'Do we know why Vulkan is the target?'

'It's just another version of the Alpharius Position,' said John. 'Horus has to win this war, and win it so brutally that the human race is engulfed and takes the taint of the Primordial Annihilator with it to its grave. The victory of Horus and the death of our species is the pyre that burns Chaos out. That means major loyalist players like Vulkan must be turned or taken out.'

'So, the spear?' asked Damon. 'Which one of Vulkan's brothers do you give it to? I mean, here on Macragge? I don't see either Guilliman or the Lion being willing to take a pop at Vulkan.'

'There is one viable candidate on this world,' said John Grammaticus.

'There's another primarch here? Who?'

'Curze,' said John.

Damon stopped and whistled. 'Curze? That maniac is on Macragge?'

'Yes, he is,' said John. 'The last thing I sensed before the Word Bearer captured me was the Night Haunter making planetfall.'

Damon shuddered. He looked up at the sewer roof.

'Screw that. I didn't sign on for Konrad Curze.'

'Well, Damon, let me put it this way... ' said John. 'Boo hoo, too late.'

He didn't hear Prytanis's sardonic reply. A fierce migraine was knifing him suddenly, almost forcing him to his knees. Tears welled in his eyes.

'John? What is it?'

John Grammaticus's psykana gift was suddenly returning in full force. The flooding rush of restored perceptions was almost overwhelming. He was registering the unmediated auras and perceptions of the Civitas around him. It was too much, like a vox floating between channels, its volume turned up full. He struggled to establish some control.

He got sharp waves of pain, anger, outrage. He looked at Damon Prytanis.

'I can feel...' he tried to explain. 'My psyk's returning. Fast. *Oh.*'

'What?'

'It's a good thing we're not relying on Guilliman or the Lion,' said John, struggling to maintain his wits.

'Why?' Damon asked warily.

'Guilliman is gone. The Lion too. They're dead, Prytanis.'

'Are you joking?' asked Damon. 'Tell me you're damn well joking!'

'I wish I was,' John replied. He was shaking with the intensity of the psyk-rush. 'The sense of hurt and loss is so strong. I'm getting it from the minds of hundreds of Ultramarines and Dark Angels.'

'Pull yourself together. Come on. If this is true, I need you sharp.'

John swallowed hard and nodded.

'Yes. Right. I will,' he mumbled. 'It's just a lot to deal with. You wouldn't understand. Imagine being deaf for a few hours, getting your hearing back, and then getting shouted at by everyone in a city all at once.'

Damon maintained eye contact, concern on his face.

'I'm all right,' said John. 'It's becoming a little more stable now.' He glanced over his shoulder.

'You didn't kill him,' he said.

'The Word Bearer?'

'Yes.'

'Damn. I thought I'd done that very nicely.'

'Well, you didn't,' said John. 'I can read him, getting back on his feet. He'll come after us. He's good at that, Damon.'

'We had better keep moving then, hadn't we?' said Damon.

They used a stone rain chute to clamber back up to street level. It was a few hours before dawn. The sky was heavy with air cover from the Fortress.

'That's a major search,' said Damon.

'Curze ripped the heart out of the Fortress tonight,' John replied. 'They're hunting for him and for Vulkan.'

'Can you find either of them?'

John paused, concentrating.

'Curze, no. It's as if I can read him sometimes, and then at other moments he's utterly invisible. As though he can cloak his mind. When I can read him, it's unbearable, but the rest of the time he's not even a shadow.'

'What about Vulkan?' asked Damon.

'Wait, I'm trying.'

'Well, we need them both,' said Damon.

They walked slowly along a quiet backstreet between two grander avenues. John focused his mind. He had been attuning it to Vulkan's thought signature since setting foot on Macragge. It was hard when that thought signature was so deranged. It was also hard in the middle of a city filled with so many agitated, unguarded minds.

He smiled.

'What?' asked Damon.

'I think I have Vulkan. He's moving south of us, south-east. Going into Anomie Deme.'

Damon nodded.

'What's he doing there?'

'No idea. He's hard to read. He's... not entirely sane these days.'

'Great. We're tracking a mad primarch?'

'Yeah. Didn't the Cabal tell you that? Didn't Gahet brief you? I hope they gave you plenty of ammo. And danger money.'

Damon scowled. 'But you found him?'

'Yes.'

'Still no read on Curze?'

'Not yet,' said John.

'Well, one of them is a start. Good job. Good job, John. You look pleased with yourself.'

John was. Focusing on Vulkan's thought pattern had revealed something else to him. The enforced psychic isolation created by Narek's torc had allowed his brain to quietly, subconsciously unpack.

Suddenly, he was able to see clearly what the farseer's conduit had imprinted on his mind. He understood what Eldrad Ulthran wanted him to do.

He understood how.

He understood why.

He took a deep breath. Finally, here was a way he could serve the forces of light. He could defy the wishes of the Cabal, and fight for his birth-race. At last he could strike a proper blow for his species, something he had been longing to do since his xenos masters first dragged him into the Horus War.

Of course, it would cost him his life, but that hardly seemed a big price to pay.

THE PAIR OF them straightened up and moved off down the street, following a route that Damon had dug up on a data-slate, a route that would get them into Anomie Deme by the shortest path.

High up on a jutting, ornamental rain spout, a crouching shadow watched them move.

Curze licked his lips.

This piece was a fascinating new addition to the spilled jigsaw of his mind. From the moment he had stepped out of the Nymphaeum pool, new visions had been coming to him. The crazed, random flow of his waking dreams had shown him a possibility called John Grammaticus. There was something curious about Grammaticus. Curze wasn't sure what it was exactly, but it was creepy and abnormal. Grammaticus was not a regular human. He was, somehow, like *many* humans all at once, or like a single human with inexplicable dimensional proportions. In particular, his fourth dimension, his time, was stretched, elongated...

It didn't matter. The latest reflections had shown Curze one especially clear thing. There was a spear, a spear that could kill Vulkan. Not only that, Grammaticus was supposed to give the spear to Curze so he could use it.

He *would* use it. He would use it to finish what he had started in the Iron Labyrinth.

It would make the night perfect. Sunrise would reveal that Konrad Curze had descended like an eclipse upon bright Macragge and, in one period of darkness, had slain three of the Emperor's sons, including the one that, apparently, could not die.

That was a fundamental achievement, a superlative *ritual* achievement, a *crushing* achievement: haughty Guilliman, the vainglorious Lion, the unkillable Vulkan.

All three, in one single night.

Horus could go burn in the warp! Nothing he had achieved was even half so impressive! Konrad Curze was about to anoint himself as the Emperor's greatest and most formidable son.

He would do it by bringing his father's Imperium crashing down more thoroughly and painfully than anything that the Lupercal had so far managed. He would do it by bringing about not a change of state or leadership, but utter galactic oblivion.

They would die. All of the primarchs would *die*, and in dying they would witness the sheer magnificence of his terror.

Curze rose. The two men on the empty street below him hurried out of sight.

He spread his tattered cloak and launched himself towards the next rooftop.

21

DREAMS AND VISIONS

*'There is only one way to see, and that is through
the knowledge of one's own eyes,
looking straight ahead.'*

– Rogal Dorn, *Principles of Sound Defence*

THE SUN CAME up fast. It was bright and warming. He watched it glinting off the waters of the bay.

He tried to relax.

The farm workers had started their toil early, wandering up the mountain slopes from the settlement below before sunrise, their scythes across their shoulders. He could hear them, as he had heard them for the last two hours, taking their blades to the grasses that threatened to choke Sotha's black halls, laughing, chatting.

He could smell the rich scent of cut stalks filling the early morning air.

Guilliman sat down on the grassy promontory, the upper slope of Mount Pharos. He wiped a hand across his brow.

Sotha was a good world, a peaceful place. All of the forces and influences that insisted he return to Macragge were somehow softened here in this summer light. Guilliman, to his shame, realised how much he craved this peace. Sotha was like a mythical Eden. For an irrational moment, Roboute Guilliman willed Dantioch to fail in his efforts to re-tune the Pharos, and wished never to return. A part of him knew that he could live out his days on Sotha in utter contentment, barebacked and tanned in the sunlight, careless, mowing the grasses with his scythe, season in and season out.

It was just a dream. Such simple, pastoral destinies did not lie in store for beings like Roboute Guilliman. Fate held, for him, a future of duty and responsibility, very different from that which might await an honest agri-worker. No common farmer would play a role in the final battle against Horus.

He heard a heavy tread crunching towards him and looked up.

'My lord,' Sergeant Arkus said, saluting. He was carrying his company's standard.

'At ease, Arkus,' Guilliman told the Ultramarine. Arkus's armour glinted in the sunlight.

'You're trying too hard,' he added.

'My lord?'

'When I arrived last night, your armour was in perfectly respectable condition, as was the plate of the other battle-brothers in your company. I remember these things. This morning, you've buffed your plate to the point of insanity.'

'My primarch is here,' Arkus said, offended. 'A surprise inspection of this post. What else would I do?'

Guilliman got up and faced him.

'I'm sorry, Arkus. My remark was petty and uncalled for. Your armour code is perfect.'

Arkus nodded, and rested the base of the standard on the ground.

'My lord,' he said. 'I am an Ultramarine. Trying too hard is the entire point of us, isn't it?'

Guilliman smiled and saluted Arkus.

'Make your report, brother,' he said.

'Warsmith Dantioch says we will be ready to test in one hour,' Arkus said.

'You can tell him I'll be there,' Guilliman said.

Arkus saluted and walked away.

Guilliman turned his face towards the sun and tilted his head back.

'Brother?'

Guilliman turned and saw the Lion walking down the mountain slope towards him. Behind the Lion, a young Scout from the 199th Aegida followed anxiously.

'Brother?' Guilliman returned.

The Lion sat down on a boulder, tired and frustrated. He locked his hands over his knees.

'Roboute,' he said, 'you should listen to this young neophyte. What's your name, lad?'

'Oberdeii, my lord,' the Scout said.

'Tell it to Roboute... My pardon, tell the primarch before you,' said the Lion, 'what you told me.'

Oberdeii looked at Guilliman.

'It's all right,' Guilliman said. 'Tell me, son.'

'The most noble Lord of the First,' replied the Scout, 'was asking me about this site, about the experience of the posting here. I may have spoken out of turn.'

'Then if the harm is done,' said Guilliman, 'you can do no more harm repeating it. Speak, Oberdeii. There will be no repercussions.'

'Well, then, about this place, lord,' Oberdeii said. 'It is an odd place to be. An odd place to garrison for any time. The Pharos... It breeds *dreams*. It is alive with them. If you stay here long enough, or live here as we do, the dreams begin to permeate you. They are as much part of this mountain as the grass, rock and air.'

Oberdeii looked up at Guilliman.

'I hope you believe me, lord,' he said.

'I do.'

Guilliman thought of the dreams he had just had, of renouncing his rule and living out his days in a careless pastoral idyll. The Pharos magnified things. It made truths and hopes seem very real. Just a night in its environs had given flesh to his private wishes of an end to duty and responsibility.

'We have begun to notice things, patterns in our dreams,' Oberdeii said. 'We have learned to pay attention. Warsmith Dantioch, may blood be his honour, has told us that the Pharos here gives light upon an empathic vibration. This would account for much. We have all felt it. My worthy sergeant, Arkus, he had a dream. He dreamed that the Dark Angels were coming to Macragge. And lo! Two days later, this very thing happened. Captain Adallus, just two nights ago, had a dream of blood, and woke up calling out the name of Curze.'

'Curze?' asked Guilliman.

'They saw it coming,' the Lion said to Guilliman.

'Thanks to this lighthouse,' Guilliman said.

'Thanks to this lighthouse and its xenos function,' the Lion agreed.

Guilliman looked to Oberdeii. 'There is something more, isn't there?' he asked.

'There most certainly is,' said the Lion.

'All in my company first thought that the dream of the Dark Angels was merely a coincidence,' said Oberdeii, 'but then the dream of Curze persuaded us there was more going on. Last night, my dear lord, I had a dream.'

'Share with me its contents, son,' said Guilliman. 'Tell me of this dream you had.

Oberdeii told him.

DAWN WAS NOT far off, a cold and dismal dawn. Drab smoke wreathed the Castrum and the high towers of the Fortress, a legacy of the bloody night that was only now passing. Aircraft and ground forces from the Fortress continued to make systematic sweeps of the Civitas's vast grid. Until they had found what they were looking for, there was no telling that the bloody night would become just a prequel to a bloodier day.

John and Damon travelled south-east across Strayko into the neighbouring deme of Anomie, moving as best they could to avoid detection by the sweep patrols. A measure of martial law had been imposed to keep civilians off the streets.

They were following John's track on the damaged thoughts of Vulkan. The pre-dawn was a pale blue hour around them. The empty, stately streets of Anomie felt like they were underwater. It reminded John of his last meeting with the farseer.

Every few minutes they were obliged to take shelter in an under-walk or beneath a portico as an Ultramarines search vehicle whined past overhead, or clattered across a junction in front of them.

Neither of them was aware of the dark shadow trailing them from roof to roof.

The more John considered the farseer's plan, the more it made him agitated. It was enervating. It was entirely the type of duty he had longed to perform, for what felt like forever. It was a contradiction of the Cabal's desires, a refutation of their philosophy and their control over him. John had a chance to fight, as a man, on the side of mankind.

It was, however, not going to be easy. John hoped he had the skill, wit and determination to see it through. The Cabal wanted Vulkan dead, for they had foreseen the epic role he would play in the final war against Horus and the warp. He was destined to be one of the most stalwart defenders of Ancient Terra. The Cabal did not want him alive to perform that conspicuous role.

Eldrad Ulthran had seen more. He had seen Vulkan's insanity, the demented state forced upon the proud primarch by the foul Night Haunter. As it stood, Vulkan was already out of the game. He was in no state to fulfill his destiny as the Cabal had predicted it. If John took no further action, his mission would be deemed a technical success.

The spear was a potent weapon. In the hands of a primarch, it could kill anything, even an unkillable being. In the hands of a Perpetual, however... Eldrad Ulthran's proposition was that under those circumstances, a different result might be obtained. Empowered by the touch of a Perpetual, the spear might *cure* instead of kill.

If John could strike the blow, then perhaps Vulkan might be restored. Rather than removing Vulkan from the war, John Grammaticus could repair and empower one of the Emperor's most powerful sons and most important allies.

There were obstacles to overcome. The presence of Curze, lurking somewhere in the Civitas, was a significant one. The Ultramarines and authorities of Macragge were another. Vulkan himself was a problem – how did one get close enough to stab an insane, hyperaggressive primarch?

Then there was the Cabal, of course, and the agent they had sent to be John's handler. John had known Damon Prytanis for a long time. They had never really been friends, but there was a lot of common ground between them. Though both Perpetuals, they were very different. John had always been very much the spy, the infiltrator, the covert operative who manipulated through disguise and dealt in information. Damon called himself a soldier, but he was a killer, pure and simple. He was an assassin, a taker of lives, and he did this with impunity. Damon Prytanis would not hesitate to take John's life if he thought John was reneging on his mission.

Or would he?

As they walked, John glanced at Prytanis, watching the easy gait, the casual demeanor, the shabby fur coat and muddy boots, the affectless manner that actually covered a hard-wired combat readiness.

There was doubt in Prytanis. There was misery. Like John, Prytanis had served too long, and against his own breed. John sensed in Damon Prytanis much of the resentment that was bottled up inside his own soul.

A Storm Eagle flew overhead, circling slowly on whickering engines, probing the lanes and back-walks between habs and insulae with cool blue-white stablight beams.

Damon and John ducked in under an arch, waiting for it to pass on.

'Can I ask you something?' said John.

'Sure. How I remain so effortlessly cool, while you're a hectic jangle of tics and quirks? It's because you're a psyker, Johnny, and I'm a fighter.'

'Well, not that, but thanks for the assessment.' John paused. Then he said, 'How do you live with it?'

'With what?'

'Serving the Cabal?'

Damon shrugged. 'They pay well,' he said.

'I thought so too, but they're using us as weapons against our own kind,' John said simply.

Damon made a face. It was an *I-want-you-to-stop-talking* face, a *we've-had-this-pointless-conversation-a-hundred-times* face.

'You really are having a problem with this mission, aren't you?' Damon asked.

'Aren't you?'

'No,' Damon replied. 'Hell no.'

He glanced out to see if the gunship had moved far enough away for them to get moving again. It had not. He pulled back inside the arch and scowled at John.

'I agreed to serve them,' he said. 'I'm a soldier. I'm loyal. End of.'

'I can read that you're not,' John replied.

Damon jerked back, eyes widening in alarm. 'Get out of my damn head, Grammaticus. I didn't invite you in.'

John held his hands up to show no intent.

'I'm not trying. Besides, you're warded against me,' he remarked. 'Very clever warp-magic, Damon. The Cabal's not above using anything, is it? Whatever works?'

Damon leaned back against the bricks, scratched his temple and sighed.

'Look, John… If you want the truth, I *am* sick of it, sick of it all. I am sick of serving those xenos pricks. I hate the fact that humanity has to take the fall to save the cosmos. I'm like you in that. But I was also telling the truth just now. I *agreed* to serve. I'm a soldier. I'm loyal. They showed me the bigger picture and I accepted it. I didn't like it, but I accepted it. They showed me the greater good. I'm a *soldier*, John. I understand expediency, pragmatism and necessary evil.'

'We were all soldiers, once,' said John. 'All that experience taught me was the power of comradeship.'

Damon sniffed. 'Yeah? Fine. I've got more heart than you think I have, Grammaticus. This whole thing hurts me more than you know. Maybe I'm not a soldier, then. Just a killer. An assassin.

That's how the Cabal has employed me these last few thousand years. I work well. I work wet. The first thing I ever killed was my own conscience. It was a mercy killing. You still have yours, Johnny, and I really pity you for that.'

He grinned at John as if he had revealed some deep and profound truth.

'Okay?' he asked.

John smiled at the use of the archaic slang. 'You sound like Oll,' he said.

'That loser?' asked Damon sourly. 'Screw it, John. If you want to see what happens to a man when he listens to his conscience, then look at Ollanius-*fugging*-Persson. That surly old bastard could have used his gifts for good, but where is he?'

John smiled, a blank kind of *well-you-have-me-there* look. He hoped to hell that the Cabal had not detected the risky clandestine efforts he had made to assist Oll Persson during the Calth disaster. Moreover, he hoped that they were blind to the new course that he had set Oll Persson upon. Unwillingly, Oll had embarked upon a thankless and thoroughly hazardous journey at John's bidding, to do something John knew full well that the Cabal would abhor...

That was why John hadn't been able to do it himself. That's why he'd had to recruit Oll.

It seemed that they were both about to strike blows for mankind *against* the interests of the Cabal. This truly was an age of rebellion and revolt.

Damon stared at John. He smiled, but there was very little warmth in the smile.

'Let's go, Johnny. You've had your moment. I get that you don't like this any more. Sorry. That's tough. "*Boo hoo, too late,*" as someone recently said. We're going to do this. We going to do it properly, and square it away. We're going to complete this damned mission if it kills us.'

'It just might,' John said.

'Comes with the territory.' Damon replied. 'I'm ready. Always have been.'

'What if I refuse, Damon?' John asked.

The gunship had moved on. Damon stepped onto the pavement. He looked back at John.

'Why would you go and do a silly thing like that?' he asked cheerfully. 'Besides, I'm not going to let you refuse. That's why I'm here.'

'I wish to serve,' said Faffnr Bludbroder.

'You have already served, brother,' Verus Caspean assured him, 'and served honourably.'

Entering the Audience Hall of the Residency, Faffnr had bowed before the new First Master of the Ultramarines out of respect. He got off his knees, and there was some effort involved. He had to lean on his axe.

'Curze left one of your pack dead, and put three more in the apothecarion,' said Caspean. 'You ought to be there too. Your service is–'

'We are hunters,' said Faffnr. 'Curze must be stopped. Allow the able members of my pack permission to deploy into the town, and we will find him.'

'For a re-match?' asked Dolor, standing at Caspean's side.

Faffnr grunted.

'Wolf, your valiant efforts are noted,' said Caspean. 'But we do not even know if Curze still lives.'

'Have you seen his corpse?' asked Faffnr.

'No.'

'Then he still lives,' said the pack-master.

'I say you should allow the Wolf to assist you,' said Euten. She stood to one side of the Legion commanders, her arms hugged around her, her face more pale and gaunt than ever.

'The Space Wolves have displayed the most devoted and emotional loyalty to the rule of law,' she said. 'I owe them my life.'

Faffnr looked at the Chamberlain Principal, and nodded in appreciation.

'I would, however, wish that the pack-master saw to his wounds before he set to inflict the same upon others,' she added.

'It's nothing,' Faffnr said.

'You leave blood wherever you walk.'

'I'll allow you to hunt,' said Caspean to Faffnr, 'but you wait an hour for our first search sweeps to be finished. Let's see what they pick up. If Curze is still out of our sight by then, the Wolves can join the hunt.'

Caspean glanced over at Timur Gantulga who was waiting nearby, fronting a group of his own battle-brothers and Eeron Kleve's Iron Hands.

'The White Scar's petition is also granted subject to similar conditions. It was astute reasoning that led you to see that Curze had switched from the Fortress to the Residency. Both you and the Wolves clearly have insight into his tactics.'

'How reassuring should we find it that the Space Wolves and the White Scars think like Konrad Curze?' asked Farith Redloss.

Dolor looked at him sharply.

'I mean to say,' said Farith Redloss, 'perhaps we can learn much from our more feral brothers.'

'Like manners?' suggested Dolor.

'My lords! Lady Euten!'

They turned to see Titus Prayto limping into the hall. His face was tight with pain. Like Faffnr Bludbroder, he had not spent anything like enough time in the apothecarion.

'I bid you all come with me, quickly,' he said directly.

They followed him out of the hall and along a banner-lined

terrace into the Reading Room of the Residency. The chamber was lined with glass-cased cabinets filled with books and slates.

'Look,' said Prayto.

An odd glow had formed in one corner of the Reading Room. It was distinctly an *other* light, the displaced luminosity that accompanied the Pharos's communication field. The curious light reflected eerily from the glass cases of the cabinets.

'I believe that Warsmith Dantioch is attempting to retune the link,' Titus said.

'This is good news at least,' said Caspean.

'We must set up a watch, to see if contact improves,' said Prayto, 'and also have patrols tour the Residency and the Fortress. There were multiple location manifestations before stable contact was originally established.'

The First Master was about to issue the instructions, but he stopped dead as the unworldly light washed over them with a brighter, flickering radiance.

The field had expanded and suddenly resolved into greater clarity. A figure stood before them, half-manifested, like a shade of the dead walking at midnight. It was impossible to identify.

'There, I knew it could be done,' a voice said, from all around them. 'Did I not say it could be done?'

'Who is there?' Caspean called out. 'Who hails us from far away Sotha?'

The communication field flickered, and then disappeared all together. The odd light drained from the Reading Room.

Caspean, Dolor and the other Ultramarines officers looked to each other.

'I'm afraid this process could take days or weeks to establish,' said Prayto.

'I do not comprehend this trickery,' said Farith Redloss, 'but perhaps–'

'–no, no, not lost!' the voice suddenly cut in, speaking out of the cabinets, out of the very books around them. 'Not lost at all! Patience! The field must be stabilised, that is all! Just a small adjustment, and–'

Silence.

'That was Dantioch's voice, I would swear it,' said Dolor.

'My Lord Dantioch? Warsmith?' Caspean called out again. 'This is Macragge! We hear you! We almost see you!'

'–I insist it is not lost! I will not let it be lost–' the voice boomed and cut away.

Abruptly, the light returned.

This time it was brighter and more steady. Everyone stepped back involuntarily as a portion of the Reading Room filled with the gleaming black mirror-stone of Primary Location Alpha, as if some ingenious mechanical scenery for a play had been rolled out across a stage.

The clarity of the background was astonishing. They could almost feel the cool black rock and the soft air. The immediate foreground was slightly out of focus, creating a hazy cloud in the shape of a man or some man-thing.

The focus popped. The figure resolved into perfect clarity to match the background.

It was the warsmith, slumped uncomfortably upon his great wooden seat on the tuning floor. He appeared tired and haggard, propped up by his crude throne. He looked like the ancient monarch of a dying kingdom – the last of his line, waiting wearily in an abandoned throne room for his life, his rule and his name to become history.

'There, as I said,' the warsmith announced, 'not lost at all. Sensitive, but not lost.'

'My Lord Dantioch,' Caspean said.

'Well, I can't do anything about the sensitivity,' said Dantioch.

'There is still so much about the process to learn and understand.'

They realised that he was not addressing them. He was speaking to one side, to a person or persons not in the field.

'My Lord Dantioch?' Prayto called.

The warsmith peered out of the field at them.

'My Lord Prayto,' he said. 'It is good to see you. Transmission was disrupted for a while.' Dantioch looked to his left. 'Move to your right,' they heard him say. 'The focus is here. I see Prayto and others.'

Other figures appeared beside him, repositioning themselves in the field: two Ultramarines, then a figure in yellow plate, unmistakably the Imperial Fist, Alexis Polux.

'How is Polux there?' Prayto exclaimed. 'How–'

His words died away.

Roboute Guilliman and the Lion loomed into the field beside the seated warsmith.

Everyone in the Reading Room dropped to their knees.

'My friends and brothers on Macragge!' said Dantioch. 'Do not make me attempt an explanation, for it is too complex. In short, I am happy to confirm that your primarchs, along with the worthy Alexis Polux, are alive and here with me on Sotha.'

'The Emperor be praised,' said Caspean.

'I feared the night's losses were too great for us to bear,' said Farith Redloss.

'There is the small matter of us returning,' said the Lion. 'We have stepped across eternity, so it seems, by simple force of will, of need. It was not a conscious decision, but rather one of the emotions.'

He stepped forward, but did not seem able to pass into the Reading Room. Every time he came too far, he simply vanished from the field. Striding back into view, he glanced at Dantioch in frustration.

'It did not promise it was a two-way process, my lord,' said the warsmith, and sighed. 'Try to focus on your greatest need, your greatest wish.'

'I should make a wish?' said the Lion. 'You make it sound like a fairy story.'

'Perhaps such technologies and their functions are the root of such stories,' said Dantioch.

The Lion scowled.

'I do not wish to be here,' he said. Again, he seemed to have no success in stepping out of the field.

Guilliman stepped forward beside him. Just like the Lion, he too passed out of sight, unable to step across. Guilliman shook his head and smiled a sad smile, regarding his failure more stoically than had the Lion. He stared out at his officers.

'I have news,' he said, 'which if I cannot cross over I must at least urgently impart to you. First, though, tell me – has Curze been captured? Slain, even?'

'Not yet, my lord,' said Dolor.

'You will update me,' Guilliman replied, nodding. 'He must be apprehended. In the meantime, I command you, at once, to prepare the fleet. Visitors descend on Macragge. You must be ready to greet them.'

'It will be done,' said Caspean.

Euten stepped forward.

'I am glad of the *sight* of you at least, lord,' she said. 'Curze told me you were dead.'

'Curze told you?' Guilliman asked in alarm.

'Curze almost killed our dear lady last night, my lord,' Caspean explained.

Guilliman started forward, grave concern plain on his face, and took her by the hands to comfort her.

'Are you well? Did he hurt you?' he asked.

She smiled.

'I am well now, lord,' Euten said. 'I am well now. Look. What did *you* wish for?'

Guilliman looked down and realised that he had stepped across.

'I did not wish for anything,' he admitted, 'except that you were unharmed. Evidently, I needed to be here, to make sure of your safety.'

He looked back at the Lion. He had never seen his brother so stricken with frustration.

Guilliman faced the field and reached out his hand.

'Give me your hand,' he said.

'I cannot!' the Lion cursed.

'I need you here with me, brother,' Guilliman insisted. He leaned in, seized the Lion's hand through the edge of the field, and pulled.

The Lion stepped through into the Reading Room.

'How did you do that?' the Lion asked Guilliman.

'I think,' said Guilliman, 'that I am more open with my needs and my hopes. I do not sequester them as you do, brother. The field could not read you. In that theoretical there is perhaps a practical that we both might heed.'

The Lion hesitated, then he nodded and placed his left hand around their already clasped right hands.

Behind them, Dantioch shifted painfully on his wooden throne. His latest efforts had sapped much of his strengths. He looked at Polux.

'Will you go?' Dantioch asked Polux.

'I think the field will permit me,' Polux replied, 'for I need to be on Terra, and Macragge is one step closer, but I fancy the mysteries of the Pharos might be more expediently uncovered if comrades work together.'

Dantioch held out his hand. Polux took it.

'I will be glad of the help, Alexis,' he said.

'As I am already glad of yours,' Polux replied.

Polux looked out of the field at Guilliman.

'I will stay here for the while, lord,' he said, 'with your permission. We will work to unravel further the mysteries of this light, and this link.'

'With my blessing,' said the Avenging Son. Polux saluted.

'Tell me about Curze,' Guilliman asked his officers. 'How close are we to finding him? What other crimes has he committed?'

'There is much to tell,' said Dolor.

'But first,' said Euten, 'you say we are to ready the fleet? For whose arrival? Who comes to Macragge, Roboute?'

'Another brother,' said Guilliman. 'Another Angel.'

22

WHERE THE
HAMMER FELL

'Death must occur so that life may prevail.'
– literal translation of the ciphered rune of the Cabal

HE CAME BACK to the place where the sky had dropped him.

Dawn had stolen in, grey and damp. Magna Macragge Civitas seemed wounded and tense, its golden lustre dimmed. Beyond the shimmer of the city shields, the coastal wind brought the grumble of thunder, and an oceanic storm threatening to blow inland and break against the sheer wall of the Hera's Crown mountains, thus shedding its rain upon the old city.

Vulkan came back to where the sky had dropped him, his mind dislocated and hurt, his garb a bloodied mis-match of purloined plate and sub-suit. His hands shook. He recoiled from shadows. His eyes smouldered. Sometimes, he chattered nonsense sounds at the sky or the earth.

The earth had once been his friend. The heat of that friendship was long gone. Vulkan's mind simmered with a fire of its own. It was hotter than any fire of the earth-rock, hotter than any magma, hotter than any core.

Sometimes he fell to his knees, and moaned or sobbed, and touched his hands to the ground and then to his face, marking his ebon skin with dust as grey as ash.

Curze had tested him by exploring the limits of his unusual life beyond its breaking point. Curze had to pay for that.

Vulkan was subliminally drawn to the object that would be pure enough to deliver his vengeance.

John glanced at Damon and nodded. They hurried across the empty street, the mumble of distant thunder in the air, and clambered their way into the burned-out ruin of a building.

The air smelled of soot and charred paper, and also of chemical fire-retardant. John could feel the heavy rain sizzling off the city shields high overhead. He wished that the shields were down, so that the rain could purge the site and wash the city clean. Magna Macragge Civitas was a city at war, however, and its armour was permanently buckled tight.

Damon Prytanis drew his pair of sling pistols. It was a deft, oft-practised gesture: *slip-slip*, from under his fur coat. He checked their loads. John knelt, and opened his carrybag.

'You think he's here?' Damon asked.

John nodded, unwrapping the parcel he had pulled from the bag.

'Hunch, or clear read?' asked Damon. 'It makes a difference.'

'Clear read,' John replied. 'This is where he landed.'

Damon looked at a brick arch above the entrance to the building's quadrangle.

'The Antimon Machine Works,' he read. 'It's seen better days.'

'He hit it like a meteor,' John replied. 'Set the place alight. It was a good thing the building was derelict.'

John rose. The fulgurite spear, unwrapped, lay in his hands.

'Is that it?' asked Damon Prytanis.

'Yes.'

'Not much to look at, is it?'

'The most potent things often aren't,' John replied.

'S'why the ladies love me, Johnny,' Damon smiled. He waited. 'Nothing? Not even a courtesy laugh?'

'Let's get on,' said John Grammaticus. 'I'm not getting any younger.'

Damon regarded him quizzically.

'I thought we had to wait for… you know… the *other* primarch,' he said. 'It's got to be another primarch who does it, right? Isn't that what they had foreseen?'

'Yes.'

'So we need the other primarch?'

'No,' said John.

'No?'

'I've thought about this,' John said. 'A primarch would be ideal, but I don't think it's essential. We can do it, either of us, you or me.'

'No, that's not what they told you,' Damon began uneasily.

'Maybe, but we're on the ground, and we're making the choices now,' John replied. 'Curze is too dangerous. He's too much of a liability. We can't control him; we can't even predict what he'll do. In fact, that's the point. Curze is psyk-invisible most of the time, so they can't have foreseen him in this situation. If the Cabal had known Curze was the only option, they wouldn't have gone for it.'

He looked at Damon.

'If we're going to do this, and do it right, it has to be us. It has to be me.'

Damon Prytanis gave him a long, probing look.

'You're not trying to pull some crazy shit on me, are you, Johnny?'

'No.'

'Johnny?'

John Grammaticus turned to look at him.

'For Terra's sake, Prytanis. We're about to do something that'll change the course of galactic history. We're about to betray our kind. *Again.* I just told you I'm prepared to do that. So give me a break, okay?'

John had the spear in his right hand. He held out his left.

'Can you spare one?' he asked.

Damon looked down at the twinned sling pistols he was wielding and realised what John meant.

'Nice try,' he replied with a dark chuckle.

'He's not likely to come quietly,' John said. 'All I have is the spear. We may need to put him down first so I can use it.'

'Well, let's see how we go. I've got your back.'

'You're not making this any easier,' said John. 'He's a primarch!'

Damon sighed, briefly holstered one of the murehk, drew his short-pattern chainsword from under his fur coat and tossed it to John.

John caught it.

'Look after it,' Damon said, drawing his other sling gun again. 'Look after it, and it'll look after you. That baby will cut through anything. Even a primarch.'

They entered the machine works.

The inner quadrangle was a rockcrete yard layered with dust, grit and shards of ceramic and glass. Each side of the quad was formed by a massive fabricatory shed, with a pillared walkway around the perimeter. The western end of the layout was flattened and smashed, as though a missile had torn through it and delivered a thermic warhead.

Damon and John crunched forward, a shabby rogue in a coat of black fur and a tall man in the dark garb of a repatriation officer, funeral watch division. *How appropriate*, John thought.

'Got a fix on him?' Damon hissed, prowling along the northern side of the quad, his guns ready. For the first time, he really looked like a soldier to John. In a million years, John could not have imitated that skill, that readiness, that capacity.

John focused.

He's all around us, John thought. *Vulkan is here, and he's everywhere. His mind is so raging, so powerful. I need–*

'Johnny?'

'Give me a second,' John replied.

I can taste the hurt. He's so wounded. I recognise that. I recognise that! What is it? What is it? He's feeling something I feel–

Vulkan came out of the shadows. He was right on them.

'Shit,' said Damon Prytanis.

Vulkan was an immense shape, eyes blazing. He looked like a massive stone statue brought to life, for he was covered in dust and dirt. He had spent the last fifteen minutes digging in the pit of the crash site. He had a hammer in his hands. It was *his* hammer – *Dawnbringer* – the one he had fallen with, the one that had brought him to Macragge. It had been buried much deeper than the level his body had been recovered from.

Howling, the maddened primarch flew at them.

'Shit!' Damon cried again, backing up fast.

Vulkan swung the hammer at them. It came cross-wise at human head-height, whistling through the air. Damon ducked. John threw himself to the right.

Both Perpetuals cheated death by a hair's breadth. The hammer-swing sliced the empty air and demolished one of the quad's pillars.

Damon had ducked so frantically that he fell. Vulkan loomed over him. Damon rolled, barely in time to avoid the next swing, which smashed the paving stones where he had been sprawled a moment earlier.

Damon kept rolling, turning fast – a combat move. He tumbled out of Vulkan's immediate kill-radius, and then rocked up on one knee, firing.

'Son of a bitch!' he exclaimed, letting rip with both of the murehk. Vulkan, four times his size, plated and raging mad, charged at him, with *Dawnbringer* raised.

Damon Prytanis expended both of his plasti-crystal ammo cores in less than four seconds. Vulkan was a big target, and Damon shot thousands of razor-rounds through his bulk.

He shredded him. The pavement behind Vulkan, for a distance of some eight or ten metres, became a huge splatter pattern of blood and ruined tissue, where separate through-wounds and impacts had gouted.

Vulkan dropped to his knees a few feet short of Damon, blood venting and squirting from hundreds of wounds.

Then he vanished, leaving nothing but the vast pooling spatter of blood behind.

Damon got up. 'What the hell?' he muttered.

Nearby, John was getting back on his feet.

'That hammer of his,' John said. 'It has a teleport function.'

'Oh goody,' Damon replied. He ejected the smoking stubs of his spent cores and loaded new ones. Then he began to circle, both sling guns out in front of him, straight-armed.

'You feel him?' he asked.

'No,' said John.

'Tell me when you feel him.'

'Obviously.'

A long second passed.

Damon looked around. 'What's taking so long?' he asked. 'Some sort of teleport lag?'

'Behind you!' John yelled.

Damon turned in time to see Vulkan appear behind him in a swirl of charged dust. He was no longer a dirt-grey statue. He was a revenant thing, painted head to foot in his own blood.

Damon narrowed his eyes and opened fire again.

'Yeah, you great big bastard?' Damon said, his pistols whipping and wailing. 'Teleport all you like. You mess with me? End of.'

A second relentless hurricane of razor-fire ripped through the primarch. John could feel the air dampening with blood mist. Vulkan staggered into the lethal streams of gunfire, but only made a step or two.

He fell, first to his knees, then face-down. His body and skull were deformed and misshapen from the sheer structural damage wrought by the murehk overkill.

Vulkan tried to rise. He was shuddering, and weeping blood like a fountain. He got halfway to his knees, using his hammer as a crutch.

'Oh, just give it up,' Damon said.

He stepped forward, put both *Guh'hru* and *Meh'menitay* to Vulkan's forehead, and blew the back of the primarch's skull out.

Vulkan dropped dead.

Damon looked around at John. Damon's face was dappled with spots of Vulkan's blood. He began to reload again. His hands were shaking.

'I don't know how many times I can kill him,' Damon said desperately. 'Will you please do it? Fast?'

John approached the fallen primarch, raising the spear. The copper stench of blood was overwhelming.

Vulkan came back from the dead once again.

It was happening faster. It was happening faster and faster each time. New life followed each death at an increasingly fearsome rate. Vulkan's rage was such that he would not let death keep him for even a second.

He lurched at them with a roar of unimaginable pain, his ruined head still re-forming and becoming whole again. Muscle, tissue, flesh and bone knitted and reconstituted in front of their eyes.

Damon let out a snarl of dismay. He hadn't even had time to finish his reload. Vulkan grabbed Damon by the throat and threw him across the quad. The Perpetual landed badly. John heard a bone break.

Vulkan turned to face John.

'I can help you,' John said. 'Please. I understand your pain. I *recognise* it. The pain of life and death, of life and death after life and death… I understand. Please, let me help you…'

Vulkan took a step forward, glaring down at John Grammaticus. He was breathing hard, wheezing through shredded lungs that were still regrowing. Blood leaked out of him, through multiple puncture wounds that were still closing.

'I understand,' John repeated, trying to sound reassuring.

+I understand,+ he sent, simultaneously.

Vulkan wavered slightly.

'I understand. Dying is hard,' said John. 'Dying hurts. Believe me, I have been there. Please, Lord Vulkan, let me help you. Let me spare you. Let me cure you.'

Vulkan paused. He was still dripping blood, and his ramshackle armour was peppered with razor-slits. Slowly, hesitantly, he held his hand out towards John Grammaticus.

Then Vulkan's head vanished in a mist of blood and brain tissue.

The shot echoed around the quad long after Vulkan's virtually headless body had fallen.

Painted with gore, John staggered back.

Narek of the Word walked into the quad, lowering his Brontos-pattern sniper rifle. He stood over Vulkan's body and put two more rounds through the torso at close range.

'He's dead,' said Narek.

'Not for long,' John replied.

'Long enough. Use the spear. Do the deed. Then you're coming with me.'

John was suddenly very quiet. The temperature in the quad dropped by ten degrees.

'He's here,' John gasped.

'Who? Who's here?' Narek asked.

An unnecessarily tall shadow leapt from the quad roof and landed between them. Slowly, it straightened up.

'*I dreamed of you,*' it hissed to John Grammaticus. 'Suddenly, I saw you in my waking dreams. You have something I need. Give me the spear.'

John shook his head. 'Never.'

Narek growled and raised his rifle to fire at Curze, but the primarch punched him aside without looking. Blood flew into the air from the impact. Narek landed several metres away.

'Give me the spear,' Curze repeated.

'Never,' said John Grammaticus.

Konrad Curze smiled.

'No one ever, *ever* refuses me,' he hissed.

'Yeah?' said Damon Prytanis from a few metres away. 'Welcome to a whole new *painful* world.'

He opened fire on Konrad Curze with both sling guns.

23

LIFE FOR LIFE

'In all things there is an exchange; of death for life, of darkness for light,
of life for death, of light for darkness. Thus is universal
equilibrium sustained.'

– Ulthrion Aledred, *Precepts of Fortitude Against*
the Primordial Annihilator (translated)

VULKAN, MONOLITHIC, HAD soaked up Damon's streams of expertly placed razor-shot.

Curze merely sidestepped them. The eldar munitions, screaming like a billion angry hornets, passed through and around the fold of smoke that Konrad Curze had become. He was untouched.

Unchecked by any object, the razor-shots screamed on, ripping a long, broad blizzard of stone chips out of the quadrangle wall.

Curze left his laugher behind him.

Aghast, Damon stopped firing for a second, turning, trying to see where his target had gone. How could anything so big move so fast, so unnaturally?

A shadow slapped the sling pistols out of his hands. Damon winced and cried out. He had broken a shoulder blade and several ribs in his fall, and the impact across his wrists jarred him badly.

His pain had only just begun.

A single metal talon slid under his chin, punching up under the jaw through the floor of Damon's mouth. He gurgled in agony, his tongue pushed sideways, his mouth and throat rapidly filling with blood. Curze laughed again and lifted Damon off the ground on the hook of his single talon.

'A *whole new painful world*,' Curze hissed, sing-song.

Damon struggled. It felt as if his face was about to be torn away.

Whining furiously, the chainsword tore into Curze from behind. John drove it in with all his might. He'd considered using the spear, but he was afraid of what that might do to Curze.

The chainsword was a more reliable choice.

Curze yelped. Blood and shreds of black armour and cloth were flung out by the sword's cycling teeth. He let Damon fall, and wheeled at John. His visage – hateful eyes, black-in-black, and a biting black maw in a spectral white face – was the most terrifying thing John had ever seen.

He didn't stand a chance.

But Vulkan did.

The decompressive pop of a teleport displacement drove John back as Vulkan materialised between him and the lunging Curze.

A hammer blow drove Curze back. A second made him reel sideways. Curze swung back with his claws, deflecting the hammer's third and fourth attacks.

The action between them began to accelerate. They rapidly

became post-human blurs, trading blows back and forth with unimaginable speed.

Vulkan abruptly connected in a fundamental way. His huge broad back and massive arms slammed the hammer into Curze's torso. Plasteel cracked like a gunshot. Curze, seemingly no more than a bundle of black rags, was hurled backwards. He brought down two of the quad's pillars in a rain of stones and dust, and smashed through the wall into one of the empty sheds.

Broken masonry slithered and dropped in the aftermath of the impact. Vulkan surged forward, using *Dawnbringer* to break the wall down further and get at his foe. Fully half of the fabricatory shed's outer wall collapsed in an avalanche of stonework and dust. Vulkan churned on in the rising dust, smashing debris out of his way to find Curze.

The Night Haunter came at him, screaming, claws wide.

'Why won't you just die? This is nothing more than the end of the fight we began months ago, brother... and believe me, it *will* be the end!'

He drove Vulkan back through another section of the shed wall, bringing down another cascade of masonry. Vulkan stepped back on his right foot, braced, and slammed the haft of the hammer around like a bludgeon, ramming the base into the side of Curze's head. Curze jolted sideways and then met the hammerhead coming the other way, and the blow sent him stumbling and flailing back into the yard.

Vulkan followed, whirling *Dawnbringer* in a vertical undersweep that struck Curze in the solar plexus, cracking him up and over onto his back.

He rolled out of the way of Vulkan's next strike, and screamed at John Grammaticus.

'*Give me that thing! Give it to me!*'

John was at Damon's side. Damon's mouth, chin and shirt-front were soaked with blood, and he was spitting out more as his mouth kept filling. He couldn't speak, but he looked at John. His eyes were wide. Curze, a rapid shadow, rushed at them to claim the spear and finish Vulkan any way that he could count on as permanent.

Damon shoved John out of the way, and pulled out the last of his four weapons. It was the small, red-glass bottle. He hurled it at Curze.

The bottle was a tiny and very precious thing. The vessel had been carefully charged by Cabal specialists with warp-magic for use in utter emergencies. Damon had learned its method by rote, and it had saved his life in the mountains, three days after his arrival on Macragge.

As it shattered at Curze's feet, it released the thing that Damon had trapped in it that day.

Ushpetkhar re-entered realspace, freed from the prison of Damon's vessel and driven mad by its confinement. There was a brief and sickening suggestion of something massive and glossy sprouting from the floor of the yard; something muscular and segmented, like a vast, jet-shelled centipede writhing with wet pseudopods. Ushpetkhar attacked the first thing it saw – it shot up in an instant, out of nowhere, curling over to collapse and constrict Konrad Curze. He fought back, astonished, screaming, shredding its noisome flesh with his claws. Ushpetkhar locked around him. The giant figure of the primarch was engulfed in the greater, more fluid mass of the daemon.

It tightened its coils. It rippled.

It squeezed them both out of realspace, and they vanished together.

Only a smear of iridescent black slime and broken fragments of red glass remained where they had been.

Damon flopped back, gurgling blood as he tried to breathe.

John rose to his feet and faced Vulkan.

'You know what I'm trying to do, don't you?' John said. 'Even in your distraction, you sense our kinship. Lives and deaths, over and over again. All that pain. We've both known it.'

Vulkan didn't respond, but he kept watching John with his burning eyes.

John stepped closer, the spear in his hand.

'Life for life, my lord,' he said. 'My life to cure yours. Take it. Take it gladly, so that you may fight for us all.'

Behind him, Damon made a wretched sound. He tried to rise. He understood what John was about to do.

John raised the spear.

Damon spat out a mouthful of blood. 'Don't. *Don't!*' he managed to splutter.

Vulkan saw the spear and recognised that he was about to be struck by a weapon. Involuntarily, he made to block it and break John with his hammer.

John was already too close.

He plunged the spear into the primarch's chest. It went in without resistance, cutting clean through what was left of his armour plate, and transfixed Vulkan's heart.

Electric fire wreathed them both. Corposant ignited and burned around the stricken primarch and the man driving the weapon into him.

Holding on, yelling in pain, John felt his life – his long, long Perpetual existence – flowing out of him through the spear into Vulkan.

He hoped it would be sufficient.

They fell. Vulkan landed on his back, the spear penetrating him. John fell across him. The lightning crackled around them for another few seconds, and then it sputtered out.

In great pain, Damon Prytanis got to his feet. He limped over to them.

They were both dead. This time, there was absolutely no sign of Vulkan rising again.

John had been wrong. Whatever madness he had been thinking, whatever had made him defy his orders, he'd got it wrong, and now, he too was dead.

'You bloody idiot,' Damon said, chewing and spitting the words, painfully, out of his mangled mouth.

He could hear gunships circling, the ominous howl of Storm Eagle engines. The fight had attracted a great deal of attention.

It was time to go. It was long past time to go.

NAREK OF THE Word stirred and sat up. His transhuman metabolism had finally clotted and closed the wounds Curze had left upon him.

He got to his feet. Further devastation had evidently swept through the machine shop quad while he had been unconscious. Curze had vanished, and the two humans were gone too.

Vulkan still lay there, however.

Narek could hear the enemy approaching, but he limped over to Vulkan's side and bent over him.

The primarch was dead. The spear impaled his chest. Narek thought to pull it out, to take it and escape so he could put it to his own purpose.

When he touched the spear, however, it was cold and inert. It no longer felt godlike. There was no power left in it. He tried to pull it out, but it absolutely refused to move.

Gunships chattered in overhead. He heard the crunch of heavy footsteps.

The Cataphractii of Guilliman's Invictus bodyguard entered the broken quad from all sides.

Narek rose to meet them. He tossed his rifle aside and slowly, reluctantly, raised his hands.

'Get this bastard contained,' said Drakus Gorod. 'Now.'

24
THE
UNREMEMBERED
EMPIRE

*'Those who urgently wish to rule are the last people
who should be allowed to do so.'*

– Konor, private writings

ON THE MORNING of the next day, the main strength of the Ultramar fleet put out from Macragge and, by the light of the Pharos, met the ships that Oberdeii's dream had foretold were coming to them.

From the bridge of his flagship, clad in ceremonial plate, Guilliman looked into the hololithic projection before him. He saw the face of his brother looking back.

Guilliman smiled.

'Well met, Sanguinius,' he said. 'I welcome you to Ultramar and the Five Hundred Worlds. It is good that you are here. Now we can begin.'

SANGUINIUS, PRIMARCH OF the IX Legion Blood Angels, entered the Audience Hall, trailing an honour guard of his finest warriors, clad in their bright crimson wargear.

He was always a breathtaking figure, dressed in golden armour and a mantle of spotted carnodon fur. His face, so noble of feature, was framed by a radiant sunburst. His great wings, of course, made him more like an angel than anything else.

Guilliman stepped forward to meet him, and they embraced. Then Sanguinius turned to the Lion and embraced him too.

'Whence come you, brother?' Guilliman asked.

'From Signus Prime,' Sanguinius replied. His voice was, as ever, like music, but Guilliman could sense pain deep within it. 'From a bloody fight and a hard betrayal. I fear that my fleet has been adrift in the warp for a long time since, and only your strange light has shown us the way out.'

'What strength are you?' asked the Lion.

'To all sensible purposes, my entire Legion,' Sanguinius replied.

'And what befell you on Signus Prime?' asked Guilliman.

Sanguinius seemed reluctant to reply.

'We faced down an enemy the like of which we have never known,' he replied. 'It cost us. It is now my dearest intention to make best speed for Terra and stand alongside our father, against the treachery of Horus Lupercal.'

'Return to Terra at this time is not viable,' said Guilliman. 'I am sorry to say that the Ruinstorm chokes all travel out.'

'We too wish to stand with Terra, if Terra still stands,' the Lion said, including both himself and Guilliman in the remark. 'For now, we must abide here, and build other strengths.'

'In what particular?' asked Sanguinius.

'I want Roboute to tell you about his efforts to keep the very essence and spirit of the Imperium alive,' the Lion said. 'I want him to tell you about Imperium Secundus.'

THE THREE BROTHERS stood and looked upon the body of Vulkan for a long time. The fallen primarch had been placed in a golden casket, fashioned by artisans of the Mechanicum.

'Vulkan. Terra, you should have told me, Roboute!' said the Lion.

'Just as you should have told me about Konrad,' Guilliman replied.

'What was it? *"You keep too many secrets, brother",* the Lion reminded him.

'Point taken,' Guilliman said. He sighed.

'It is a preservation capsule,' Guilliman told his brothers. 'It is intended to sustain our dear brother Vulkan's body in the slightest hope that his extraordinary gifts may yet return him to life.'

The top of the casket was clear glass. Vulkan's body had been dressed in fresh wargear taken from Guilliman's armoury and decorated in the livery of the Salamanders. His hammer, *Dawnbringer*, lay upright across his breast. No one had been able to remove the spear lodged in his heart.

'It is a sorry sight,' whispered Sanguinius. 'How many more of us must fall? How many more of us will Horus take?'

'Vulkan lives,' said Guilliman. 'This is the cry of the Salamanders, and I heartily uphold it. Even in his state of death, he represents the will in us to survive.'

'It is still a sad fate,' said Sanguinius, 'to be held in a casket here in the cold cellars of your Fortress, consigned for all eternity.'

'It is not a fate I would wish,' Guilliman agreed. He gestured towards the figures of Zytos and the other Salamanders survivors who had blown to Macragge from the bosom of the storm. They knelt around the golden casket, forming a mourning vigil.

'I have pledged that, once the storm has abated, good Zytos and his brothers will transport our brother's body back to Nocturne and inter him in the clean soil of his home world.'

'This is more fitting,' the Lion said.

They withdrew from the vault. Guilliman turned and took a last sad look at the casket.

Engraved upon it, on a gilded scroll, were the words '*The Unbound Flame*'.

'WILL HE DO it?' Euten asked.

'I believe the Lord Sanguinius is somewhat unwilling,' said Farith Redloss.

'Well, they are talking at least,' Dolor pointed out.

The three primarchs had withdrawn to the seldom-visited chamber where Guilliman had set the long table and the twenty-one seats draped with banners. The broad doors were closed. Euten and the ranked officers of all three Legions were obliged to wait in the hall for a verdict or command.

'He is the most suitable,' Euten said. 'To see him up close... Lord Sanguinius is the most...'

She searched for a word.

'He is angelic,' said Dolor.

'He is numinous,' added Farith Redloss. 'He is more like his father in that respect. Some of the primarch lords are very much of the flesh. Horus is one, and your lord Guilliman another. They have physicality. But the Emperor... To be in his presence is to be in the presence of that which is spiritual, and has no constant form. It is said the Emperor appears to each man in the image that man wishes to see. I think Lord Sanguinius has inherited much of that trait.'

Euten nodded.

'It is true. I do not think of him as a face or a figure. I think of him as a light. The very colour of his hair and his eyes seems to change with his mood, and with mine.'

'This has been noted by others,' Dolor agreed. 'Several of the primarchs have this quality beyond simple physical stature, but none more than Sanguinius.'

'He would be perfect,' she said.

'Many think so,' said Farith Redloss. 'Just as many wonder why Horus and not Sanguinius was chosen as Warmaster after Ullanor. If Horus was preferred, and yet has revealed such mortal flaws since, one wonders what secret flaws reside in the Lord of the Blood Angels?'

'IMPERIUM SECUNDUS REPRESENTS continuity,' Guilliman said. 'Since Calth, it has been all I can do to hold the fractured parts of the Five Hundred Worlds together. Ultramar is all that we know we have. If the Imperium endures, then we will re-join it when the storm dies, but if it has not endured elsewhere, then we have preserved it here.'

Guilliman had sat in the seat marked with the cobalt-blue banner of his Legion. Likewise, the Lion had placed himself in the seat covered by the Dark Angel's proud flag. Sanguinius had chosen to remain standing. He paced, troubled but thoughtful.

'Roboute has made this argument to me at length,' said the Lion, 'and though I have been troubled by some of its details, I find myself seeing the value of it more and more.'

'How so?' asked the angelic lord.

The Lion sat back, his hands flat upon the edge of the table.

'The events of last night alone,' he said in a quiet tone, 'have made me value life and kinship more than ever. We have lost another brother, and Macragge, great heartstone of the Five Hundred Worlds, was almost brought low by the deeds and machinations of just one demented traitor. I have witnessed the venom of our enemy, and I have seen the sad fragility of those assets and lives that remain to us. Roboute and I do not think alike on many subjects. We disagree. But we also stand together, loyal. We fight for the Imperium, and this is all of the Imperium that we have.'

'But regent?' Sanguinius said. 'That smacks of usurpation...'

'It smacks of necessity,' replied Guilliman. 'If Terra and our father have gone, then so has Malcador. We must rally our shattered strength before it is too late. Neither the Lion nor I can stomach the other assuming the role, but we are unanimous when the choice is you.'

'You always were the most like our father,' said the Lion.

Sanguinius looked up at the light of the storm spilling through the chamber's high windows.

'Let me say, brother,' said Guilliman, 'you showed no great delight in being delivered from the storm and reunited with us. You seem troubled and burdened. That tear marked beneath your eye? Is that a new notation of your anguish?'

'We have all seen troubles,' said Sanguinius. 'Brothers fight and fall, and the stars die. Daemons walk abroad. I fear that Old Night steals in upon us anew. I would rage against that.'

'Then make your stand here, for now,' said Guilliman. He stood up. 'Take this oath of moment, and I will make a pledge. The first moment the storm abates, the first moment we see the light of Terra or hear word that she still stands, I will light my ship-drives, and, with all measure of my forces, guide your Legion back to the home world. There will be no delay or argument. We do not build a second empire here. We maintain the original, founded anew on this globe as circumstance demands.'

'You would make this pledge to me?' asked Sanguinius.

'With all solemnity,' Guilliman replied.

'And you will back this?' Sanguinius asked the Lion.

'With my blood,' the Lion replied.

Sanguinius sighed.

'I notice, in the hours since I set foot upon the soil of Macragge, that there are no remembrancers in your court, nor in the retinue of the Lion.'

He regarded them.

'Is this mere coincidence?'

'Discretion,' Guilliman replied. 'If Terra stands, then future generations may see, whether true or not, a heresy and usurpation in the foundation we make here. I would not stain the memory or legacies of the loyal sons with such a smirch, however unintentioned. Therefore, I did conclude early in my deliberations, that no piece of this undertaking should become history until history it needs to be. No chronicles will be made, no remembrancers charged to observe this business and commemorate it. If Ultramar is all the Imperium we have, then in due time and with great effect, its histories will be written and will become the single Imperial record. But, if Terra yet survives, as I most dearly hope, then this will become, in future days, an unremembered empire, an unthinkable act undone and unthought.'

Sanguinius took a deep breath. 'Then it is down to us? We three decide?' he asked.

'There is only us,' said the Lion, rising to his feet.

'Tell us, Sanguinius,' Guilliman said, 'which seat will you take at this table?'

IT MAY HAVE been the moment, or merely his imagination, but Magna Macragge Civitas seemed to glow, as it had done in more glorious years. The great towers and spires of the city shone with a golden lustre, as they had done in the first era of the Five Hundred Worlds.

The sky was full of ships. They moved overhead, in series and formation, a procession of honour and a display of might. High up, illumined by the light of the Pharos star, the great capital ships drifted like leviathans. Below them, in the lower atmosphere, formations of fighter craft and gunships made fly past after fly past. The six great war horns of the ancient Battle Kings sounded across the storm-lit Civitas in unison.

The streets were full. Cheering crowds filled every via and

avenue, and processions of the Legiones Astartes, Army, Mechanicum and praecental forces converged from their various barracks and fortresses on the broad space of Martial Square.

Guilliman took the salute of the roaring crowds on the platform of the Propylae Titanicus.

He turned to the Lion at his side.

'This we do?' he asked.

The Lion nodded. 'This we do, for it is right,' he said.

Guilliman stepped to the side of his brother Sanguinius. He grasped his right wrist and raised his hand to the sky in triumph.

Sanguinius raised his head and looked out over the cheering sea of faces and punching fists. He allowed his hand to be thrust aloft. He spread his mighty wings in a salute, like the sign of the aquila.

At the top of his voice, Guilliman declared the regency, but the noise of the multitude was too great for the words to be heard.

25

ENDS AND BEGINNINGS

'Alpha and Omega, the first and last, each within the other.'
– The Apocrypha Terra, date unknown

LIGHTS CAME ON. The heavy cell door opened. Titus Prayto stepped into the chamber.

Seated upon a metal bench and shackled by the throat, ankles and wrists to pins set in the rockcrete floor, Narek of the Word looked up, but did not speak.

'So, friend. We begin again,' said Prayto. 'Will you say more today?'

'There is no more to say,' replied Narek.

'You are hard to probe, Word Bearer, and hard to open,' said Prayto. 'I am impressed. Others would have broken days ago.'

'There is nothing in me to break,' said Narek.

'Did you slay the lord primarch Vulkan?' asked Prayto.

'Asked and answered,' Narek grumbled.

'For the record today.'

'No, I did not. Though I would have if I had possessed the means.'

'Who did?'

'I don't know. I can only offer the conjecture that it was the immortal human known as John Grammaticus, or perhaps his unknown confederate.'

'We have no record of a John Grammaticus on Macragge, or–'

'I told you,' said Narek. 'Where he passes, he does not leave traces. I do not know what happened to him, but his aim was to slay Vulkan.'

'What was the weapon he used?'

'I do not understand it. A spear, forged from the power of the Emperor.'

'And this is what he employed?'

'Perhaps he did. Perhaps it was Curze. Curze was there too.'

'What happened to Curze?' asked Prayto.

'I know not.'

'Were the eldar present? There were clear signs of eldar munitions.'

'No. Grammaticus's confederate used those weapons. Though it was told to me that their masters are eldar-born.'

'Anything else?' asked Prayto.

'Nothing else,' said Narek of the Word.

Prayto stepped out of the cell, and closed the hatch. It slammed shut. In the gloomy corridor outside, one of the lowest level spurs in the Fortress of Hera, the Avenging Son stood waiting for him.

'Has he changed his story?' Guilliman asked.

'There is not a hint of variance, my lord,' Prayto reported. 'He maintains this strange tale of immortal assassins and Curze. I cannot tell if it is true or false, but it matches the physical evidence, and from my read of him, he believes it utterly.'

'He does not lie?'

'He appears, my lord, to have no reason to do so.'

Guilliman shook his head.

'I don't understand. He's a Word Bearer, reviled by our Legion more than any other. He's on Macragge, alone, after Calth, yet he seems to display no guilt or shame or deceit, nor even fear.'

'I think he is a very singular being, lord,' said Prayto. 'I think perhaps, he is a little similar to Warsmith Dantioch. A good man drawn by fate on the wrong side.'

'He's an ally?' asked Guilliman.

'Not like the warsmith. Dantioch has come over to us and renounced his Legion. Narek is still dangerous. He sees us as the enemy, and he remains true to his Legion. But he is loyal.'

'What do you mean?' asked Guilliman.

'Each day, as I ask my questions to occupy his mind, I probe deeper to unlock the hidden truths. He is loyal to his Legion, but it is a loyalty to the spirit and foundation of his Legion, not to what his Legion has become. I see two things clearly.'

'And they are?'

'First, he is remarkably single-minded, determined. There is a fixed purpose in him that is almost frightening to read. The second thing is what that fixed purpose is. He wants, with an urgency that is alarming, to kill your brother Lorgar. It is all he lives for.'

'Is this an act?' asked Guilliman.

'If it is, it's the best piece of psychic conditioning I've ever read,' Prayto replied. 'What do we do?'

'Come back tomorrow and ask him the same questions,' said Guilliman. 'Keep doing that, every day, until we have the truth.'

'And then, lord?'

'And then,' said Guilliman, 'I will order his execution as a traitor and a heretic.'

✠ ✠ ✠

HE WOKE UP, and knew the pain of life again. Without even opening his eyes, he knew that he was on a craftworld.

He could smell the eldar.

He sat up. The chamber was small. He was on a cot which, like the rest of the room, was made of wraithbone. It glowed with an inner light that he found nauseating.

'You brought me back,' he said.

'Oh, I had to, Johnny,' said Damon Prytanis. 'Never leave a man behind, and all that.'

'I mean, to life.'

'Yeah, that was their choice. After what you pulled, Johnny, I think they want you alive enough to punish you soundly.'

John sighed.

'Vulkan?'

'He stayed dead. Your trick didn't work. Plus, it killed you. It was stupid, Johnny. Technically, you completed the mission. But they know what you were really trying to do.'

'Why? Because you told them?'

'I didn't have to,' Damon Prytanis replied. 'Gahet's waiting for you. Slau Dha too. They want to know who you've been talking to. They want to know where you're getting these ideas from. They want to know what *else* you might have done.'

He paused. He rubbed the dressings on his throat and jaw.

'Basically, they want to know *how* you've betrayed them,' he said, 'and why.'

'Because I'm human,' said John Grammaticus.

Prytanis laughed.

'Funny, actually. Because that's true now. That crazy stunt? Pushing your life energy into Vulkan? It took everything out of you. It took *everything*, Johnny. They brought you back to life, but it's the only one you have left. They can't do it again. You're not a Perpetual any more, Johnny, you're just a man. You've got one life remaining, and they're going to tell you exactly how you're going to spend it.'

The door behind Damon Prytanis hummed open.

'They're ready,' he said. 'Shall we?'

THE DEEP VAULT was silent. The memorial flame fluttered on its stand. Zytos knelt beside the golden casket.

The sound came and went so quickly that Zytos thought it was in his imagination. He waited, listening. It did not come again.

He waited longer, willing it to return.

It did not repeat.

It *had* merely been in his imagination.

For a second, he thought he had heard a heartbeat, the *du-dunt* of a single heartbeat.

But no. It was wishful thinking.

Zytos of the Salamanders bowed his head and resumed his mourning vigil.

REALSPACE TORE OPEN like a gut wound. A bloody, mangled figure tumbled out, lean limbs flailing, and left red stains on the mountain snow as he rolled down the slope. Behind him, the realspace tear bulged and spasmed. The torn and wet mass of Ushpetkhar, choking on its own black ichor, shuddered and died, collapsing backwards into the warp and closing the tear behind it.

At last. Dead at *last*. The combat had been far too long and far too gruelling. How many days, how many *weeks* had it lasted in that no-place, no-time wasteland of the immaterium?

Almost dead, cadaverously thin, and soaked wet-black from head to toe in daemon blood, Konrad Curze got to his feet. He was shaking with cold, pain and hunger.

He looked around with his wild, black-within-black eyes, struggling to identify his location. He was high in a range of mountains, huge mountains, snow-capped. A single toxic star shone in the storm-ruined sky.

His visions began to flow again. They ran through his demented mind like shadow-play. They showed him that a city lay not far off, perhaps just a fortnight's trek through the mountains. It was a great golden city on a coastal plain, watched over by a mighty fortress.

Magna Macragge Civitas.

His visions showed him the cheering crowds, the streets full of people, the great triumph of the declaration. He saw the Lion and Guilliman, alive after all. *Alive after all.* He saw Sanguinius between them, proclaimed as master of mankind.

They were trying to save the Imperium by shoring it up on Ultramar and the Five Hundred Worlds, and declaring it re-founded.

Curze began to laugh.

It was nothing. It was pitiful. It was an empty gesture made by desperate men obsessed by notions of nobility.

It was just another empire for him to raze to the ground and annihilate.

He started to walk.

He left many bloody footprints in the snow behind him.

ACKNOWLEDGEMENTS

The author would like to thank the following, variously, for ground work laid down in other novels and stories, for plot threads, for brainstorming, for questions answered... and in many cases all of the above – Graham McNeill, Gav Thorpe, Jim Swallow, Aaron Dembski-Bowden, John French, Rob Sanders, Graeme Lyon, Alan Merrett, Nick Kyme, Neil Roberts, Alan Bligh and Laurie Goulding.

Thanks, love and appreciation to Nik for her supportive work editing copy, delivering feedback, and generally putting up with me and the whole process.

ABOUT THE AUTHOR

Dan Abnett is a multiple *New York Times* bestselling author and an award-winning comic book writer. He has written almost fifty novels, including the acclaimed Gaunt's Ghosts series, and the Eisenhorn and Ravenor trilogies. His Horus Heresy novel *Prospero Burns* topped the SF charts in the UK and the US. In addition to writing for Black Library, Dan scripts audio dramas, movies, games, comics and bestselling novels for major publishers in Britain and America. He lives and works in Maidstone, Kent.

Chris Wraight

SCARS

The Legion divided

An extract from Scars
by Chris Wraight

MALCADOR THE SIGILLITE had none of the grandeur of his companions. His robes, though richly made, were simple. The staff he leaned upon looked to be made of little more than iron, though the aquila device that topped it was artful. His voice gave away his physical weakness – it sounded destroyed by age. None, save perhaps the Emperor himself, knew just how old he was. He had no known birthplace, no cultural identity. As far as the wider Imperium was concerned, he had just *always been there*, as solid a presence as the Palace itself.

Malcador and the Emperor. The Emperor and Malcador. They were like light and dark, sun and moon – each as inscrutable and unknowable as the other.

Except that the Emperor was gone, locked away in the deep Throne chambers, his unmatched power deployed to an end that even the Lords of Terra did not speak of openly.

'Let me tell you again,' said Dorn. 'Perhaps you have forgotten where it is that we stand. Magnus has broken the wards around the Throne, and now this, the mightiest fortress in the galaxy, sits upon a foundation of madness.'

'It is contained once more,' insisted Malcador. 'For now the world knows little of the actual truth.'

'It is contained only because the Emperor binds Himself to the hidden war,' Dorn replied. 'This respite has been bought with the sacrifice of a thousand souls. *That* is why the world does not know.'

'Not yet,' said Valdor bleakly. 'But they will. Perhaps a few more weeks, perhaps months, but it will spill out eventually. Rumours are already running wild.'

'It will do,' agreed Malcador. 'But as long as He holds firm…'

'Yes, as long as He holds firm,' said Dorn, bitterly. 'That is what we are reduced to. No actions, no movement – just hope.'

'We cannot help Him,' said Valdor. 'We know this. So let us turn to what we can do.'

Malcador chuckled dryly. 'I never asked you how it felt, Constantin, to see Prospero burn. Did even your callous soul blanch at that?'

Valdor didn't miss a beat. 'No. It was necessary.'

'Was it?' sighed Malcador. 'I did not give the order. I wanted Magnus censured, not destroyed. What was it that made Russ do it? You never could give me an answer.'

Dorn exhaled impatiently. 'You know all of this, Malcador. You know all that happened there, just as we do.' He was coldly furious. 'Does this need repeating? The Warmaster is at the heart of it, poisoning everything we do, and now he has the blood of three more Legions on his hands.'

At that, Malcador seemed to wince. The slaughter of Isstvan V was still raw. None of them, save the implacable Valdor perhaps, could refer to it without provoking that hollow, draining, sense of loss.

'Ferrus is truly gone, they tell me,' admitted Malcador. 'Vulkan and Corax missing. Eight Legions declared traitor, even now carving the void apart to get to us.' He smiled grimly. 'Shall I go on? The ether in turmoil, blighting the Astronomican and making us blind? No word of Guilliman or Sanguinius. Are they with us? Or have they also turned?'

'Not the Angel,' said Dorn, firmly. 'And I will not believe it of Roboute.'

'But they are lost to us, for now at least,' said Valdor. 'So we must survey what we know. Russ is at Alaxxes. When I left him, they were badly mauled, for the Sons gave us a hard fight, but they will hunt again.'

'And the Lion,' said Malcador. 'What of him?'

'He pursues his private feuds,' said Dorn. 'And when has he ever been anything but his own master?'

Malcador smiled. 'You brothers – such a nest of rivalries. I warned him to make you sisters, that it would make things more civilised. He thought I was joking. I wasn't.'

Dorn didn't smile. His face seemed permanently rooted in a kind of frozen tension.

'There is one other,' said Valdor quietly.

'Ah, yes,' said Malcador. 'So easy to overlook the Khan. Why is that?'

'It is his gift,' said Dorn dismissively.

'The Khan was in the Chondax system,' said Valdor.

'Which, like so many others, is beyond our reach,' said Malcador, his voice bleakly humorous.

'What of Jaghatai's loyalty?' asked Valdor.

'I did not know him, not well,' said Dorn.

'None of us did,' said Malcador. 'That was the point of him – in any system there needs to be uncertainty.' He smiled at Dorn. 'You, my friend, were an exercise in the opposite. No wonder you two did not understand one another.'

'So who was he close to?' asked Valdor.

Malcador thought for a moment. 'Horus, of course. They were so similar. I believe they conferred on Ullanor.'

'Magnus, too,' said Dorn, somewhat hesitantly. 'They fought alongside one another for a long time.'

'Yes,' said Malcador, nodding pensively. 'The Librarius – the Khan, Magnus and Sanguinius were behind it. That was the root of their connection, such as it was. They all believed in the need for psykers within the Legions.'

Valdor took a deep breath. 'So there it is. The Khan's known allies, Horus and Magnus, traitors both.'

'All of us trusted Horus,' said Dorn.

Order the novel or download the eBook
from *blacklibrary.com*
Also available from

and all good booksto